Mended Legacy

Mended Legacy

by D.S. NASS

MILAN
BOOK PUBLISHING

For inquiries, contact: DSNassauthor@gmail.com.

ISBN (Hardcover): 978-1-7373113-5-5
ISBN (Paperback): 978-1-7373113-8-6

Cover Design by A. Osh Designs: www.alekseyosh.com
Interior Design by Milan Book Publishing LLC

Printed in the United States of America

To my incredible children — Nic, Zak, Skylar, Creed, and Erick, and to my beautiful granddaughters, Daisy and Scarlett. Your strength, resilience, and courage in the face of life's challenges inspire me every single day. You have endured, grown, and continued to love with open hearts — and in doing so, you've shown me what true bravery looks like. You are my purpose, my pride, and the legacy I'm most grateful to leave behind.

AUTHOR'S NOTE

I've always loved stories where the main character undergoes a transformation—where they emerge from the other side changed, perhaps scarred, but stronger. And if there's a great romance in the mix? I'm all in. That's the kind of story I wanted to tell. What I didn't expect, though, was how much this story would transform me in the process.

When I started this sequel, I thought I knew where it was headed. I had a plan. But these characters—Grace and Erick—had a different idea. They grew and changed and pulled me right along with them. It felt less like writing and more like herding toddlers playing soccer... or maybe cats. Sometimes both.

Honestly, the story kept evolving and surprising me. What began as one thing turned into something deeper, wilder, and more honest than I planned. That's part of what I love about writing—it teaches you to let go, to trust the process, to just keep going.

Every detour, every rewrite, every moment of doubt—it was part of the journey. And even when I didn't have the full map, I knew I had to keep moving forward.

This book is personal. The themes—healing, redemption, love after brokenness—are more than just plot points. They mirror parts of my own life. Writing it brought up things I didn't expect, but it also reminded me how far I've come.

I couldn't have done it alone. I truly believe some people come into our lives to guide us—to hold our hands through the shadows and help us rise from ashes to beauty. For me, those people have been the readers who supported my first book, my family, and my incredible coworkers.

If there was ever a trail guide through this journey, it was Stefani-Ann Milanese-Brousseau, **Owner, Milan Book Publishing**. I am so grateful to get to work with her and call her my friend.

Without her, there wouldn't be any published books at all, let alone a sequel.

Don't wait until you're not afraid to dive into your dreams. Just take the first step. But take it with the people who believe in you. *The ones who won't let you give up.* I'm so grateful for *my* people—and for all of you who've come along for this wild ride.

With love and gratitude,

D. S. Nass

"You were born for more than just mediocrity. You were born to be a light—to love and to serve."
—Richard Paul Evans

Prologue

E rick adjusted the cuffs of his silk beige tuxedo. The fabric was smooth against his skin as he watched the guests settle into their white folding chairs. Summer in New England carried a scent of radiant blooms and stunning sunsets as the warmth of the late afternoon sun cascaded through the leaves, casting a serene glow over the assembled crowd. The venue had an understated elegance to it, with lush green fields bordered by towering oaks, providing an idyllic backdrop for the occasion.

"Is everything all right?" Erick whispered to Daniel, who gave a slight nod. His hands gripped the wheels of his wheelchair.

"Perfect," Daniel replied, his voice steady. "I'll just lock it here." As Daniel secured his wheelchair at the head of the aisle, Erick straightened his posture, ready to perform his duties as best man. Daniel was marrying his best friend, Sky, and Erick couldn't be happier for them. The music softened to a gentle hum, signaling the start of the procession.

Luna, Daniel's loyal golden retriever, led the way, proudly walking down the aisle. Loose pale pink petals and daisies were woven into her collar. With each step, the golden retriever moved down the aisle as the petals sprinkled out in the wake of her path. Jace, the other four-legged member of the wedding party, sported a black bow tie and had the wedding rings tied to a small pillow on his back.

Sky's sister, Charlotte, wore a sage chiffon gown that caught the light and swayed like the green leaves above. She moved with grace, her smile warm as she made her way up the aisle.

Isabelle, Sky's friend from UConn, came next, her smile barely contained as she beamed at Jonah, one of Daniel's groomsmen from high school.

A sage organza had been woven through the rungs of the wooden archway at the end of the aisle, helping to frame the ceremony space. The fabric gently flowed with the warm summer breeze.

Erick glanced at the guests, all present in honor of the union about to take place, and he felt a swell of pride for his brother. He nodded to his office manager, Joyce, and her husband, Don, who sat up front.

In that instant, amidst the beauty of the wedding and the joyous celebration of love, Erick's mind briefly wandered to Grace Evans, his first love. He'd spent the last year helping her recover physically and mentally from a hiking accident that had left her with amnesia. The concealment of his identity had brought them closer, only to tear them apart again once her memories returned. She'd asked Erick for space and to complete her recovery on her own. He'd hoped she would have been at Daniel's wedding, but she was not. From what he'd heard, she was finishing her book and was about to go on her book tour that fall. He quickly refocused, remembering he was next to Daniel, and he had a big job to fill. He was ready to witness the vows and the beginning of a new chapter in his brother's life.

The sun dipped lower, casting an amber glow over the Connecticut farm, transforming the scene into something ethereal. At that moment, Sky appeared at the far end of the aisle. The warm light haloed her silhouette, the delicate fabric of her dress seeming to absorb the sunset itself. Erick watched as Sky's father proudly escorted his daughter. Benjamin Rawlings' weathered face, unusually stern from years on the ranch, softened into a wide smile as he looked at Daniel.

Erick couldn't resist a glance at his brother, whose eyes were fixed on his bride. Daniel's eyes glistened as Sky approached. When they reached the archway, Sky paused to offer her father a tender kiss on the cheek.

Sky then turned to Daniel, taking her place by his side, as the guests settled into a hushed expectation. Erick cleared his throat, trying to steady the swell of emotions inside him.

Next, Daniel and Sky began to recite their vows, words they had written themselves. Erick's thoughts drifted involuntarily again to Grace. The longing for her presence overwhelmed him, and he desperately wished she were here, witnessing this joy alongside him. Daniel spoke with conviction, and his voice was unwavering as it carried the weight of his promises. Then Sky reciprocated, her voice full of laughter and tears.

Amidst the fluttering confetti and a chorus of jubilant cheers, Daniel sealed his union with a tender kiss that spoke volumes, his adoration for his bride as clear as the golden sky above them. Sky responded with a radiant smile, her happiness infectious. Then, with a playful wink to the crowd, she hiked up the hem of her elegant gown to reveal a pair of well-worn cowboy boots. The guests erupted into a boisterous celebration, clapping and whooping, their joy mingling with the rustic charm of the farm.

In one smooth motion, Daniel reached out and gently lifted his bride onto his lap, her voluminous tulle skirt cascading around them like cotton candy. Daniel and Sky rolled toward the barn that had been lovingly transformed for a rustic reception, and Erick realized in that moment that his brother and Sky's relationship represented a picture-perfect moment of love overcoming adversity. Erick's heart swelled with pride at the thought.

The newlyweds reached the barn's threshold just as the sunset cast an orange glow over the scene. Erick lifted his glass of sparkling cider, the slender stem of the flute cool between his fingers. He raised the glass higher, catching the light of the amber bulbs that dangled like stars above from the barn rafters. The soft clink of his fork against the glass drew the attention of expectant faces toward him. He cleared his throat, and the room fell into a hush.

"Daniel and Sky," Erick began. His eyes, dark blue and earnest, focused on his brother and new sister-in-law on their special day. "What a miracle your love has been to each other and everyone you come into contact with." He looked over the beautiful, enchanting venue. Pink and white peonies arranged in burlap-covered mason jars wrapped with an artist's touch complemented the magical sunset that shone through the windows.

"Sky, you not only bring light into Daniel's life, but also to everyone that you meet. Your dedication to your work and our youthful patients never fails to amaze me, and I'm inspired by you and strive to be better with my clients because of you."

There was a rustle as people shifted in their seats, their attention on Erick's sincerity.

"The only thing you love more than your work is my little brother." The words were a nod to their bond, visible to all present, a truth that resonated in the shared smiles and knowing glances exchanged around the room. "We are all blessed to welcome you into our crazy family."

As Erick spoke, a loneliness welled inside of him. He pushed the thought aside, focusing instead on the love that filled the space, a love that promised hope and renewal. Sky's smile anchored Erick's as he looked toward her, acknowledging their mission to heal others.

"Daniel, I'm so happy to call you my brother," Erick said, his voice thick with emotion. "Look at you," he paused. "You are all grown up now, buddy!" His throat tightened as he realized just how much Daniel had grown in both maturity and character. He was bearing witness to another milestone, feeling both pride and a twinge of melancholy for the moments they

would no longer share, and for the people who would not celebrate with Daniel today, like his mother and father.

Erick raised his glass higher, his arm steady despite the
storm of emotions within him. "To Daniel and his new wife!"
he toasted, his eyes meeting his brother's, willing him to understand the depth of love behind each word. "May your days be
long and filled with the joy you bring to others. I love you both
for your perseverance and dedication in your lives, helping others daily." His voice was thick but did not falter. "You inspire *me*
to be a better man, Daniel." He watched as Daniel's eyes softened, an understanding passing between them. "You both have
shown me that love was possible, and the two of you together
means the world will be a better place. You two are living exam-
ples of how to do it right, and I'm honored to share in this special day. This day, where love truly wins. Mom and Dad would
be very proud and are here with us celebrating." Erick paused.
"To love! God bless you both." Then he laughed. "I better not
see you two at work until *after* the honeymoon!"

Just then, Jace and Luna both let out a loud bark of agreement, breaking the tension, while everyone laughed and clapped.
Erick slid back into his chair beside Daniel, who was busy receiving congratulatory pats on the back and shaking hands with
wide-grinned guests.

"You're still the sappy one!" Daniel's voice cut through the
clapping and resumed chatter.

The laughter and applause thundered through the air, and
Erick's grip on the glass tightened as he brought it to his lips.
The effervescence tickled his nose before the liquid warmth
spread down his throat. The glow from the lights caught the
edges of the glass, casting a dance of light across the linen tablecloths.

The DJ announced the first dance, and Sky and Daniel's
wedding song, 'Thinking Out Loud' by Ed Sheeran, filled the
room. Daniel placed Sky on his lap again and spun the wheelchair around the dance floor.

Erick found himself lost in the moment as his gaze drifted over to Brook and Finn's table. He set the now-empty glass down just as a waiter came by with another filled glass and set it down by Erick. A shadow of disquiet crept over Erick, who had a sinking feeling of an unwelcome weight on his chest. His mouth felt dry, so he picked up the fresh glass and downed his sparkling cider. It felt different than the last one, and he instantly realized it was champagne as he felt a warmth in his stomach.

"Hey man, you okay?" Daniel returned from the dance floor as Sky hopped off his lap and began line dancing with her friends.

Erick forced a smile, nodding. "Yeah, just—"

"Thinking about Grace?" Daniel finished for him with that knowing look in his eyes.

"Can't hide anything from you, can I?" Erick moved the empty glass away from Daniel and chuckled weakly, but the smile didn't reach his eyes. He scanned the room again, half-expecting Grace to materialize from the shadows. He leaned back into his chair beside Daniel.

"Give her time," Daniel said, squeezing Erick's shoulder reassuringly. "She's got to deal with her stuff, just like we all do."

"Beautiful speech, Erick," a voice came from across the table from Sky's friend Isabelle, pulling him back from the edge of his thoughts. His gaze met Isabelle's. He didn't know her well, only from sharing a light conversation with her the night before at the rehearsal dinner.

"Thank you," he replied.

She took the empty seat to his right and offered a tentative smile and a hopeful look. Her hazel eyes sparkled under the fairy lights overhead.

"Would you like to dance?"

He studied her and hesitated. She was not Grace, but something about her—the way she held herself, expectant and slightly nervous—stirred something within him. It was a longing for connection, a momentary reprieve from the ache that gnawed at his soul.

"Sure," Erick replied, his voice steadier than he felt. He rose, and the chair scraped gently against the wooden floor. He extended his hand to her. Together, they stepped onto the dance floor, the music enveloping them in its gentle embrace. He held her and led with a practiced ease, and each movement reminded him of his lessons in his youth. As they danced, Erick's mind wandered. He envisioned Grace's red hair catching the sunlight on one of her long treks, her smile wide with adventure. Yet he was moving to a new rhythm with someone else, trying to match the beat of another's heart when his own was with the woman he couldn't seem to forget.

He and Isabelle moved together into the sea of dancing couples, stepping in time to the melody that filled the air. With each turn, Erick contemplated what roles he was expected to play: the supportive brother, the intelligent colleague, and the man who had it all together on the surface.

"Daniel and Sky are perfect for each other," she commented, her smile unwavering.

"They sure are, aren't they?" he remarked. And then the song drew to an end, the last notes hanging in the air like unfulfilled promises. "Thank you for the dance, Isabelle." His voice expressed gratitude for the dance, distraction, and a fleeting sense of normalcy instead of his constant emotional turmoil.

"Thank *you*," she echoed, her smile lingering as they moved off the dance floor and returned to the reality of the celebration around them. "I have to admit, I'm impressed you remembered my name."

Erick managed a half-smile, noticing how the flickering candlelight made Isabelle's skin glow. As she stood before him, he was momentarily struck by her natural beauty.

The conversation lulled, and Erick's attention drifted, captivated by the ambience of the room. "Thank you again for the dance, Isabelle," Erick said, his voice barely audible above the crowd. He started to feel lighter on his feet for the first time that day.

"Any time, Erick," she responded with a hint of reluctance in her tone. Sky wagged her finger, calling Isabelle to her. "Excuse me for just a moment," Isabelle said, stealing away toward Sky, and Erick returned to his seat.

Left alone with his thoughts, he watched the happy faces around him. He marveled at the ease with which they embraced the joy of the occasion. Erick wondered if there would ever come a day when he could join them without feeling like an impostor in his own life. He saw Brook and Finn dancing and was surprised that Daniel had even invited them. *How could they make their marriage work?* he wondered.

A waiter came by with glasses of champagne. Erick took another glass, and the gentle fizz of champagne caressed his tongue before slipping like a silk ribbon down his throat. He had nothing to lose. His bloodstream hummed with lightness, and he could finally breathe again. *Why not? It wasn't like he was actually an alcoholic.*

At that moment, Isabelle returned.

"Well, I'm back, and I'm all yours."

"Let's get some air." Erick gestured toward the exit as a waiter handed both of them fresh flutes of champagne.

"Let's," she said, her smile wide as he guided her into the humid night air. Isabelle's eyes held his—a mirror reflecting a hunger for connection—and then her lips met his in a kiss that whispered promises Erick knew he couldn't keep.

He pulled back, the taste of champagne now a bitter reminder of his own demons. "Isabelle, I can't—I'm not ready for anything serious right now."

"Who says it has to be serious, Erick?" The vulnerability in her eyes and the champagne made him want to stay with her a little longer.

Part One

Chapter 1

6 months later...

Grace traced the cover of her book, *If You Only Knew*, with her finger. The book was artfully displayed in a stacked tower at the *Written Word* bookstore. The book title's irony was not lost on her; so many parts of her personal story remained a mystery. Her story intertwined her life with the wisdom she learned from her biological mother's journal.

All at once, Grace felt uneasy. A prickle of awareness crept up her spine. She felt an eerie sensation of eyes upon her, examining and intrusive. She straightened her posture as her gaze swept over the room. A lone figure lingered by the history section, thumbing through a book on ancient civilizations. There was nothing remarkable about this man, who instantly averted his eyes. Grace shook it all off, attributing the attention to being a well-known author. She'd been through so much mental and physical trauma in the last decade: feeling trapped while dating Finn, losing all of her memory, having to use a wheelchair after her fall last year, and thinking she may never walk again. Grace felt the anger rise within her again while her fingers brushed over the locket her father Robin had given her last year.

"Quite a turnout you had tonight," Mr. Limbo commented from behind the counter, bringing Grace's thoughts back to the present.

"Thank you," Grace said, glad for the distraction from her racing thoughts. She turned away from the display, and her eyes landed on the corner of the room where she had just read excerpts of her book to an attentive audience. The tour ended in her hometown, and she'd been welcomed warmly here. Because of Erick's unexpected kiss tonight, this book signing was different from any other.

Once again, Grace felt butterflies as the memory of the kiss lingered on her lips, sweet yet confusing, as if it belonged to another lifetime—one where she could allow herself the luxury of being loved without fear or doubt. Erick's touch had been tender and reassuring, but as she replayed the moment, her heart filled with conflicting emotions. Grace wanted to be with him more than anything, but it was too soon. She couldn't be with anyone until she followed the new leads about Raven's death and learned who her biological father was.

Grace's team had left, and now she waited for her ride to the airport, where she would meet Pala. Grace recalled his long, grey ponytail, his kind eyes, and the heartfelt conversation she had with him at the end of the book signing.

"I was hoping you'd sign my book for me. I traveled across the country and missed the initial signing. Make it out to Pala." He handed her the book. Grace paused at the mention of his name and then looked up at him, recognition moving over her face. "I think you and I have a lot to talk about," he said.

"I have so many questions," was all she ended up saying. Grace was stunned to see Pala in the flesh, seeking to find her. She wanted to ask him everything about Raven right then and there.

"And I could answer them, but maybe I should just show you," Pala said as he pulled an envelope from his pocket. "I know this is presumptuous of me, but I talked to your assistant, and she said this was your last book signing." The warmth of his eyes made her feel at ease.

Grace opened the envelope, revealing a one-way ticket from Hartford to San Diego.

"This flight leaves *tonight* in only two and a half hours."

"I know it's short notice, but I thought I would take a chance," Pala said. "This was the last flight out." Pala took his now signed book and held it in the crook of his arm. "We can book your return flight whenever you like."

The bookstore owner sealed up the last box of books with long tape and looked over his shoulder toward Grace. "This is the last of them."

"Great, thank you!" Grace turned to the owner while she placed the ticket in her pocket.

"Have a good night, then." Mr. Limbo shook her hand, picked up the box of books, and brought them to the back. When he returned, he had her two bags and a suitcase. "These are yours, I'm sure." He waved goodbye and made his way back to his office.

I have no excuse not to go, she thought to herself. *My bags are with me, and I have no obligations for the coming week.* Then, she suddenly remembered that Erick was waiting for her at Café Bella. She hesitated as her thoughts warred with each other. *I can't be with Erick fully until I know who my father is. He's going to hate this.* She cringed, knowing he would be confused and hurt. *What if he doesn't understand?* Grace took a deep breath and closed her eyes.

"Are you okay?" Pala asked, breaking into her thoughts.

"Um, yes." Grace opened her eyes determinedly. "I just need to reschedule something I had planned for tonight." *I won't get another chance like this again. He has to understand.* But her stomach twisted into a knot because she was certain Erick would be disappointed. He'd waited so long for her already.

"I can't believe how much you're like her," Pala mused. "Anyway, our flight leaves at 9:35 p.m. I have to check out of my hotel and make some calls. I can meet you at the gate."

"I hope my car arrives soon or I won't make it on time."

Grace's phone beeped, and she looked at it. "Well, look at that. Right on time. My car is almost here."

Pala gently took her phone and started tapping the keyboard. "Here's my number in case you have any issues. I'll see you there. I know it will be worth your while." He smiled as he handed her the phone back and left the bookstore. Another notification chimed, indicating that her ride would be there in a minute.

Guilt seeped into her thoughts, and she thought of Erick waiting for her at Café Bella at this very moment. Then Grace remembered the last time she saw him at HigherGround. She had mixed feelings about Erick, and a few reservations tumbled into her mind just then. Being with Erick was going to be wonderful, but at the same time, Grace couldn't deny her fear whenever she looked at him. She knew it wasn't fair to Erick, but his face was a mirror image of his twin brother Finn—the man who left her with scars. She would deal with all that when she returned from her trip to California. She just hoped that a week or two would be enough time to figure out who her father was and the truth about Raven's death.

The path to California beckoned, and Grace felt the enormity of the decision that lay ahead. Her father's bloodline could either redeem or condemn her. How could she start a life with Erick when her family roots were unclear? After all, Grace had just recently learned that Raven was her mother, not her estranged aunt.

When she stepped outside, a frigid wind caught her hair. Snow hugged the sidewalk edges, typical for late winter in Connecticut. The moon highlighted the night while she looked around the well-lit street.

She was at a crossroads between her past and her future. Her gaze drifted toward the street corner cafe where Erick would be waiting. She approached the street, looking for the car that would soon take her to the airport. She hoped she would find the answers she so desperately sought, and that this trip would be the final journey to confront her past and a chance to shape her future, one where Erick's place remained uncertain.

Her phone chimed, and Grace glanced at the screen, noticing an alert flashing. Her eyes locked on a car as it pulled up and then parked. She checked the app that showed the driver's photo, a square-jawed man with dark eyes and a thick mustache. The driver exited the car and leaned against the black sedan, waiting. His derby hat concealed most of his face, so she couldn't be sure, but he matched the image well enough.

Her gaze fell on the car's make, model, and license plate, which matched the phone application.

"Are you Grace Evans?" the driver asked as he moved to the passenger door and opened it with practiced professionalism.

She nodded.

"Ready when you are."

"Thank you," Grace said, sinking into the faux leather backseat. The door closed gently, and he placed her bags in the trunk.

The driver settled behind the wheel, turned the key, and started the engine. Grace started to relax. She had decided to risk it all, and the car would take her to her next step. She was pulling away from her future possibility of a relationship with Erick and toward a journey that demanded that she confront her past. She peered out the window and wrapped herself in silence as the familiar sights of the town faded.

"Quiet night for a drive," the driver commented, adjusting the rearview mirror.

"Quiet's what I need," she confessed, watching the bookstore shrink in the distance.

"Running from something or toward it?" he inquired.

"Both," Grace admitted, the honesty of her response surprising even herself.

"Life's a mystery novel sometimes, ain't it?" the driver said. "Full of twists and turns."

"Exactly," Grace agreed, feeling the weight of her own story pressing down on her. "But I'm ready to turn the page."

"Where are you headed?" he asked, focusing on the road ahead.

"San Diego." Grace shook off the queasy feeling in her stomach and turned her attention to the rolling landscape.

"Ah! I love it out there. I might find my way out there soon."

"Do you have family out there?"

"Turns out, I just might. I just found some family I didn't know I had," the driver answered as he turned onto a new road.

"I hope you can connect with them. I'm on a similar journey." Grace closed her eyes. She couldn't shake off thoughts about her perplexing family lineage, her mother's sudden death, and the mysterious figure known as Jack Stone. California just might hold all the answers she was seeking. As the miles and scenery passed, her heart raced with anticipation for what awaited her at the end of this journey.

No matter what truths lay in wait, Grace knew one thing: she needed to see the truth before moving on. Grace needed to know whose blood ran through her veins and if she was still in danger. If she were honest, Grace would admit that, in her heart of hearts, she hoped all this would lead her back to Erick.

Chapter 2

Erick opened the door to Café Bella, his red scarf tucked into his long coat. He remembered when he brought Grace here for the first time after her accident. They had been there so many times when they were kids, and later when they had worked together on her recovery. The memory brought a smile to his face. He recalled his wild idea to be Grace's physical therapist while she was recovering from amnesia and learning to walk again. Before she regained her memory, he almost blew his cover several times. One incident happened at this very cafe. They had ordered hot chocolates, and the barista had topped Grace's with cinnamon. Erick knew she was allergic to it and had to say something. Even though the lies became stacked even higher, he felt that the ends did justify the means. Grace could walk now and remember everything from her past. Meeting here tonight was their chance to start their relationship fresh *without* the lies.

A familiar barista named Marie immediately greeted Erick when she heard the cafe door chime. The aroma of roasted coffee beans and freshly baked pastries filled Erick's nose. He eyed his favorite table, tucked away in a secluded corner by a window. It was quiet, and there were little twinkly lights above the window where he could see the street view. Unfortunately, there was no sign of Grace yet.

"Good evening, Erick," Marie said cheerfully, her eyes crinkling upward in a smile. "The usual spot?"

"Thank you, Marie. Yes, that would be perfect." His voice was low, and he could barely hide his excitement.

"Just you today?" she asked, placing a menu in front of him.

"No, I'm meeting someone, so please leave two menus." Erick situated himself so he faced the entrance, and then he unwound his scarf.

"Would you like something while you're waiting?" Her lips pressed tightly together.

"Just two cups of hot chocolate, no cinnamon, and extra whipped cream, please." Erick scanned the menu.

A tinkling of the chime above the door caught Erick's attention, but it was just another happy couple entering the cafe. He let out a heavy sigh and opened his coat, letting it fall behind him on the chair. His gaze flickered impatiently to the entrance every few seconds. *She's going to be here any minute!*

"You want me to wait to bring out that hot chocolate? Or would you like it now?" Marie asked, her eyes falling to the empty seat next to Erick.

"Um, you can bring it out," Erick confirmed, looking toward the door. "She'll be here soon."

He leaned back in his chair, his fingers intertwined as he replayed the kiss at the book signing in his mind. It was a kiss that whispered of promises and an abundant future. A scripture came to mind just then. Jeremiah 29:11. *"For I know the plans I have for you," declares the Lord, "plans to prosper you and not to harm you, plans to give you hope and a future."* These words had comforted him all these months as he waited for the right time to see Grace again. Even now, he closed his eyes and prayed he would say the right things when she arrived, hoping he would not mess things up yet again.

Erick heard the door chime again, and his thoughts danced with anticipation. She would finally be here with him. He allowed his mind to wander as he relished the memory again of Grace reading passages from her novel, her voice beckoning to his soul. He remembered how her lips felt on his and how the world stood still for the moment.

A ceramic mug clinked onto the table, breaking his reverie. Steam curled up from the hot chocolates. Maria looked at him expectantly as she set the second cup down.

"Thank you." He offered a grateful smile. Erick reached for the warm mug and took a deep breath, allowing the rich sweetness of melted chocolate to fill his senses.

Erick pictured Grace walking through the door. Her smile, reserved only for him, would light up the room more brilliantly than the full moon outside. *Grace will be here any second,* he thought to himself. *What will I say to her?* He picked up his phone and saw no messages. It was getting late, and he was starting to worry. It had been over a year since Grace had taken time apart from him, needing space to process the lies she discovered during her recovery. He had waited patiently for her to heal and decide if a future together was possible.

It was a miracle that Erick stumbled onto her website a few months ago and saw that her book tour schedule was ending in her hometown. He could not stay away and recalled his excitement when he stood in the back while she read from her first published book, which told their actual love story.

He saw Grace's beautiful, wavy, red hair as she stood up front, her voice filling the bookstore. Erick remembered how his heart beat faster with each word she spoke. When she paused, he felt compelled by an unseen force to weave through the crowd of enraptured listeners to reach her. As their eyes met, he confidently strode all the way to the front and joined Grace, quoting a passage from her book but altering the words slightly to make it a grand romantic gesture. His heart pounded as he took her in his arms and they shared an electrifying kiss.

Lost in the moment, Erick didn't even notice when the waitress brought a glass of ice water to the table. It wasn't until she winked at him that he returned to reality. But before he could fully process what was happening, his phone rang and startled him out of his blissful state.

Erick glanced at the caller ID and saw that it was his twin brother Finn. Over the past year, he had been by his brother's side every step of the way as Finn battled addiction. Erick had acted as his unofficial sponsor, and it had been a minute since they'd talked, so he answered. Finn began yelling in his ear before he could even say hello.

"Brooke is trying–" Finn started.

"Sorry, Finn, I can't talk. I'm about to go into a meeting. I'll call you tonight." Erick's heart raced as he pressed the phone off. Nothing was going to get in the way this time. He prepared what he would say to Grace. He had dreamt of this moment for years, envisioning a life where they could be together and start a family. This was the legacy he had been working toward his entire life, a purpose greater than anything he had ever imagined. As the door chimes echoed through the small cafe again, Erick looked up, his heart racing with the wild anticipation of Grace's arrival. But immediately, his world caved inward, his breath sucked out of him. It wasn't her. A thought came over him as he swallowed down the truth. He had read the situation wrong yet again. And maybe, just maybe, she wasn't coming after all.

Chapter 3

race thought about all the book tours and the traveling she had done over the last year. Her adoptive parents, Robin and Faith, were kind enough to attend several book signings to support her. They had always been there, and even though she still wanted answers about her biological parents, it did not mean she had forgotten all they had done for her. She decided to text her parents just to keep them in the loop.

Grace: I'm going to California tonight with Pala. He has answers about Jack, and I want to learn more about Raven. I plan to be there a week, maybe more. I'll call you when I get out there.
Robin: Are you sure this is what you want?
Grace: It's what I need.
Robin: Okay, pumpkin. Know your mother and I will always be here for you.
Grace: Thanks, Dad.
Robin: Be safe. Love you!

As they merged onto the highway, Grace leaned back, closing her eyes against the glare of the street lights. Behind her eyelids danced images of Erick, his face a soothing reminder of what she could have or what she might lose. Grace knew she'd have to text him, but she didn't know what words would ease his inevitable pain.

"We're almost to Bradley International Airport. What terminal and airline are you taking?" the driver asked, tapping his tungsten wedding band against the steering wheel as he waited.

"I'm flying American through Terminal B to San Diego," Grace responded, briefly opening her eyes and gazing at the screen of her phone. She was torn between gratitude for Erick's unexpected arrival at her book signing and the looming guilt of leaving him behind.

As the airport drew closer, Café Bella was long gone along with the hope of being with Erick. Each passing second tested Grace's resolve and threatened to break her heart. Erick's father had torn Erick away from Grace once, landing her into Finn's arms. How could she choose between her present love for Erick and her past trauma with Finn? How could she resolve any of her relationship issues without unraveling her family ones first?

Grace knew that whatever lay ahead, she had to do this, not for anyone else but for the woman staring back at her in the mirror each morning. The airport would be the gateway that would lead her to the answers she so desperately sought.

Grace's fingers hovered over the screen of her phone as she contemplated her words.

Grace: Erick, I'm so sorry. I have to go to San Diego. I can't make it to the cafe.

Erick: San Diego? What? What's going on? Alone?? Right now?

Grace watched as bubbles appeared and disappeared several times before another text message from Erick came through.

Erick: You promised. I waited a year for this, Grace. A year.

Grace: I know, and I'm so incredibly sorry. It's...complicated. Not alone. I'm with Pala.

Erick: Complicated? Is that what you're calling this?

Grace: I said I was sorry.

Erick: You know... you were kissing me back, Grace! Did I misinterpret something?

Grace: No! God, no. It's not like that. I found out something huge about my adoption. About my mother.

Erick: What? What are you talking about?

Grace: Raven. Her death wasn't an accident. I need to find out what really happened. I have to go to San Diego now. This may be my only chance to find out the truth and who my father is.

Erick: So you're leaving? Just like that? Again?

Grace: I need answers, Erick. I can't just move on without knowing.

Erick: So... what are you saying? What about us?

Grace: I don't know, Erick. I truly don't. I just... I need time. I need to go to San Diego.

Erick: Time. Right. So what am I supposed to do? Wait here while you're off chasing ghosts?

Grace: I'm not chasing ghosts, Erick. I'm finding my family. I'll keep in touch, I promise.

Erick: Promises. Yeah, I've heard those before. Look, Grace, I don't know what to say. But I find it weird that you couldn't pick up the phone and give me a heads up before I made a fool of myself waiting for you.

Grace: I know, and I'm so, so sorry. It was just too painful. I'm sorry I let you down.

Outside, the world passed by in a blur of white and grey colors, the trees barren during this season. Grace felt the tears rim her eyes as she thought about Erick's biting text messages. With each mile, the reality of Grace's departure settled deeper into her bones, an ache that was both freeing and terrifying. She closed her eyes again and leaned back against the plush seat, allowing the music to wash over her. In her mind's eye, she saw her cottage in the woods, the sanctuary she had created after her recovery, and her memories returned from the past. But even within those walls, the shadows lurked with unanswered questions about what really happened to her mother, about Jack Stone, and where Pala fit into the mix. Pala was here now and might help her find her biological father's identity.

The car slowed, navigating the New England roads that snaked around Bradley International Airport. Grace gripped the handle of her small bag, feeling the smooth leather beneath her fingertips. Her heart thrummed in sync with the turn signal's click as they approached Terminal B.

"American Airlines, right?" the driver asked, confirming her earlier statement.

"Yes," Grace replied, her voice steadier than she felt. "Terminal B."

"We're here." He navigated the vehicle with a practiced ease, pulling up to the curb outside the bustling entrance. Grace reached for the door handle.

"I'll get that," he offered. The driver jumped out of the car and placed her bags on the curb and then opened her door to let her out. "Safe travels," he said, tipping his hat. "May you find what you're looking for."

Grace's eyes narrowed as she stepped out into the biting cold. She heard the door close, and then the car disappeared into the sea of travelers, leaving her alone with a fierce determination burning in her chest. The smell of exhaust filled her nose as she marched forward, ready to take on whatever challenges lay ahead. California held answers, ones that would define her past and shape her future. Grace carried her bags to the entrance, where her journey began with the push of a revolving door and the roar of airplanes overhead.

Chapter 4

E rick looked down at his phone again, hoping she would change her mind. He dialed her number, but it went straight to voicemail. *Who the hell is Pala?*

Dread flooded his veins, and his phone rang again. He sighed and closed his eyes when he saw it wasn't Grace but his little brother.

"Where have you been?" Daniel asked before Erick could speak.

"I went to a book signing," Erick said, slumping in his seat. It was too late now. Perhaps if he had just stayed with Grace at the bookstore, he could have at least talked to her and convinced her to take him with her. He kicked himself for not just waiting there. What if something happened to her in California, and he wasn't there to protect her?

"Of course, you can't stay away from that girl! How did it go?" Daniel teased.

"Well, it started off great. Grace was up there reading from the book and…"

"Please tell me you didn't do anything crazy," Daniel interrupted.

"Define crazy?" Erick coughed. He squeezed his phone to his ear and grimaced. "So, I saw Grace," he said slowly, "and I may have recited some lines from her book."

"Of course you did," Daniel chuckled. "And?"

Erick could hear Sky in the background asking if he was with Grace.

"We ended up kissing," Erick said, stroking his beard absentmindedly.

"You *kissed*? Where?" Erick heard Sky's voice and knew he was now on speakerphone.

"Right in front of everyone. They even clapped," Erick said with a cringe.

"That's straight out of a rom-com!" Daniel exclaimed. "So, are you two official now?"

"It's complicated." Erick sighed. Daniel's voice sounded muffled for a second, as though he was saying something to Sky that he didn't want Erick to hear. "Look, I didn't plan to see her and kiss her. It just happened," Erick defended, feeling the need to justify his actions.

"Of course," Daniel responded, calm and collected as always. "Love hasn't been smooth for you, brother. I just don't want you to get hurt again." He paused for a moment. "What now?"

"We were supposed to meet at Café Bella. Let's just say, I'm here, and she's not."

"What happened?"

Erick heard the door chime again. "Actually, she…" He hesitated, his throat tightening around the words. The silence stretched between them, filled only by the distant murmur of conversation from nearby tables.

"Come on, Erick. Talk to me," Daniel prodded gently.

Erick drew in a breath, tasting the bittersweet flavor of reality. "She's gone." The admission felt like defeat.

"Where?" The question came out flat, almost resigned, from

Daniel.

"To California. She sent texts, and that's all I got."

Erick heard nothing on the other end of the line for a few seconds. Finally, Daniel said, "Man, I'm sorry. Wait, what did she say *exactly*?"

"That she's sorry. That she has some quest to go on or something like that. I get that she's determined. It's one of the things I love so much about her, but a text message saying she's sorry kind of feels like a punch in the gut. And it doesn't change the fact that she's out *there* somewhere… and not *here*." Erick felt the familiar nag in his chest. It was a constant pull, like an anchor tethering a ship that was trying to sail. He wasn't sure he could keep up this dance for much longer.

"What did the texts say?" Daniel asked again after a long pause.

"She's with some dude who knew her mother. I mean if this was so important to her then why didn't she tell me at the book signing? I have zero clarification on us. And from what I do know, she didn't choose me." Erick was just rambling now, speaking his thoughts for all to hear. He ran his hand through his hair in frustration. *How was this happening again?* "I can't do this anymore." Erick wasn't one to cry, so, when he felt his eyes burn with tears, he quickly wiped them with a napkin. This whole thing with Grace was taking an emotional toll on him. "I think we're done for good this time."

"It sucks," Daniel said. "I hate that you have to keep going through this, and I'm here for you, bro. Look, I like Grace. She's… amazing, and I get that if we were in her position, maybe we'd leave everything to go on a quest to find our parents too, but I stand by you. My brother. And I don't like that she's making you feel bad." He paused before continuing. "Despite what you say, I don't think it's over. So, you do what you need to, and if that means you're done with her, that's okay by me. And if you two are meant to be, that's great. I support your relationship. Either way, Grace needs to meet with you face to face. You've known each other too long for serious conversations to happen through text message."

"The back and forth is overwhelming, Daniel. I tried so many times to stop loving her, but… I can't. And that's insane, because she drives me crazy!" Erick rubbed his forehead. He'd put his love life on hold for Grace and knew he should move on with someone who actually wanted to be with him.

"Did she say how long she would be in California?" Daniel asked.

Erick sent Daniel a screenshot of the texts from his phone. "Sent you the text exchange. I don't know. Besides, I'm supposed to do the Beyond Limits Therapy conference presentation in a few days in Boston." Erick took a sip of his hot chocolate with his free hand and swallowed the pain down as he waited for Daniel to say something. "Daniel? Are you there?"

"I'm here. Dude, go to the conference," Daniel said finally. "Enjoy yourself. Then figure it out after that. And like I said before, maybe Grace *is* the one, maybe not, but you shouldn't miss out on other opportunities for love if Grace isn't emotionally available right now."

Erick pondered Daniel's words for a minute. "You know what, Daniel? You're right. I need to focus on the conference and figure out all the Grace stuff when I get back."

"First things first, brother," Daniel began, and Erick could almost see the reassuring smile on his face. "Breathe. Then we'll figure out the rest." Daniel's voice crackled through the phone.

Erick paused, the screen's glow casting shadows across his face as he reread Grace's messages for what seemed like the hundredth time. An unending ache throbbed in Erick's temples.

"I'll figure it out after the conference," he whispered, more to himself than to Daniel. He squeezed his eyes shut and said goodbye to his little brother. Before Erick put his phone in his pocket, he texted Grace one final time.

Erick: And you don't want my help? You know I would do anything for you and help you in any way I can.

Grace: I'm very sorry, but I need to do this on my own, Erick. Please forgive me. I'll keep in touch.

He shook his head in frustration. When was the waiting going to end with this woman? He pulled some bills out of his pocket and hastily threw them on the table next to Grace's untouched, and now cold, hot cocoa. Grace wasn't coming. He couldn't believe it. After all they'd been through, all they'd overcome, and now they were right back at square one.

Chapter 5

G race looked at her phone one last time. She hoped Erick would wait for her, but there was no way to be sure. She took a deep breath and realized the finality of it all. Only after she found her answers could she even think about opening herself up to Erick or *anyone*, for that matter.

She found her flight on a departure screen, passed through security, and then headed toward her gate. Grace's eyes darted around the area looking for Pala among the travelers waiting for the flight.

"Flight 437 to San Diego is now boarding at Gate 12," bellowed the announcement overhead. It was time.

Clasping the boarding pass tight enough to crease the paper, she inhaled deeply and saw Pala standing there waiting for her.

"I was hoping you didn't change your mind. Are you ready?" he asked as Grace approached.

"As ready as I can ever be." She walked with Pala toward the flight attendant who was collecting tickets.

"Boarding pass, please," the attendant said with a practiced smile. Grace handed it over, her gaze catching sight of a family embracing a few feet away.

"Enjoy your flight, Ms. Evans!"

The flight attendant returned the boarding pass and ushered her toward the jet bridge.

"Thank you," Grace murmured, stepping forward. The narrow corridor seemed to constrict around her, and the aircraft's hum grew louder as she approached the plane's entrance.

Finally, she settled into her seat by the window and gazed outside at the tarmac, the ground crew moving about in the night. She relaxed as Pala slid into the middle seat next to her.

"Is this your first time in San Diego?" Pala asked.

"Yes," Grace confessed. "I've been flying and traveling the last few months for the book tour, but only as far west as Las Vegas."

A white-haired man with an LA Dodgers hat entered the aircraft holding his leather bag with his right hand and walked down the aisle to his seat. She felt a strange sensation of déjà vu. His lips curled into a smile under his white mustache. He was probably someone's grandpa. She suddenly missed Bran, her grandfather. Soon after, the father and daughter she had seen in line while waiting to board walked down the aisle past them.

"Here," Pala said, and Grace's gaze turned from the passengers boarding to a piece of gum held out for her. "For your ears when we take off."

"Please fasten your seatbelt. Flight attendants prepare for take off," instructed the voice over the intercom.

With a gentle lurch, they took off, climbing higher until the twinkly lights on the buildings below shrank to mere specks.

"You should rest," Pala suggested. "The flight is long."

"I can't wait to get to know you and learn more about my mother, but I need to know if Jack Stone's blood runs through my veins. I need to know if his insanity is also a part of who I am. It would be great to find out that you're my biological father."

"Blood isn't destiny, Grace," Pala counseled, his tone in-

41

fused with wisdom from years of navigating life. "I can't wait to get to know you as well. No matter what we find, you are my family now."

The plane climbed in altitude, and as she contemplated what lay ahead for her in San Diego, Grace knew that sleep would not come easily.

Chapter 6

Erick stared out his bedroom window into the night, recalling the days when he used to run with Jace. Lately, though, it seemed like he spent so little time with his beloved companion. Daniel and Sky were happy to watch Jace when Erick traveled. Even now, he would be dropping Jace off again in the morning so that he could attend the Boston conference. Last year he kept himself busy with a lot of travel and various meetings for his physical therapy franchise, HigherGround. This should've felt like a dream come true for Erick, but for some reason, it only left him empty inside. In fact, his whole life suddenly felt meaningless. And the largest void was the place in his heart where Grace had been for so many years. But she was gone. She'd run away from him too many times. This time, all the way to California.

Erick reluctantly opened his suitcase and carefully packed a week's worth of folded clothes and one plain suit into the bag and zipped up his carry-on. Erick always traveled light. He preferred the minimalist lifestyle even before it became trendy to do so.

A notification beeped on his phone just then, reminding him of his conference set up tomorrow. Then he remembered he needed to call Finn back. As the phone rang, he waited, but it went straight to voicemail. Giving up, he tossed the phone down on the side table when it immediately rang. It was Chris Callahan. He hesitated for a beat before answering. "Chris. Didn't expect to hear from you until tomorrow. What's up?"

"Erick! Always straight to the point. I like that. Listen, I'm just checking in to see if you're still coming to the conference?"

"Yeah, I already confirmed that I'll be there. What's up?" Erick ran his hand through his hair and then tapped his foot rapidly.

"You know me too well. I've got an idea that's going to blow the lid off physical therapy as we know it. I'm talking about next-level stuff. And I want you in on it."

Erick sighed. "Next-level, huh? What's the angle?"

"Customized and adaptive algorithm programs for patients, real-time feedback, predictive analytics—the works. Imagine scaling what you do at HigherGround to a global audience. We're talking partnerships, funding, the whole nine yards."

"Are you talking about artificial intelligence software for therapy?"

"I am," Callahan answered.

"That's… a stretch. My clients come to me because they want that human connection. Besides I'm not too sure about all this technology stuff. It depersonalizes everything."

"Come to my presentation while you're here for the conference. You won't be disappointed."

"I'll think about it."

"Oh, and congratulations on being nominated for the Malley Award. You deserve it."

"Thanks, Chris."

"See you there then. Don't forget to stop by my table."

"Sure thing," Erick said and then hung up. He couldn't help but shake his head, imagining robots conducting physical therapy. Sure, on the one hand, it could free up time for the things he wanted to do, but HigherGround was all about the human and spiritual connection.

As he sat there, Erick reflected on his career briefly. He had two franchises and that was enough. He wanted to take a break and focus on what was important.

The cabin was silent now, except for Jace's snoring or the distant hoot of an owl outside. He could feel a shift in the air. It felt like he was headed for a crossroads moment, and he knew whichever road he took would not only define his future relationships, but also who he was as a man.

Chapter 7

Grace's eyelids were heavy with jet lag as she and Pala got their bags and headed toward Pala's parked car. In silence, he drove, but she was so tired she could barely see the terrain in the moonlight. She allowed her eyes to close as Pala navigated his Land Rover Defender EV over the smooth asphalt. Grace woke again when Pala pulled up to a bookstore. As she stepped out of the car, she glanced up at the still-dark sky, faintly lit with the faded hues of the rising sun. Her internal clock was off due to the time change, leaving her feeling disoriented and drained.

"Here we are," Pala said softly, breaking the silence as he shut off the engine. His voice was raspy and thick. They unloaded their bags, the wheels thumping rhythmically over the cracks in the sidewalk. "My apartment is above the bookstore." Pala led her up the stairs and unlocked the door, revealing a cozy space.

"Guest room's this way." Pala showed her the way.

She entered the room and placed her belongings on the bed. The walls were adorned with striking, framed black and white photographs that captured majestic landscapes and a few of Raven herself. Grace's eyes lingered on the photos of her mother, memories flooding back to her. She then noticed the shelves that housed an odd array of books, some standing upright while others lay on their sides. Grace wondered which of these were her mother's favorites. With a gentle thud, she rolled her suitcase to the corner of the room. Placing her other bag on the neatly made bed, Grace felt a sense of comfort wash over her. Her mother's spirit was there, and she could feel it.

"Raven took those photos," Pala said, hovering in the doorway. "Need anything before I turn in?"

Grace shook her head, then hesitated. "Actually… could we talk? Just for a minute?"

"Of course." Pala entered, settling himself into the armchair by the window as Grace perched herself on the edge of the bed, her hands fidgeting with the leather-bound journal she had brought with her. She looked up at him. "This journal… it's my mom's. She mentioned you in it."

"I hope she said nice things," Pala said with a half smile. "I wondered if she would tell you about me someday. I'm thankful you have the journal. It's like having a little piece of her." He paused, collecting his thoughts. "We were close, once. We met while I was working at a bookstore in Connecticut to save money to hike the Appalachian and Pacific Coast Trail. We hiked together on my days off. Then, we parted ways because I needed to get back to California. She showed up unexpectedly months later, and I had just finished my solo hike of the PCT. You see, I'm not just part owner of the bookstore downstairs, but I also run many guided hikes for tourists and locals. It was a life and a peaceful time for me until…" He trailed off, not needing to complete the sentence.

"Until my mom showed up," Grace finished for him.

"Yeah." Pala's gentle eyes met hers.

"If you loved her all those years ago, why did you leave her in Connecticut, pregnant with me?" Grace rubbed her eyes, which were feeling heavy again.

He hesitated to answer. Pala sighed, adjusting his loose hair tie. His voice was thick with emotion and regret. "The thing is, your mother never told me she was pregnant, and we were together only that one night back then. I left her because I had my own demons to face, and I needed to conquer mountains," he continued, his words measured. "When she came here, I changed in so many ways I never thought possible, and losing her last year tore out a piece of my soul. I still feel the pain."

Grace absorbed his words like a puzzle piece clicking into place. Here, in the guest room's soft light, with the morning's first whispers beginning to peek through the blinds, she felt the first stirrings of understanding. "Thank you for telling me," she said, her mind unable to take much more.

"Anything you want to know, I'll tell you," Pala promised, and she believed him.

Grace's fingers turned the yellow pages of her mother's journal, each entry a fragment of the past she was desperate to understand. Pala watched her from across the room.

"Jack Stone," Grace said, uttering the name like a curse. "She was terrified of him."

Pala nodded. His face seemed to crinkle with lines of regret. "Raven confided in me about Jack, how she fled from Connecticut, and the pain of leaving you with her brother, Robin, and his wife, Faith." He paused, looking away. "She stayed as long as she could in the cottage there, but every time she spent time with you, she feared Jack would find a way to get to you. Raven was never the same after that, but she was safer here with me, away from that monster."

"Safer," Grace echoed, her voice hollow. She couldn't imagine the fear that must have lived in Raven's bones. And they both knew that in the end, she wasn't safe at all.

"Your mother… she was so distraught when she came to me," Pala continued, his gaze finding hers again. "I couldn't turn her away, and I still cared for her. Our relationship grew over the next two decades. You should know she did have moments of happiness. We shared something beautiful, but she always thought about you."

Grace absorbed his words. "So you did know about me?"

"Yes, Raven did eventually tell me about you," he admitted. "I don't blame her for not telling me right away. She loved you fiercely, enough to keep you a secret, to protect you from Jack. I always wondered if you were mine, but it didn't matter because your safety was paramount."

"Before... before she fell," Grace stammered. "You mentioned she changed. What happened?" Her speech slurred as sleep tried to take her over with a force she tried to resist.

"She became paranoid just before she died, convinced someone was following her. It wasn't like her at all." He looked down. "She eventually locked herself away, not just from the world, but from me, too." Pala tenderly leaned over Grace and placed a woven blanket over her, and she let her eyes close. "Sleep, child. We have plenty of time to look into the past," he whispered.

The weight of memories and unspoken words left Grace exhausted. Physically and emotionally drained from carrying it all, Grace finally succumbed to sleep. As she drifted into dreamland, her mind was filled with questions and fragmented memories, each waiting to be connected. Despite the overwhelming burden on her shoulders, there was only one thing for her to do now and that was to rest. She knew that tomorrow would bring just as many challenges, and she needed all her strength to face them. Tomorrow, she and Pala would create a plan of action. Until then, Grace allowed herself to dream of endless possibilities and untold secrets waiting to be uncovered.

Chapter 8

Erick woke to the sound of rain pattering against the cabin's roof. He stretched, feeling the dull muscle ache from yesterday's stressful events. Jace was curled up at the foot of his bed, snoring softly. After getting dressed and packing his remaining belongings into a duffel bag, Erick grabbed a cup of green tea and headed out to his front porch, Jace trudging behind him. He sat down and took a sip as Jace settled beside him. A fresh snow had fallen overnight, and it glistened as the sun rose over the horizon. Erick savored the peace he felt at sitting there with Jace, overlooking the woods where they used to run side by side. Back then, he ran to escape a guilt that wasn't even his to bear. His thoughts drifted to Finn, and Erick wondered why his brother had called him the other night. Come to think of it, Finn hadn't called back.

The rain had stopped, but dark clouds still loomed over the horizon in central Connecticut. He sipped his tea slowly, watching as the wind pushed droplets of rain off leaves and branches. It was tranquil here, far away from the chaos and demands of everyday life. But it was also lonely. It felt like it had been so long since he had prayed deeply to God for answers. He'd spent so much time climbing the ladder of success, life had flown by at a rapid rate. Everything changed since that day on the dock when Grace recalled her memories.

Jace woke up and ran around the deck several times before returning to Erick's side with a soft whine. "I know," Erick said with a small smile as he scratched behind Jace's ear once again. "It's time to go see Luna." They both piled into the Jeep, and he dropped off Jace at HigherGround.

Before he could leave the parking lot, Erick's phone buzzed. It was his travel agent, Scarlett. "Listen, all the roads are closed due to the severe snowstorms in Massachusetts. I'll keep you posted when they're cleared for travel."

"Oh, okay," Erick's mind switched gears. "Send me the information when you can. If the schedule changes, we will have to notify the attendees and presenters."

"Already working on that. Talk soon." The call ended, and Erick knew his agent would take care of all the details. Scarlett had been recommended by his previous travel agent, who had changed careers and wanted to ensure Erick was cared for.

Erick looked over his shoulder and backed out of his space noticing the sign, *Dr. Erick Finn, DPT*. Suddenly, the soft glow of the dashboard illuminated the name *'Daniel'* on the car's digital screen, cutting through his thoughts. He put the car in drive and tapped the Bluetooth button embedded in the steering wheel.

"Hey, brother," Erick answered. *Was it Jace?* Erick rolled to a stop at the stop sign at the end of the parking lot. There was a heavy pause on the other end before Daniel's voice broke through, strained and unfamiliar. This was serious. "Is Jace okay?"

"Yeah, he's fine." Daniel, on the other hand, did not sound fine. "It's about Finn. I don't know what to do. Finn is in trouble, and Brook is gone."

"What do you mean... gone?"

"I mean, like, packed her bags and left for London."

Erick's jaw clenched because he realized he should have taken the call from Finn when he had the chance. "I… I had no idea. He tried calling me the other night at the cafe while I was waiting for Grace."

"Finn's slipping back into old habits, Erick. It's bad."

The soft click of the turn signal seemed to grow louder in Erick's ears as a plan formed in his mind. Time was ticking away—time that Finn might not have if his descent continued to spiral unchecked. "What exactly do you think is going on with him?" he asked, the car veering smoothly onto an exit ramp. Erick should have been paying attention, but his career had pulled him away from steering his brother onto the straight and narrow. He'd been pulled into so many different directions—meetings with eager inventors, showcasing their latest prosthetic innovations, calls that ran late into the night, conferences, and seminars that flew him across the country. He had left Finn to navigate his sobriety alone. Now his twin was floundering.

"Something is happening with him and Brook, but I'm not sure what. I'm fairly certain that he's drinking again."

"I'm on it," Erick said, more to himself than to his brother. "Just let me sort it out."

"Don't you have a conference to set up?" Daniel reminded him.

"God works in mysterious ways!" Erick's smile returned. What he thought was a setback turned into an opportunity to help Finn here and now. "Massachusetts is under a state of emergency due to the heavy snowstorm they got last night. I may only have a small window of time to get through to Finn. I'll keep you posted." Erick drummed his fingers on the steering wheel.

"Since Brook is out of the country," Daniel said, relieved, "she shouldn't get in your way."

"Good. That gives us some space to work with," Erick replied, his mind already racing through scenarios as he merged onto the highway. "When she's around, only bad things happen. I bet she was the one who switched out cider for the champagne at your wedding last year." He recalled the slip at Daniel's wedding, how the champagne flute had felt like a live grenade in his hand. It was a stark reminder of how fragile trying to be in control really was.

"All those years you dated Brook, you of all people should know how manipulative she can be. You need to guard yourself whenever she's in the room. Fool you once and all. I really wish I could help with this situation right now, but Sky and I are headed to a charity gala tonight, and I can't miss it. I'm already in the dog house because she wants to move out of the apartment and buy a new home in Georgia to be near her family. I'm not sure about any of this. What do you think I should do?"

Erick winced at the possibility of not seeing Daniel every day, but there was nothing he wouldn't do for his little brother, no matter the cost. He glanced at the dashboard clock. "You two will figure it out. Don't worry, Daniel. We will have a franchise in Georgia, but we should talk about this," he insisted. Erick couldn't afford to go down that rabbit hole yet. "And don't worry. I'll manage things with Finn." Erick felt the weight of responsibility settle firmly on his shoulders. "Do you know if he is at FINNLondon or Finn Manor?"

There was a brief pause before Daniel answered. "Finn Manor. Brook insisted after the wedding that they would live there full-time. Remember?"

"Of course." Erick rolled his eyes recalling Brook pushing for the ceremony to be on the lawns of Finn Manor and suspected she was up to something. Brook had always been scheming, even since they were kids. Their small wedding had been abrupt, a whirlwind of decisions that left everyone else dizzy. They were only engaged a few weeks before Brook insisted on a small, quick wedding that she planned all herself, right there on the grounds of Finn Manor. Erick had recalled thinking the reason might be that she was pregnant, but no one understood her urgency, even now over a year later.

"Thanks, Erick. I owe you one," Daniel said with gratitude.

"Hey, we're family," Erick replied.

"Finn should be at home dealing with the decorators Brook

hired."

"Decorators?" Erick scrunched up his nose. The family house was where Erick had to say goodbye to not only his mother as a boy, but also his father last year. He hadn't been back since. Now, with Finn's wavering sobriety, it was his duty to offer his help, even though it was just last year that Finn and Brook tried to take everything from Erick. He still hoped Finn had some good in him.

He passed Amaryllis Lane, where he spent the better part of last year helping Grace learn to walk again. *I wonder what she is doing in California with Pala.*

Erick signaled again and turned onto the quieter street that led toward the grand entrance of the Finn manor. As the estate came into view, its towering presence was a stark reminder of the secrets it housed. The tree at the gate brought back the memory of the car crash that night after the graduation party, more than a decade ago. He still vividly remembered the screech of metal on metal, the world spinning out of control, and then the bone-jarring impact that changed everything. After years of having nightmares, he'd finally uncovered the truth about the accident. But Daniel's life-altering injuries had fueled his guilt and propelled him to sobriety.

Erick dismissed the memories and parked. He quickly made his way to the front steps when suddenly, he had to duck to avoid being knocked down to the ground by a large sofa carried by burly men through the entrance and the foyer.

One of the men shouted, "Watch it, dude!"

Erick gathered his resolve and managed to avoid the movers. He needed to find Finn and pull his brother back from the edge.

Entering the house, Erick could hear the muffled sounds of arguing. He walked around the foyer and followed Finn's voice, which was coming from their father's study. Erick eased the large oak door open slowly, unsure what he would find behind it. He noticed books strewn across the floor and his brother's back was facing away from him, leaning on the window, slumped over in defeat. Erick's heart sank when he saw his brother's hand firmly gripping a crystal glass with amber liquid sloshing around while he held the phone with the other. *God, please have mercy on me,* he thought. *I know we haven't spoken in a while, but I could use some help.*

"You can't do this!" Finn spat his words and didn't even flinch or make any indication of realizing another person was there. Erick thought about what to do next because any sudden moves might cause Finn to act out like a wild caged animal.

Chapter 9

race stirred awake as the early afternoon sun filtered through the windows. Disoriented by her surroundings, she slowly slipped out of bed and made her way to the shower. The bathroom was stocked, and several fluffy towels were neatly folded on the vanity for her. Grace reveled in the hot water cascading over her body before emerging, feeling refreshed and rejuvenated. She dressed for the day, a sense of calm washing over her as she was ready to start her search.

The aroma of freshly brewed coffee wafted into the room, drawing Grace to the kitchen, where Pala greeted her with a large steaming clay cup of the brew topped with a foamy cream. She took a sip.

"It's good, right?" he asked. "How did you sleep?"

"Yes, it *is* good. I haven't slept that well in a long time," Grace confessed, grateful for the peaceful rest she had experienced.

Pala set out a plate of large muffins and an assortment of fresh fruit, explaining that he had picked them up from the bakery downstairs earlier that morning. The colors and scents of the fruit reminded Grace of a farmer's market, and she eagerly dug in, enjoying every bite as they discussed their plans for the day ahead.

Her fork pierced a piece of juicy pineapple, the succulent fruit releasing a burst of sweetness. She sipped her coffee to calm the emotions swirling within her.

"Where do you want to start first?" Pala asked, his voice gentle and understanding.

"I think we should try to go on a hike and maybe retrace where Raven took her final steps," Grace replied, her words catching in her throat. "What do you think?"

"I agree," Pala said, nodding thoughtfully. "How much time do you need to get ready?"

"I'm already dressed, but I still need to grab my hiking shoes," she said, picking up a muffin filled with plump blueberries. Everything in California seemed fresher compared to back home. "Is it close by, or will we have to drive?"

"The trailhead is within walking distance," Pala reassured her. "We can take our time and enjoy the scenery."

Pala packed two small backpacks with water and food and handed one to Grace after she laced up her trail runners. "It's a moderate hike; it could take us a few hours up and back. Are you sure you're ready for the heat? The temperatures are fairly consistent here all year round, but you're not used to the dry heat." He picked up a small bottle of sunblock and tossed it to her.

They set off down the stairs and onto the street below. Grace couldn't help but take in the stunning view of the nearby mountain range. The sun above cast a warm glow over everything, making it all feel like a scene from a movie. She followed Pala's lead and pulled a baseball cap over her head to shield her from the intense sun.

As they crossed the street and passed a large building that housed several apartments, Grace couldn't help but wonder what it would be like to live in this charming western town. But Pala's words and warnings about the hiking trails and rattlesnakes brought her back to reality.

"People come from all over to hike these trails, but they really need a guide because we have rattlesnakes, coyotes, and other wildlife to watch out for. Even our weather can sometimes be challenging if you don't know what you're doing. Fires. Mudslides. Of course, Raven had an instinct for these things." It was like he was reading her mind.

With the mention of Raven's name, Grace was reminded of why she was here. She tried to keep up with Pala's steady pace. Soon, she would see for herself where her mother fell to her death. Grace was sure there would be some evidence of Jack Stone somewhere, and she would do everything possible to find all the answers over the days to come.

They kicked up desert dust as they walked away from the small western town and headed north to the trailhead. "You do this for a living?" Grace invited Pala to share.

"Yes, for many years. I love it. I can feel my ancestors here. It's quite a spiritual experience. That's why Raven also loved it here." Pala mused.

"The weather here is amazing," Grace said. "I've been stuck in snowy Connecticut for too long."

"It's great, but this time of year also brings a dry season and the threat of wildfires, but we are due for some rain," Pala replied with a nod to a passing hiker. Despite the potential dangers, he seemed entirely at ease in his element.

"I wish I had known you growing up," Grace said after they'd walked while. "I love hiking. In fact, I just started leading a women's group called 'Healing Hikes'. We go up to the summit, and it's such a cleansing experience."

"Yeah, I took Raven on that trail years ago. But there's nothing like being out here in the fresh desert air." Pala picked up the pace. After about an hour of hiking, they stopped for a water break. Pala pointed out the 3,648 ft. summit of El Cajon Mountain as one of the most strenuous hikes in San Diego. "Today, we'll have just enough time to explore this trail and return before dark. We can take a walk on the beach tomorrow."

He pointed out more interesting facts while they walked. "That pine you see there is one of the rarest pines in the world, by the way." Pala and Grace walked on together. "Hey, when we get back, I'll pick up some of the best food from my favorite vegan Mexican place."

"That sounds great." Grace was mesmerized by all the natural features, mountainous regions, and the salt air. The ground beneath her feet was sun-beaten brown sand and clay.

"The sandstone has been here for over fifty million years. Check out this tower viewer. It works like a telescope." Pala turned off the trail and gestured to a spot overlooking the Pacific Ocean. "Sometimes you can see leopard sharks from here." He peered into the viewer and then stepped back to allow Grace some room to look.

Above, sea birds flew gracefully down to the beaches. After another hour or so of hiking through various terrains—from rocky inclines to lush meadows—they finally reached their destination: a stunning overlook with panoramic views of the desert landscape and beaches below.

"Did you ever want children?" Grace asked as she took in the breathtaking scenery. Several tourists were there taking pictures.

Pala paused momentarily before responding, "I'm more of a wanderer myself. I never really thought about having kids. Now that my parents have passed, my fellow hikers have become my family. But when I found out about you, I couldn't help but wonder what it would be like to have a real family. Over the years, Raven and I never had children together, though we did discuss it at one point. I think she may have had a medical condition that made it too risky to have any more children, but she never shared all the details with me. We just agreed that it was safer not to have children and continue our nomadic lifestyle. Your mother was wild and beautiful, just like this place." His voice softened as he spoke of Raven. "She blossomed here, away from Jack's control. When I first met her, she was closed off and guarded. But over time, she opened up and embraced the freedom that nature brings. She truly had a beautiful soul." Pala's words were filled with admiration and love for Raven, but there was a hint of bitterness when he mentioned Jack's name. He pointed to the cliff. "This is the spot where the authorities found her."

Grace was speechless as she looked over the ledge. The salty water and the waves crashed around large black jagged rocks creating tide pools adjacent to the beach. She was standing in the very space where her mother walked. As more questions flew into her mind, she knew in her bones that she was exactly where she needed to be at that moment. She suddenly wished Erick was with her on this journey, but she realized that he would only be a distraction. Pala truly had a kind soul and knew the land like the back of his hand. She hoped this journey to find answers would help her get to know this man and maybe find out he was her father after all.

Chapter 10

Erick was on his own mission. He could hear Finn's booming voice as it bellowed through the foyer and Brook's voice screaming from the phone. Erick could see the chaos as he entered his father's former study—the crystal decanter on the table was tipped over.

Finn's appearance shocked Erick the most. His brother's suit was crumpled and wrinkled as if he had slept in it, and his shirt sleeves were rolled up exposing the circular scars on his arms, a reminder of the abuse he endured from their father. Finn's hair was disheveled as he turned around. His eyes were bloodshot, and he had a wild look on his face. Erick cautiously approached Finn, aware of the caged animal within him.

"We need to get you to a meeting," Erick said calmly, trying to diffuse the tension in the air.

Finn's response was bitter. He gulped the last of his drink and threw the glass toward Erick causing him to jump and instinctively move his head just in time. Finn's crystal glass shattered against the wall behind Erick.

"Let's go outside and talk," Erick said with a firm tone. "Just you and me." He desperately wanted to get Finn out of this room.

"You wouldn't understand," Finn spat, still gripping onto the remnants of his anger.

Erick moved closer and placed a gentle hand on Finn's shoulder. He softened his tone now. "I may not understand everything, but I'm your brother, and brothers are for life, remember?"

But Finn jerked away from him, shaking off Erick's touch.

Erick couldn't help but look around and recall this house's memories. He was shocked to see that Brook was renovating every room, but their father's study was left untouched, leaving it exactly the way it was when they were all kids. It was a reminder of everything they had been through, and Erick knew he would do whatever it took to help his brother heal and move forward.

"I might not understand. But then again, I might. How will you ever know if you don't talk to me?" Erick pleaded with his brother.

Finn's voice was strained as he sat down behind the desk, his hands gripping the armrests of the leather chair so hard that his knuckles turned white. "Everything is falling apart. My childhood home is being torn apart, and Brook won't stop nagging me about my company. Now FINNLondon is being sued. And to top it off, Becker Publishing is trying to steal our business right from under us, and we might lose everything." He leaned forward in his seat, burying his head in his hands. "I can't handle any of this."

Erick sat on the desk's edge. "That's a lot to deal with. Becker Publishing? I thought they were in the insurance business."

Finn stood up abruptly, his face contorted with rage. "Yes, James Becker and his daughter are trying to steal the family business. All they needed was Brook to marry one of us. Don't pretend you actually care! You never wanted anything to do with this family or the business." Finn stood up. "I don't need you or your judgmental religious beliefs getting in my way. You're all the same. This was my last shot at leaving a legacy and now that is gone, too."

Erick was confused. "What are you talking about?"

Finn sneered. "Brook was pregnant."

"Oh, no," Erick said quietly, unable to imagine Finn's pain. Realization dawned on Erick. She must have lost the baby. He went to hug his brother, but Finn pushed him away.

"Don't touch me! You'll never understand."

"But I want to try," Erick pleaded, stepping back to give Finn some space. "Miscarriage is tough for anyone."

"It wasn't a miscarriage," Finn snapped, walking toward the door.

"What happened?"

Finn had his back to Erick as he opened the door and looked out at the moving trucks in the distance. "I didn't think Brook wanted children," he said through gritted teeth.

Erick's mind raced as he tried to process this new information. "Are you saying she…?"

"Hell, I don't know what to believe anymore. Honestly, I don't think there ever was a baby," Finn cut him off, his voice cold and distant. "She didn't even ask me what I felt about all of it, but we got married because of the baby. Now she and her father are taking FinnLondon away from me. They planned this as soon as Declan left his shares to me."

Erick was stunned by all that was said. He was about to say something else, but Finn stormed out of the room. Erick quickly followed him, reaching the front door just as a car pulled up for Finn. As his brother got into the service car without a second glance, Erick knew that something was seriously wrong. He needed to find a way to help Finn.

With a heavy heart, Erick took out his phone and dialed a number he never thought he would ever have to call. Erick closed his eyes as the phone rang on the other end. He knew full well that this conversation would be one of the most difficult ones he would ever have. But Finn needed help, and Erick was determined to do whatever it took to save his brother from this downward spiral. Only one person could set the record straight once and for all.

"Brooklyn Becker, here," the voice boomed through the phone with a cold, professional tone.

"Brook, it's Erick," he said, his voice low.

"What do you want?" Brook snapped, her tone dripping with annoyance.

"I'm not sure what's going on. Finn seems to be spiraling out of control," Erick managed to say before she cut him off.

"We're in the middle of a legal battle at the publishing house. The one that you wanted nothing to do with," Brook retorted snarkily. "Why do you care?"

"Finn needs help. He needs to get to a meeting," Erick pleaded, trying to get through to her.

"Oh, so that's what this is about!" Brook yelled into the phone. "Erick to the rescue! You need to stay in your lane and leave us alone. Don't you have someone else to chase after?"

"This is about Finn's sobriety." Erick ignored her jab about Grace and gritted his teeth, but his patience was wearing thin.

"Stay out of our business, Erick. You made your choice when you left me for that girl. Now I'm taking what was always going to be mine," Brook sneered. "I'm redecorating Finn Manor and it will be unrecognizable when I'm done. If he doesn't like it, he can go back to his penthouse in New York, alone."

"What happened between you two? I thought we were past all the pettiness. How did it come to this?" Erick couldn't help but ask, despite knowing he wouldn't get an answer.

"That's none of your concern! Mind your own damn business and stay away from me and Finn," Brook spat back. "He has his own demons to deal with, and I have my plans for FIN-NLondon. Yeah, go ahead and tell him. He already hates his life anyway. Maybe if you tell him, I won't have to."

"You're unbelievable." Erick felt disgusted by her lack of empathy. "How can you even live with yourself?"

"Thanks for the chat," Brook said. "Next time, save us both the trouble, and don't bother calling. It's too late." She cursed Erick before hanging up.

Erick slammed his phone down, his face ablaze. Regret set in as he wondered why he thought Brook would ever be reasonable and help him. He sped out of Finn Manor in his Jeep, desperate to get to Daniel and figure out a plan. Grace was off doing her own thing, and he needed to make things right with Finn before heading to Boston. He had to focus on saving Finn before it was too late and he lost another person he cared about.

Chapter 11

Grace didn't know what she expected to find on the trail where Raven was last seen alive. The weather was sunny and warm as she gazed out at the vast expanse of mountains and ocean from the edge of the rocky ledge. Below, the waves crashed against the rocks, their spray a majestic crescendo. The scent of the sea air filled her nostrils. A memory suddenly flooded her mind of when she had fallen off a cliff back in Connecticut and how Erick had saved her. She shook off that memory and focused on the fact that she was here to find answers about Raven's tragic death and her own paternity.

Her eyes caught a glimpse of a lone black raven flying gracefully in the distance. Pala stood beside her like a steady force, keeping her grounded, safe. *Could Pala be my biological father?* Her thoughts were interrupted by his voice.

"What are you thinking, Grace?"

"There's no great way to ask this question, but I have to ask anyway." Grace frowned. "Are you interested in taking a DNA test?" Grace couldn't help but feel grateful for Pala's support, regardless of any potential biological connection.

"Of course, I would love to. For you, anything," he replied. "But no test is going to show me how to be a father. Honestly, I'm just starting to think of you as my daughter." Pala kept his eyes fixed on the ground as he spoke. "Grace, I always wonder if I could have done more to protect her."

"You did everything you could. I know it," Grace replied.

Pala didn't respond, just gave her a simple nod thanking her for understanding.

"We should head back," Pala said abruptly.

Once they returned to the apartment, Pala suggested washing up before eating dinner. After showering and changing into fresh clothes, Grace joined Pala in the living room. Just like he had promised, there was takeout from his favorite vegan restaurant. As they ate, they discussed potential leads and theories, with Pala sharing what little information he had gathered from previous visits to the police station.

Feeling exhausted and frustrated by their lack of progress, Grace picked at her food more than eating it.

"Is the food okay?" Pala asked.

"Oh, it's delicious, but I'm too anxious to eat," Grace admitted.

"That's okay." Pala wrapped up her burrito, put it in the fridge, and placed their dishes in the dishwasher. "If you're up to it, we can head down to the beach. It was one of Raven's favorite places to be at this time of day during the *golden hour.*"

Pala carried two blankets and walked with Grace down to the beach. The wind played with wisps of Grace's red hair as she stood at the edge of Torrey Pines State Beach, gazing at the horizon. The sun had begun its slow descent into the Pacific, which mirrored the fiery oranges and purples in the waves. She dug her feet into the soft golden sand.

"Your mother loved photographing and capturing moments like these," Pala said as if he were back there with Raven on this very beach. "She had an eye for the way light danced on the water. This was her sanctuary."

Grace turned to look at him, searching his face for traces of the man who might be her biological father. His features were calm, etched with the kind of serenity that came from a life lived in sync with nature's rhythms.

"Did she come here often?" Grace asked, as she looked out over the ocean. The roar of the waves drowned out her voice. Large rocks jutted to the north near the cliffs where they had hiked the day before.

"Whenever she could," he replied, his eyes not leaving the sunset.

"Do you still have her camera?" Grace asked suddenly, wanting to see the images her mother had taken.

"When she went missing, she must have taken the camera with her," Pala said. "It's gone now. I had a custom strap made for her in purple and yellow embroidery with her name on it. She found peace in the stillness here, watching day turn into night." Pala put a blanket down for each of them, while a seagull cried overhead, circling before it soared away toward the cliffs. Pala watched it with a gentle smile. "I guess *we* are creating new memories now," Pala suggested. "The past is a canvas, but the present... it's the paint we hold in our hands right now."

Grace nodded, considering his words. She noticed how Pala's expression softened when he spoke of the present and how his hands gestured gracefully while sharing his deep connection to the world around him.

"Being here with you, it feels like I'm walking in her footsteps," she said.

"More than just footsteps," Pala corrected gently. "You're walking alongside her spirit, her legacy."

"Is that why you brought me here?" Grace looked up at him, seeking the truth.

"Partly," he confessed. "But also to share something I'm passionate about, because I believe in conserving the beauty of places like this." His arms opened slightly, encompassing the expanse of the beach and the cliffs beyond. "I want to protect and nurture the land."

"Because of your roots?" She tilted her head, curious about the depth of his conviction.

"Exactly." Pala nodded. "My heritage teaches me to respect every creature, every plant. The vegan lifestyle isn't just about how I eat. It's my way of minimizing the impact I make."

Grace felt a surge of admiration for the man beside her, a man who walked and talked with such quiet dignity. She watched as he bent down to pick up a piece of driftwood, examining it with careful fingers before placing it back exactly where he found it.

"Every action matters," he said, meeting her eyes again, a gentle challenge in his gaze. "Even the small ones."

The sun dipped lower, and the sky was a breathtaking display. Grace realized she was witnessing more than just a sunset; she was seeing the world through Raven's and Pala's eyes. A world where every footprint counted, where every life had value, and where the past and present were intimately connected by the earth beneath their feet and the vast sky above their heads.

Chapter 12

Erick drove back to HigherGround and parked outside of Daniel's apartment. He was getting nowhere with Finn, and he needed reinforcements. Daniel opened the door, and Erick could feel the weight of the news he carried like a heavy storm cloud ready to burst. He took a seat as Daniel wheeled into the living room.

Erick wasted no time getting to the point. "Daniel, we need to talk about Finn."

"What's happened now?" Immediately, Daniel's relaxed posture straightened.

"He's spiraling out of control again, and it doesn't look good." Erick felt his cheeks warm, his blood pressure rising as he spoke. "Brook is up to her old tricks again."

"What happened, Erick?" Daniel asked again.

"She not only tricked Finn into marrying her by claiming to be pregnant, but she's also trying to destroy the entire company that our father left him. It's no mystery Finn and I have had our differences, but for God's sake, even he doesn't deserve this."

Daniel let out a low curse in frustration. "How is he handling all of this?"

"Not well," Erick admitted, remembering his brother's shattered state that still haunted him. "He's drowning himself in alcohol. If we don't do something soon, we might lose him."

"Okay, let's think this through," Daniel said, determination sparking in his eyes. "What if we get him out of Connecticut? Away from Brook and all this chaos? Maybe New York could offer him a fresh start."

The idea floated around them for a moment before Erick spoke up. "New York… it could work. I'm not sure if that is far enough, though, as the loft apartment is the first place Brook would look and it may be tied up with FINNLondon's assets. What Finn needs is a discreet rehabilitation this time. A place where Brook can't find him. This would give him some distance and a chance for a new beginning if he's even willing to go. We'll have to convince him together."

"Then that's what we'll do," Daniel declared.

Before they could discuss their plan further, Erick's phone buzzed in his pocket, a welcome distraction from the heavy atmosphere. His agent was on the line. "The conference in Boston is postponed," Erick reported to Daniel after ending the call. "They're in a state of emergency still and now the airports are closed. I'll check back in a few days to see if I can reschedule."

Erick felt a small glimmer of relief at the unexpected delay that would give him more time to focus on Finn. "Another complication, but this will give us more time."

"More time to save Finn," Daniel said, trying to inject some optimism into the situation. "Then you can go to your conference"

"I bet Finn went to FINNLondon," Erick said, a plan forming in his mind. "We should head over there before it's too late."

"I hope we can get in. Finn's receptionist may try to stop us." Daniel had a mischievous look on his face. "You do have an uncanny resemblance to him…"

Erick smiled at the thought, though his heart still was worried for his twin brother. They would do whatever it took to help Finn find his way back from the edge. Then, maybe, he could work on his next idea—finding Grace and bringing her home.

Chapter 13

Grace found Pala the next morning sipping coffee in the kitchen looking at the weather app on his phone. There were muffins and fruit set out again, but she didn't want to waste any time.

"Ready to go to the police station in town?" Pala asked as if reading her mind.

"Yes, let's go. The sooner we get more information, the sooner we can find Jack Stone." Grace put on her light jacket, and they headed out the door.

Pala navigated the road smoothly as they merged onto the busy streets of San Diego. Grace fidgeted with her hands, her gaze fixed on the road ahead. She was determined to find out the truth, and Pala was right by her side, a solid presence of support. They passed by the towering public library, its glass windows reflecting the sun. Grace couldn't help but think she might find some answers there, and it was conveniently located just a few blocks from the San Diego Police Department. The tension of expectation in the car was thick as they continued on their journey.

Pala parked the car. The building was adobe brown outside with a Spanish tile roof and arched doorways. Large palm trees in the front swayed in the breeze. Grace thought it looked more like a fort than a police station. The two quickly entered the dimly lit station, which was buzzing with people already. The receptionist greeted Pala and Grace as they approached the front desk. Grace's heart started to race when she wondered what they might find out. She was there to get a copy of Raven's autopsy and the police report surrounding her death. Grace hoped these documents would hold answers and maybe confirm her worst fears.

"May I help you?" The clerk looked up, her expression neutral behind thick glass.

"I'm here for the autopsy report of Raven Evans," Grace said, trying to keep her voice steady. "On or about the first week in September, about two years ago?"

"Name?"

"Grace Evans. I'm her daughter."

After entering information on the keyboard, the clerk disappeared into the back office. Pala stood beside Grace, silent but supportive, and his presence made her relax.

"Here you are." The clerk returned, reviewed the documents, and placed them in a manila envelope before she slid it through the opening beneath the window. "These are copies, so you can take them with you."

"Was there any evidence of foul play?" Grace asked, fingers already prying open the envelope.

"Cause of death, accidental fall from a cliff," the clerk read, devoid of emotion. "No evidence suggesting otherwise."

Grace scanned the report, the words blurring. Accident. *No foul play. Case closed.* "Who signed off on this report?" she inquired, thinking about her next move.

"Officer Lawrence Keating," the clerk answered, pointing to the second page. "But he retired last year."

"Do you have an address for Keating?" Pala asked, and the clerk wrote down the information. "Thank you for your help."

Pala tapped the desk before leading Grace to the exit.

"Retired?" Grace said to Pala as they left the precinct.

"Let's go talk to him," Pala said, hopeful.

With the address in hand, they were able to track the retired officer down just a few miles away on the outskirts of town, in a modest home with a well-kept garden.

"Mr. Keating?" Grace said when he opened the door. The man who answered didn't look anything like she expected. Grace felt it was odd that he retired. He seemed much too young for retirement.

"Sorry for the intrusion. Can we ask a few questions about a case you worked on? It's about Raven Evans." Pala asked, polite but firm.

"Cliff accident, I believe, a couple of years back," Keating stated curtly, leaning against his door frame, not interested in letting them in. "Nothing more."

"Is there anything else you can tell us? Anything at all?" Grace pushed, looking for any flicker of memory. She saw his eyes darting around the neighborhood nervously. "Did you interview any witnesses?"

"Nothing really to tell. We did what we could. There wasn't much evidence to start with, and there were issues about the data being collected properly. The weather didn't help either. Rain washed away whatever was left up there." He shrugged, a gesture that seemed to carry the weight of unresolved cases and unanswered questions he had put to bed years ago. Keating's eyes darted around the street again as if he were expecting someone.

"Could anything have been overlooked?" Pala pressed, his gaze sharp enough to cut through the haze of any forgotten memory.

"Listen, I've done my job for many decades. When I say it's an accident, it's because nothing is pointing to otherwise."

"Have you heard of a man named Jack Stone?" Grace pressed on.

"No, that name doesn't ring a bell. The chief told me to

put this case to rest, and someone had the body shipped to the east coast." Officer Keating's eyes widened, and he lowered his voice. "There was something unusual, though."

"What?" Grace held her breath waiting.

"There was another hiker. It didn't make the report because the other officer was a rookie assigned to the case and forgot to ask for his name. An older gentleman, maybe in his early 60s was hiking out there and had called the accident in, but he didn't make the report, and I thought that was odd. I mentioned it to the Chief, but he wanted to resolve this case and avoid any widespread panic. It was an election year, and we are proud to have San Diego as one of the safest places to live and visit."

"Thank you for your time," Grace said, as they turned to leave.

Pala and Grace returned to the bookstore lot. Grace looked up at the clear sky, and suddenly, a flash of light came from a window across the street. She looked up just as the curtains were drawn from the inside. Grace felt like she was being watched as she exited the vehicle carrying the police reports. They were back to where they started, the truth slipping away. But she knew one thing for certain—this wasn't the end, not for her. Grace knew that Jack Stone was somehow involved, and she suspected that he was the hiker that called the police that day. But there was more to it than that. Grace had a strong feeling that Jack Stone had killed her mother. Now, all she had to do was prove it.

Chapter 14

Erick and Daniel drove to the FINNLondon offices. Once Daniel was situated in his wheelchair, they both went into the tall glass building, entered the elevator, and pressed the button for the top floor. The elevator door opened, and Erick walked to the reception area.

"Hello, may I help you?" A sleek-looking blonde greeted them with her eyes never leaving the computer. Finally, she looked up and addressed Erick, "Oh, sorry, Mr. Finn. I didn't see you there." Her face flushed with embarrassment.

"Uh, that's okay," Erick said, not correcting the receptionist. "I just haven't been getting my messages."

The receptionist frowned and scrolled through the computer messages. "I'm so sorry, Mr. Finn. Athena asked us to hold all your calls and not to disturb you." She printed the messages and handed them to Erick. Athena was Finn's executive assistant, and Erick knew that even if they got past the receptionist, they would still need to deal with her.

"Thank you and no worries. I haven't been myself lately. I'm the one who should be apologizing to you." Erick smiled his million-dollar smile, a hint of dimples just underneath the beard. Phones rang intermittently in the background.

"You're too kind." The woman's eyes widened with worry. Then she mouthed sorry again as the phone rang. "FINNLondon publishing…"

Erick darted his eyes from Daniel to the side door that suddenly opened. When the receptionist turned away from them, Erick pushed Daniel through the open door, and they rushed down the hall, adrenaline pumping. Erick couldn't help but laugh because of what a sight they both must have looked like running down the long hallway.

"We don't have much time," Daniel said laughing, pushing himself faster. They reached the end of the hallway and found Athena standing there with her hands on her hips, frowning.

"What are *you* two doing here? Finn *doesn't* want to be disturbed." Athena stood her ground.

"Finn's in trouble and we're here to get him out of it," Erick spoke up while Daniel slowly rolled closer to the corner office door. Down the hall and through the glass walls, they could see Finn slumped over his desk. Without waiting for permission, Erick ran after Daniel and threw open the door to Finn's office. Athena helplessly protested and followed them into the office.

"I'm so sorry!" Athena held her hands up at the doorway. She gave up and closed the door, leaving the brothers alone to talk.

Finn was there with his head on the desk, crying. When he saw Erick and Daniel, he stood up. Erick saw Finn's blood shot eyes that suddenly narrowed. "I *said* I don't want your help!" he growled.

"Well, too bad. We're family! Brothers for life, remember?" Daniel rolled to the side of the large mahogany desk. "What do the lawyers say about getting FINNLondon back?"

"Brook tricked me. Being married meant she was entitled to half of Dad's shares. The lawyers said it was all my fault." Finn ran his hand through his hair. "I had no idea she was planning all of this. She and her father have been behind this plot ever since

Dad passed. I should've seen this coming."

"Well, maybe it's a good thing." Erick sat in the opposite leather chair, the desk an island between them.

"You and your stupid silver lining. There's nothing that can save this business now. Becker lawyers are out there firing people and shredding any opposing evidence. It's too late."

"Can I ask you a question?" Erick calmly asked Finn. "Do you really want to run a business right now when everything is so crazy? Maybe we get you in front of a judge and get you out of this marriage. Unless you still want Brook?" Erick focused his eyes on Finn's reaction.

"Brook is a monster. I thought she and I could build a legacy for the next generation. But, I never had time to get a prenuptial agreement, and she had me sign papers for the renovations, but they were actually papers that gave her sole ownership of my majority shares." Finn covered his face with his hands. "I know I don't deserve anything after what I put both of you through, but I just want a life that Dad could be proud of."

"The apartment in New York… is that part of FINNLondon, or did Dad give that to you? She can't touch that, right?" Erick asked.

"Yeah. I'll have to call my lawyer and get that sold without Brook noticing and taking it. She took everything else from me."

"Let's get you to an AA meeting, and then you and I can make some calls," Erick suggested.

"Listen, bro, we're family, and we have to look out for each other, but this addiction is killing you faster than Brook ever could. You need to get yourself together and prepare for battle," Daniel interjected as he moved over to Finn.

"I don't need a meeting. I need to go to rehab again. This thing is too hard to fight alone." Finn stared out the window, overlooking the buildings below.

Erick stood up. He knew they had to act fast. "I have just the perfect place in mind. They're very discreet, and Brook won't be able to find you."

"Ok," Finn conceded, and the three brothers left the office

together. Before they were out the door, Finn turned to his be-wildered assistant. "I have to go away on business, Athena. Just forward my calls to the work phone, please."

Once they made it down the elevator and past the lobby area, Erick looked back and mouthed sorry to the receptionist, whose mouth gaped open seeing the real Finn. Outside, they all piled into the Jeep, and Erick connected his Bluetooth and pressed a number into his phone.

Chapter 15

Grace was restless all night, tossing and turning, her mind consumed by thoughts of the mysterious police officer Keating and his involvement in the case of Raven's so-called accident. It didn't make sense. After all, Raven had been an expert hiker. Unable to sleep, Grace rummaged through Pala's kitchen drawers and found some push-pins. Returning to her room, she was determined to piece together the events leading up to the accident, so she began hanging up the reports she had obtained from the police station and photos she printed at the bookstore. Next to the report, she placed a photo of Officer Keating.

With Pala gone for the day on a guided hiking trip, Grace called for a car through her phone app and headed to the San Diego Central Library. As soon as she stepped inside, she was astounded by the place's grandeur. Sunlight streamed in through floor-to-ceiling windows, casting a warm glow over everything.

Grace remembered that Raven had written in her journal that Jack Stone had been admitted to a mental institution in New York. Lacking any other leads, she decided to start there, hoping her research would yield more information about him. Making her way to the information desk, Grace inquired about where she could find research on mental hospitals in New York. The reference librarian led her to a computer with database archives specifically focused on this topic. With expert guidance, Grace immersed herself in the records of public and private institutions, as well as an index of births and deaths.

One particular entry caught her eye as she combed through the databases: *Established in 1952… ceased operations in 1998…* It was a psychiatric hospital in New York that had long since been abandoned. Now, it was nothing more than a ghostly remnant of its former self; its legacy lived on only through old news articles and an empty building.

"That was about the time Raven would've been pregnant with me," Grace whispered to herself, her eyes narrowing.

She printed photos of the psychiatrist and the mental hospital, along with an article about the building being abandoned. Next, Grace researched the doctor and found his contact information, which showed he had a small practice just outside South Salem, New York that bordered the Connecticut state line. She printed information about this doctor and planned to call when she got back to the apartment. Grace thanked the librarian, left the library with papers in hand, and then ordered a car on her phone app to bring her back to Pala's apartment.

Outside, the cloudless sky stretched a hazy blue. The sun caused Grace to shield her eyes while the wind whipped her hair around her face violently. She held tightly onto the papers she had collected at the library. Every fiber of her being was consumed with uncovering the truth about Raven's supposed hiking accident and finding Jack Stone.

Finally, a car pulled up, and Grace quickly got inside, giving the driver Pala's address without a second thought. Her heart raced with anticipation as they drove toward the apartment.

Once inside, Grace tore off her jacket and headed straight to her room, which she had turned into a makeshift investigation headquarters. Papers adorned every inch of wall space above the desk, and she meticulously combed through each one, searching for any discrepancies or clues.

What am I missing? Grace stared at the array of papers and hoped for patterns to emerge or things that didn't quite add up or make any sense at all. Officer Keating's statement seemed sketchy at best. *What was he hiding?* Grace couldn't shake off the feeling that something much more sinister was at play.

A knot of frustration and urgency coiled in her stomach as she stood back and took in all the information. She knew she needed to eat something, but her mind was too consumed trying to connect all these pieces together.

After reviewing the information obtained at the library, Grace located the name of the psychiatric physician, Dr. Allistair, and dialed his number. After Grace explained who she was and what she was investigating, the receptionist reluctantly agreed to have the physician call her back after his appointment. Feeling both relieved and anxious about finally getting some answers, Grace forced herself to grab an apple off the table. But as she sat down at Pala's kitchen table, she just couldn't take the first bite. An ominous feeling settled over her like a dark cloud. She was afraid that the closer she got to the answers, the more likely she would encounter Jack Stone. Her intuition was definitely warning her that danger loomed just around the corner. Even though Grace knew she should pay attention to her intuition this time, she was still determined to uncover the truth no matter what the cost.

Chapter 16

Erick connected a call on Bluetooth. "We should be there at the designated time."

"Great! Glad you all are on your way then," the voice on the other end replied.

Erick looked over at Daniel in the passenger seat and nodded. Next, he glanced at Finn in the rearview mirror. His brother sat in the back, broken, but Erick was optimistic that Finn had chosen to get help.

"I know I don't deserve any of your help. Not after I helped Brook drug you, Erick. That damn party, which caused Daniel's…" He winced. "I've been a terrible person for so many years. God, the way I treated Grace was just awful and I was killing myself at work trying to impress Dad. Brook can't find me here, can she?" Finn started coughing between sobs, his face ghostly white. "I'm going to be sick."

Daniel and Erick looked at each other. Erick pulled over and let Finn empty the contents of his stomach on the side of the melting snowbanked highway. This was going to be one rough trip and Finn could be in the early stages of detoxing.

Finn jumped back in the Jeep, and Erick handed him a water bottle. Taking small sips, Finn leaned his head against the back window.

"You've done this before," Erick said, "and it'll be just as difficult, but you have our full support now. What's going on with Brook isn't right, and I know I don't care about the family business, but if you want to get it back, I can help."

"I don't know what I care about anymore. I thought I'd messed everything up when Grace left me and who could blame her?"

Erick's insides twisted at the thought of Finn and Grace together. He wasn't sure why it bothered him so much. It was like picking at an old wound he had thought had healed over.

"But it really took a spiral down when Brook and I married," Finn continued. "I just wanted a chance to start over. To become a father like the one I never had. A good father would really listen to his son. I didn't even know I wanted kids until Brook made it a reality. Of course, she probably made the whole thing up. It wasn't like we even talked about it or discussed anything. She was a different person instantly. But *I'm* the one to blame. I caused all this mess. I don't even know why you two care if I live or die. God, I'm not sure if I'm cut out for this life."

"Finn, that's the alcohol talking," Daniel interrupted. "You don't have to apologize to me about anything. All of that is in the past. As long as you get the help you need, we don't have a problem helping you through this mess. But if you're going to keep drinking, then we *will* have a problem. We can only untangle this mess if you do the work and put your whole heart into the process." Daniel turned and looked right into Finn's eyes. "The choice is yours."

"How did you get so mature?" Finn laughed. "I don't know how you could ever forgive me."

"I already have, and I am one lucky man," Daniel countered. "Sky is the greatest thing to ever happen to me. If you want to do something good, then you need to get the most out of this experience, and then when you get back, we can work on getting

Brook out of all of our lives once and for all."

"Amen to that!" Erick chimed in. "Don't worry about us, but it will take hard work on your part. You can't just throw in the towel when things don't go the way you thought. It's normal to repeat rehab several times for it to stick. I personally think your attitude will take you farther this time. You didn't fight us to go, and now you'll have our full support this time. Use this time wisely and figure out how you want the rest of your life to be. What kind of man you want to become."

Finn sighed deeply and closed his eyes. Erick's gaze flickered from the road to the rearview mirror, then to Daniel. They only had sixty more miles to go. "We should be there on time," Erick announced to everyone. "There will be more battles to fight, but now it's time to conquer this addiction head-on."

Chapter 17

Grace's voice was steady despite her heart pounding when the psychiatrist's caller ID appeared on the screen and she answered the call. "Dr. Gerry Allistair?"

"Yes," the doctor replied.

"I'm Grace Evans, and I'm looking into the death of my mother, Raven Evans. I need information about Jack Stone, one of your patients?"

"There isn't much I can say due to HIPPA that protects patients, Ms. Evans," Dr. Hensley stated. "I cannot discuss any individuals, living or deceased."

"Even if it could shine light on a crime?" Grace pressed the phone to her ear, unwavering. "Doctor, we believe you worked with a patient in 1998, connected to a series of crimes that may be ongoing now as we speak. Did you treat a patient named Jack Stone?" The line went quiet, but Grace waited a few minutes. "Are you still there?"

"I'm here, but as I stated before, I cannot confirm a patient's name or discuss anything about his sessions."

"Even if your testimony could have the power to bring this man to justice."

"It's out of my hands." Dr. Allistair was not budging. "I've lost everything after the fire at the mental hospital. I just want a quiet life here, helping people with mild depression or family issues. I can't help you. I do recommend you stop looking, though, because if this character is as bad as you say he is, you could be in danger, too."

"I think the real reason you're not talking has nothing to do with your code of ethics. Did Jack threaten to do more than burn the hospital down if you talked?" Grace was quick to the punch.

"I'm sorry, I can't help you," the doctor repeated.

"Then why would you even bother calling back?" Grace wanted to scream in frustration into the phone.

"My receptionist told me what you needed. I called you back because I wanted to warn you that you are in grave danger. You need to drop this while you still have time." Grace heard a click at the end of the line as the doctor ended the call.

Grace stood frozen in her room, staring at the photo of Dr. Allistair with a mix of fear and confusion. He wouldn't have warned her about danger if he didn't know who Jack was or what he was capable of. Lost in thought, she jumped when the phone rang with an unknown number flashing on the screen.

"Hello?" she said hesitantly, wary of who might be on the other end.

"Ms. Evans?" a woman's voice whispered urgently. "I have the answers you're looking for."

"How did you get this number? *Who are you?*" Grace demanded, trying to keep the panic out of her voice.

"I can't say. Just call me Barb," she replied cryptically. "Your mother, Raven, called here a little over a year ago looking for answers and I couldn't help her. I still happen to have an archived file of Jack Stone's sessions. Do you want it?"

"Of course." Grace breathed a sigh of relief. Hope flooded through her. "Where are you?"

"I can't tell you that," Barb said, sounding just as anxious as Grace felt. "But please, don't tell anyone we spoke. Jack has already warned us that he'll come after us if anyone asks about him."

"I won't say anything," Grace promised. She was right, the doctor had been hiding something.

"We can meet, maybe. Are you in Connecticut?" Barb asked.

"No," Grace confessed. "I'm in California this week."

"Well, I'll print out the documents and send them overnight. They're transcripts from sessions that prove he set many fires, including the one that killed his adoptive parents. Just give me an address. Also, take down this number to contact his sister Rebekah. She should know more."

Grace gave her the address of the bookstore below the apartment and took Rebekah's number down. She thanked her profusely before hanging up. As Grace processed all the information she had just received, she couldn't shake off the nagging feeling that digging into Jack Stone's past could provoke him into coming after her next.

But there was no turning back now. She dialed the number Barb had given her for Rebekah Silverstein and it was for the corrections facility. Grace left a message, hoping that this woman could shed some light on the fire that caused their parents' death.

As she hung up the phone, Grace couldn't help but feel like she was one step closer to finding the truth. But at what cost? Her heart raced with a mix of determination and fear, knowing that all this digging was sure to draw Jack Stone out of hiding. But she couldn't back down now. She had come too far, and she would stop at nothing to find out the truth about Raven's death.

Just then, Pala entered the apartment, and Grace couldn't wait to fill him in on all her progress that day. But when she saw his weary eyes and his crossed arms, she was unsure how he would take the newest development that had unfolded about Jack.

Chapter 18

Erick, Daniel, and Finn finally arrived at a large wrought iron gated entrance, and they were instantly buzzed in. As they pulled up to the Legacy Healing Center, they all took in the grandeur of the entrance. Erick carefully helped Daniel into his wheelchair while Finn slowly exited the vehicle.

"Whoa!" Daniel let out a low whistle. "This place looks like a celebrity hideout!"

Erick took the lead as they approached the entrance, with Finn and Daniel following closely behind. A man with strawberry blonde hair emerged from the building, dressed in crisp white pants and a collared shirt embroidered with a green tree logo. He met them under the vestibule.

"I'm Atlas. Which one of you is Mr. Finn?" The man greeted them with a wide smile, shaking hands with Erick and Daniel.

"Technically?" Daniel remarked. "We all are."

"*I'm* Dominic. I just go by Finn, though, and I'm checking myself voluntarily into your facility." He admitted his defeat with the exhaustion of the drive evident in his voice.

"Welcome," Atlas said warmly to all three of them. "Unfortunately, only Finn can come in with me. But I'll give you all a few minutes." He returned to the front entrance, but waited at the front door.

Erick gave Finn an encouraging tap on the back. "You've got this, brother! You have my number. If you need anything, just call, and I'll take care of it for you." Finn turned and hugged his brother tightly as tears filled his eyes.

"Take as much time as you need, Finn," Daniel reassured him. "We'll handle the insurance and finances for this place. And we'll get to work selling the loft in New York while you're here. When you're stronger, we can take on the Beckers in court *together*." Finn bent down and embraced his younger brother.

Meanwhile, Erick handed Atlas his business card, promising to take care of everything as he had indicated when he had called earlier. The man assured him that they would take good care of his brother, but there would be no communication for the first few weeks due to the detox process. He told Erick the case worker would call after 72 hours.

Atlas escorted Finn inside, and Erick and Daniel stood there for a moment.

"She can't find him here, right?" Daniel asked.

"No," Erick replied. "I'm sure of it."

"Good," Daniel nodded.

After Daniel settled into the car, Erick carefully placed the wheelchair in the back.

"Now what?" Daniel asked as he fastened his seatbelt.

"I have to get back to prepping for the conference," Erick replied with a sigh. "Can you call your real estate agent friend and figure out how we can sell the loft in New York? Finn is going to need money if he's going to go up against Brook and James Becker. The legal stuff may be out of our hands for now, but we can build up reinforcements so Finn can rebuild his life when he gets out."

"Yeah," Daniel nodded.

"I can't imagine how hard it's going to be for Finn to detox." The long ride back to HigherGround had been too quiet, and Erick's mind raced, trying to process what Finn may face in the coming days.

"I'm just glad he didn't put up a fight when we got him at the office complex." Daniel smirked. "It was fun getting past reception though."

"We made a great team didn't we?" Erick smiled just as a call came through. He swiftly pulled into the HigherGround parking lot. He knew he needed to answer the call, but a part of him hesitated as he was enjoying this moment with Daniel.

"Sorry, it's the hospital. I have to take this." Erick sighed, shifting the Jeep into park and picking up the call from Sherri from the hospital. Daniel waited patiently, his expression unreadable.

Once the call ended, Daniel spoke up. "I know Sky still has Jace and Luna inside the studio, but we can keep Jace longer if you need to see a patient."

"A patient of mine is in trouble, but I'll swing by later to get Jace," Erick said, forcing a smile and retrieving the wheelchair from the back. "Thanks again. I couldn't have pulled this off without you."

Daniel nodded. "Stay out of trouble, will ya?" He waved and rolled himself up the ramp to his apartment. Erick couldn't help but think about everything that happened last year. He was glad Daniel had found his true love.

Erick returned to the Jeep and turned up the volume on the radio and tried to drown out his thoughts with music. But when "I Believe It Now" by Sidewalk Prophets came on, it only served as a reminder of his unwavering faith in God. He desperately wanted things to work out for his family and Grace, but it seemed like every step forward was met with three steps back.

While parking at the Saint Mary's Hospital, Erick closed

his eyes and breathed deeply. He prayed for his brother Finn's recovery and for Finn to find a way out of Brook's grasp. He also prayed for Grace, and he prayed for himself because his heart felt heavy with all these burdens. He felt God's presence, and he found solace in knowing he wasn't alone in his struggles.

As he walked into the hospital, Erick couldn't help but wonder about the patient he was about to see who was on an involuntary psychiatric 72-hour hold, which could hamper his physical therapy treatment. He realized that everyone around him was fighting their own battles, and sometimes it felt like no end was in sight. But deep down, Erick held onto his belief that God was bigger than any problems and that nothing was impossible.

Chapter 19

Grace's pulse quickened, as her phone screen notified her that she was getting a call from the correctional facility in Connecticut. Grace averted her eyes away from Pala.

"Is this Grace Evans?"

"Yes!"

"This is Rebekah... you left me a message about Jack?" The exhaustion in Rebekah's voice sounded as though jail had worn her out all these years.

Pala's apartment felt like it was shrinking, the walls inching closer each second, every fiber in Grace's straining to hear Rebekah was making her dizzy. Grace moved into the guest room to hear better.

"I know you are serving time for a crime you did not commit. I saw the article on the fire at your parents' business," Grace said as her gaze locked on her wall of papers. "I think Jack killed my mother, Raven, and if I can prove it, they will see he was behind the fires and maybe prove your innocence. He may have even set the fire at the mental hospital in New

York."

"You are the child, aren't you?" she asked. "Well, then, you must know what you're dealing with. My parents and their business are all gone. It was an inferno, Grace. An act of pure evil."

Grace's hand tightened around the phone, trying to imagine all the fire and smoke—a living nightmare that Rebekah could not escape while serving time.

"Tell me everything you know," Grace urged.

Rebekah's next breath seemed to drag. "I was there, trapped in the blaze like a fly in a spider's web. Jack… he started it," her voice resumed. "I don't know why. Our parents gave him everything. I was the one who found them." Her words stumbled over each other. "And I had to identify them." A sob caught in Rebekah's throat. "I barely escaped with my life. When I woke up in the hospital, bandaged and broken, Jack was there," Rebekah said quietly as if someone could overhear, "looming over me like the devil himself. He caught me on the phone trying to warn Raven."

Grace's eyes darted to the corners of her own room, half-expecting to see Jack's menacing figure emerge out of the shadows.

"He told me, 'If you speak a word of any of this to anyone… I will finish what I started.'" Those words had sealed Rebekah's fate in silence and fear. "I guess I really have nothing to lose anymore."

"Keep talking, Rebekah," she urged gently. "Do you have evidence or proof he set the fire that killed your parents?" Every muscle in her body tensed as she waited for an answer that might change everything. "Rebekah? I need to know." Her pulse quickened with the hope that they were finally on the brink of a breakthrough. She took a deep breath to steady herself, keeping her focus on the phone still pressed against her ear.

Rebekah's voice lowered to barely above a whisper. "The truth is that all the evidence was destroyed in the fire, but what evidence was left, he planted at my apartment. Mostly, the paint thinner is what he left for the police to find. I'm sure there were other things, but I forgot after all this time. But I did find out he changed his name to *Luke Silver.* He was obsessed with your mother… I think he felt she was the only person that loved him. But, because he is who he is, his ideas about love were not normal. To him, love meant submission and control. And when Raven wouldn't give that to him, he made punishing her his quest. I did get a letter from him once about ten years back, and I saw a return address with the name Luke Silver on it. He's been living in San Diego, Grace, but I don't know where. That's all I can remember."

Grace scribbled the details feverishly onto a notepad. "Thank you, Rebekah," she said with gratitude, but also apprehension. Somewhere out there, she knew that Jack was closer than ever. A shadow in the night hunting his prey. The thought of him watching her made her skin crawl. No longer was this just about proving who Grace's father was, but now Rebekah's innocence was at stake. It was also about stopping a predator who had slipped through the cracks. She was the hunter now, and she was getting closer.

"Jack has been in San Diego all this time?" Grace asked in disbelief.

The recorded operator injected its warning. *"You have thirty seconds remaining on this call."*

"Yes," Rebekah confirmed. "My little brother Dov warned me about Jack's obsessions. When Jack found out Raven was having an affair, it drove him crazy. Then he got word of a baby, and he made it his mission to find the child. Dovid is all I have left, and he knows I'm innocent. He used to be close with Jack and keeps me informed on things and in the real world. Just trust me. Jack will always be three steps ahead of you. Be careful," Rebekah warned before the line disconnected.

Grace remained motionless, staring at her notepad as she laid her phone down on the desk. With this new lead, Grace realized what she had to do next. Grace wouldn't stop until the truth was unearthed once and for all.

With a deep inhale that did little to calm her racing heart, Grace stared at the collage of old and new evidence. She made a promise to free an innocent woman sentenced to life behind bars and a vow to Jack's victims who could no longer speak for themselves... victims, like her mother.

Chapter 20

Erick entered his patient's room and quietly closed the door. Silence filled the small room as he noticed his patient, Michael Latrell, perched on the bed, one foot idly swinging back and forth while his back faced Erick.

Erick gently broke through the silence, aware of the fragility of the moment. He walked over with measured steps, maneuvering around the bed to be face-to-face with Michael. Erick paused to follow his gaze to the window.

"What do you see out there?" His words were carefully chosen with years of training not just to inquire, but to connect, to bridge the gap between them.

"Hey, Doc." Michael glanced at Erick and then back to the scene out the window. "I guess you heard." He lowered his sleeve self-consciously to cover the bandages.

Erick sat down next to him on the bed. His eyes landed on the prosthetic leg that was leaning against the side of the bed. Michael wore a blue sweatshirt, black shorts, and white sneakers. The scars on his knee were deep and still red. "Has it been a year already?"

"Doc, I just can't…" Michael's eyes filled with tears.

"It's a tough road," Erick said wistfully. "It's the toughest actually. I've been helping people for years but have never been in your shoes. But, what I do know is disappointment and that life can be cruel and unforgiving. Can I ask you something?" Erick turned and looked him right into his brown eyes. "Before the accident, what were your plans for your life?"

Michael's head slumped before he hopped off the bed, grabbed his prosthetic, and snapped it on. His shorts fell long over the top, his back to Erick in defiance. "I already have a shrink, man! I don't need this."

Erick moved closer. "Michael," he said so firmly that he turned around quickly. "Listen, I didn't come here to make you feel worse than you already do. But, I also know that the doctor has placed you on a 72-hour hold because you are a danger to yourself. From my calculations, your time is not up until tomorrow morning. You have nowhere to go. So why not just tell me why you're here first?"

Michael tightened his lips. "You already know everything. Why don't you tell me why *you're* here?"

"You're my patient." Erick shrugged.

"You *were* my physical therapist," Michael shot back.

"Well, that's true." Erick moved toward the door. "I get it."

"You don't get shit! No one understands me. You can shrink me all you want, but you lied to me."

"How did I lie to you?" Erick raised his eyebrows, curious about where this was going.

"You told me I could *walk* again." Michael's fingers trembled as they wiped the tears from his face, the bandage on his wrist stark against his skin.

As Michael moved about the room, Erick remained silent, absorbing the blow. His movements were not as fluid as they once were, but there was a determined grace to them nonetheless. One step followed another. Erick watched Michael walk past him and toward the window. "So what do you call what you're doing right now?"

"You *made* me believe," Michael said, then sank in defeat in the single chair by the window.

"What did I make you believe?" Erick challenged.

"You made me believe that everything was going to go back to the way it *was*." Michael brushed another tear from his cheek. "I just don't want to be here right now."

"Where do you want to be instead?" Erick asked just then.

"Anywhere but here. I feel trapped in this life and in this room."

"Well, they have a policy…"

"I don't give a shit about the policy. I should *not* be here. I should have my leg. I should be starting my senior year in college. Getting married…" Michael choked the words out. "Stefani left me because I have no future."

"Ah, women… that *is* something I *do* know about," Erick said, as he remembered his struggles with Grace. He felt he, too, should have been married by now. "Can I ask you something?"

"I guess," Michael conceded.

"If I can get you out of here, will you help me with something?"

"My hours aren't up yet." Michael looked confused. "They won't let me leave until I talk to the shrink again."

"I got us a special pass. Are you in or are you too scared to break the rules?" Erick tipped his head to the side, waiting for an answer.

"You're crazy!" Michael's face lit up briefly. "Wait… are you serious?"

"Dead serious," Erick affirmed. "But if we do this, you'll have to trust me. Can you do that?"

This question went unanswered as Michael thought about what Erick was saying.

Erick shrugged and headed to the door. "If you'd rather stay here and feel sorry for yourself…"

With a sudden burst of energy, Michael walked closer to Erick, his movements jerky as he adjusted to the weight of the prosthetic. "Let's bounce."

"Good, because there's something you really need to see." Erick already had a plan for Michael to bring him back to a world that still held possibilities, however far they seemed to be at the moment. He tossed Michael his jacket. "You're going to need this."

Erick led the way, and Michael followed, each step a silent declaration that he was more than his injuries, and more than the heavy despair that weighed down his spirit.

"Okay," Michael finally said, his voice barely above a whisper, yet it resounded with newfound determination. "I'll trust you."

Chapter 21

Grace was lost in thought as she traced her fingers along the contours of Jack's deceiving smile in the photo she had mounted on the wall. This photo was featured in a newspaper article she found at the library and it had to be taken before she was born. She suddenly felt dizzy and settled into the small chair by the desk. A chill spread through the room as her mind swirled with the theories she'd woven together like a mental puzzle. How many times had she sifted through these articles, searching for the truth about what really happened? The lines blurred before her eyes as she fought to maintain focus.

Pull yourself together. The image of Jack mocked Grace from the wall. She had an eerie feeling that she was being watched as the hairs on the back of her neck tingled. Grace got up and closed the blinds over the window. She was becoming painfully aware that this relentless pursuit had consumed her waking hours and invaded her dreams. *Jack may have set a trap for me, but I will be the one to finish it once and for all.* There was no turning back, and Grace couldn't stop now, even if she wanted to.

In Raven's photo, her bright smile was frozen in time, but Grace knew the story and the info she'd already found made it all seem even darker. The journal her dad gave her from Raven held the secrets of how Jack was so evil from the beginning. It wasn't until Pala had come along that her mother realized how he kept her like a caged bird. Grace imagined the fear that gripped Raven in her final days here—a fear that had ultimately been justified. Once vibrant and full of life, Raven was now reduced to a memory because of Jack.

Grace's eyelids were heavy, and more tears threatened to spill over as she realized she too felt that same fear now. With each breath, she tried to fight against the swell of emotions and the fatigue that enveloped her. She stared blankly at the wall of photographs and despite all her effort, her eyes fluttered shut.

A sudden noise caused Grace to open her eyes and turn sharply as Pala slowly pushed the door open and stood there. His presence had been an anchor for her the last several days. He looked pained and worried, his eyes reflecting a fierce protectiveness over her.

"Are you okay?" Pala's voice was gentle as if he was speaking to a child.

Grace attempted a reassuring smile but she felt confused and foggy at the same time. She nodded, not trusting herself to speak just yet, afraid her voice would reveal how far down the rabbit hole she'd fallen searching for Jack. Pala was a lifeline back to the world, and Grace prayed it was *his* blood that ran through her veins.

"We're missing something," she finally said, her voice shaky. "It's right in front of our faces, but I can't see it yet." She gestured to the photographs and all the documents hanging on the wall.

Pala offered a silent nod of solidarity and Grace was grateful that they were in this fight together.

"I found Rebekah, Jack's sister. She all but confirmed that Jack hunted Raven down and pushed her over the edge. Quite literally, actually." Grace's voice was raspy and strained as she forced herself to recount the conversation. She watched Pala's face closely, the deep lines of his forehead tensing in response, his eyes never leaving hers.

"He's been living right here in San Diego, but under another name, Luke Silver," Grace continued as a shiver went down her spine. "He was the one who set the fire that killed his adoptive parents and framed his sister. He… he knows about me and you." The words were a bitter reminder that time was running out. Grace was convinced more than ever that her mother's death was no accident.

Pala's expression darkened, he clenched his fists briefly and tightened his jaw.

"And Rebekah needs our help," Grace added. "Only one way to get evidence now…" Her throat constricted knowing it was just a matter of time until she would inevitably have to confront Jack himself. She swallowed hard, the terror momentarily subsiding. "We have to find him before he finds us. Because he's watching. Always watching."

Nodding grimly, Pala absorbed the new information and leaned forward, determined to figure out their next course of action. "I may have someone to contact in Connecticut about Jack. Might lead us to a clue."

"Thank you, Pala," she said, her words holding genuine gratitude. Grace looked at him, a tight smile on her lips as she watched him.

"Don't thank me yet," he replied grimly. His eyes were dark and deep in thought. "This could get very dangerous." The reality of Pala's warning settled upon her.

"More dangerous than it already is?" She let out a worried laugh.

"Much more," Pala warned, stepping closer to her. His brow was knitted, and his mouth set in a thin line. "We're stirring up a viper's nest, Grace. We can't be sure when he'll strike."

She found herself looking around the room. "Jack…

Luke…whoever he is, isn't just a ghost from the past anymore. He's real and closer than we thought."

"Too close," Pala confirmed. He moved to the window, peering through the blinds onto the quiet street below. "Which is why we need to be smart about this. No more reckless moves."

"Reckless?" Grace's voice rose to justify her plan. "Finding the truth isn't reckless."

"It is when it puts you in his crosshairs." Pala turned back to her, his expression softened. "I know how much this means to you. But we have to tread carefully now. Promise me, Grace," Pala pleaded, taking her hand. His grip was firm, grounding. Promise me you won't lose yourself in this. Raven lost herself with same obsession. I *can't* lose you, too!"

"Okay," she said finally, knowing that Pala would be devastated if anything happened to her. "I promise."

Pala released her hand, but Grace noticed his shoulders remained tense. His eyes narrowed. "I fear it might already be too late. When was the last time you ate or even slept, for that matter?" he asked. "This quest is killing you, and I feel like I'm reliving the last week I spent with Raven."

"I'm just not hungry, but I'll be fine. I guess I should lie down now. I'm pretty tired." Grace tried to hide her trembling hands.

After he left the room and closed her door, she could hear Pala on the phone. She lay on her bed and stared at the ceiling, knowing full well that sleep wouldn't come. Rain pattered against the windowpane. With each passing minute, the room felt like it was growing colder and darker. The muscles in her body tensed with an anticipation that bordered on desperation. Grace knew she couldn't back down now or keep the promise she had just made to Pala, when the truth was within her grasp. She was so close it was maddening. Grace let out a deep and heavy sigh, went over to the window, and stared outside at the street below. She heard every little noise and then a deafening quiet.

All the waiting felt like it could bury her. Suddenly, a car passed slowly outside and Grace paused as she watched the vehicle disappear around the corner. Each sound outside seemed amplified in her ears as she strained to hear everything, and every shadow was a potential threat. Grace wrapped her arms around herself, trying to dispel the paranoia that was building inside her. Jack had been a master of manipulation, always one step ahead, and even hiding in plain sight.

"Grace." Pala's voice startled her from her spiraling thoughts. He stood by the now-opened door to her room.

Grace turned sharply, her gaze locking onto his. "Did you hear something?"

He shook his head, his expression unreadable. "No. It's just… You've been watching the street like you will see someone. I don't think he's out there."

"Jack *is* out there somewhere," she said, her voice low and firm. "We can't underestimate him."

"Maybe you should try to rest—"

"Shh!" Grace held up a hand, her eyes focusing beyond the window again. A figure walked past, obscured by the rain in the afternoon light. Grace thought she saw Jack's silhouette in every passerby for a breathless moment, feeling his eyes boring into her from every direction.

"Grace," Pala said gently, drawing her attention back inside.

"I'm sorry. All this waiting…" Her voice trailed off and betrayed the toll it took on her nerves.

"I know," Pala agreed. "All of this can wait until tomorrow. I am really concerned about you."

Grace silently settled back onto the bed, a heavy blanket of apprehension settling over her. The storm outside intensified, thunder echoing. Pala sat beside her on the bed and placed a blanket over her.

The shrill ring of Pala's phone shattered their moment of solace. They both flinched, their nerves strung tight. Grace sat up and watched him, her heart pounding, as he retrieved the device from his pocket and glanced at the caller ID.

"Hello?" Pala answered cautiously and moved to the kitchen as Grace followed him.

Chapter 22

Erick and Michael exited the hospital after they signed the papers for a short reprieve from the hospital and what time to return.

They drove through town and arrived at a community park entrance and parked by a weathered basketball court surrounded by a discolored chain-linked fence. Erick watched Michael exit the Jeep, and then pulled an old basketball out of the backseat.

"What is this?" Michael crossed his arms over his chest.

Erick unlatched and pushed open the gate, its rusted hinges groaned in protest. The basketball court was empty, grey, and cracked. Around the perimeter were patches of dirty snow. Small puddles pooled where it had melted in the late afternoon sun. Michael hesitated, his gaze shifting between Erick and the ball in his hand.

"I don't play," Michael said and was unfazed when Erick threw him the ball. The ball hit the ground and then rolled away from Michael.

"Now, who's lying?" Erick ran over, stole the ball, and laid it up for a perfect shot.

"Dude, *what* is your problem? You aren't happy in your life, so now you have to punk the disabled person?"

"Who's the disabled person?" Erick passed the ball to his patient.

"Stop asking me dumb questions," Michael protested, holding onto the ball. "We're wasting time." He threw the ball and missed as it clanged against the rim and then bounced off.

"We can go back to the hospital if you want." Erick shot a three-point shot and got all net.

"Nah, I won't let an *old man* beat me," Michael smiled, despite himself, as he took the ball away from Erick. He jumped and took the shot. The ball rolled around the rim and fell through the net.

"I'm not *that* old!" Erick laughed as he rebounded the ball. "I thought you said you can't play," he scoffed.

"I can't play like I *used* to play. I was on the varsity team in high school." Michael blocked Erick's shot and finished with a layup.

"I know," Erick said as he dribbled the ball back.

"If you know everything, then why are you going to let me beat you?" Michael taunted Erick, a new spark in his eyes.

"Because the only disabling thing I see is your *ego*, my friend. You play just fine from where I am standing. So what's really holding you back?"

"Come on, man!"

"Why did Stefani leave you?" Erick countered and then dribbled past Michael for the shot.

"Nope, *you* first. Why is your girl not with you?" Michael held the ball now.

Michael's reflexes kicked in, and muscle memory guided his hands in intercepting the ball mid-air. His fingers gripped it tightly as if holding on to a part of himself he thought he'd lost.

"Come on," Erick urged, nodding toward the net. "You *do* want to play don't you?" Without waiting for a response, he passed the ball to his patient.

"Been a while since anyone's passed me the ball," Michael confessed.

With a swift motion, Erick closed the space between them. He pivoted left, then darted right, his movements sharp and practiced. Michael barely registered the shift before the ball was swept away.

As Erick drove toward the basket, Michael turned on instinct, his body responding despite the protest in his mind. He was a step behind because just then, almost in slow motion, Erick propelled himself upward, arm extending, and laid the ball up for a perfect shot. It kissed the backboard and slipped through the net with a whisper.

"Bring it on," Erick challenged.

Michael's gaze darted from the doctor's taunting smile to the ball as it smacked into the ground with a thud. "Old man," he scoffed, the corner of his lip perking up. He snatched the ball from Erick's unsuspecting grasp with a swift motion, more from stubbornness than skill.

Next, Michael sprang into action, as he rose into the air. He released the ball, watching its arc while holding his breath. The ball tumbled through the net. "I won't let an old man beat me," he said.

"I thought you said you can't play!" he scoffed, wiping sweat from his brow with the back of his jacket sleeve.

"Can't or won't?" Michael countered, a smirk playing at the edges of his lips. "Life was much simpler when victory was measured in points scored and games won."

Erick's eyes held a glimmer of understanding. "Now, it's about overcoming the battles you're fighting against yourself and your own body. Show me what you got." Erick was aware of the unspoken duel unfolding between them. He stooped slightly to ready himself for whatever Michael might throw his way. "I can't believe you've still got a great shot!" he exclaimed, while he tracked Michael's movements with an equally challenging and supportive intensity. As Michael maneuvered around him, every pivot and push was a battle between the man he had been and the one he was becoming. Erick was witnessing the transformation right before his eyes.

Chapter 23

race followed Pala to the kitchen and sat down at the table where Pala had moved to take the phone call. She leaned on her elbows and strained to hear fragments of the conversation, noticing the tension in Pala's shoulders.

"Understood," Pala said, clearing his throat. He ended the call and met Grace's expectant gaze.

"Who was that?" Grace began, her voice trailing off, hopeful for some new evidence.

Pala moved closer, his presence a solid reassurance. Yet when he finally spoke, his voice was grave. "I found something out," he said, the words heavy with implication.

"What?" Grace asked, unable to wait any longer.

"More than we bargained for," Pala continued, his eyes searching hers. "I spoke to my old boss from the bookstore I used to work at in Connecticut," Pala said finally. "I remembered him mentioning something strange to me once, and I didn't put it together for a long time. About a hiker who was passing through, an old friend asking about me." Pala shook his head.

"The hiker wanted to know all these details about my life, about Raven, and Karl was hesitant to provide him with any, said the guy just seemed off." Pala paused. "That's all I heard from Karl about that. I actually thought it was a friend I met hiking. But then Karl was weird about the whole situation, and the more I thought about it, something about the hiker's description always threw me. At the same time, I knew Jack was after Raven and would go through me to get to her. And it turns out, I was right. I had to press him for information, but Karl gave my info to a hiker named *Luke Silver.*"

"He gave your information to him? Why would he do that?"

"Because Luke Silver threatened him. Karl isn't the type to just give out personal information about employees. He tried to dig deeper, get info on this hiker, but he came up empty. And just when he was about to go to the police, Luke Silver threatened his life, and Karl got scared. This was all around the time that Raven had moved in with me." His forehead folded into deep lines. "Karl is still afraid," Pala continued, though a tremor in his voice threatened to betray the calm facade he tried to maintain. He shook his head. "Jack threatened to burn down his bookstore if he said a word. Karl has a wife and two kids! I can't imagine what kind of stress he has endured all these years being silent."

Grace leaned forward, her own fears momentarily paused by the concern she saw etched into Pala's weary features. "Your boss… " Grace started, her words faltering as she tried to process the implications. "He's afraid for his life because of what we're doing?"

"Yes and no. I feel responsible because of what I've dragged him—and now you—into," Pala said, his lips pressed into a thin line. "This is spiraling out of control, Grace. It's no longer just about finding the truth. People are getting hurt. For all we know, Jack has probably been stalking us this whole time! Here I thought this was a safe place for Raven, and now I've also put you in danger." Pala looked pained again.

Grace could see the conflict that raged behind Pala's gaze.

His need to know the truth and his desire to protect those around him was tearing him apart, piece by piece. *Rebekah had been right about everything.*

"It really *was* Jack all along," Pala said. "He's been living as Luke Silver, stalking Raven and me, setting up a twisted game for all these years."

Grace rose from the table, the chair scraping against the floor. "We're so close, I just need to do a little more research. I'm sure they have more records at the library. I have an address and… " Grace trailed off knowing it wouldn't end until she had confronted Jack once and for all.

Suddenly, Pala jumped up from his seat, his movements sudden and decisive. "We have to stop all this before it's too late." Pala froze, then reached for his phone. "At the very least, we need to be careful from now on." In his eyes, Grace saw the determination and shared understanding that this search was drawing to its inevitable conclusion. She watched as Pala looked up the phone number. Grace assumed this would initiate a chain of events that would finally bring them face-to-face with the monster behind everything.

Grace felt her fear dissolve as the phone connected, replaced by the sense of ending this once and for all. The time for waiting and second-guessing was over. Now, they would strike back.

Chapter 24

Erick stood in awe as he watched Michael successfully make a three-point shot. "Still got some moves, I see," Erick teased, yet beneath the banter was the utmost respect for his patient.

The ball left Michael's hands in an arc toward the basket. It hit the rim with a bang that rang throughout the park, but his rebound was swift. "Your turn," Michael said, passing the ball back to Erick. "So did your girl leave you because you suck at basketball or what?"

"My girl's in California at the moment," Erick said, lost in thought.

Michael took advantage and stole the ball easily and scored.

"What did you do to chase her away?" Michael asked, as he passed the ball back to Erick and waited.

Erick thought for a moment, "I honestly have no idea, this time."

"You're leaving out all the good stuff. You must have done *something*, or why are you two not together?" Michael pressed on.

Erick ran to get two water bottles from the cooler and removed his fleece jacket. The time was going by too fast. When he returned with the bottles, he handed Michael the other bottle.

"It's a long story. Let's just say I helped her after her accident when she lost her memory."

"That seems like a nice thing to do."

"And then she found out I lied to her."

He took a swig of water.

"Ah, so you *are* a liar!"

Michael crushed the water bottle to punctuate his thought.

"It was for a good reason at the time," Erick defended. "I hadn't seen her in a decade, and I was the one who found her after she fell down a cliff."

"Whoa, that is complicated. Please tell me she wasn't one of your patients?"

"Well…" Erick began.

"Oh my God! You *are* crazy! Isn't that like some sort of ethical issue?"

"Yeah, it was." Erick sighed at the admission.

"She kicked you to the curb when she found out?" Michael asked.

"Pretty much." Erick took another sip, wondering why he was talking about his love life.

"Stef didn't want to be with me anymore." Michael looked down at his legs as he spoke.

Erick changed the subject. "Do you believe in God?"

"Not really. Why would I believe in a God that can take away my leg? If He was so great, then why would He have caused that drunk guy to hit me while I was riding my motorcycle?"

Erick thought for a moment. "We can only see what we see now. But if we look back, we can usually see God working out things. The hard part is being patient and taking the time to see."

"Well, I lost my leg *and* my future wife. What else can this *God* take from me?"

"Well, for one thing, you're alive and breathing today. That itself is a miracle, don't you think?" Erick looked directly at Michael. "Second of all, you just played basketball for the first time in years. How did that feel?"

"One game isn't going to give me back my basketball scholarship or change my life." He stared ahead. "But it did feel good to be back out there. I'll give you that…" Michael shrugged. "Now what am I supposed to do?"

Erick considered Michael's situation for a moment. He knew the game they played today was mending something for each of them. They were two men who held on to the remnants of their former lives, and both were searching for meaning. "Perhaps it isn't just about winning or losing, or even about the past. Maybe it's about the here and now," Erick said. "It's also about moving forward, despite everything we've both been through and finding your purpose. You have to figure this path out for yourself. I can only show what is possible."

"Man, I guess we're both at a crossroads," Michael said. "We both know what it's like to lose parts of yourself to circumstances beyond your control. I assumed Stef would no longer love me, so I pushed her away after the accident last summer. It was all my fault."

His confession was part of letting go. With every word, he painted the picture of his life and the one he had now and how it separated him from someone he still cared for deeply. "With all the recovery I had to do, I knew it would be too much for her. I feel robbed of the life I dreamed of." His fingers tightened around the ball, knuckles whitening. "I had it all figured out, and I had the most perfect girl by my side. I used to be someone. Now I'm just a college dropout." He let the ball roll from his hands, watching it bounce away.

"Hey." Erick reached out, stopping the ball with his foot. "You're more than what happened to you."

"Easy for you to say." Michael retrieved the ball. "But how do you move on when every part of your life reminds you of what you've lost?"

"By not letting the loss define you," Erick said, knowing the truth of his words was something both of them needed. "We find a new game plan and change up the plays."

"Sounds like coach talk." Michael tried a smile, but it didn't reach his eyes.

"Maybe it is," Erick admitted, standing up. "But maybe it's time we *both* start listening to our inner voice." The skies had darkened, and he knew their time was nearly up.

The lights buzzed as they flickered on, and just then, Michael looked up to the sound of pounding feet and the noise of youth as they spilled onto the court. Five boys came running, their laughter piercing the quiet dusk like firecrackers. Erick and Michael turned toward the sound. Among the group, a boy in a wheelchair navigated the terrain with ease. Behind him, two others matched his speed. Their energy was infectious and jolted Michael from his introspection.

"Look at them," Erick said, nodding toward the newcomers. A smile tugged at the corners of his mouth. "Life doesn't slow down for them, does it?" Each boy had something different about them.

"No," Michael uttered, watching the dynamic scene play out. The boy in the wheelchair executed a sharp turn. Erick could feel a shift in the atmosphere and he noticed something within Michael also stirred.

"Doesn't seem fair, though," Michael added quietly.

"Fair's got nothing to do with it," Erick replied. "It's about playing the hand you're dealt."

Erick looked over at Michael while he watched intently as the boys took possession of the court, eager for their game to begin. And at that moment, Erick observed Michael breaking down the barriers and opening up to a world of possibilities he never never thought possible. Michael realized he might be able reclaim a part of himself he once thought was lost forever. "Maybe," Michael conceded, "it's time I stopped focusing on what I lost and just got back in the game."

"Well," Erick replied, a smile forming on his lips and a spark of mischief in his voice as he leaned back and stretched his arms in front of him. "I did say I wanted to show you something…"

Chapter 25

Grace's body surrendered to the crushing weight of dehydration and exhaustion. Her limbs felt heavy, her mind hazy, and soon, consciousness slipped away.

The faint smell of smoke suddenly filled her nostrils, jolting Grace awake. She snapped into alertness, her heart pounding with the immediate threat of danger. Flames danced wildly against the walls of Pala's building. Through the haze of heat and fear, she caught a glimpse of Jack Stone's retreating figure, darting away from the chaos he had ignited. Grace called out to Pala, but her eyes burned, and the heat grew intense and hot on her face.

Driven by an unseen force, Grace ran, her feet pounding against the cold pavement as she wove through the crowded streets of San Diego. Panic fueled her as Jack's form grew smaller ahead, but she kept after him.

The small town fell away behind her, giving rise to the wild coastal trail she and Pala had walked together when she first got to San Diego. Her heart thundered in her chest. Grace lost sight of Jack Stone as the path wound upwards, the mountain challenging her with its steep incline.

Below, the ocean roared fiercely as waves crashed against the unyielding rocks. The moon was high in the sky, lighting her path. No matter what she did, she could never catch up to Jack Stone, but she pressed on until a voice filled her head.

"Grace!" The sound pierced through like a beacon of hope. It was Erick! It felt warm and real as she stumbled toward him, arms flung wide open with a longing that seeped into every fiber of her being. Their embrace was like heaven on earth and filled her soul. Grace swore she would never let go again. She wanted to stay in Erick's arms forever and forget everything. It had been a mistake coming here. Pala was right about it being too dangerous.

"I'm so sorry; I'll never leave again!" Grace cried into Erick's chest.

But peace was fleeting, because Jack Stone came out of the dark like an omen. She clung to Erick like a solid fortress against evil, and when she let go, she faced Jack. "I know what you did to Raven!" Grace accused Jack. Her words were like sharp blades aimed at his heart. Jack laughed, and the sound echoed like a cold wind, chilling her to the bone as he lunged toward her with malice in his eyes.

"You're just like her. You are my daughter! But now you'll suffer the same fate as your mother." Suddenly, Jack pulled out a gun, and a thud followed the horrific noise. Erick fell to the ground and his blood spilled everywhere.

"No!!!" Grace ran over to help him, but as she approached, it wasn't Erick at all; it was his brother Finn. She knelt down, and Finn's blue eyes stared blankly at her. It was too late. She fell back as Jack lunged at her. Then her balance betrayed her as the ground vanished beneath her feet, and she was falling. Grace tumbled through the air with only the harsh rush of the sea and the inevitable impact of the sharp, ragged rocks below.

Then, with a jolt that sent shockwaves through her body, the rocks and the icy water swallowed her. Grace gasped for breath as she choked.

Suddenly, she was awake, and all that remained was the salt that lingered on her tongue as she struggled to find her bearings.

Chapter 26

Erick smiled as a man approached them and gave him a high-five. The lights on the court illuminated their faces in the night.

"Doc, thanks for joining us tonight." The man walked with a limp, but he didn't seem to notice.

"Michael, I'd like you to meet Richard. He's the coach of the Farmington's Unified Sports middle school boys' basketball team."

"But they all are…" Michael looked confused but shook Richard's hand.

"They're what?" Richard asked.

"They're like… me." Michael stared in disbelief. The boys were happy to play and very competitive despite some having prosthetic legs or wheelchairs, and one boy had one arm.

"Would you like to join us?" Richard asked, turning to Michael.

"I don't play much… anymore." Michael looked down at the metal on his own leg.

"Suit yourself." Richard blew the whistle and began practice.

"But if you change your mind, we're looking for an assistant coach."

"Do I look like I can coach?" Michael scoffed and then scratched his head.

"These boys give everything they got five days a week. I just show up and make sure no one gets hurt." Richard blew the whistle again. "Jaxon was wide open, and you *must* block that shot, Creed!"

"Why don't you sleep on it, Michael?" Erick gently tapped his shoulder.

"I just don't know what I have to offer anyone." Michael slumped his shoulders again. "I appreciate you checking in on me, but I just don't see what good I can do." The boys shot and missed, sending the ball flying toward the bench where Michael was sitting. He caught the ball as a boy with a prosthetic leg ran up to him.

"Nice leg!" the boy said. "I'll be getting a new titanium one after the season."

"I was fortunate to get this one," Michael said, tossing the boy the ball.

"We better get you back, Michael," Erick said, standing up and high-fiving Richard. "We'll be in touch."

"See you at the church fundraiser over the summer," Richard said to Erick after handing Michael his card. "Michael, when you're ready, give me a call."

"Take care now. We need to go," Erick said, and they both climbed into the Jeep. Once at the medical facility, Erick dropped Michael at his therapist's office at the perfect time and turned to leave.

"Thank you," Michael said, suddenly stopping Erick short.

"Of course," Erick said and spun around. "You *will* survive this, and it'll make you stronger. Let me know what you decide about the coaching gig. I'll call you next week to check in, if that is okay with you?"

Michael put his hand out and shook Erick's. "I'll let you know."

Erick saw something in Michael that he had not seen in quite some time. Hope shone brightly in the young man's eyes. Over the years, Erick had saved many people who had experienced devastating injuries. It was only recently that he needed to save himself from his past. Now, if only he could plan the future he wanted—a future with the woman he loved. If she would only give him the time of day. Maybe he should take her absence as a sign to move on, but Erick wasn't quite ready to let go.

Chapter 27

Grace awoke from the nightmare, confused. *What had happened to her? Where was she?* Her blurred vision tried to focus on the structure above her head. How did she get under the small desk? Still dizzy, her hand clawed the underside, trying to get leverage to pull herself up, but her hand felt something soft instead.

Eventually, after several attempts, she was able to carefully pull herself upright. She flipped the switch on the wall, turning on the overhead light. Next, she turned on the flashlight on her phone and knelt down and peered under the old maple wood desk.

She ran her hands under and toward the back of the desk, and she discovered a folder that was covered in duct tape. Without tearing it, she peeled it off the bottom of the drawer and placed it on top of the desk. She looked up at the photographs and documents pinned on the wall above, then back down at the folder. Grace opened the folder and found handwritten notes.

October 31st

Jack Stone is here, lurking in the shadows. I guess deep down I knew it would come to this one day… I just wanted a simple life with Pala here in nature. Then, recently, handwritten scraps of paper started appearing. At first, I did not know what it meant. Each note had a scrawled message. The first one I found under the rubber wiper blade pinned against the car window. Then, another one was tucked in with the bills and flyers in the mailbox. Sometimes, the phone would ring late at night, and all I'd hear was the sound of someone breathing on the other end. My gut tells me it's Jack.

I've been following clues to see what actually happened to Jack. I went to the library and used their computers, and I discovered the mental institution where Jack was admitted to after the fire. The building is just ashes now, destroyed not long after he was released. I remembered his face flickering across the news, speaking of legacies and a future family with his girlfriend. It was a warning. He was coming for me.

Every word I'm writing down here is a piece of my soul, a metaphorical and literal map for Grace to avoid falling into the same trap. All I want is for her to discover her true legacy as my daughter. I could feel it in my bones that Jack is back and after revenge. I fear she may be next in line, and I'll give my life to protect her from that fate.

Grace could not believe the words on the paper. There were more handwritten pages from Raven to read. She knew this might be the answer to all her questions and the proof she was looking for to finally release herself from the grip of a madman who may very well be her father.

Chapter 28

Erick rubbed the bridge of his nose. The beginnings of a headache throbbed behind his eyes as he hugged the phone between his shoulder and ear. He had picked up Jace and was glad to be back in the cabin, but it no longer felt like a sanctuary of solitude. It was too silent, too empty, even though Jace was content on the rug, waiting for the next adventure.

The persistent buzz of missed calls had been an undercurrent to his evening, news that he could no longer ignore. Erick's agent was giving him the itinerary for tomorrow as the conference was back on in Boston.

"Okay, I understand. I'll head to Boston first thing, and once I reach the convention center, I'll go ahead and make sure our presentation is set up smoothly for the kickoff events." Erick disconnected the call and saw more missed calls. There even was one call from Grace, but when he played back the message, all he heard was breathing. He called her back immediately, but her phone went right to voicemail.

It's Grace, you know what to do after the beep.

Disappointed, he closed his eyes and left her a message.

"Hey, I saw that you called. I hope you're doing well. Call me when you can."

Next, Erick pressed Daniel's name in his contact list and waited for his little brother to answer.

"Hey, the roads are open now, and the conference is back on. I'll be headed out tomorrow morning," Erick informed Daniel.

"Come on over tonight. Sky made chili. And bring Jace so you don't have to worry about him in the morning," Daniel suggested.

"Are you sure it's not too late?" Erick asked as Jace's eyes darted around, ready for adventure.

Daniel would not take no for an answer, so Erick and Jace jumped into the Jeep and headed over to his brother's apartment.

"Come on, Erick!" Daniel's voice nudged him from his thoughts as he and Jace approached the apartment. "Sky's culinary magic won't stay warm forever."

The crisp evening air greeted Erick, his breath visible in front of him. The cold had lingered over not only the town but within him as well. New England winters seemed to last forever, but spring was right around the corner. Once inside, the smell of cumin, garlic, and chili powder filled his nostrils.

"Daniel, do you ever think about—" Erick trailed off.

"About what?" Daniel asked.

"About knowing when to hold on to something or whether to let go? Do you think some things are meant to be left behind?" Erick was conflicted.

"You'll know what to do when the time comes," Daniel spoke matter-of-factly.

Erick pondered Daniel's words as he caught the aroma of the sweet cornbread in the the kitchen. "You're right," he conceded.

Erick took a seat at the kitchen table, and immediately, the men took hearty scoops of the chili. The blend of herbs and spices promised comfort, a temporary haven for Erick before he began his new journey.

"You've outdone yourself again," Daniel complimented Sky, his demeanor giving way to a light-hearted anticipation of the meal.

"Thank you!" Sky said, fixing herself a bowl. Then she passed the salad and cornbread. At the conclusion of dinner, Sky announced, "I need to take the dogs out for one last walk." She kissed Daniel and patted Erick on the shoulder for reassurance. "I'll leave you to it then."

The warm aroma of spices lingered in the air as Erick pushed his empty bowl of chili aside, a satisfying heat lingering on his tongue. Daniel leaned back in his chair, an eager gleam in his eyes.

"Man, that was good!" Daniel said, wiping his mouth with a napkin. "So, Erick, do you have your speech written for your presentation in Boston?"

"Yes, that was the easy part. Can you and Sky still come to the awards ceremony?"

"We wouldn't miss it for the world," Daniel replied, fixing his gaze on Erick. "Listen, have you thought about what you'll do after the conference?"

Erick knew Daniel was asking if he was going after Grace when he got back.

"I missed the one call I got from her, but I did try to call back, and she didn't answer. If I haven't heard anything by the time you guys come up to see me, then yes, I'll take the next flight out to San Diego and see what's going on. But anyway, I should get going."

By this time, Sky had returned from her short walk with the dogs.

"Thank you for the delicious meal, Sky!"

"Of course," she replied. "Have a safe trip, and we'll be seeing you at the ceremony."

Erick nodded, feeling a mix of anticipation and nerves knotting in his stomach. He hugged Sky first, then Daniel, and told Jace he would be back soon. The conference was a big deal, yet he knew his heart was no longer into these kinds of events.

Once Erick was back at the cabin, he put his duffel bag by the door and hoped to get some sleep. He needed his mind sharp, but the anticipation of his upcoming presentation and thoughts of Grace kept him awake. He knew his deep love for Grace would never wane, but he couldn't live half a life waiting for her to decide. He deserved to be happy, and it seemed like it was time for him to move on.

Chapter 29

Grace could not stop reading the pages her mother had written. She was also aware that following Raven's footsteps could very well lead to a confrontation with Jack Stone.

When that first note appeared, my life crumbled into pieces. Even though Pala was my rock, I couldn't quell the rising tide of panic in me.

Fear had a way of sharpening my instincts. Jack's essence shone through his scrawls on the paper. I documented each discovery and every unveiled threat.

The last note, though, held an address: 1374 Unit #67 ------h Street, which was burned into my mind.

Grace squinted and tried to read the smudged street name. No matter how much she tried, she couldn't make it out.

I couldn't wait for the predator to strike. Pala witnessed me as I began to deteriorate. His concern was not unfounded. I couldn't eat, couldn't sleep as I prepared to enter Jack's place.

*The lion's den. I refused to risk Pala's life. If things went wrong…
I needed him to watch over Grace. The only thing that kept me alive was
the hope of protecting Grace, and I write these pages to document all of
my fears—a map for those who might come looking for me if I don't
return. And now, I stand ready to follow the trail to its end, to face the
ghost that refused to die.*

*I anticipated the confrontation with Jack Stone. It was time to end
this, one way or another. For Grace. For Pala. For ME. I went to the
address, and I felt his presence there. He'd been here, watching, plotting.
The walls were plastered with photographs, a collage of my life with Pala,
and each snapshot felt like a violation. Every trail we had walked, coffee
shops we sat in, and every friend we talked to. Jack had documented all
of our comings and goings.*

*A cold dread settled over me when I found a photograph with a large
red X scrawled over my face. Pala's kind eyes looked back at me from
another image, his smile unaware of his danger. The air seemed to thin,
making it hard to breathe in Jack's apartment. This was no longer paranoia. It was real, and it was a chilling confirmation of my fears.*

*I discovered a final note tacked under my photo that said, 'Raven,
READ ME.' I carefully opened the note, painfully aware that he could
return at any minute. He wanted me to see all of this. I read the com-
mand: meet me at dawn on Monday. The words danced before my eyes,
each one a silent scream. I knew that I wouldn't stop until I could see his
face; I could not let fear dictate my fate.*

*My heart was heavy with the weight of what might come, and this is
why I'm writing it all down for someone to find.*

*This writing will serve as proof of both my resolve and desperation.
Let these notes bear witness to the truth in case I do not return. Let them
guide Grace away from the shadows cast by Jack Stone. Every message I
found and every threat captured within these lines are my legacy of love
and protection for Grace. Jack has to be faced and stopped, no matter the
cost.*

Grace looked at the paper again. The street name was
smudged, which prevented her from making out the address

completely. How many street names would end in an *h*? She could search the internet, but she didn't need Pala interfering. No, she would go to the library to figure out this location.

The last time Grace recalled feeling safe was when Erick was with her. She was in over her head now and needed him. She'd tried to call him, but it went straight to voicemail. He was angry with her for leaving, and she had to respect that.

Grace felt a wave of exhaustion wash over her and could not speak. She was tired from chasing her past and running from the one man she needed the most.

Chapter 30

Erick maneuvered his car into the valet lane in front of the Boston Convention Center. He emerged from the driver's seat and faced an attendant in a red jacket. "Good morning!" He nodded curtly to the valet attendant and tossed the keys to him. As the cool morning air sent a chill down his spine, Erick zipped up his jacket. With bags in hand, he strode up to the counter, where a staff member greeted him.

"Dr. Erick Finn?" she asked, her eyes briefly glancing at her clipboard before ushering him to the conference room.

"Yes. Thank you," he murmured, stepping into the large expanse of the main ballroom. It was still relatively quiet except for the echo of his footsteps. Erick's thumb tapped against the screen of his phone, bringing up the document with this year's conference schedule. His gaze swept over the digital collage of panels, keynotes, and roundtable discussions. The meet and greet caught his eye, slated for that evening—an event designed for networking.

Erick made his way to the side of the stage and set his things down on a nearby table covered in a white tablecloth. He sank into a chair and opened his laptop. The laptop display showed a plethora of unread emails and meeting reminders. He closed the laptop, feeling the confines of the room closing in on him. Erick closed his eyes momentarily, seeking solace in a dimly lit room. Then he ran a hand through his hair in a gesture of frustration.

He was still a little worried that he hadn't heard back from Grace, so tonight, after the reception, he would reach out to her again. Yes, their relationship was emotional chaos right now, but Erick could still feel the pull, a magnetic force drawing him back into Grace's world. His love for her was like a heavy anchor. He could get only so far before it dragged into the deepest depths of the ocean again. He looked up and saw his team coming in.

Hours later, Erick and his team had finished setting up the glossy programs and plastic name tags attached to navy lanyards on the tables just outside the ballroom. Next, he went upstairs and rested.

After he showered and got dressed, he looked in the mirror and smoothed his beard into place. Erick ran his hands through his sandy brown hair a few times to smooth out some of the waves, and when he was pleased with his look, he slid a sweater on over his dress shirt. Then he headed out of his hotel room and pressed the down button on the elevator.

When the doors opened, Erick made his way to one of the banquet rooms for the reception, where he noticed several of his colleagues with drinks in their hands and a huge buffet spread on the far table. Erick walked over to the fruit and cheese station and turned when another doctor he'd met once before approached him.

"Erick, great to see you," the doctor said, shaking Erick's hand.

"You too, Garrett."

"Heard you were up for an award."

"So they tell me," Erick said.

"Good stuff. Catch you later, man," Garrett said, and then he headed away from the table.

Alone again, Erick picked up a small plate and, and using a toothpick, picked up a few cubes of cheese and strawberries. *I am not drinking tonight. I need to keep a clear head if this convention is going to be a success.*

"Save some for the rest of us!" a warm female voice greeted him.

Erick's heart skipped a beat as he whirled around, the voice instantly igniting a memory within him. There she stood, bathed in the warm glow of the crystal chandeliers. Isabelle's presence was a jolt of electricity, sparking life into the formal atmosphere of the reception.

"Hey!" Erick managed to stammer, his usually composed demeanor giving way. She was a vision in pastel blue. The sight of her brought back a vivid image of them swaying to music, laughter mingling with dance music, and for a moment, Erick was transported back to Daniel's wedding.

Before he could say more, Isabelle's arms wrapped around him, her embrace a familiar comfort. The sensation of her warmth against him dissolved whatever remnants of professional decorum he clung to. Her skin radiated heat despite the earlier chill.

"Hey," he repeated, softer this time, as if afraid to break the enchantment of their reconnection.

When she finally stepped back, Isabelle's eyes met his with a knowing twinkle. "I knew you'd be here," she said, her voice carrying certainty and a hint of something more.

"Did you now?" Erick mused with surprise as he held Isabelle's gaze. The room's soft lighting sparkled in her hazel eyes, suggesting she knew far more than she let on. "You look great!"

Isabelle's response was immediate. Her lips curved into a smile. "As do you!" Her highlighted hair shimmered like strands of amber honey.

Erick leaned against the white cloth-covered table, his small plate balanced in one hand while the other nonchalantly speared a cube of Gouda. He popped it into his mouth, savoring the rich creaminess.

"So, what brings you here?" he asked, striving for casual conversation despite the quickening pulse he felt at her close proximity.

"My boss sent me over here for the week," she explained, her voice bubbling with the same effervescence Erick remembered. "His wife went into labor last night. So here I am!" She laughed and then continued. "I just got back from two weeks in the Maldives." Her words painted a picture of azure waters and white sands. "Destination wedding."

"Your wedding?" he asked.

"No, no. A friend's."

Erick couldn't help but admire the ease with which she laughed, a spontaneous burst of genuine joy. He looked around the ballroom, which had filled up, and he could hear the low hum of conversation and clinking glasses. Together, they navigated through clusters of fellow attendees toward the gleaming open bar.

"An espresso martini, please," Isabelle requested, her wink playful as she leaned comfortably onto the polished surface. "And for you?" There was a hint of challenge in her voice as if daring him to match her choice with something equally bold.

Erick considered for a moment but quickly decided against anything alcoholic, as he was mindful of the long evening ahead and the mental clarity he sought to maintain.

"Guess you're going to be up late tonight!" Erick chuckled, his eyes alight with the playful banter. He gestured to the bartender, "I'll have a club soda with a twist of lime, please." As the bartender nodded and turned to fulfill the order, Erick slid a crisp twenty into the large tip glass with a casual flick of his wrist. "Thank you," he said, knowing Beyond Limits was picking up the tab.

With drinks now in hand, Erick and Isabelle navigated through the crowd of convention attendees. Familiar faces emerged from the sea of industry professionals; there were other physical therapists whose methods Erick had long admired, salespeople whose innovative prosthetic products often sparked new ideas, and marketing reps who wanted to get their products into the hands of therapists.

Isabelle's presence at his side made him feel relaxed because she was a part of this secret physical therapy world. Her easy laughter and insightful comments were seamless. And her light touch on his arm guided him to conversations with industry icons.

As the evening wore on, they exchanged looks, slipped out the large banquet doors, and headed to the courtyard outside. Stepping out into the fresh air, Erick took a deep breath, feeling the coolness fill his lungs. The contrast between the warmth of the indoor festivities and the crisp Boston night was invigorating.

An array of twinkling lights and stars illuminated the pathway above them as they strolled along the cobblestone pathway. It was a relief to be away from the crowd, to share this moment of tranquility where words seemed unnecessary. Erick felt a kinship with Isabelle that went beyond the shared laughter and professional camaraderie—it was as if their paths were meant to intersect here, in this moment.

Erick's breath clouded as he exhaled. "Beautiful night tonight."

"God's masterpiece," Isabelle whispered as her eyes lifted to the starry heavens above. On her wrist, Erick noticed a delicate gold bracelet, its links joined by a small cross.

"You believe?" he asked, stunned by this new revelation.

"Of course I believe. God touches everything around us. My parents took me to church since I was little. Every summer, we attended Vacation Bible Schools." Isabelle shrugged, gently rubbing her fingers over the bracelet. "I believe He helps me with my patients, and I've seen many miracles over the years. How about you?"

A woman who had a passion for her patients and God, just like him… was it possible?

"I couldn't agree more. I just feel distant from His presence lately," Erick confessed.

"Well, maybe you'd like to go to church with me on Sunday? Close that distance between you and Him?" Isabelle suggested.

Erick paused as the invitation caught him off guard, stirring a blend of curiosity and anticipation within him. "Around here?" he asked, sipping his drink as if to buy a moment of time.

"There's one about 15 minutes from here," she said, her voice a soft melody against the backdrop of the night. "I like it. I go there when I can."

"You never told me that you lived in Boston," Erick admitted, his tone filled with genuine interest.

"You never asked," she said, her voice floating on the night breeze, "but I hope to move to a quieter place. I need to get out of the city. I prefer quieter places like Connecticut."

Erick couldn't take his eyes off her.

"I prefer the quiet, too," he said, smiling widely as he thought about quiet time with Jace, the birds, and his sanctuary in the woods.

He wanted more of that.

"Let's get inside," he suggested. "You look like you're freezing, and I don't have a jacket to give you."

Erick led the way, opening the door for her as they stepped out of the biting night air and into the comforting warmth of the indoors.

"I saw some chairs by the fireplace in the lobby," Isabelle said. "Would you like to continue this conversation?"

"That would be great!"

The dimly lit lobby area enveloped them, revealing an intimate corner where two soft, high-backed chairs faced each other across a small square table. The orange glow of the firelight cast a serene ambiance over the space. Isabelle chose the chair closest to the hearth, sinking into it with a contented sigh as Erick settled into the opposite seat, appreciating the sudden change in temperature. "So," he began, leaning forward slightly, elbows resting on his knees to bridge the gap between them. "Tell me more about what drew you to physical therapy."

Isabelle's face brightened as she launched into the story of her own calling to their shared profession. Erick listened intently, nodding as she spoke of challenges and triumphs, her words filled with the same dedication and compassion he himself felt. He chimed in with his own experiences, finding common ground in their desire to heal and improve lives. He couldn't believe they shared so much in common, especially their impact on the world, one patient, one breakthrough at a time.

Later, he said good night, and they parted ways. Exhausted from the long, busy day, he made his way up to his room and went to bed. The penthouse suite seemed enormous just then. Erick reached for his phone in an attempt to quell his loneliness. There were still no messages from Grace.

"Here we go again," he whispered to no one in particular. This love he had for Grace held him captive, and reaching out to Grace now was to open himself up to a familiar pain. Erick quickly texted a simple text. **Are you okay?**

Erick waited a few minutes, and getting no response, he felt his heart aching all over again. Then suddenly, a text came through.

Isabelle: So are you in for church tomorrow?
Erick: How did you get this number?
Isabelle: I have my ways. You in or what?
Erick: Of course, send me the address and time, and I will meet you there.

After Isabelle sent the address, he put his phone down on the side table and closed his eyes. Each direction felt like a thick fog, and Erick stood motionless, caught between his head's logic and his heart's longing. Maybe love didn't have to be complicated after all.

Chapter 31

Grace was so exhausted that she decided to lie down again and allowed herself a few hours of sleep. She awoke early the next day and slipped out of her room. There was no sign of Pala this morning, but perhaps he was still sleeping. Her eyes came into focus, and she noticed a stack of mail on the table and a large manila envelope addressed to her. Careful not to make any noise, she opened the envelope with her finger. Her stomach growled, but it would pass. Now was the time to learn about Jack Stone.

Jack was seeking counseling because he was struggling with his anger. After several suicide attempts, he went on medication, and then at age twelve, Jeremiah and Sarah adopted him. His brother Dovid was away at Yeshiva University, and Jack had just found out his sister had killed his adoptive parents and burned down the family business. Recently, on top of all that, his girlfriend had cheated on him. He located his biological father, Luke Stone, who had been incarcerated for serial murders in New England and was on death row. When he tried to visit him in prison a few years back, his father refused to meet with him.

Diagnosis: *Borderline personality disorder (BPD), Dependent personality disorder (DPD), and schizophrenia.*

The patient exhibits an intense fear of abandonment and difficulty regulating his emotions, particularly anger. The patient also shows signs of extreme codependency, manipulative behavior, and wild mood swings. He states he is unable to make decisions without reassurance from others, and feels helpless or uncomfortable when alone. When he is left alone, he locks himself inside for days, trapped in his thoughts. The patient hears voices, has disorganized speech when talking about hurting others, and has abnormal hatred for women. He claims to have had several incidents in foster homes with women physically and sexually abusing him, although it is difficult to decipher reality from his delusion, as there is no physical evidence corroborating his story.

It went on to show the list of medications and the treatment plan Jack was on and how he didn't like the medication because he felt like a zombie, but once adjusted he felt better.

This will have to be monitored very closely. I'm not confident he will maintain the medication treatment plan.

In the latest sessions, he spoke of the things that happened when he raged, but didn't act out anymore. Despite concerns, Doctor Allistair has concluded that he can be discharged from the facility and monitored on an outpatient basis.

Next, Grace read that he had been discharged from the hospital, but there were handwritten notes about Dr. Allistair receiving threats just before the building burned down. He suspected that Jack was responsible for all of it. According to the doctor, Jack was still a danger to himself and others.

Grace had come this far, and now she needed to see this through to the end, despite the danger. Even if she didn't survive to tell anyone about it.

Chapter 32

Erick looked at his reflection in the mirror early the next morning and smiled. He was eager to meet up with Isabelle at church. Once he parked the Jeep in the parking lot, he checked his phone, but there were no new messages. He ran up the stone steps of the church and opened the door, leading him into the foyer where he could hear voices singing praises to God. He turned into the sanctuary and saw Isabelle standing in the back pew, happily singing with all of her heart. Erick slipped into the row next to her and began to sing the well-known hymn, "It is Well with My Soul." His tenor voice blended with her soprano voice. Once the worship music was over, they both took a seat next to each other.

"I'm so glad you came," Isabelle whispered in his ear as the pastor started to talk.

Erick nodded at her and looked back up at the pastor. The message was about prayer and the story of Esther, who risked her life to save her people. The pastor's parallels to their lives today were interesting. It was a heartfelt sermon, and then they got to sing again before it was over. Isabelle introduced him to a few people before exiting the church building, and then he offered her a ride back to the convention center, which she accepted.

"What did you think of the message?" Isabelle asked Erick as they made their way onto the main road.

"I thought it was very thought-provoking. I realize that it's time for some changes." Erick kept his eyes on the road.

"I was thinking the same thing. I work way too many hours at the hospital. I would like to get into a smaller practice and work one-on-one with various clients," Isabelle confided.

"I'm opening a new franchise of HigherGround, so if you're interested, I could set something up whenever you decide." Erick offered.

"Sure, that would be great!" Isabelle looked out the window as the conference center came into view. The traffic seemed lighter today.

"Well, this conference is getting underway in a few hours." Erick parked near the valet station and came around the Jeep to open her door while handing the keys over.

"Thank you, I hope you enjoyed your morning as much as I did. Would you like to get coffee or something else before it starts?" Isabelle walked beside Erick as the automatic doors opened and the intimate setting vanished into the bustle of a crowded lobby.

"Unfortunately, I won't be able to. My team is waiting on me right now, but I can see you after the event if you like. Maybe dinner?" Erick waved to Isabelle, who nodded before heading over to the coffee cart. Once in the elevator, Erick realized Isabelle was incredibly easy to be with. She was present and not confined by the past or any past mistakes he might have made. It was so refreshing.

He changed out of his casual attire into his black suit and a crisp, freshly-pressed white shirt. Then he hung the lanyard holding his laminated nametag around his neck. Erick descended in the elevator and made his way to the grand ballroom. The room was empty, with chairs set up in neat rows facing the stage. His eyes scanned the room for any sign of Isabelle.

Erick walked up to the stage and stood behind the podium, looking out at the grandeur of one of Boston's most prestigious hotels. His laptop was all ready and open for him as the hum of conversation from his team filled the spacious conference room while the banners emblazoned with <u>Beyond Limits Physical Therapy</u> hung high over the stage. He clicked through his presentation on his laptop, images of innovative prosthetics and therapy patients flashing across the screen.

He had come so far since his days at HigherGround, professionally and personally. The spotlight seemed blindingly brighter now. *HigherGround* and *Erick Finn* were renowned among the inner circles of physical therapy. His triumphs were a result of his relentless dedication to his craft and his patients. Yet even with all the success, the sold-out events, and the accolades, an unresolved chapter was still waiting for him.

The one with Grace.

Erick snapped his laptop shut. His presentation was a triumphant fusion of technology and the human spirit. The conference room buzzed with his team's subdued chatter as they adjusted microphones and tested the sound system, but Erick stood still amidst the bustle, hands clenched on the podium.

"Hey boss, everything's set. You're gonna kill it," one of his team members said, offering an encouraging thumbs-up.

"Thanks, Justin," Erick replied, the words automatic. His gaze drifted to the windows, where the Boston skyline melded into the horizon. The Beyond Limits promotional flags flapped gently outside, promising boundless potential. Yet here he was, being pulled by the weight of a single question that refused to release its grip on his heart.

What if this is it with Grace? Erick thought as he rubbed his temples. *Where are these headaches coming from? Some kind of doctor I am!*

His pulse throbbed in his ears as thoughts of Grace's face flashed in his mind. The curve of her smile could eclipse the very sun. He knew because he had flown too close. Erick wasn't new to rehearsed speeches for a large audience, but no amount of preparation could steady his nerves for the one conversation that mattered most—the one he would have to have with Grace when he returned home.

"Rejection is a real possibility," he whispered to himself, his voice barely audible over the hum of the room's heating system. Doctors, researchers, reporters, and other attendees filed in and found their seats. He saw Chris Callahan, the sponsor of the event, wave from the back of the room.

"Sorry, what was that?" Justin tilted his head, his eyes wide with confusion.

"Nothing, just… going through my opening line," Erick lied smoothly, flashing a practiced smile. But the facade felt hollow, starkly contrasting the authenticity he spoke about in his seminars.

Erick took a deep breath and reminded himself why he was here, now, at the pinnacle of his career. He had scaled mountains of adversity, and each rung on the career ladder brought him closer to this moment.

Just then, Isabelle walked in wearing a cream colored pant suit, and her presence seemed to illuminate the whole room. He watched her find a seat in the front row and put her notebook on the seat next to her. Erick could not take his eyes off her and wondered if perhaps relationships didn't have to be so difficult after all.

"Ready when you are," Justin said, pulling Erick back to reality.

Erick closed his eyes and leaned on the podium as the light grew dim. *God, please be with me. Help them to see you and not me. Remove my ego, Lord. Please allow me to be useful… in Your Son's name.* Erick opened his eyes and enthusiastically responded, "Let's do this." His response was firmer this time and decisive. He left the stage and felt the familiar surge of adrenaline as the Master of Ceremonies asked everyone to find their seats.

The excitement in the room was palpable as "Walk on Water," from Thirty Seconds to Mars pumped through the speakers. Strobe lighting swept across the audience and finally landed on the center stage.

Erick approached the front of the room, taking two risers at a time, reaching center stage once again. Then he looked out at the sea of faces before him. This was his element, his stage. Erick took a sip of water from a crystal glass as the song faded.

"Good afternoon!" he began, his voice clear and resonant, "and welcome to the Beyond Limits Physical Therapy Conference. I'm Dr. Erick Finn."

Erick delved into his speech, showing slides on each breakthrough and case study that year. With a deep breath, each word was full of conviction as he told stories of patients who had defied all odds under his care. Each slide projected on the large screens above was everything he imagined it would be. Then the lights came up. The audience clapped when he demonstrated his technique on the stage while introducing a previous client, Antony, who was fit with a new prosthetic leg. Erick turned the podium over to his patient to tell his own story and made his way to the empty seat next to the most intriguing woman there.

Isabelle.

Chapter 33

Grace's hands shook, a mix of fear and anger consuming her as she clutched the crumpled papers. Every fiber of her being wanted to unleash a scream and run straight to Pala with the new information she'd found in Raven's papers, but he had asked her to be careful. She hesitated, but there was no way he was going to let her confront Jack herself. Pala would want the police to handle it, but she was too close to the truth, and she wasn't going to back down now.

She smoothed out the creases on the pages and read through them again. Raven's story of feeling disconnected from reality and constantly living in danger hit too close to home because now, Grace was also part of that dangerous world. She saw her reflection staring back at her in the dim light of her phone screen—a face she did not recognize. Dark circles had formed under her eyes, causing her to look ghostlike. And even though she was fatigued and stressed, Grace was determined. Glancing at the clock on her phone, Grace absently wound her hair into a long braid, put a hair tie in it, and formulated a plan. Pala always took his morning walk before opening the bookstore at 10 a.m. This gave Grace the perfect opportunity to sneak away unnoticed. He would be leaving soon, and she waited until she heard the front door click shut. Then she slipped out of bed, got dressed, and ordered a car to drive her to the library.

Once the library opened, she found the public computer and typed *Jack Stone* into the search engine. The results showed there was a warrant out for his arrest and a number to call the FBI if anyone had any information. Grace was able to find Jack's biological father, Luke Stone, who had been connected to a series of killings all over New England and was now serving a life sentence.

She typed the partial address she found in Raven's journal into the computer, and a map appeared. Grace zoomed in on the satellite image and narrowed her eyes at the computer screen. Next, she got help searching addresses that ended with the letter 'h' that had unit numbers. The librarian printed out a list on a page of potential places within a five-mile radius. Grace took the papers with the addresses and took a car to the first location on the list. It was almost too easy to find, which should have been a relief, but she realized that maybe Jack *wanted* her to find this place.

"Please wait for me. I'll only be here for a few minutes," Grace said to the driver, who nodded.

Grace approached the apartment and saw the door was ajar. She knocked.

"I know you're in there, Jack!" Grace said as the door swung open, revealing a completely empty space. Inside, the darkness was illuminated by the faint glow of sun filtering through the broken Venetian blinds. Her eyes flitted around the room, looking for life as they adjusted to the dimness. She smelled something that resembled paint chemicals.

"Can I help you?" A voice from behind her startled her so much that she stumbled back.

Grace whipped around to see two men in overalls with paint

buckets. "Oh! I'm sorry," she stammered. "I thought…"

"If you want to rent this place, you'll have to contact the real estate agency. But you shouldn't be here." One of the guys handed her a business card from the pile on the kitchen table.

"Oh, yes, of course. Thank you." Grace left the apartment, the door clicking shut behind her. "Well, that was a dead-end," she said, getting into the car and heading back to Pala's apartment.

Once inside, she crossed off the first address and scanned the other addresses; only a few looked like they could be the right one. She took out the card the painter had given her, picked up her phone, and dialed the real estate agent. At this point, she had nothing to lose.

Chapter 34

Erick took the seat next to Isabelle. Together they watched the demonstration and testimonial on stage. He looked over at her and then glanced down at this program in his hand. She beamed next to him, completely enthralled with the transformation on stage.

"That was so exciting." Isabelle leaned over and whispered in his ear. "Did you sign up for the breakout sessions?"

"I'm teaching one," Erick whispered back.

"I know. I signed up for yours." Isabelle smiled. "Lower Limb Prosthetics: Empowering through Mobility."

"It's going to be a great one, I think." Erick's eyebrows lifted.

The two watched the rest of the opening session and then walked out together.

"I'll see you soon!"

Isabelle grabbed a water bottle from the table and headed down the corridor through the crowd of people.

Erick found his team and led them to the breakout session room. As the clock ticked down to the start of his presentation, he meticulously arranged the tables and set up the smart board in the brightly lit classroom-style setting. The scent of freshly printed paper filled the air as his team laid out neatly organized folders and handouts for the incoming physical therapists. He was focused, determined to deliver a session that would resonate with his audience.

"Erick!"

Erick turned to see the CEO of Beyond Limits, Chris Callahan. He approached, his expression a mix of hope and urgency. With an enthusiastic tone he said, "Have you thought any more about my proposal? The newest physical therapy venture? I really think we could make it big."

Erick paused, glancing up from his laptop. He took a moment to collect his thoughts, knowing Chris had been obsessing over this idea ever since their last conversation. "Chris, I appreciate you thinking of me, but I've given it a lot of thought," he replied, his tone measured. "Right now, I'm focused on my current business. I'm looking to train more people to help expand what we've built. Look, the bottom line is, personalizing treatments and focusing on human connection have been really successful for us. And that's the model I'd like to keep."

Disappointment flickered across Chris's face. "I understand, but this could really be a game-changer for both of us. AI is the future, Erick, and physical therapy is a perfect model for this innovation."

Erick shook his head gently. "I get that, Chris, but my priority is to deepen the relationships we have with our clients. As I said, personalization is key to what I do. I want to empower my team to deliver that same level of care and human connection."

Chris sighed, defeated but trying to mask it. "Well, I respect your decision. Just keep it in mind, okay?"

"Of course," Erick replied, offering a reassuring smile. "I wish you the best with it."

With a curt nod, Chris made his way to the front of the classroom, settling into a seat next to Isabelle. Erick couldn't help but notice the way Chris leaned into her, but he quickly pushed the thought aside.

The moment had come. He took a deep breath, centering himself as he glanced at the clock. It was nearly time to begin. As the first attendees filed into the room and settled in, Erick turned his attention to the smart board, ready to share his vision and insights on the power of human connection in physical therapy and in the modality of prosthetics. This was what he was passionate about, and today, he hoped to inspire others to embrace that same philosophy.

After a flawless PowerPoint presentation and an inspired Q&A, Erick signed off on each therapist's Continuing Education Credits. The attendees left the room and headed to dinner. The convention staff were itching to break down tables for the next event, so Erick and his team began to clear the room, folding chairs and stacking them neatly against the wall. Just as he was about to grab a few more chairs, he noticed Justin approaching him, a serious look on his face. Justin had been quiet during the presentation, but now his expression had a look of urgency.

"Hey, Erick, can we talk for a second?" Justin asked, looking around.

"Sure, what's up?" Erick replied as he set down the chair he was carrying.

"I saw you talking to Callahan earlier," Justin said, his tone lowering to a conspiratorial whisper. "I don't want to alarm you, but I've heard some unsettling rumors about him."

Erick raised an eyebrow. "Well, I'm not a man to listen to rumors, Justin."

"I wouldn't have either, except it might impact Higher-Ground."

Intrigue flickered across Erick's face. Justin wasn't a gossip, so if he was bringing this to Erick's attention, he supposed he should pay attention. "What kind of rumors?"

Justin leaned in closer, his voice barely above a murmur. "From what I understand, Callahan is buying up small physical therapy franchises, one by one. Consolidating power and eliminating the competition."

Erick frowned. "That doesn't sound good. He seemed genuine when we met."

"Trust me, I thought the same thing at first," Justin replied, his voice firm. "But I've done some digging. And it's all true. I've isolated seven companies so far that he's done this to. He's got a reputation for being a snake. He lures people in with charm and big promises, but he's really just looking to expand his empire at the expense of small businesses. Don't let your guard down."

Erick felt a knot tighten in his stomach. "Thanks for the heads up, Justin. I appreciate you looking out for me."

"Of course. If he approaches you with any proposals, think twice," Justin warned, his eyes scanning the room once more before settling back on Erick.

"I will," Erick assured him. "I'm not looking to change my approach anytime soon. What we're doing works. We'll have the Georgia franchise up and running by this time next year."

"I'm looking forward to it," Justin replied.

As Erick helped the convention staff break down the rest of the tables, his mind raced with thoughts of Callahan and the implications of Justin's warning. His gaze caught Isabelle lingering by the doorway.

"Are you still up for more?" Erick asked, approaching Isabelle.

"Of course, but I'd like to take a walk and show you around the city. That way, we can build up an appetite."

"What do you have in mind?" he asked, his eyebrow lifting playfully.

"You're going to need your coat," she said, flashing a bright smile at Erick. "Meet me by the front entrance in ten minutes."

Moments later, Erick was at the front door. Isabelle looked adorable in her pink puffer jacket and matching knit hat; her eyes sparkled as she approached. She expertly hailed a taxi and directed the driver to go to Beacon Hill, where they walked along the street to Boston Common Frog Pond, stopping to watch a few brave ice skaters navigating the slick surface.

"Come on." Isabelle reached for Erick's elbow and pulled

him over to the street vendor selling hot drinks. "Let's get something hot." She handed Erick a hot chocolate and pulled out several bills to pay for it.

"Thank you!" Erick was grateful to wrap his hands around the paper cup as steam rose from the small opening in the cover.

"Ah! The cinnamon is spicy tonight." Isabelle laughed and slipped her hand through Erick's arm. "Let's check out the carousel!" She sounded like an excited child.

His thoughts turned to Grace for a brief moment, sipping the hot beverage as he felt the warm aromatic cinnamon on his tongue. "I don't think they're running it because of the snow." Erick didn't want to disappoint Isabelle when they got close and noticed the lights were off. "But we can keep walking."

"Yes, let's walk this way," Isabelle said, leading him down another street. The street lamps flickered on and illuminated their walk over historic cobblestone streets. Sparkly lights wrapped around large trees, making it seem like another world.

They walked in silence as Erick looked around at the sights. They finished their hot chocolate and tossed the empty cups into the trash. They ended their walk by the Charles River Esplanade and sat together on a park bench.

"This is lovely," Erick admitted out loud as his warm breath filled the air. The snow made it even more magical and having Isabelle close was a bonus. "I appreciate the tour. You really know your way around this city. I've been here once or twice for other conferences, but I never had the time to stroll around. It's magical here, especially at night."

"Well, it's a good thing I know the good places to go. You don't want to be wandering around Boston at night in certain places. But if you're hungry, I know just the place!"

"I am," he replied. Erick stood up and extended his hand, and Isabelle gratefully took it as she hailed another cab. "It's my turn to treat you to something delicious."

Chapter 35

Grace typed in the number of the real estate agent, and it went straight to voicemail. She decided to leave a message. But when her phone rang shortly after, she quickly answered it.

"Hello?" she said.

"Hi, I'm Natalia from Sunset Canyon Leasing Agency returning your call about the apartment on Windcrest Lane. Are you interested in renting the place?" Natalia got to the point.

"Actually, I was trying to locate the previous tenant who lived there. It's a long story, but I think he is my estranged father that I located on one of those DNA sites," Grace said, unsure how far to take this ruse. "I have a partial address as well."

"Why don't you tell me what you have, and I'll see if there is a forwarding address? It would have to be part of the public record for me to access that information. If not, I could at least help you figure out the partial address. I could have an answer for you in half an hour. Will that work?" Natalia sounded very upbeat.

"I only have a street name that ends in 'h' and the numbers 1374 Unit #67. " Grace promised to meet her and hung up the phone, grabbing her light jacket.

"Where are you going?" Pala asked as he entered the apartment.

"Just going for a walk," Grace lied. "I want to clear my head. I'll be back in an hour or so."

"Okay," Pala replied, although he didn't look convinced. "No more Jack Stone stuff though, right? We have an agreement."

"I know. I'll be fine. Just going down to the beach. I won't be long."

"I'll be at the bookstore if you need me." Pala got a water bottle from the fridge, headed toward the door, and then turned. "We can have dinner together tonight if you want."

"Yeah. Sure," Grace said, unsure if she would live to tell about what happened after confronting Jack, let alone make it for dinner. Pala left for the bookstore, and then Grace ordered a car and gave the address to the driver.

"Can you wait for me?" she asked the driver once they reached the real estate office. "I'll only be a minute."

"Yeah, okay."

Grace smiled at the driver and hurried into the office.

"So glad you could make it!" Natalia said as she pulled out a document with a map of the town and placed it on the counter for Grace to look at. She highlighted the address. *1374 Nevaeh Street, Unit #67* "The street ends in the letter 'h'. I couldn't find any forwarding information, and the information would ultimately be confidential. However, I did a search of your partial address, and this is what came up in our archive listings. I hope this helps."

"Thank you," Grace said, putting the address into her phone. "You don't know how much you're helping me. I've been waiting for this reunion for a very long time."

"Glad I could help." Natalia smiled.

Grace hurried out of the office and back into the car that was thankfully still waiting for her. She settled into the back seat and studied the map on her phone, pinching the image closer until the satellite image became clear on her phone screen. There it was, a nondescript building just a stone's throw away from her temporary home—the location was right across the street from the bookstore! She could not believe it.

Within minutes, the driver parked, and she exited the vehicle. She was standing in front of the apartment complex and potentially Jack's apartment. She stood there gazing at the bookstore, and then looking back up at the building, suddenly feeling sick because all this time, *Jack had been hiding in plain sight!* The car drove off, and she was alone. She closed her eyes and took a deep breath. Without further hesitation, Grace went to the entrance. The main door was locked, but thankfully, a young woman was leaving out the door, and before it could close, Grace grabbed the handle and slipped inside. There were long, shadowed hallways in both directions, an elevator, and signs showing unit locations. She immediately realized Unit 67 was on the top floor, which would give an eagle's eye view.

Grace pressed the up button and waited for the elevator. The doors opened, and her heart stopped when she thought someone might be exiting the elevator, but the small area was empty. She could smell the damp, salt air and noticed sand on the floor as she pressed floor number six. The elevator reopened on the top floor outdoor hallway. The concrete walls ran only halfway up, allowing air to circulate and providing an unobstructed view of the outside world. She finally found the unit number she was looking for and could not believe she was finally here. She suddenly felt a wave of nausea and wished she had told Pala where she was. She blinked her fears away and knocked on the door. There was no answer, but the door slid open on its own when she knocked again, as if by magic.

"Hello?" Grace slipped inside the dark apartment, fumbled for a light switch, and then shut the door. "Is anyone here?" The room was silent.

Across the room, by the side window, was a computer. She walked over to get a closer look. To her horror, Grace saw that all the walls were covered in photographs. Each was meticulously arranged in a timeline spanning over two decades. There were pictures of Pala laughing under the sun. Raven was photographed looking up to the sky, lost in thought, moments captured from a distance.

An expensive-looking digital camera was propped on a tripod and stood by the window, its very presence an intrusion into the lives it spied upon and the great lengths that Jack went to hunt Raven down. The realization hit Grace like a physical blow when she saw *her* picture. She was behind the podium at each venue of her book tour. Several candid shots of her and Pala from just this week were also displayed. Her heart jumped to her throat, and she stared at all the photos of her recently at the library, her walking around town with Pala, and their day at the beach. Jack had been watching her, cataloging Grace's existence as if she were a specimen under a microscope. Finally, her gaze fell on what looked like a hiking map pinned to the wall, trails highlighted and small notes by each. It depicted the same network of paths where Raven had taken her last breath. Her eyes continued to scan the room.

Holding her breath, Grace unpinned the map to take a closer look, and just then a slip of paper fluttered to the floor. She snatched it up, her eyes scanning the bold handwriting:

You've been looking for me, daughter. Guess you are more like me than you thought. Meet me here at sunrise. Alone.

It was a dare from Jack himself. Anger and fear warred within her as she shoved the note into her jeans pocket. All of this was the evidence Grace needed to prove to Pala and the police that she was right all along about Raven. She took photos of the room with her cell phone.

Turning to leave, she paused at the sight of an open closet door. Grace walked inside the large closet and gasped. Inside were a collection of wigs and disguises organized in neat rows, the tools of a chameleon who had slipped through crowds unnoticed. Each wig represented a different character, a different lie. She shuddered to think that every casual encounter and every fleeting interaction could have been him hidden behind one of these false faces.

Grace felt dizzy again and stepped back from the closet; her world was spinning from the chaos of her discoveries. Jack had played a cat-and-mouse game, but Grace knew that the time for hiding was over. It was time to confront the monster once and for all. She needed to face the man who claimed to be her father and demand the truth.

Crash.

A sudden noise startled her, and she dove under the desk, her breath coming in shallow gasps. When she heard nothing more, she peered out to see a black cat saunter by her; the flick of its tail had knocked over an old coffee mug. Grace attempted to catch her breath when her eye caught a slight irregularity in the paneling under the desk. Her fingers pried it open, revealing passports and various IDs. One in particular caught her attention. It was an employee card from the driving app. *What was his name? John?* Her mind recalled the driver who picked her up in Connecticut. The next ID photo jarred her mind as it clearly was the grandfather she'd encountered on the airplane. Grace closed her eyes and remembered the guy at the bookstore at the end of her book tour. Her mind then played back to one of the patrons she saw at the San Diego library. He had been everywhere!

Grace picked up the cat and shut the door behind her, sealing away the shrine to Jack's twisted surveillance. In her pocket, the crumpled note seemed to burn against her skin, a warning of the perilous journey ahead. This was her one chance. Maybe, at last, all her questions would be answered.

Chapter 36

rick followed Isabelle into the cab, feeling a rush of excitement as the car darted through the historic streets and pulled up to the entrance of the Liberty Hotel.

"A hotel?" he asked, his eyebrows shooting up at Isabelle as he held the door open for her.

"This place has the best Italian food you'll ever taste." She smiled and followed Erick into the main lobby leading to the entrance of the restaurant named Scampo.

At the hostess podium, a young woman dressed in all black greeted Isabelle.

"Hi, I was hoping to get a table for two," Isabelle said.

"Do you have a reservation?" the hostess asked.

"No, I don't."

Before the hostess could respond, a well-dressed man with dark hair appeared.

"It's good to see you again, Miss Boyton," the man said to Isabelle, nodding. He whispered something to the hostess, and she nodded before smiling widely at Isabelle. "Enjoy," the man said to both Isabelle and Erick before disappearing, and Erick guessed he was either a manager or the owner of the establishment. Isabelle and Erick were seated instantly at a table with white leather-backed chairs. The old, brick-faced walls and dim lights gave the restaurant a romantic, chic feeling.

"How did you get a table this fast?" he asked, looking over the menu as the waiter poured water into their glasses.

"They know me here." Isabelle winked and removed her hat as a man came for their coats.

"I can see that," he added playfully. "Feel like I just walked in with a celebrity."

"I'm the one here with an award-winning celebrity, Dr. Finn."

Erick raised his eyebrows again and put the menu down on the table, musing over the fact that Isabelle was such an independent woman. He watched as she whispered something into the waiter's ear.

Erick took a sip of his water. He was enjoying her company, and the restaurant was fancy but still had a cozy feel.

"What can I get you to drink tonight?" the waiter asked.

"I'll have a glass of your best merlot," Isabelle requested.

"I'll have club soda with lime, please," Erick said, looking across the candlelit table.

"Do you want to share a bottle of wine?" Isabelle cocked her head.

"You go ahead and order what you like. I'm okay with the club soda."

"Suit yourself. Just one glass then." Isabelle put her menu down. "I've been meaning to ask you something."

"Ask me anything. I'm an open book." Erick's eyes met hers.

"Do you have a girl back home? Sky mentioned someone." Isabelle leaned closer to Erick. The candlelight made her eyes look golden.

"You've been talking to Sky?" Erick stalled. He didn't want to ruin the night talking about things he couldn't control. For the first time in what seemed like forever, he just wanted to be himself and in the moment.

"Of course, you know we are friends. But you're not answering the question." Isabelle clearly wasn't going to let this one slide.

"I know." Erick took a deep breath, and the waiter filled Isabelle's wine glass. "Where do I begin?"

"Do you have a girlfriend, Dr. Finn?"

"Not exactly. There *is* a girl that I've been chasing since we were kids, but our timing is always off, and every time we keep finding our way back to each other, something… there is always something that gets in the way."

"What do *you* want?"

Erick thought for a moment because he hadn't been asked that by anyone, let alone Grace.

"I just want to share my life with someone whom I don't have to chase after," he replied. "I want a family life and to be a great husband. Something that isn't complicated."

The waiters placed several small plates of spaghetti carbonara, meatballs, salad, wagyu skirt steak, and broccoli rabe on the table.

"I ordered for us, and before you talk about treating me, I want you to know that I know the chef personally, and these are samples of the best dishes they have. Everything has been arranged." Isabelle took a confident sip of her wine and poked her fork into a meatball and then retrieved a side of spaghetti. "I'm a woman who knows what she wants and isn't afraid to ask for it."

Erick nodded in approval.

The dinner was simply amazing, and Erick didn't want the night to end. After sharing a slice of cheesecake, they left the restaurant and headed back to the Boston Convention Center and Hotel.

The two of them exited the cab as snow began to lightly fall. Inside, they made their way through the bustling lobby to the golden mirrored elevators.

"I had a lovely time, but it's getting late," Erick said unconvincingly, looking down at her face.

"Maybe we should finish what we started at the wedding."

She cupped her hands around his jaw and drew his face to hers.

Chapter 37

Grace, with no time to waste, fled across the street as a car blared its horn in warning and nearly hit her, causing the cat to dart from her arms. She walked through the entrance to the bookstore, and the cat ran through the door. Grace looked everywhere to find Pala so she could tell him what she had found and how she had been right about everything! Her eyes searched everywhere for him. *Where are you?!*

She finally spotted Pala, but he was helping a customer. Grace pushed her way past an older man who was waiting for his receipt.

"Excuse me, this is an emergency!" Grace was surprised by how rude it sounded.

Pala frowned, and gently taking her by the arm, walked her to the other side of the store as several more customers came in. "I know you said to let go of the Jack stuff," she said, "but I learned something new. Something extremely important."

"You're making a scene, Grace," he interrupted her, dismissing her claims with cold finality and steering her back upstairs to their apartment. "We talked about this, and you promised you'd stop. You're going to get yourself *killed!* Please stay in your room. I *have* to work to pay for this place. You can't be scaring customers away. I need you to rest and be *here* when I get back, and then we'll talk about all this Jack stuff. Can you do that for me?"

Grace sat on her bed, feeling like a child who had just been scolded. She noticed the black cat slinking into the room. *Jack's cat.* Pala waited for an answer, and when she didn't respond, he continued softly. "I want you to know that I think of you as my daughter now, and I'll do anything to keep you safe. I don't want to have to lock you in your room, but I don't want you to get yourself killed either." Pala looked pale. "I'll check on you in a few hours when my partner comes in. Promise me you won't do anything stupid until I get back. Then we can talk about *everything.* And you can then explain to me why we have a cat." Pala waited for a beat before leaving the room. Grace didn't say anything and just stared ahead, stroking the cat, whose purring was loud in the silence.

Panic gave way to resolve as Grace tested the door. It wasn't locked, thankfully. She could busy herself until Pala was finished, she decided, and she could find something to do, like combing over Raven's notes for one. She had forgotten where she'd put them. Exhaustion clawed at her, but she persisted, scavenging every corner until she saw them tucked away on the bookshelf. Fingers trembling, she flipped through the pages, absorbing the words again that spoke of Raven's findings and her last, determined pursuit of Jack Stone. Then she found the original trail map that was just like the one she found in Jack Stone's hideaway. The black cat wove his body through her legs.

"You're safe now, kitty."

Grace remembered the note in her pocket and the instructions to meet Jack on the trail the next day at sunrise. It would be hours before it was dawn, but she knew she was going to meet him no matter what the cost was. She'd left that detail out when she was spilling information about Jack earlier, and she didn't plan on telling him her plans. She had to be smart and make Pala think she was fine. All she had to do was get through dinner, and maybe he wouldn't notice when she left in the morning.

A few hours later, Grace picked at her food with her fork, but she was still too anxious to eat. She wanted to tell Pala about everything she discovered in his apartment, but she knew he'd be upset if he knew that she was sneaking out to meet the devil himself.

"So, how was your day?" she asked, trying to sound casual.

Pala looked sick, picking at his own food. His eyes met hers before his fork clattered onto his plate. "I'm sorry, Grace," he said, shaking his head, "but I have to call Robin tonight. I'm worried."

Grace's eyebrows shot up. "Why? About me?"

"You haven't eaten in over a week, Grace." His eyes fell to her untouched plate.

"I'm fine. What are you even talking about? So… what, I'm a burden to you now? For God's sake, Pala, it was *your* idea for me to come out here!" Grace's tone was icy. "You're just as much in this as I am."

"I just… I can't… I can't do this anymore." He looked like he was about to cry when his gaze fell on the cat. "I saw Raven go down this road, and we know how that ended. I'm afraid I can't keep you safe anymore. I have to call Robin to come get you as soon as he can fly out. I'll take you home myself if I have to."

Grace was furious now. "I'm *not* a child!" She slumped in her chair, and although she was angry, she could see how Pala might view her behavior as childish.

"You lied about ending the search for Jack for one thing. Jack clearly knows you're here, and we both know he won't stop until he gets to you, just like he got…" His voice cracked and he stood up. He threw their meals into the trash and turned back to her. "I can't protect you. And you need help."

Grace's eyes narrowed, and she repeated. "I'm not a child."

"And… where did this cat come from?" Pala looked pained as he found his phone on the counter. "He needs a new home. You both have to go."

"I'm not going anywhere," Grace said, standing up. She couldn't tell him that this was the cat she found in Jack's apartment and how it was only across the street. "Neither is this cat. You can't just throw us out because you are afraid of the truth. If we stop now, Jack will win."

"I'm not going to be responsible for you getting yourself killed. I owe that much to Raven."

Pala wouldn't listen and faced with that fact, she stormed out of the kitchen and went to her room, slamming the door. She lay on her bed looking up at the ceiling fan, and as the plan took shape in her mind, she knew this was it. This was the moment she had been waiting for since she arrived, and all she had to do was wait until tomorrow. Then she would finally have the truth she desperately wanted.

Chapter 38

rick woke up early the next morning, put on his running attire, and hit the streets of Boston just as the sun was coming up. He rounded the corner and passed by the ice-skating rink and the carousel from the other night with Isabelle.

He finally made it to the water's edge and stopped to take a breath. He was thinking about Isabelle, still feeling the heat from the unexpected kiss the night before. Here was a perfectly good woman, someone who shared his beliefs, his passion for helping others, and his desire to leave the world a better place. Isabelle certainly understood the demands of the profession, and she even thought they could take HigherGround to global levels. But was this really what Erick wanted, or was he so trapped in the past he couldn't even take the first step toward a promising future? A future where a woman actually *wanted* to be by his side.

He took a deep breath and ran as fast as he could back to the convention center. Once he got into his room and took a shower, he looked at the schedule of events on his program. The Beyond Limits crew had planned something unusual for the attendees that day—some sort of mixer-workshop where they could get to know their colleagues and have some fun after the intense classes. They also had the afternoon off to go explore the city and all of its history. Erick didn't even know what he was going to do this afternoon, but he figured Isabelle had probably already planned something for them to do together.

Erick made his way down to the lobby and stopped by the coffee cart. When he placed his order, he found himself ordering two cups and a couple of croissants. Several attendees were milling around the room talking in groups. He put the bakery bag on one table with the coffee and took a sip from his cup. He scanned the room looking for Isabelle, but she was not in sight. This seemed odd, even though he didn't really know her. She seemed like a morning person, but he couldn't be certain.

"Ladies, and Gentlemen!" A woman leaned over the microphone, trying to garner their full attention. "Please walk around and find your *special* name tag. You each will be assigned a number."

Erick found his name tag at table five.

"Once you find your name tag, please turn it over," the woman instructed.

He did as he was told; his tag revealed the number #28.

"Now find the person in the room who has the same number as you. You have ten minutes!"

Erick walked around the room, moving systematically through the crowd. He was looking down at this card when he accidentally collided with a woman in a royal blue sweater and light jeans.

"Oh, I'm so sorry!" he blurted.

The woman turned around, her smile as wide as the Boston Harbor.

"Watch it!" she said.

For a split second, he hadn't recognized her, not with her hair up in two small space buns.

"Isabelle!" he exclaimed.

She stood there with her card facing out with the number

#28. "I suppose you rigged this event?" Her smirk was hard to miss.

"I swear, I did not!"

Isabelle grabbed his arm and gazed at the coffees in Erick's hands. "And... you brought me coffee!"

"How did you know?" Erick asked, puzzled by her.

"When will you realize that I know *everything* going on around here?" She took a sip. "And you guessed how I like my coffee!"

He was stunned and wanted to ask her more but got interrupted by the announcement.

"Now that you have found your partner," the voice boomed over the PA system, and everyone looked up. "You and your partner have to find a stack of ten cups. The first ten people to stack their cups without knocking them over will move to the next round!"

"I never back down from a challenge!" Isabelle declared, and without a doubt, they were one of the first few couples to finish.

Erick and Isabelle easily crushed the competition over the next few challenges, eliminating all but one partnership. The final challenge was to create the best Gingerbread house. A panel of judges was going to vote for the most creative.

The partners huddled together, whispering their ideas to each other, and when the bell rang, they began. Erick could not remember laughing so much. Isabelle wanted to design a physical therapy studio with a Gingerbread man who had a broken leg and held a candy cane as a crutch. She picked up a gumdrop and put it in his mouth, and he didn't complain. *This must be what it's like to have a relationship I don't have to work at.*

"Come on, Dr. Finn! We have to..." Isabelle held her stomach from laughing so hard when Erick accidentally caved in the graham cracker wall trying to place the pretzel rod parallel bars. She quickly fixed it and playfully punched him in the arm, quoting the movie *Sandlot*. "Easy there! You're killing me, Smalls!"

The buzzer went off, and they both lifted their hands in the air. The other team had built an elaborate hospital complete with an ambulance. The judges came by with their clipboards and studied each one.

"And the winner is–"

Chapter 39

race stared at the ceiling when suddenly she heard a muffled conversation coming from the kitchen. She climbed out of bed, peered out the door, and saw Pala slumped over the table, talking in hushed tones.

"I don't know what to do. It's happening all over again, Robin." Pala paused and was quiet for a moment. "How soon can you get here? I know, but I just can't make another call to you with tragic news. I wish I had called you sooner, then maybe even Raven would be..."

Pala had followed through with what he said he would do. He betrayed her and had called the only father she had known for nearly three decades. *Why couldn't he trust what I am doing? Why does everyone have to control me? I'm a grown woman, after all.*

There was no point in talking to Pala now. For all she knew, Robin was already on a plane to come get her. Everyone was trying to save her when all she wanted to do was save herself. She had to play it cool, though, if she had any hope of following through with her plan.

She went back to bed and tried to sleep for a few hours

and awoke to a missed call from Erick. It was still dark out as she stared at the bright screen. She was even more determined to talk to him, but it would have to wait until she got back. If she called him back now, he would try to talk her out of what she was doing, and she was too close to turn back now.

Grace knew there was only one thing left to do. She would leave now and make it to the top before Jack even got there. This would give her the advantage. She wouldn't leave until she had her answers, even if she had to force them out of Jack. After quietly getting dressed, she laced up her hiking shoes, and when she quietly walked by Pala's room, she could hear him snoring.

Grace slipped out of the building into the night and felt for her phone in her pocket. She flipped the hood over her head as she jogged past the looming apartment where she knew Jack could be watching. This was her last chance to find out everything. She approached the hiking trail, the same one where, nearly two weeks ago, she and Pala had walked aimlessly through the trees along the Pacific. She had gotten quite close to Pala, and she knew deep down that he was only trying to protect her. The DNA test results would come in a few weeks, and even if they didn't share the same blood, Grace knew they shared the same love—they both loved Raven. Now, this quest seemed like it was tearing their bond apart. Grace heard her shoes crunching on the sand and rocks as her eyes scanned the ground, searching for something, a clue that everyone else had missed.

"Come on, Raven," she whispered to herself, "show me something."

At that moment, a glint caught her eye. It was a small, metallic object partially buried under a tuft of grass. She crouched down, her pulse quickening as she unearthed a keychain, its surface scratched and weathered. It looked a bit familiar, but it wasn't Raven's.

"Who did you belong to?" she said aloud, turning it over in her palm. The keychain felt significant, but it was just someone else's lost treasure.

Grace rose, sweeping her gaze across the panorama of

towering trees and rugged terrain. A faint hint of morning sun shone as a single brush stroke across the sky. This spot, a breathtaking trail that Raven had adored, now seemed to taunt her with its tranquility. She wanted answers; this was the entire reason for coming here.

"Raven wouldn't just slip," Grace said to the open air, her fists clenching. "She was too careful, too…"

Her thoughts trailed off as she let the sentence hang, unfinished. Raven's fall was no accident, Grace was certain. But it wasn't enough; she needed proof, evidence that would reveal the hidden treachery lurking beneath this picturesque setting.

As she stood there, the sun began its slow ascent. All she could imagine was Raven, her mother, lying broken at the base of the cliff. Just then, a large black bird appeared and circled the clouds above. The clouds were moving fast now and bunching together, a warning that a storm was coming.

"Mom," Grace said, her voice soft but firm, "I'll find out who did this to you. I promise."

With renewed determination, Grace strode along the path, each step a silent vow to uncover the truth, no matter how painful it may turn out to be. She was on her quest alone, but the thought of justice for Raven and Rebekah propelled her forward, no matter how long it took. She knew Robin would come soon enough to try to convince her to come home.

Grace stepped lightly over sharp rocks, afraid of twisting her ankle with every footfall. The trail curved ahead, and she could hear the crashing of waves, the waters colliding in a crescendo of salty spray. She was getting closer to the spot where Raven had fallen.

"Raven," Grace murmured out loud, "what did you see in your final moments?"

She scanned the terrain, noting how the first rays of light pierced the foliage, creating a kaleidoscope of light and shadow. Her gaze followed the jagged outline of the cliffs.

Focus. Look closer.

Grace stumbled on a rock and face-planted on the sandy

trail. The wind picked up and blew sand in her face. She got up and wiped the sand from her eyes. Suddenly she saw something poking out from the ground. She reached down and examined it, releasing more sand. It was a camera, fixed into a waterproof case, caked in dirt.

Attached was a bright purple and yellow strap faded by time, but the name *Raven* was still visible on one side. It had been over a year and a half since Raven's death. Surely the battery would be dead. But she had to try. She pressed the power button.

Nothing. Dead.

Grace let out a sigh as she popped open the side panel. The SD card was still in tact. She put it back in and tried the power button again.

This time, the camera slowly powered on, and Grace's heart began to race as digital images slowly came up. *Oh my God! It survived all this time! This has to be Raven's camera and the photos that she took just before she died.* Pala would have to take her seriously now!

Grace wanted to run down the trail to the safety of Pala's apartment, but she honestly didn't think he would care at this point. No, it was up to her to follow this to the end. She wrapped the camera around her neck and continued on her journey. With her phone in her hand, she sent a scheduled text of her location and information about the camera to Pala. It would arrive in Pala's messages in about an hour, just in case she never made it back. Then she put the phone back in her jacket pocket and climbed up the path. Each step and every minute was one closer to her destiny. She was determined to finish this thing once and for all.

Chapter 40

Erick laughed when the other team came in first, and he felt satisfied with the second- place trophy he and Isabelle won.

"We would have been first if your hands weren't so clumsy!" Isabelle hugged him with her little trophy in her hand. They congratulated the other team for winning.

"Now go and have some fun. This is your fun day off!" a voice exclaimed over the PA.

Isabelle and Erick retrieved their jackets and hats from the coat check and then picked up to-go sandwiches from the marketplace in the hotel lobby.

"I'm going to show you one of my favorite things to do this time of year," Isabelle remarked, a mischievous sparkle in her eye.

"Well, everything you've suggested so far has been fun!" he admitted.

"Come on!" Isabelle was like a kid full of energy. "We are going snow tubing!"

After their adventure, several hours later, they were sitting at a cafe warming up with steaming hot cider.

"I have to say, I've never done that before!" Erick admitted before he took a sip of the sweet, spicy cider.

"When your tube flipped upside down, I thought we were both going to wipe out."

Erick wore a grin the size of New England. "I'm sure they can run the conference just fine without me." He looked wistfully out to the slopes. "Honestly, I'm thinking of taking a step back after this conference is over."

"Why would you do *that*? You're about to go global and be number one in the *world*!"

"I'm missing my dog, and my family needs me more than ever."

"Ah," Isabelle shook her head. "I think that's a mistake."

"Why?"

"The way I see it, we only have so much time on this earth, and if everything is going well why stop now? Why don't you see how far you can go? There will always be time later to take a step back. Now is the time to go after all that you can." She frowned.

"Maybe, but it's a lonely life."

Isabelle reached out and held Erick's free hand. "It doesn't have to be. I think we make a great team, even if we came in *second* place this time."

"We're that!" Erick looked back out the window, unsure where this conversation was going.

"It's the girl, isn't it? You can't set her free, can you?" Her lips pressed together, and her eyes narrowed. "I'm willing to do whatever it takes. Even uproot my life and move to Connecticut for a chance to be with you. If I'm being real, I haven't stopped thinking about you since the wedding, and I think you should give *us* a chance."

"You're great, Isabelle, and I'm having so much fun." He squeezed her hand, but let go to finish his cider. "It's just... a bit complicated for me at the moment. My family needs—"

"What about what *you* need? Don't you want to be happy?"

Isabelle pressed on.

"It's not that simple." Erick didn't like the full-court press he was getting and stood up. "I think we should go."

"Okay," Isabelle walked along with Erick, and then she stopped as he kept walking down the sidewalk. "Hey!"

He whipped around, noticing she was no longer by his side. A large round snowball hit him in the chest. "Oh, is that how you're going to play this?" Erick bent down and packed a snowball, throwing it, but it missed, shattering at her feet. After their snowball fight, their laughter returned, they called a truce, and finally got a cab back to the hotel.

They entered the elevator together, Isabelle pressing her floor, Erick pressing his. They didn't say anything, but when the doors opened, Isabelle turned.

"If you want to be with me, I'll be in room #1251. She winked. "You won't be disappointed." Isabelle handed him a spare keycard to her room and disappeared down the corridor as the doors jolted shut and the elevator continued its ascent.

Erick leaned against the wall and tried to untangle the dilemma he found himself in, as he tightly gripped the keycard.

The card left a shallow impression on his palm, but it was nothing compared to the one Isabelle left on his heart and mind.

Chapter 41

Grace remained determined and kept walking at the break of dawn as hues of pink outlined the rolling clouds. Her stomach growled loudly, and she wanted to kick herself for not bringing any water, but soon she would find out why she came here. Her phone began to chime, and it had to be Pala. By the non-stop calls and chimes of text messages, she knew he was looking for her, but she couldn't turn back now. She lowered the volume, and put the phone back in her jacket. Her vision blurred, causing the trail to look slanted and warped. She stopped and put her hands on her knees. Why had she decided to do this on her own? She couldn't help but feel a twinge of longing, wishing that Erick was with her now. He would've stood by her side, if only she had let him in, but she'd done what she always had, shut him out. What if she'd stayed, met him in that cafe, and abandoned her crazy quest? Raven's camera dangled from her neck, reminding her why she was there. She swallowed, breathed deeply, and blinked so she could see clearly once again. When her dizziness subsided she pressed on higher and higher, determined to get to the top.

Grace heard a rustling sound and snapped her head to the right. Her heart pounded and she screamed as her eyes adjusted to what she saw. A light brown rattlesnake stopped, coiled itself, and shook its tail in self defense. Grace was certain it was going to attack her, but by the grace of God it slithered away. Dark clouds loomed overhead, revealing the cliffside and the choppy ocean below. Wind gusts sprayed a salty mist on her face as low thunder rumbled in the distance.

Still unnerved by the rattlesnake, Grace felt a prickling feeling up her back, making the hair on her arms stand up. She wasn't alone. Someone was there, watching, waiting. It was him, had to be him. Her breath caught, and she slowly turned around, bracing herself for whatever awaited her.

"Show yourself, you coward!" Grace screamed with a desperation that only comes from too many days spent chasing ghosts. She planted her feet firmly on the slick ground, knees slightly bent, ready for any threat that might emerge.

The silence was deafening until she suddenly heard a distant call of a raven. She looked up as the large black bird circled above. Another rustling noise caused every muscle in her body to tense. Suddenly, a dark figure emerged from the shelter of a gnarled tree, stepping into the shadowy light as it filtered through the ominous clouds.

"Well, well, well! I see you got my message, *Grace,*" the figure said. Jack Stone was there, in the flesh. He wore a derby hat, the brim shadowing his eyes.

"*Jack!*" Grace screamed through the wind as rain began to beat down from above.

Chapter 42

Erick stood motionless in the hallway, holding the cold, plastic keycard to Isabelle's hotel suite. Its sharp edges were digging into his palm as a silent reminder of the choice he was about to make. It was almost like a metaphor for the crossroads he found himself in now. He leaned against the wall, staring at Grace's contact photo on his phone.

With great anticipation, he dialed Grace's number again while his heartbeat was pounding with every passing second.

"Pick up," he muttered under his breath, a silent prayer cast into the void. But the ringing ceased abruptly, cut off by the cheery voicemail greeting that grated on him.

You've reached Grace! Please leave a message, and I'll be sure to get back to you as soon as possible.

Erick's shoulders slumped as he ended the call, the finality of the unanswered attempt to reach her weighing heavily upon him. It was the end of something he had chased for far too long. For decades, he had been consumed by an unrequited love for Grace. It defined him, drove him, and tormented him all at the same time. Each attempt to be with her felt like he was pushing a boulder uphill, only to have it roll back down. Yet, despite the pain and and after all this time, he wasn't sure if he could ever let go. *Could he live with himself if he walked away? Was there a limit to the agony one man could bear before he broke?*

With a resigned sigh, Erick turned and walked toward the door that stood between him and Isabelle. His mind paralyzed him, and his thoughts ripped him apart as he stood gazing at her suite door. He squeezed his eyes shut and gritted his teeth. His anguish felt like a knife piercing his chest. As he stood in the hallway, clutching at his chest as if trying to hold the pieces of his shattered heart together, he knew there were no easy answers.

He suddenly sensed Isabelle's presence behind the door. She was here, now, and Erick couldn't deny the contrast between her straightforward desires and the endless uncertainty he had with Grace.

Isabelle's pursuit of him was a welcome sensation. She offered a chance at something genuine, free from any expectation and history. In her eyes, he saw a future unmarred by the scars of past traumas, a possibility of being chosen rather than settling for his usual role of being the pursuer.

His hand tightened around Isabelle's key again, grounding him in the present. The choice lay before him, and undoubtedly, someone would get hurt by whatever decision he made. Erick drew a deep breath, steeling himself against the pull of old habits and worn-out dreams. It was time to step through a new doorway that led not to the ghosts of yesterday but to the promise of now.

He pressed the key against the door before he could change his mind. A sharp electronic beep cut through the fog of Erick's hesitations. A small green light flickered on, signaling the unlocked door and effectively the permission to enter into uncharted territory. He exhaled a breath he hadn't realized he'd been holding and pushed the door open. As the door swung inward, Erick stepped over the threshold. The soft click of the door closing behind him felt final, like the end of a chapter written.

Isabelle represented a chance at new beginnings. A shared journey where he was wanted, not merely accepted. Erick moved forward with the courage to love and be loved completely in return.

Chapter 43

"**G**race," Jack Stone said to her again. As he moved closer, she could see his weathered face clearly. His dark eyes regarded her with an intensity that made her skin crawl.

"I knew you would come," he said, his tone returning to casual, but with an obvious edge.

She played along, but her voice was defiant. "Why did you want me to meet you *here?*"

"I wanted to meet *my daughter,*" Jack countered, but his gaze never left her face. "Parents have rights, you know."

Grace's fingers curled into fists at her sides, and then she thrust them into her pockets. "There are easier ways, you know, and for the record, you made sure Raven doesn't have rights anymore."

"Accidents happen, Grace. You, of all people, should know that."

"Just stop," she said, as she withdrew her hand from her pocket, and pointed a finger accusingly at him. "Don't talk about it like it was some random act of nature. This place," she gestured around them, "doesn't hide the truth. It will reveal it."

"Sharp, just like your mother was," Jack's lips twisted into a semblance of a smile.

"I know what you did and I know what you are still doing. It stops here and now." The unspoken threat was highlighted by the sea mist rising from the ocean below and several black ravens circling just below the dark clouds above.

"Careful, Grace," Jack warned, his smile fading. "Some truths can't be unseen. And some cliffs are unforgiving," he said as he looked away from her and toward the jagged edges of the cliffside.

"Is that a threat?" Grace's heart pounded, yet her exterior remained calm as she felt the rain that fell steady now.

"Take it as you will," Jack said, backing away slowly and deliberately. "Just remember, we all have secrets. Even you."

"Tell me what happened to Raven!" she demanded. Grace put her hand in her pocket and felt for the security of her phone.

Jack's eyes narrowed, glinting with something dark and unreadable. "You really want to go there, Grace?"

"I'm not leaving until I get the truth! You owe me that much." Her pulse quickened and the rain became steadier.

"The truth? The truth is that you *are* my daughter," Jack smiled sardonically. "See for yourself!" Jack lurched forward and thrust a crumpled piece of paper into her hand.

The earth beneath Grace's feet turned to thick mud. She quickly took the paper to see what it said before it got wet as Jack moved to close the gap between them. Every instinct in her screamed to flee, to put a distance between herself and this man who claimed a bloodline that she denied, even if the proof was right there in her hand.

"Listen, I don't want to hurt you. I just want to get to know my *daughter*. I've been denied a relationship with you for your entire life!" He looked at her intently as he pleaded with her. "It's not fair!"

Grace's heart hammered against her ribs as she looked down at the damp paper with The Medical Genetics of San Diego's logo. She focused, her eyes scanning the clinical text, each word a punch to her gut. *99% match.* The impossibility of it screamed within her head, a denial that clawed up her throat. She crumpled the document roughly and jammed it into the empty pocket of her jacket, her movements jerky with the adrenaline that flooded her system. Her breaths came out in short, sharp gasps as she retreated from Jack one slow step at a time. She could feel the slick earth beneath her boots, threatening to betray her balance if she moved too hastily. The wind howled as lightning illuminated the jagged peaks, momentarily blinding her.

"There's your proof!" Jack Stone's eyes were cold and calculating. The rain beat down harder, making him seem inhuman.

"You are *not* my father!" Even if the paper in her pocket could prove it, she could never allow him to be in her life. Rain plastered her tangled red hair to her face, tears burning her eyes from all the sleepless nights, haunted by this menace. Now, here she was, face to face with him and she would get his confession even if it killed her. Her mother's memory and her own sense of self hung in the balance. She willed herself to stand firm against all the darkness he represented, even if they shared the same DNA. At this point, it didn't matter. She realized she had a choice and could be anything she wanted to be despite any facts he could present. "This proves nothing! When did you even get my DNA for this test?" She desperately fought her fear to stand firm against the storm both above and inside her.

Jack's words slithered through the rain-soaked air. "Remember that one book tour venue in Las Vegas you did?" he said, a twisted sense of pride in his smile and tone.

What could he say that would convince her that this was true? He is a pathological liar!

The damp earth beneath her boots gave way slightly, making her feel as though her whole world was dangerously unsteady. How could she not know he had been there? Piecing together fragmented memories, Grace realized with a sickening jolt that he had been everywhere, a chameleon among the crowds. She recalled the closet full of wigs and disguises, all laid out for her to see. Jack had left the trap, and she walked right into it. Each book signing, every hand Grace shook, every driver, and even the bartender! It dawned on her now that he had been there.

"Yeah!" he continued, pleased with himself, "Maybe you can remember when you had that glass of wine at the bar. Who do you think was the bartender?"

A chilling shiver coursed through Grace's body, the kind of fear that rooted itself deep in the gut and clawed at the insides. The revelation made her mind race. It stole the very breath from her lungs. A montage of faces of strangers morphed across her mind, and it all seemed possible that they all could have been the man who stood before her. But, he could *still* be lying about the results at the lab.

Jack raised an eyebrow, a flicker of amusement in his eyes. "I know everything." His tone was flat, devoid of emotion.

"You're insane." Grace stepped closer.

"Am I? Or are you just in denial?" Jack countered, eyes narrowed.

"Why have you been stalking me for a year, Jack?"

"I just wanted you here with me." He paused, his eyes darting away from hers.

Grace felt a surge of icy dread. "What about my mother?"

"She was… a problem. She didn't want us together. But you're my daughter, and I deserve to be with you." His words were a mumbled start to a confession as he moved even more dangerously close to her. Jack's expression shifted, becoming an unreadable mask as the heavens continued to open above them, drenching their small world in a relentless deluge. Every inch he moved closer to Grace felt like danger. A flash of lightning illuminated his face, making his eyes seem almost vacant.

"I admit it," Jack said, his voice trembling, "I pushed Raven because she wouldn't listen to reason." He grasped her hand.

"It doesn't justify pushing her off the cliff!" Grace screamed as she pulled away from him. "No matter what happened between you two, she didn't deserve to die."

"You can't begin to know the truth," he countered.

"You sent cinnamon in a package to her knowing she was highly allergic and could have died. If that wasn't enough, you followed her across the country to San Diego, photographed her and Pala like it was some sick game. You belong in a mental hospital."

"I just wanted her to take me back, let me meet my child. I brought her up here to talk sense into her. I'm your father! I have rights to my kid. She refused to let me get to know you."

"Can you blame her? She was protecting me from *you!* And how did you find me, anyway?" Grace asked.

"I saw you online. I went to all your book shows," he said, as he continued to move closer to her.

Instinctively, Grace retreated from the edge, mud slick underfoot, the earth threatening to betray her with every step. Rain mingled with the tears that welled in her eyes, while the storm seemed to be unending. She bravely took a halting step toward Jack, driven by some unseen confidence running through her veins. Grace tried to muster all the strength she had left. The fabric of her jacket, now soaked, clung to her skin, and a chill made its way through to her bones.

"I just want a chance to be your father." His voice was filled with desperation as he lifted his hands in the air in surrender. His eyes were both piercingly dark and imploring as if he was searching for any glimmer of acceptance.

Grace knew he was incapable of having a healthy relationship with anyone and that this was far from over. She was going to get a confession from this psychopath one way or another.

Chapter 44

Erick jogged through the thawing snow on the Boston streets, consumed by thought. He realized he wasn't meant for the rat race life. Sure, he'd been successful and reached more people, but it was at the sacrifice of a simple life filled with joy and authenticity. Isabelle had asked him, *"What do you want?"* and the truth was, he didn't know. All he knew was he missed the days when he could set his own schedule, see his patients at his studio, and then spend time in nature with Jacey Boy. The *simple* life. That's what he missed.

After an hour, he bounded up the steps to the hotel and pressed the elevator button. As he waited in the lobby, out of the corner of his eye, he saw Chris Callahan sitting at the bar nursing a drink, even though it was still early in the morning. Chris waved him over, and Erick joined him at the bar.

"Erick! Just the man I wanted to see." Chris wore a collared shirt, embroidered with his company emblem. "Did you get a chance to see my presentation?"

"I did," Erick said, searching the room. After what Justin told him, Erick didn't want to discuss his business with Chris any longer.

"Well?" Chris asked, taking a sip of his drink. "Was I able to change your mind?"

"I'm afraid not," Erick said, motioning to the bartender to bring him a water. Even though he knew Callahan's real intentions now, he still entertained his proposition. "You really think a computer can match... you know, the personal touch? Next, you'll have robots doing the physical therapy."

"Think broader, Erick. Moving beyond limitations means we can reach so many more people. Why limit ourselves to a local practice? It takes way too long from the time patients get their referrals and insurance authorization to their first evaluation. With AI, they can have their authorization immediately. "

Erick wasn't sure how to respond. He didn't agree with Callahan, but the guy was merely stating his thoughts on the inevitable future of the medical field.

"Picture a world where therapy is just a click away," Callahan said. "No matter where you are. That would open so many doors. You'd be helping people who never could get help before."

"That's the dream, but isn't there something... lost in all that?" Erick took a sip of his water. "I mean, personal interaction is key."

"Exactly. I totally agree! That's where you come in. With all your talent, we can make waves, right? HigherGround could be a global name!"

"But at what cost?"

"Patients will have lower out-of-pocket expenses, and automation means efficiency, Erick. It can complement your personal vision and make it accessible to everyone."

"I appreciate the talk. I really do. And your presentation was really cutting edge stuff. But my mind hasn't changed. As I said before, I've got my own philosophy and a way of doing things."

"Which is?" Chris took a sip of his drink.

"People first, *always*. Look, there's just something sacred about training one-on-one. I use innovative holistic techniques tailored for each person like music therapy, meditation, visu-alization, power of prayer and unique locations like basketball courts. I've had many successful outcomes, especially with cases that have shown no previous success in the past. How do you replicate that online?"

"With your help, you could bring that to each client. Just think about it. Keep an open mind."

"Yeah, I'll think about it." Erick said it mostly to get Callah-an to stop nagging him about it. He checked his watch. "Look, I'll catch up with you later."

"Of course, man. See you later."

Erick strode over to the elevator and waited for the doors to open, and pressed the PH button. Just as the doors started to close, Isabelle entered the elevator.

"You okay? I must have just missed you on your run this morning." Isabelle looked up at him. "You look… upset."

"I'm fine." He forced a brief smile.

"Saw you talking to Chris Callahan. What'd he have to say?"

"Guy's ahead of his time, but his philosophy doesn't mesh with mine."

They didn't speak as the elevator reached his floor, the doors opening into the living room. Isabelle walked over to the win-dow and looked out over downtown Boston.

"Whoa, what an amazing view you have!" she said, sitting down on the couch and removing her jacket and gloves as Erick headed into the kitchen to get them two glasses of water.

"Isabelle, I wanted to tell you," he said, returning to the liv-ing room, "I've really enjoyed the time we've spent together." Erick took a big sip of water and set the glass on the table.

"Are you trying to break up with me when we aren't even together?" Isabelle laughed.

"Not at all. Honestly, you are a beautiful soul, and I think we could have an adventurous life together." Erick ran his hand through his hair.

"But…" Isabelle interjected.

Erick closed his eyes, willing his heart and head to work together to find the right words..

"Your heart is still with the redhead?" Isabelle guessed.

Erick moved to the window and looked out over the city. "My heart is all over the place."

Isabelle intertwined her arm with his. "I was living in Connecticut with my Aunt, taking classes at UConn when I met Sky. My life changed after she completed her clinicals for graduate school at the physical therapy office where I was working. She convinced me to apply to Boston University after I graduated. She helped me with my classes that first year, and I was hooked." Isabelle moved away from Erick and sat down on the white sofa in the living room. "I asked Sky about you. She told me your heart was broken since high school. Correct me if I'm wrong, but after all these years, you still seem stuck in the same place."

Erick sat on the ottoman and winced. "You're not wrong."

"Explain to me why you can't just move on? What does she have over you?"

"It's just me. I have to make a change."

"Maybe it's time you stop chasing ghosts." Isabelle moved to sit next to Erick. She looped her fingers in his and put her head on his shoulder. "Have you asked God what His plans are for you?"

"Yes. I had a patient, a young man in college who I met with a year ago. He was hit by a drunk driver, and he not only lost his leg but everything, including his fiancé." Erick recalled the recent basketball game with Michael. "I could only teach him how to walk again, but it wasn't enough, and he couldn't bear to wake up another day after losing the only life he knew. I just met with him before I came here. Thank God the conference was postponed, and I was able to see him. I'm not sure what might have happened to him otherwise."

"I'm so sorry." Isabelle squeezed his hand.

Erick stood up and walked over to the window. "There are people who need more than a physical therapist, or prosthetics, or new innovations. They have hearts and losses that we cannot even imagine." Erick looked down at the people and the cars bustling about the city. "I need a change. I want to get back to being the man I was, and no matter what happens with my love life, I need to go where God leads me. I feel this is my path now."

Isabelle walked over to him. "I'd love the chance to explore all this and more with you," she said, placing her hands on his face. "I don't think walking away from what you have spent years building is your destiny. With me by your side, I believe we could have it all!"

Instead of kissing her, he gently took her hands, removing them from his face. "You're at the beginning of your career, and just starting your life. You don't strike me as a woman looking to settle down anytime soon."

"I think we have something worth pursuing, even if it's long distance." She let go of Erick's hands. "You don't have to decide today." Isabelle then flashed a smile. "All you need to do is follow your heart." She turned and kissed him.

He didn't stop her because she was right. He needed to know what he truly wanted from life, and for now, it was to be with her. Isabelle broke away from him this time and walked toward the elevator door. "I should get ready for tonight. I'll see you soon."

Once Isabelle was gone, Erick checked his phone for any new calls and threw it down on his bed when there were no notifications. This didn't go the way he'd planned, but he was sure of one thing. He didn't want to wait around for anyone anymore. He was the author of his own life, and today was the beginning of a new chapter.

Chapter 45

G race felt the weight of Jack's gaze, but the intensity of his plea stirred something inside her. *How could she even consider letting this man into her life after what he did?* An untamed defiance swelled inside her.

"I'll *never* be your daughter!" she screamed, the words slicing through the air like daggers through his heart. She continued despite the uncertainty of how her rejection would be received. "I don't care what this paper says. All those people you hurt and killed! How could I ever trust you after what you did?" Her voice rose above the waves that crashed dangerously below, and Grace could no longer hide the disgust she felt for this man. He claimed that he was family but had shown only hatred and evil to the ones he loved.

Jack's eyes narrowed to near slits, unable to mask the simmering anger beneath. Yet Grace stood firm, rooted to the spot by an inner strength that would not allow her to back down even if what he said was true.

"You're an ungrateful *bitch*, just like your mother!" Jack shouted angrily as he advanced toward Grace. She stumbled back, her boots slipping in the mud, and then she fell hard on her back, dangerously close to the cliff's edge. Jack continued, revealing his pain and anger, saying that his mother abandoned him and that everyone he loved left him. "In fact," Jack continued. "You're all the same! That's why they all needed to die. Setting the fire and Rebekah taking the fall was pretty genius of me to pull off. Raven didn't see it coming, and neither did you. You *all* deserve to die for thinking you're better than me."

Grace crawled up to her feet again, and as soon as she planted herself on the ground, listened to the confession she had waited all this time to hear. "Actually, *you* will be the one getting everything you deserve!" She had everything she needed to put this man away for a long time. All she had to do was get this information to the police. She tried to sidestep his advances, but he was too quick for her as his hand grasped her arm.

"Let go of me!" Grace's voice was fierce, and her arms and legs engaged in the struggle, hoping to use her elbows or knees to her advantage. Panic surged through her veins as he pushed her once again to the edge. She tried to break free of his grip, flailing her other hand around, seeking something, anything, to halt her descent. Her fingers finally grasped a jutting rock, the uneven surface biting into her hand. The perilously close edge fueled her sheer desperation as she realized she was mere inches from a fatal fall.

"Stop this madness!" she screamed over the thunder, scrambling for control. "You don't want to do this!"

"Madness?" Jack spat the word out, his eyes filled with malicious intent and a cold fury that chilled her to the bone. "This is retribution!" He came at her again, but Grace had found her center now; the terror that had threatened to paralyze her had transformed into an otherworldly determination.

"Grace, why can't you understand? I'm all you have left!" His plea was lost in the wrathful wind, his words distorted and hollow.

Defiantly, she answered, "You don't know what love is!"

His next attempt was frenzied, a man blinded by his own evil delusions. But in his reckless determination, he miscalculated his grip, and Grace twisted out of the way. Now, the tables had turned. Jack looked wide-eyed as he teetered on the unstable edge. His arms flailed wildly for balance, but gravity held no mercy.

"Jack!" Grace gasped as she instinctively reached out to him, but there was no chance to alter the course of what seemed inevitable.

Jack's heel of his boot skidded down, stopping before falling off. His body staggered precariously. He caught himself, his fingers wrapping around a frail twig sprouting from the side of the cliff. His feet dangled against the smooth surface of the cliff rock. *"Grace!"* he gasped in sheer panic. *"Help me!"*

Chapter 46

Erick needed to talk through his thoughts with someone, and his little brother knew his heart better than anyone. But Daniel's number went straight to voicemail, so he called Sky next. She would know where Daniel was.

"Erick!" Sky answered on the second ring. "How are you?"

"Not too bad. The conference is going well. When are you guys leaving to come up here?" Erick sat down on the bed and decided against talking to Sky about Isabelle.

"Daniel's getting fitted for his tux right now, and we're going to leave tomorrow afternoon." Sky changed the subject and asked, "Is everything okay over there?"

"It's going fine." He wasn't lying because he was enjoying himself.

"You aren't telling me something, darling, I can feel it. I'm your sister-in-law. Out with it. Wait! Did you ever hear from Grace?" Sky was asking questions he didn't want to answer.

"No, I haven't heard from Grace." Erick rubbed his beard and willed this conversation to end.

"What?" Sky sighed audibly. "I need to get a hold of that

girl!"

"She's busy finding her biological father or getting to know one. Not entirely sure. But I'm just going to keep moving forward."

"Any updates on the Atlanta franchise?" Sky asked, changing the subject.

"Still opening sometime in late fall, but this will be the only other franchise. We have to get back to focusing on seeing patients. I need to take a step back from all this research and all that's involved in developing these franchises. But Atlanta's already in the works and should open next year as planned."

"Oh, I see," Sky said.

Erick wanted to ask her if she was still pressuring Daniel to move to Georgia, but this wasn't the time, and without Daniel there, it didn't seem right to ask.

"This conference can't get over soon enough," Erick continued. "I really miss my dog! How is he?"

"Jacey boy is great. My pediatric patients love seeing him. As a matter of fact, he's here with me now at the studio."

"Woof!" Jace barked loud enough to carry across the line.

"Hey buddy!" Erick smiled. "Sky, please tell Daniel I'm looking for him, but I guess I'll see both of you tomorrow night at the award ceremony. I have to go. There's a closing event I need to attend tonight."

They hung up, and Erick thought about Isabelle and the future. Maybe instead of always planning ahead, he would just let go for once and enjoy life just as it unfolded. How long had it been since he felt this free? A message came through on his phone. His team wanted to meet up with him before the event. He knew his path going forward, but he needed to show up fully for what mattered most. And right now, that meant finishing what he'd started.

Chapter 47

Grace looked over the side of the cliff, and for a heartbeat, their eyes met as Jack flailed around trying to find a foothold. Despite everything that had happened, she couldn't allow herself to let him fall. Besides, she'd rather see him rot in prison than die this way. She dropped to her knees, her arm reaching for his hand.

"Give me your hand!" She lay down on her stomach on the ground to get closer to him. Her fingers found his, and she grasped one hand as he held the vine tightly with his other hand.

Next, Grace heard a loud crack as a lightning bolt illuminated the sky and pierced the ground between them, forcing their hands to separate.

Quickly, she crawled closer on her elbows to the edge again and saw that the twig had given way. Jack's eyes widened in terror for a fleeting moment before he plummeted down the cliff's edge. The silence that followed his descent was more deafening than any thunderclap.

Time stood still. Grace felt her hands ache and burn as she peered down the cliff through the veil of rain. Jack descended to the raging ocean below, his eyes piercing hers, and his hand still reaching desperately for her. His body contorted as it horrifically impacted with a jagged rock, while the sea sprayed in a crescendo, washing away all that was and would ever be of Jack Stone. A shuddering breath escaped her lips, and it was then she realized she nearly died facing the darkest part of her legacy.

"Jack!" Her voice croaked with an emotion she couldn't name. Grace quickly sat back, fearful she might slip and suffer the same fate. Heart pounding, she scrambled for her phone still in her pocket, hands shaking as she dialed 911. Her breath came in ragged gasps while the operator promised a rescue.

"Stay where you are. Help is on the way," assured the dispatcher.

"Please, be quick," Grace whispered, ending the call. She put the phone back into her pocket, her gaze fixed on the path from where she'd come, straining to see through the fog now that the rain had subsided.

"Grace!" Voices barely audible called out from the dark shadows. Robin and Pala emerged like angels through the mist. They ran to her, enveloped her in their arms, and held her tight. Grace felt relief flow through her body when she saw both of them there by her side. "Sorry," she murmured to Pala as a rescue helicopter muffled her words.

"Hey, no apologies. You're safe now. That's all that matters," Pala said, stepping back, his voice firm, almost commanding her to believe it.

Whumpa-whumpa-whumpa-whumpa pulsed louder and louder in Grace's ears as the helicopter loomed closer. The cold ocean breeze whipped across the cliffside, and the rolling clouds illuminated the scene with a somber palette of blues and grays. Police officers and emergency rescue workers emerged on the scene to assess the situation.

"One victim in shock exhibiting flash burn injuries on the dorsal hand," a paramedic said as he looked over at Grace.

"Another victim went over the cliff. Unlikely, he'll survive. We need a forensic investigation now that this is classified as a search and recovery mission." He wrapped Grace with a blanket and bandaged her hand, while Robin stood vigil by her side.

"Miss Evans, I need to ask you a few questions," said an officer.

"Does she have to *right now?*" Robin asked, standing between the officer and Grace.

"Who are you?" the officer asked.

"I'm her father," Robin said with authority.

"We need her statement here, or she can come to the station." His eyes were piercing, and Robin eventually relented by moving a few inches away. Continuing his questioning, the officer looked back at Grace. "Your name is Grace Evans?"

"Yes." Grace started shivering despite the blanket.

"What were you doing out here in a storm?"

"Jack asked me to meet him up here," Grace confessed.

"What?" Pala's eyebrows shot up in disbelief.

"Sir, I'm going to have to ask you to stay back while I question the witness. Please step over there where I can see you." The officer crossed his arms and spoke louder and sharper. "Again, what were you doing up here with the victim?"

But before Grace could muster the energy to respond, the scene shifted rapidly as the FBI descended upon them, asserting control and authority. Her heart hammered against her chest as the last remnants of the storm tapered off and the clouds dissipated. She looked back toward the edge of the cliff.

"Grace, you're bleeding," Robin pointed out, his voice steady despite the calamity, as he pointed out her other hand, raw from the ordeal.

"Miss, I'm going to need you to step back!" One female agent instructed firmly. Her eyes scanning the area, she placed herself between Grace and the cliff edge. Yellow caution tape was being unrolled with a sense of urgency as it fluttered about like a kite in the rising wind.

"Special Agent Cortez," another agent introduced himself,

flashing a badge briefly before tucking it back into his coat. "We'll be handling this from here on out. I'll need a statement from the witness."

"Let's move somewhere out of the way." Agent Cortez gestured. "We'll need your full cooperation."

It was all happening so fast—too fast for Grace to process. She was caught in a barrage of flashing lights, urgent voices, and the relentless crash of waves that served as a constant reminder of the events that had just occurred.

"Come on, Grace. Let's move over there," Robin urged gently, guiding her away from the cliffside.

Pala, Robin, and Grace moved toward the array of official vehicles parked haphazardly along the trail. She tried to process all that had happened, including Jack's confession, his crimes, and his fate intertwined with her own story. She reached into the pocket of her rain-soaked jacket, fumbling momentarily before finding her phone. She hesitated as she eyed the throng of FBI agents moving about the scene.

Chapter 48

Erick headed down to the hotel restaurant and sat alone at a table overlooking the street. He ordered a medium rare filet with buttered rosemary baby red potatoes and steamed asparagus. He pulled the event website up on his phone and looked at the program information. In about an hour they would be setting up for tonight's keynote speaker. Her name was Aimee Mullins, an athlete born with a medical condition that required an amputation of both of her legs below the knee. The description said she was a Paralympian and held the world records in the 100-meter, 200-meter, and long jump track events.

Normally, Erick would be excited about hearing a patient's story, but now he just felt tired. He took a few bites of steak and tried to swallow when Isabelle bounced in and sat across from him, his fork still mid-air.

"Are you having dinner without me?" Isabelle joked and looked up at the waiter to order a glass of wine and the chicken marsala. While she waited, she took out her silverware and placed her napkin on her lap. Next, she took her fork and boldly stabbed one of Erick's red-skinned potatoes. "Mmm. These are good!" she said, her mouth full.

Erick put his fork down. "You can have the rest."

"Why are you so broody? It's the last night before the awards ceremony tomorrow. You should be having fun!" Her wine arrived at the table, and she took a sip and looked over at Erick. "Do you have to do anything else with your team? Or is your part over now?"

"I'm done after this last closing ceremony, but I still have to attend the awards as one of the nominees and all." Erick shrugged. He didn't want to win any awards—not anymore.

"I hope you win! Then maybe you'll change your mind about going global with HigherGround. I heard Sky and Daniel are coming tomorrow night."

"Yeah, they'll be here." Signaling the waiter, Erick asked, "Can I get a cup of green tea, please?"

"Green tea?" Isabelle raised an eyebrow.

"I'm pretty tired." His eyes were half closed. "You had me all over the city doing things I've never done before. It has been quite the adventure here," Erick said, feeling his spark returning. Even though he was ready to get back to his real life, he wasn't sure if he wanted to close this chapter with Isabelle.

"I've had the best time ever, and we should connect after the conference. Maybe you can give me a recommendation because I'm looking to get out of this city. Who knows what state I will pick." Isabelle's food came, and she dug right in.

"As I said before, I'd be happy to help you." Erick rubbed his beard, and his tea arrived.

"Do you want some?" she asked, passing him the wine glass.

"Nah, thanks, though. I don't drink." Erick sipped his tea and looked out the window.

"Oh, that sounds like a story," Isabelle said, taking more bites of her food.

"Let's just say whenever alcohol is involved, something terrible happens." He didn't want to talk about his family's issues with her. "We have less than an hour before the presentation starts."

"What do you have in mind?" She tipped her head and looked into his eyes.

"I'm sorry, but I need to start getting ready. Can you save me a seat?" Erick wished his life were less complicated. A life where he was free to enjoy life as it unfolded.

"Fine, of course. I can save you a seat." Disappointment flickered across her eyes.

Erick stood up and threw some bills on the table. "See you there!" As Erick made his way back up to his room, he felt fatigue like he had never felt before. Once in the sanctuary of his suite, he lay down on the bed and fell asleep. He felt happy and dreamt of what more success might feel like with Isabelle by his side. They had everything anyone could ask for. But even in his dream, Erick felt a flicker of unease. A quiet ache tugged at him—an old, familiar grief. He still saw *her* in the distance, the girl he'd loved since childhood. Her emerald eyes, usually filled with wonder, were now wide with fear. She was somewhere out there, possibly in danger, and in the eerie silence, he swore he heard her crying out his name.

Chapter 49

"**G**race," Robin said, his voice low and insistent, "you don't have to do anything without legal counsel."

"I need to," she insisted because the truth couldn't wait for lawyers or courtrooms. "This ends today." Without another word, she handed the phone to Agent Cortez.

"What is this?" Agent Cortez asked.

"Jack's confession is recorded on my phone," she said, her gaze fixed on the agent's eyes, feeling victory for the first time. "He admitted to everything—the fire at the family business, framing Rebekah, and killing my mother."

Cortez's expression shifted as he listened to some of the recording. "Wow, this is pretty damning evidence." The recording finished. "I have one last question for you, Ms. Evans. Did you kill Jack Stone?"

Grace's mouth dropped open and shut.

"Miss," a different agent began, breaking the silence that had fallen over them, "you had a motive to kill Jack Stone and every reason to want him dead. That makes you our prime suspect."

"God, no!" Grace suddenly recalled the camera around her neck. "Here's my mother's camera. I'm certain there are photographs on here. Maybe your forensic team can check the time stamps on them." She met the agent's gaze without flinching. "Yes, I wanted to see him pay for what he did to my mother, to *all* of us. But not like this." She glanced back toward the cliff. "He was trying to kill me, but he slipped. I tried to save him, but the lightning hit... I wanted him to spend the rest of his life behind bars. It wasn't supposed to end like this."

The agent eyed her skeptically before his attention was drawn to the charred remains of the small tree near the cliff's edge. Her burn marks, the camera, and all of the physical evidence had to be enough to corroborate her story.

"Her account matches the scene," Cortez confirmed, looking back at Grace with a newfound respect. "It seems Mr. Stone's end was... an act of God."

Even though the rain had stopped, and the promise of sunlight was breaking through the clouds, Grace felt a shiver pass through her. "Let's get you somewhere warm," Pala said, retrieving a dry blanket and wrapping it around her shoulders. Next, he guided her toward the waiting emergency vehicles.

"Grace, just a few more questions, if you don't mind," another agent called out.

"No, she's been through enough," Robin interjected firmly as he positioned himself in front of Grace. "You'll have to wait for her lawyer."

But Grace lifted a hand, signaling for Robin to pause. "It's okay, Dad. I'll answer," she said with a weary resolve.

"What more can you tell us about your last interaction with Jack Stone?" the agent persisted, his pen poised above a small notepad, ready to record every detail.

She recounted everything she had learned in the nearly two weeks she had been here, sharing his alias, Luke Silver, and the address where they could find more evidence of all the surveillance equipment, disguises, and photographs. Her voice grew fainter with each sentence, and the emotional toll was getting too much to bear.

"Oh my God, Grace!" Pala placed his hand on her shoulder as she tried to steady herself against the barrage of questions being thrown at her. Her thoughts swirled chaotically. The world tilted precariously, and a wave of dizziness swept over her.

"That's enough!" Robin put his palm up as Grace started to lose focus. "Grace! Grace, can you hear me?" She blinked rapidly, trying to clear her vision. Robin's voice sounded distant, as he called her name.

Everything faded into silence as Grace's knees buckled beneath her. The grip of exhaustion, stress, and trauma proved too much, and darkness claimed her before she fell to the ground.

Grace awoke in a sterile hospital room, her chest rising and falling with the mechanical rhythm of her breaths. She noticed that Robin and Pala were sitting at her side, as she heard the endless beeps of medical equipment in her head. "Jack... he..." she choked out while Pala's hand rested gently on her shoulder, a silent gesture of comfort.

"Jack's dead. You're free now, Grace. There's nothing he can do to you now." Pala assured her.

Grace tried to sit up, only to be met with a gentle but firm hand on her shoulder.

"Take it easy, Pumpkin," Robin soothed, helping her find a more comfortable position. "You're in the hospital because you fainted. I know this has all been overwhelming, but it's time for you to come home. Get away from all this. We can leave tonight if the doctor releases you. I've already taken care of your return flight, and Pala went back to pack your things." Robin reached for her hand. "If that's what you want, of course."

The memory of Jack's confession echoed in her mind, and she closed her eyes briefly, letting out a sigh of relief. "I'm ready," she agreed. "Let's go home."

"How's my patient?" a female doctor asked, entering the

room and observing the monitors for a moment. "Your blood work came back normal after the second blood draw. Your electrolytes and albumin were pretty low the first time, but I don't see why you can't be discharged once you finish the fluids." The doctor glanced at the hanging I.V. bag. "I'll get the nurse to get the paperwork. Do you have any questions?"

"No, I'm feeling much better and would like to go home now," Grace said.

Robin breathed out. "I'll bring the car around."

When the nurse finally wheeled Grace into the lobby, Pala approached her with wide eyes and hugged her once again. "I promise to be here for you whenever you need me." Pala agreed to stay in touch and fly out for a visit as soon as he could. "I want you to know that I did cherish our time together. Even if our DNA test results show you aren't my daughter, I feel blessed to have gotten to know you."

Grace reached for his hand. "I know now it doesn't matter who my biological father is." Grace stood up and put her hand in her jacket and remembered that Jack's DNA results were still in her pocket.

"I'll always love you as a daughter, Grace, and I won't forget what you did for Raven and me." He hugged Grace with tears in his eyes and said goodbye. "I'll take care of the cat you saved. Also, the FBI returned this. I know Raven would have wanted you to have it." He reached into a weathered olive-green knapsack, pulled out Raven's camera, and handed it to her. A small, endearing smile played at the corner of his lips. "Guess what? There is some good news. They were able to download the images and submit them as evidence."

"Thank you, and I love you too," she whispered in his ear.

Robin returned with the car and shook Pala's hand. "We make a great team. Please keep in touch. We're family now." He then loaded the bags in the back.

"Are you ready to go home? Robin asked, standing by his daughter's wheelchair.

"Thank you, Dad. I'm glad you came to get me. Thank God,

I don't need this wheelchair!" Grace was glad it was all over, but she knew today that family wasn't found in blood test results. It was the human connection and the healing power of love that made a family.

Chapter 50

Erick woke up and realized he was late to the closing conference. He quickly got his things together and headed down to the main ballroom. True to her word, Isabelle had saved him a seat.

"You're late," she whispered in his ear. He still wasn't sure if he'd made the right decision last night. Her soft scent still lingered, soft and cozy, a blend of cashmere, gardenia, and possibility.

He tried to focus as he listened to the former athlete's story, but could only think about all the things he had been through in the last decade. So much had gone wrong, yet so much had gone right. God had made it clear to him that the only way back was to slow down and see where the road took him next.

He listened to the keynote speaker with a newfound sense of inspiration. He was captivated by the story of the former athlete, while the memories of his own life filled his mind— both the struggles and the triumphs. He had been through so much, but now it was time to focus on his next step. Erick couldn't help but feel a sense of peace wash over him. The keynote speaker's words about how slowing down and seeing where the road would take her next resonated deeply with Erick. When the keynote speaker was finished, Erick found his way up to the stage. Standing in front of his colleagues and peers, he felt a sense of clarity. He knew that it was time for a change.

"Thank you all for being here today," he began, "and thank you to all the presenters who have shared their knowledge with us. It's because of people like you that we are able to make a difference in the lives of others. Your time here was well served, and I know that you'll take what you learned and help others in need. Countless people will benefit from the new innovations we've had a rare chance to see in this field of therapy." He paused to take a breath and looked at the audience, filled with people like him wanting to make a difference. "I know many of us are eager to get back to our patients and continue making an impact one person at a time, as am I. Before I finish, I just want to remind everyone to fill out the survey in your program and drop it off at the box located next to the exits. I hope you all can leave with a renewed passion for helping others. Without you, these events are not possible, which is why we are excited to have you join us at the awards gala tomorrow night. Dinner is sponsored by the Beyond Limits Team, followed by the award ceremony. Thank you again!"

The crowd stood up and erupted in applause, and Erick walked through, stopping to shake hands with his colleagues. His eye caught Isabelle as she turned and exited the ballroom. At that moment, he realized this was no longer the career path he wanted to be on. Even though he was going to miss the connections he made over the years, Erick knew what he wanted and wasn't concerned with the future. Once out of the ballroom, he saw Isabelle waiting by the elevators.

"Thank you, Isabelle. I want you to know that you helped me realize what mattered, and I appreciate you inviting me to church the other day. I know all things will work out now as long as I stay close to Him." Erick pointed to the sky.

Isabelle hugged him and said, "I'll be a phone call away if

you need anything. Maybe I can come visit you in a few weeks. I would love to see HigherGround."

"Let me know when you're in town, and I'll give you the tour," Erick smiled. He wasn't closing the door on a future relationship with her.

"I will." She leaned in closer to his ear. "Of course, you still have my key if you want to spend more time together." She winked at him, and when she pulled away, she said, "I'll see you tomorrow, Dr. Finn."

Isabelle disappeared into the crowd, and Erick pressed the button for the elevator, feeling free, not bound by the constraints of life. He knew what he needed to do, and he was going to let God take the reins this time. It was time to let go.

As the elevator doors closed, Erick felt a sense of peace settle over him. Everything was going to work out as it was meant to. He was ready to embrace whatever miracles were in store for him. It was time to get out of the way and watch life unfold just the way God intended.

Chapter 51

Grace and Robin boarded the plane back to Hartford, Connecticut. Because they'd be getting home late, Robin suggested she stay at the house. "If you would like, Mom and I would love to have you over again. I can make you your favorite pancakes!"

"That would be great, Dad," Grace replied. She looked out the window as they taxied down the runway.

After a long day of traveling, Grace's heart relaxed as Robin's new truck rolled to a stop outside the familiar white picket fence that bordered her childhood home on Amaryllis Lane.

"Home at last," Robin murmured from the driver's seat, his voice soothing Grace's frayed nerves.

As if summoned by the sound of their arrival, the front door swung open, and Faith emerged.

"Grace! Robin!" Her mother's voice cried out with relief and joy.

In two strides, Grace found herself wrapped in a hug. Faith's embrace reminded Grace that no matter how far she'd traveled or what trials she endured, this place and family would always be her safe haven.

"I'm so glad you're back and safe," Faith said, pulling back just enough to look Grace in the eyes. "Come inside, both of you. You must be exhausted."

Faith ushered them into the house that brimmed with memories of a life once lived. Once settled in the living room, wrapped in the warmth of familiar surroundings, Grace recounted the events in San Diego.

"It was so surreal," Grace began, tucking a strand of hair behind her ear. "Pala and I investigated so much. Eventually, I ended up on the cliffs overlooking the ocean. Jack… One second he was right there." She paused, swallowing the lump that formed in her throat. "And then he just wasn't. He slipped, lost his footing, and grasped a twig. I tried to help him. I did."

Faith's brows furrowed with concern, and she clasped her hands tightly together. "That must have been horrifying for you to witness." Her tone filled with worry. "Grace, my dear, you've been through an ordeal." Faith reached out, looking at Grace's bandaged hands. "I think you should consider seeing a doctor and getting yourself checked out physically. And perhaps—"

"Perhaps what?" Grace asked, but she knew what her mother meant.

"Perhaps talking to Dr. Hopkins or another therapist again?" Faith finished gently. "You've experienced something traumatic. It's important to take care of your mind as well as your body."

Grace considered her mother's words. It was true; the weight of all that happened hung heavily on her shoulders, and the images and emotions still swirled chaotically in her mind. Perhaps seeking help was the responsible thing to do, the necessary step to begin processing everything that had happened. "I agree," she finally said.

"Good," Faith replied, squeezing her hand. "Now, let's get you settled in for the night. You need to rest."

"Before I turn in," Grace said, turning to Faith, "there's something I need you to do for me." She reached into her bag and handed her the crumpled paper.

"What's this?"

"This is a DNA report. Jack gave it to me before—before everything happened." She pushed on. "Can you look at it? Authenticate it? You know people, right? Someone who can verify its legitimacy?"

"Grace," Faith began, "you know that whatever this paper says, it doesn't define you. DNA might tell us where we come from, but it doesn't dictate who we are."

"I know," Grace replied, but she wanted to close the chapter on Jack once and for all.

"Even if he is your biological father, Jack's actions are not a reflection of you. You're not responsible for his choices or his mistakes." Faith held her daughter's gaze. "You're your own person, Grace. Remember that."

"Thank you." Grace smiled briefly, feeling a sense of peace settle over her. "Can I borrow your phone? The FBI still has mine."

"Of course. Good night, Grace." Faith went into the kitchen and then handed her the phone.

"Good night, Mom." Grace's reply was softer still as she turned and slipped into the sanctuary of her childhood room, the door clicking shut behind her.

Moonlight filtered through the curtains, casting a silvery glow on the familiar walls. Her gaze swept over the room, lingering on the antique dresser, the photo collage from high school with Erick, and the business card for HigherGround. She removed the card, then flipped it over and saw Sky's familiar handwriting. Sky had given it to her when she got her memory back and wrote down her personal number if she needed anything.

The sight of her old bed, with its quilted comforter, begged her to lie down. It was a vivid reminder of days spent as she recovered within these four walls, healing from her fall. It felt like both a lifetime ago and only yesterday. Grace picked up Faith's phone. She glanced at the time and hesitated, but the need to set things right gnawed at her. She dialed the number, and the ring cut sharply in her ear.

"Hello?" a muffled voice answered.

"Sky? I'm sorry for calling so late," Grace began, her voice barely above a whisper.

"Grace? Are you back? Is everything alright?"

"Yes, it's just… " Grace paused, exhaling, "I need to ask if Erick will be at work tomorrow. I feel terrible about how I left things… I want to make it up to him."

"He's in Boston for the week." There was a rustle on the other end followed by a muffled yawn. We're driving up tomorrow for an awards ceremony, and Erick has been nominated. Why don't you come along? It'll be about a two-hour drive."

Grace blinked, the offer too good to pass up. A surprise for Erick—a chance for redemption. "You sure it wouldn't be an imposition?"

"Absolutely not," Sky assured her warmly. "I think Erick would love to see you. It could be the kind of surprise he'll never forget."

"Thank you, Sky. This means more than you know," Grace said, a smile finding its way to her lips, an unexpected lightness lifting her spirits.

"Great! We'll pick you up around three o'clock. Get some sleep, Grace. Tomorrow's a new day, and it sounds like it's going to be an eventful one, too."

"Good night, Sky." Grace ended the call, a sense of purpose slowly replacing the weariness inside her. As she settled under the covers, the shadows of the past faded away, giving way to the promise of a brighter tomorrow.

Chapter 52

Erick's penthouse suite was dark, but the morning light filtered through the heavy curtains with an almost intrusive glow. His limbs felt heavy as he pushed himself up, his muscles aching from the long week spent presenting and absorbing knowledge at the physical therapy conference. As he sat on the edge of the bed, his thoughts drifted toward Isabelle. She had been a constant, welcomed presence here this past week. With her, he found a camaraderie that went beyond professional respect; there was an ease to their relationship, and he enjoyed every minute with her.

But, how would this work with her? He lived in Connecticut; she was in Boston. The logistics were a puzzle with pieces that didn't quite fit, yet the life they could create together held an allure he couldn't ignore. He decided to call Daniel. He knew he would understand. He always did.

The phone rang once or twice before Daniel's groggy voice answered, "Erick, hey man. What time is it?"

Erick gave a wry chuckle. "Yeah, sorry about that. I just..." He trailed off with a sigh, unsure how to articulate what he needed to say.

"Girl trouble?" Daniel supplied knowingly.

"Something like that."

Before Erick could elaborate further, a feminine voice was talking in the background.

"Daniel, who is it?" Sky's voice rang out.

Daniel sighed. "It's Erick. But we're kinda in the middle of something here..."

"Oh, let me talk to him!" Sky exclaimed. There was a fumbling sound, and then her bubbly voice came clearly through the phone. "Erick! We can't wait to see you. We're already packed for the road trip. See you tonight!" There were more muffled noises. "Daniel, it was supposed to be a surprise..."

"Talk soon!" Daniel said just before the line went dead.

He huffed in frustration, tossing the phone onto the hotel bedspread. Of course. they were busy. It was thoughtless of him to call so early. His eyes caught the flyer on the nightstand advertising a high-end clothing boutique. That gave him an idea. He picked up his phone again, typing out a text to Isabelle.

Erick: Hey, I need something nice to wear for the award ceremony tonight. Want to come shopping with me? Maybe you could help me pick something out? Something without a tie. Let me know.

He hit send before he could overthink it. Her response came quickly.

Isabelle: Ooo fun! I'd love to. Meet you in the lobby in 30 minutes?

Erick smiled, the prospect of seeing Isabelle already lifting his spirits. Tomorrow, he could worry about everything else. Right now, he just wanted to enjoy the day.

They met up in the lobby. Erick wore a leather jacket over his khakis and a HigherGround collared shirt. He glanced at his watch and shifted nervously as Isabelle approached him in the lobby. She wore jeans and a yellow sweater and had a bright smile on her face.

"I hope you're ready for an experience! Fashion waits for no one." Isabelle led him outside and hailed a cab. They arrived at the high-end formal store, one side with men's apparel and the other side with women's. "You first," she said as she steered him into the men's side. "Let's find you a shirt that makes you look like someone who actually cares about winning this award," she joked.

"I care! Just not about ties. Those things choke me." Erick crossed his arms, suddenly unsure about this shopping trip.

"Never heard of anyone who had *necktie-a-phobia!* You should see a therapist." She pulled him by his hand further back in the store.

"I *am* a therapist, and that's not a real word, you know. But seriously, my dad wanted me in ties every day at FINNLondon. That's just not my style."

"No way. That doesn't fit the image of the calm, collected physical therapist vibe you've got going on. So it's an act of rebellion then?" Isabelle laughed and then gestured toward a rack of shirts with mandarin collars. "This style will look great on you."

"I prefer my collared shirts and khakis. It's practical." Erick rubbed his beard and looked through the shirts.

"Practical? More like a middle schooler's uniform." She stopped short and pulled hangers with different shirts on them and several dress pants. "Come on, try these on."

Isabelle directed Erick into the dressing room, and he closed the heavy burgundy curtain with her on the outside. He changed into the dress pants and tried on several shirts, but he liked the black one with gold embroidery on the collar. Just as he was putting it on, Isabelle slipped inside his private dressing room and pulled the curtain closed.

"Let me help you with that." Her fingers moved swiftly over the cloth buttons.

"Pretty sure you're not supposed to be in here," he protested playfully.

"A little risk never hurt anyone. Now, stand still while I tuck this shirt in." Her eyes locked on his.

"You're dangerous," he said, as the playful tension built between them.

She stepped back and looked him over and then turned him around toward the mirror. "You have no idea. Besides, I think you like it."

"Careful, I may never dress myself again if you keep this up."

"Let's just say we make a great team," she said, looking at Erick through the mirror. "This is the one! Now you look like an award-winning therapist."

"You really are good at this," he said and admired himself in the mirror. "I may have to keep you around permanently."

"It's a gift, but I'm not quitting my day job or anything. Come on, let's go to my side of the store." She exited the dressing room while he changed into his street clothes.

Once they arrived on the women's side, Isabelle quickly chose several dresses, and Erick waited while she tried them on. Finally, she emerged, twirling around in a gold shimmering strapless number.

"That dress looks perfect on you. Like a living treasure." His breath caught in his throat.

"It's a bit much, don't you think?" She stood on her barefoot toes.

"No. Tonight, you'll outshine every chandelier in the room. It's perfect."

When they paid for their purchases, Erick added the jacket that matched his pants. They hailed a cab and found themselves back at the hotel once again. In the lobby, he stopped, still holding all their garment bags.

"You know, you're almost too good to be true." He looked into her eyes. "Why do I feel like there's a catch? You're funny, beautiful—more than I expected."

She smiled and leaned in to whisper, "Just think about this… I can't wait to take that shirt off you after you win the award tonight."

"You just keep making things more complicated, don't you?" He handed her the garment bag with her dress in it.

"Only because I like you, Erick."

"Now that's something to look forward to."

Chapter 53

Grace went home the following morning, showered and packed for her trip. She chose a shimmery emerald green evening gown for the ceremony. Its brilliant color brought out her eyes. Butterflies filled her stomach in anticipation. She hoped that Erick would be as excited to see her as she was to see him. When Sky pulled up to her house exactly on time, Grace slid her garment bag into the back seat.

"Hey there, girl!" Sky called out.

"Got everything?" Daniel asked, grinning from the passenger seat.

"Everything and more." Grace beamed.

As the car pulled away from the cottage, Grace felt a fluttering in her stomach.

"Are you okay?" Sky asked, glancing at Grace through the rearview mirror. "What happened to your hand?"

Grace met Sky's gaze in the mirror. "Oh, that's sort of a long story." She swallowed the knot that had formed in her throat before changing the subject. "Are you sure Erick will be happy to see me? I hope he isn't too angry about how we left things the last time we saw each other."

"Yeah, he didn't take you ghosting him well," Daniel admitted. "But I'm sure he'll be glad to see you, and you guys can talk things out." Daniel paused before saying, "Why *did* you ghost him by the way? I thought you two were working things out?"

"It's complicated," Grace replied. She wouldn't say anything more, and she was thankful when the conversation shifted.

"We both read your new book, by the way," Daniel said, turning slightly to make eye contact with Grace in the back seat.

"Really?" Grace raised an eyebrow.

"Cover to cover," Sky confirmed, pride evident in her voice. "You've outdone yourself, Grace. The details were incredibly vivid."

"Almost like you lived them," Daniel added, his tone half-teasing, half-serious.

Grace's heart skipped a beat, and she looked out the window, watching the landscape blur and pass by. "I did," she murmured. The words from her latest novel were part of her story, her mother's, and the healing that followed.

"Tell us there's a sequel," Sky said, breaking the brief silence. "And, by the way, what happened in San Diego?"

"I will write another book, but San Diego was…" Grace trailed off, searching for the right words. "I'm not ready to talk about it." She paused, the image of the Pacific's desert and beach terrain flashing before her eyes. As the hotel loomed into view, her heart began to race once more. This night was not just about a reunion or attending an awards ceremony, but it was about a new beginning. One that she hoped would bring her closer to Erick. Grace stared out the window as they pulled into the hotel's parking lot.

"Life has a way of giving us a second chance to choose a different outcome," Sky mused.

"Or maybe to prove we've learned from our mistakes the first time around," Grace added.

Daniel turned his head to look back at Grace. "You know who else deserves a win tonight? Erick. He's put everything into his work, and I can't think of anyone else who deserves to win that award more than him."

Grace nodded, her heart swelling with affection for the man who had become an integral part of her story. "He's the best, isn't he?" she agreed. "Erick's dedication is something I've always admired. From the first day we trained together, he's been nothing but passionate about helping people believe in themselves."

"Yep, my big brother has set the bar high," Daniel said with a chuckle.

"Here's to Erick," Sky chimed in, lifting an imaginary glass in the air. "And to new chapters, for all of us."

They pulled up to the valet, and the car came to a gentle stop. As they stepped out, Grace took a deep breath, the cool evening air calming her nerves. She was looking forward to tonight's celebration, and she thought this was the perfect setting for the beginning of her next great adventure.

Daniel's phone buzzed, breaking her train of thought. "Looks like the coast is clear," he lowered his voice, scanning the message as his eyes widened. "Erick's out with the big dogs doing VIP things."

"Perfect timing," Grace breathed, relief washing over her. They stepped inside the hotel lobby, the hum of soft conversation and canned music filling the air.

Daniel wheeled himself over to the front desk, exchanged a few words with the clerk, and returned with keycards in his hand and an envelope with passes to the gala that night.

"Let's get ready, ladies," he said, his voice low as he looked around.

Grace nodded, her pulse racing with anticipation. The last thing she wanted was to spoil the surprise that had been meticulously planned for Erick. The secret that might just turn the evening into something magical.

Once inside the suite, Sky began to unpack while Grace carefully removed her garment bag and hung it on the back of the bathroom door. The delicate emerald fabric of her dress glistened under the hotel lights, adding to the magic.

"Remember, darlin', tonight is about joy," Sky said, setting the rest of the bags down and setting up her beauty supplies in the bathroom. "Let's have a little fun!"

She closed the door and changed into a one-shoulder gown with a Grecian gold-leaf belt. She wore a matching gold-leaf pin that held some of her hair back on one side while the rest of her hair flowed in long, cascading loose curls.

"Sky, I… I'm so sorry about missing your wedding," Grace finally confessed, as Sky zipped up her dress.

"Grace, stop that! No need to apologize," Sky answered gently. "You were healing and on your book tour then. You don't have to apologize for anything, sweetheart." She stepped back and looked at Grace, stunned. "Honey, you're a real looker tonight." Sky's Southern drawl soothed Grace like a warm hug.

"Thanks, Sky." Grace smiled, touched by her friend's unwavering support. "I just hope Erick gets the recognition he deserves."

"Hey." Daniel knocked on their door and Sky answered it. "Whoa, you are a vision, babe!" He locked eyes with Sky as she adjusted his tie. "Erick's gonna win that award. And when he does, we'll all be there cheering him on—just like we always are. And Grace, he's going to be so surprised when he sees you!"

The three of them headed to the elevator. Grace pressed the button, and her heart raced with excitement. She self-consciously hid her bandaged hand with her gauzy scarf. She hoped Erick felt the same excitement when he saw her for the first time tonight.

Chapter 54

Erick thanked Isabelle for her help, and they agreed to meet downstairs in the lobby in an hour. The memory of their shopping trip flickered through his mind, a carefree day of laughter and easy banter. He was starting to fall for her. The conference and their time together would be over soon, and then real life would come crashing down on him. Before he knew it, he would have to return home. *Alone.*

As he descended down the elevator, adjusting the mandarin collar of his black shirt and smoothing down the lapels of his black jacket, he caught sight of Isabelle.

"You look… stunning." Erick thought she was breathtaking. He put out his elbow for her to take, and Isabelle held his arm as they made their entrance into the grand ballroom. He reveled in every moment he'd shared with Isabelle this week, from spontaneous adventures around Boston to deep conversations for hours. Their connection was undeniable yet undefined, which was thrilling but also a little terrifying.

A quiet buzz of conversation filled Erick's ears as he gazed at the expanse of the ballroom. Tonight, the atmosphere was intimate but exquisite, bathed by a warm glow of candlelight flickering on each table. Callahan had hired a private chef to prepare an exclusive dinner menu, setting the stage for this high-end event.

Erick planned on savoring the rest of the time he and Isabelle had left together. His phone vibrated discreetly in his pocket, and he excused himself to glance at the screen. Daniel's name flashed with a message.

Daniel: We've arrived.
Erick: Keys are at the desk.

He slipped the device away again and turned to Isabelle, his expression apologetic for the interruption. "That was Daniel. He and Sky just got in. I told them to get ready and meet us tonight in the main ballroom."

"I know. I'm presenting the Innovation Award tonight. I can't wait to see them."

Even though he knew that time was slipping through his fingers like grains of sand, for now, he chose to dwell in the present moment and to focus on the evening ahead with the most captivating woman he could wish for.

Erick and Isabelle hugged after dinner, and she promised to see him after the ceremony. He went to meet his team while she left through the lobby as guests began to arrive and take their seats.

Several awards were given out, and applause filled the ballroom. Erick wanted to see Daniel in the audience, but his manager Justin had asked him to stay put while he and Isabelle presented the last award. From Erick's vantage point, he could only see partially onto the stage, and Isabelle was smiling off to the side, holding a large award in her hand.

"We're here to honor the significant strides one man has made in the last decade. He's one of the most honorable men I have ever met, and he has taken innovation to a whole new level. His unique style has helped thousands of patients recover when they themselves believed there was no hope. Tonight, we are here to honor *Dr. Erick Finn* with the highest award in Physical Therapy. Please give a round of applause for Dr. Finn, who created partnerships between research and education and executed it all seamlessly in his practice and newest franchise of HigherGround."

Erick winced when he heard his name, but made his way onto the stage. "It's My Life" by Bon Jovi's chorus rang out, and everyone stood up from their round tables, toasting him with their crystal drink glasses. Justin discreetly moved to the side of the stage, while Isabelle approached Erick smiling as she held the polished plaque of the H.P. Maley Lecture Award, which gleamed under the spotlight. Isabelle wrapped her arms around him and kissed his cheek. "I've known all this time!" she squealed.

Justin nodded toward Erick, and when their eyes met, he handed the microphone to him to say a few words.

Taking the microphone, Erick looked out over the crowd. "Thank you all, truly," he said, blinded by the spotlight. "First, I couldn't do this without giving God all the glory. He is the reason I'm here at all tonight. I also want to thank everyone dedicated to our cause, especially the brilliant minds I've had the privilege of working with. I would like to thank my family, Daniel and Sky, who are here tonight! I am who I am because of them. In the coming years… " The crowd was hushed, hanging on his every word as he spoke of new innovations in physical therapy and how, as better doctors, they could also change lives. "This has been an honor… "

He stopped suddenly when he saw Daniel smiling widely in the front row with Sky. But what caught his eye was an emerald green dress on a woman sitting next to Sky. Erick's breath caught in his throat.

Could it really be?

He stammered, trying to finish his acceptance speech. "I've, uh, always believed that true honor lies not in this recognition, but bearing witness to the resilient human spirit of our patients.

That's what HigherGround was built on." He was stunned for a moment as the crowd erupted in thunderous applause.

How could Grace be here?

Time seemed to move in an endless slow motion.

Isabelle kissed his cheek.

The way Grace's brows drew together twisted something in Erick's chest.

Daniel's eyes widened.

Sky grimaced.

Erick's eyes landed on Grace as she stood, stumbled back and then headed for the exit, the expression on her face punctuated by her eyebrows drawn tight together in utter shock.

"Thank you!" Erick said to the crowd, and then, with his heart twisted in a pain sharp enough to tear him in two, he jumped down from the stage and ran after Grace. He had to get to her before it was too late.

Part Two

Chapter 55

Grace, Sky, and Daniel had found their seats up front by the stage moments before Erick began his speech. The bright lights illuminated the banquet hall and the excitement grew with every name announced until, at last, they called Erick to the stage. A swell of pride rose within Grace as she watched him stride forward, confident in every step, to accept the award that was so rightfully his. His smile captivated the audience, and all their eyes were on him—especially hers.

But then, amidst the thunderous applause and the camera flashes, there was a shift in the atmosphere. A woman materialized beside Erick, her golden dress shimmering under the chandeliers. Grace's breath hitched as the woman handed him the award and then wrapped her arms around Erick in a congratulatory embrace that seemed to last *too* long for a colleague. The woman's lips found Erick's cheek, and a hollow ache bloomed in Grace's stomach. The sight was too much for her, but she couldn't look away.

Her stomach lurched and she thought she was going to be

sick. Grace closed her eyes, then looked over at Sky, hoping for reassurance that what she'd seen was innocent. But Sky stood frozen, mouth slack, eyes wide, equally locked onto the scene playing out on stage. Daniel was oblivious to their silent exchange, caught up in the fever of celebration. His fist pumped the air as he couldn't contain the joy he felt for his brother's triumph.

Grace couldn't breathe and stood up abruptly and stumbled back. Finding her balance once again, she quickly headed for the exit. She could hear Sky calling out to her. The ballroom suddenly felt stifling, and the air thickened around her as she moved through the crowd of formal-dressed guests all emersed in the excitement of the moment. The room shook with deafening applause, and she felt like she was running through water in her high heels. Her green gauzy scarf floated behind her as she escaped the ballroom and caught her breath in the lobby.

Grace's eyes darted around until she found the elevator and repeatedly jabbed at the button with almost violent force. As she waited for the metal doors to slide open, time seemed to stand still, her chest heaving. She couldn't stay here any longer, not with Erick or that woman who clearly wanted to be with him. The scene replayed over and over in her mind. *Why is the elevator taking an agonizing amount of time to open?* Finally, with a chime that signaled both relief and dread, the golden mirrored elevator doors opened. A stream of people spilled out, their lively chatter and laughter in sharp contrast to Grace's mounting anxiety and the fact that she knew she would have to face everyone at some point.

She stepped inside and leaned heavily against the cool wall of the elevator, allowing her breathing to return to normal. The smell of perfume lingered in the air as she closed her eyes and gave herself a moment of peace.

Grace tried to push away the doubt unraveling her from the inside. Even Sky's reaction had confirmed her suspicions.

Maybe the woman was just an admirer, drawn to Erick's wealth and charm, she thought. But deep down, she knew they both had unresolved issues that needed to be addressed. She had stood him up at the cafe, and maybe he had grown tired of waiting for her. Her fear that he had finally decided to move on was coming true. Grace would have to face the music eventually, but she just needed space to think about what to say. She jabbed the "PH" button multiple times, and she braced herself for what was to come. She had to admit that she was exhausted running away from every conflict.

As the elevator kicked into gear, Grace exhaled the breath she hadn't realized she'd been holding. Finally, she had a moment alone to process her thoughts.

Suddenly, a hand shot through the doors. They jerked open, and she tensed up at the intrusion.

Not now. Please. Not him.

All she wanted was some time alone to process her feelings, but instead, she would have to face this unpleasant situation head on, here and now.

A figure stepped inside, and his eyes locked on hers, unflinching. Grace's breath caught as her eyes met his, and time stopped as a cascade of emotion swept over her: confusion, heat... *betrayal.*

She had to face this head on.

Now.

But the truth was, she wasn't ready, and she didn't know if she would *ever* be.

Chapter 56

Erick called out to Grace as the door began to close. *"Grace! Wait!"* Erick thrust his hand between the doors, and the elevator opened once again. He stepped inside as the doors sealed them in together, and tension filled the small space. There she was—the woman whose image had been burned in the corners of his mind for an eternity, standing there breathless, her cheeks flushed and streaked with tears.

"Please, I need a moment alone," Grace whispered.

"Grace," Erick said as he placed the award on the floor beside him.

She looked up, her eyes hollow and wide with shock and something else he couldn't decipher. Erick noticed her chest rising and falling with rapid, shallow breaths. The sight of her being in a panic because of him was something he couldn't live with.

"Grace, what are you doing here? Are you okay?" His voice was filled with concern, as his heart hammered against his ribs.

She looked like she was fighting for air. "I wanted to surprise you," she said quietly, her whole body shaking.

"You did surprise me!" He stepped closer, instinctively reaching out to steady her, as though she could collapse at any moment. *She does not look well,* he thought. The elevator glided smoothly upward, and being so close to Grace reignited a familiar ache, longing, and regret that had been simmering within him all these years—the same feelings he tried desperately to forget this week. Clearly, he was unsuccessful yet again.

As Grace's shoulders began to shake with quiet sobs, his arms moved instinctively, wrapping around her. She buried her face against his chest, her tears dampening his shirt.

"Hey, it's okay," he said with a soft and reassuring voice. "You know I care for you, right?" The words were valid despite the circumstances. Grace nodded against him, and Erick continued, "I'm deeply touched that you came to see me." He was honored, but at the same time, there was so much unsaid between them. Drawing back just enough to look into her eyes, Erick searched for understanding. "I guess Sky and Daniel were in on this," he surmised.

"I just felt so terrible standing you up at the cafe," she confessed between sobs. She looked up into Erick's eyes again. "I know now that I should have asked you to go with me, but instead, I ran *again*." Her admission was filled with regret. "I ran from my feelings for you, and I thought that if I could find my father and know the truth, then we could be together. But then I discovered that Jack might not only be my father, but that he was also my mother's killer. I was afraid that if there was a chance I shared the same blood in my veins as that monster, that I, too, was damaged in some way. And you deserved better than that. But then I realized that despite our heritage, we all still have choices. I was hoping that if you loved me once, you could still love me despite where I came from. So, when I flew home yesterday, I reached out to Sky about how to make it right. She suggested I ride with them to see you win this award." She gestured toward the trophy on the floor.

"Where you come from doesn't matter to me. My family

isn't the greatest either, but they taught me about who I didn't want to be." He looked at her for a long moment, then spoke again, softer this time. "So, did you find out if Jack was your father?"

"No, not for sure anyway." She shook her head.

"But none of that matters now. What matters is that I'm too late." Her voice broke, and she swallowed hard. "You've found someone else."

The elevator gave an ominous lurch. The walls moaned, and for a brief moment, the fluorescent lights flickered. They both looked up, and Erick held her closer. The elevator halted its ascent with a gut-wrenching jerk, leaving them suspended between floors, and then the elevator plunged into darkness.

Chapter 57

G race's eyes attempted to adjust to the sudden blackness. Her heart raced, and she clung to Erick tightly just as small yellow emergency lights illuminated their faces with distorted shadows. She was so close to him that she could smell his cologne.

"Great," Grace muttered, lowering herself to the floor. She leaned back against the wall with her arms crossed and her dress spilling to one side.

"Well, it's not like we haven't been through worse, right?" Erick tried to lighten the mood and reached for her hand, but she pulled it away. In her mind she replayed the scene on stage that had happened moments earlier.

"True, it was worse that one time we got stuck in the storm at HigherGround when Finn tried to kill you," Grace said, rolling her eyes. "At least this time we're not drenched and fighting for our lives."

"That's true." Erick pulled out his phone. "Let's see if I can get us out of here." He tapped his phone several times but nothing happened.

"Let me guess—no signal?"

"Just give me a sec... " Erick sounded concerned.

"I shouldn't have come tonight." Grace sighed.

"What does that mean?" He put his phone back in his suit pocket."

"It doesn't matter now if you've already moved on." She huffed.

He didn't respond. Instead, he reached for the emergency phone mounted on the wall, its red casing visible in the dimly lit elevator. "Come on! Come on... " Erick murmured, his thumb pressing the button with urgency, making Grace feel nervous because he was usually very calm and collected in situations like this.

The line rang twice before the connection cracked and filled the small space. "God, please send us help," Erick said so softly that Grace wondered if she had heard him correctly.

"God is going to help us out of this?" Her arms still were folded tightly across her chest.

Erick visibly winced at her words just as the receiver finally connected. Grace could hear a muffled response, and then he said, "Yes, hello! We're trapped in the elevator in the south tower." Erick paused. "Just myself and a woman."

Grace saw his eyes dart over at her. He relayed details precisely, and then he stopped to listen. "What're they saying?" she demanded, feeling left out of what was happening.

"Fire rescue will be here soon," Erick finally repeated what he heard on the other end of the line. "There is a power outage at the moment." He placed the phone back in the box and closed the metal door. Then he sat down next to Grace to wait for help. "I'm just curious, why *didn't* you ask me to go with you?" Erick ran his hands through his hair. "You always have to do things your way and on your own. I could've helped."

"You love playing that hero role, don't you?" She leaned forward to see his face.

"It's not about that." He paused, listening intently.

"Then what is it about?"

240

Erick looked into her eyes and sighed. "It's about being part of your life. We were a great team. Plus, I would like to get us out of this mess."

"And then what? Back to pretending everything's fine as if you haven't moved on already?" Grace looked away. "It still wasn't enough for you to wait for me. You don't know what it's like for me."

Erick took her hands into his and leaned toward her ear whispering, "Then help me understand."

"I just wanted you to understand what I was going through. I'd just regained my memory, lost who I thought I was, and grieved the death of my mother. It was all too much to process and I needed to find my father!"

"So, are we just going to keep doing this dance? You know I've waited years…"

"What do you *want* from me, Erick?"

Erick hesitated and finally said, "I want you to see yourself through my eyes. We're great together if you just stop running away. Let me help you. Just let me in your life, for once."

Grace looked down as Erick's fingers moved to her face. "Maybe… maybe we just need to get through tonight first."

"Let's just focus on that," he whispered as his hand caressed her face.

"And then?" Grace asked, her heart racing.

"Then we can figure it out."

Chapter 58

Erick had spent years wishing for more time with Grace, but not like this. He had a nagging feeling that the only reason she was there was because they both were trapped. He always felt the need to protect her at all costs, but she still wanted to walk away. He knew getting angry with her would solve nothing. Erick closed his eyes and prayed. Calmness filled him once again as he held her close, waiting for the rescue team.

Grace whispered in his ear, "Remember when you found me in the hospital that day?"

"Of course. I remember it all." Erick let out a sigh like he hadn't breathed yet that day. "I'm sorry that I lied to you when you deserved the truth."

"I know you were just trying to help me. I don't think you understand what I've been through. If I'm being honest, I still see Finn sometimes when I look at you," Grace confessed, moving out of his embrace and pressing her back against the wall.

"I can't imagine what you've been through." Erick slumped lower, feeling the warmth of their arms together.

"I know we can't change the past. All we have is here and now." Grace reminded him. "You should have trusted me with the truth at some point. My parents all lied to me. If they'd just told me Raven was my mother, I might've been able to save her. Perhaps she would even be alive today." A tear fell from Grace's eye.

Erick remembered his own mother's passing, and the familiar ache returned in his heart. He moved closer so that his face was now inches from hers, and he brushed away her tears with his free hand.

"After all the mental and physical therapy, it still isn't enough to piece me back together. I feel like I'll never be the same!" Grace cried.

"Let me help. I just want to be a part of your life," Erick said. "We can face things together."

"Sometimes, I still think the only person I can trust is myself." Grace paused, her eyes not wavering from his. "So, be honest now. Are you in love with that other girl you were with onstage?"

Erick let out a deep sigh. "Isabelle is a friend of Sky's, a colleague I met at Daniel's wedding. I thought you and I were over. You left me, Grace. You made it seem like I didn't have a place in your life. I tried to reach out, but you wouldn't talk to me. I called you and you never responded. What was I supposed to think? You *never* let me in. Every time things get hard, you run. Run *from me*." For a long moment, neither spoke. Then, despite his best efforts to stay a safe distance from her, he leaned into her, and the next thing he knew, his fingers grasped her hair. Grace's lips were on his, kissing him back, making his head dizzy. He wanted her always, like a hunger he couldn't satisfy, as if his life depended on it. It felt like they were falling from twenty stories high, and he never wanted to hit the ground.

Suddenly, a loud banging noise startled them, and Erick moved back to assess the situation but kept his arm around her.

"Sounds like help is on the way," Grace said breathlessly, looking up at Erick. He wiped her tear-streaked face with his hand and prepared to face the outside world again.

"Did you enjoy our romantic elevator getaway?" Erick asked.

A laugh escaped Grace's lips.

Erick's dimple emerged as he smiled mischievously. Yet, he also knew that in the last several days, he had only been thinking about a life with Isabelle, and it would be difficult to juggle his conflicting feelings once they got out of this elevator.

"Sometimes I wish we could go back to high school, and I wonder what would have happened if we had just talked to each other back then. We could have found a way around our parents. I would have never gotten mixed up with Finn. That's when things went very wrong for us," Grace mused.

"Give yourself a break, Grace. We were kids, and it was a long time ago." Erick sighed again. "Maybe we can untangle it all… together," he suggested. "I believe everything happens for a reason. God is the author of our story, and He isn't finished with us yet."

"I'm not sure if I can believe like you do. I wish I could leave the past behind." Grace frowned. "I guess I'd be willing to try and see where this path with you goes."

"Is that what you want?" Erick's eyes searched her for the truth.

"Yes," she said, her voice barely above a whisper as Erick intertwined his fingers with hers.

Erick wanted to get out of this elevator and to the safety of his room. His heart loved being this close to her, but his mind was cautious. Would she stay with him or run off again when they were freed from the temporary confinement? One thing was certain: *He knew he could not go through another heartbreak with her.*

"Okay, I am ready to stop running. But I have one condition that is a deal breaker." Grace put two hands on his face.

"Anything, Grace." Erick felt his resolve melting like an ice cube on a hot July day.

"Promise you will always talk to me and tell me the truth. Lies break relationships. I don't think I could handle another betrayal. It has to be us and *only* us." Grace smiled up at him.

Erick laughed. "I promise to tell you the whole truth, even if it costs me everything. We should take it slow and start over." His face was ablaze as her hands were still on his face. He also knew he had to be honest about Isabelle. "I do have to tell you something, though."

Grace pressed her lips to his again. Her desire for him filled his soul, and he leaned into her. The world outside ceased to exist. Unseen and obvious obstacles held them back, but now they had a chance to be free. He needed to protect her heart, but he also wanted to show her how much he still loved her.

Suddenly, the elevator doors opened with a deafening, scraping noise. Firemen spilled into the elevator, breaking the spell. Erick swiftly helped Grace up, held onto her, and assessed the situation. One fireman winked at Erick and said, "Let's go, love birds!"

Chapter 59

Grace was hoisted out of the elevator first, followed by Erick, and they both headed toward the stairwell after being checked out by paramedics. They climbed up two flights of stairs until they reached Erick's room. He guided her inside, and she could feel the fatigue coming over her again.

"Sit here," Erick murmured, extending his hand to the cream-colored sectional facing the Boston skyline that lit up the clear and starry night. "Are you hungry?"

"Starving," Grace replied.

"Let's get some food. What are you in the mood for?"

"Pala was a vegan, so I've been mostly eating plant foods lately. What I could really go for is a juicy burger," Grace suggested. She retreated to the bathroom, where she stared at herself in the mirror, reflecting a disheveled look. She could still feel Erick's hands in her hair, and tried to fix herself up. Returning to the living room, she heard Erick on the hotel phone.

"Okay," Erick said. "I'd like to order four cheeseburgers, fries, and four house salads for room 3444." He hung up the phone. "It'll be up shortly."

"Four?" she asked him, consciously touching her hair.

Erick's phone rang before he could answer, and he turned away to answer it.

"We're fine. Seriously, everything is okay. Why don't you come up to the room? I ordered some food." He placed the phone in his pocket and looked at Grace. "Sky and Daniel are on their way," Erick announced and handed her a throw blanket from the chaise lounger. Grace wrapped the blanket over her arms while the elevator dinged its arrival.

Sky stepped in first, her gaze sweeping over them both. Grace could feel the tension in the room and the air of unspoken questions as Daniel wheeled himself into the kitchen to join Erick.

"Hey, what happened?" Sky asked as she walked into the living room, her sage tulle skirt swishing back and forth with every step she took. A frown creased her usually bright features as she glanced back at Erick in the kitchen.

"Congrats on the award!" Daniel approached Erick, and they clapped hands in a high-five.

"Thanks, buddy!" Erick handed Daniel the award so he could get a closer look.

Grace looked from the men to Sky, who sat down next to her and looked as confused as Grace was at the moment.

"What happened to you guys? The entire ballroom lost power before the generators kicked on," Sky said.

"Did you guys get caught in the dark?" Daniel asked. "We tried texting you, but there was no signal."

"We got stuck in the elevator, but we're okay now," Erick said.

"That must have been terrifying!" Sky covered her mouth with her hand.

"Erick handled it all." Grace looked up at him just as there was a knock at the door. It startled her at first; she worried it might be Isabelle. She hadn't even had a chance to ask Sky about her.

Erick strode over to let the server in, signed the check, and handed him several bills before pushing the cart toward the large table. The scent of creamy cheddar cheese, grilled beef, hot french fries, and the freshness of the crisp greens filled Grace's nose.

"Who's hungry?" Erick asked as Grace took a small bite of the burger.

She closed her eyes and tasted the savory flavor of the food.

"Good?" he asked, and she nodded.

"I was hungrier than I thought I was," Sky announced.

"I can always eat." Daniel used a napkin to wipe his face and slurped his soda gleefully.

As she ate, Grace looked around the room at Erick and his family. This is what she craved now, to be near family. Even if it wasn't her blood. The peacefulness of the moment was interrupted by the patter of rain against the enormous window.

"You guys should stay over and not drive home in the rain," Erick suggested after sipping his soda.

Sky looked at Daniel. "Okay, but we'll have to leave early in the morning. I have a client at 9 a.m., and I need to text Ashley to let the dogs out tonight and to feed them in the morning."

"Thanks, man." Daniel smiled at Erick and then looked over at Sky, who, as far as Grace could tell, was sending him a silent message of some sort. "Well, I'm tired. We should be turning in for the night." He wheeled away from the table, and Sky collected their dishes and placed them back on the cart.

"I can drive Grace home," Erick suggested.

"That's fine," Grace said. "Thank you. I appreciate that."

"Good night, you two. Safe travels back if we don't see you in the morning."

She could tell they were leaving to give them space to talk. As Sky and Daniel hugged Erick and congratulated him, Sky leaned over to her and whispered, "I hope this night is all you were hoping for." Then Daniel lifted his wife, placed her in his lap, and wheeled her to their bedroom.

Grace had no idea how this night would turn out, but for the moment, she didn't care because there was no other place she wanted to be right now than in this room with this man. For the first time in a long time, she finally felt safe.

Chapter 60

Erick put the rest of the dishes and food on the cart and placed them outside the room. When Erick returned, Grace was sitting on the couch staring out into the night, quiet and unreadable.

"I don't have anything to sleep in," she said.

"No worries," he said, going into his room and returning with a large T-shirt and sweats. "The room is yours; I'll be here on the couch."

She took the clothes in her arms and asked Erick if he could just get the clasp on her dress. "Sure," he said, as she turned her back toward him. He carefully lowered the zipper, and his fingers traced the silvery thin flat scar on her lower back. He could see the outline of her bones and wondered what had happened to her in California.

"That's good. Thank you," Grace said, retreating to the bedroom. She returned, wearing just a soft grey HigherGround T-shirt with "Where You *Can* Walk on Water" on it. It hovered just over her knees. "The sweats were too big. Thank you, though."

Grace moved closer to Erick and laid her head on his chest. He was sure she could feel the steady beat of his heart. His strong and sure arms encircled her, and he felt her relax into his embrace, grateful for her warmth. "It's getting late, and we have a long drive tomorrow," he reminded her softly, his lips kissing her forehead.

"Mmm," she murmured, half-asleep, "I guess I'm still jet-lagged; I feel so tired."

"You're welcome to use the bed in the primary suite. I can stay out here if you prefer."

"I don't want to get up." Grace stretched her legs out on the large sectional couch. Erick spread the large throw over her, and her eyes slowly closed.

"Sleep well," Erick whispered and slowly began moving away.

"Please don't leave. Will you stay with me?" Grace's voice was a small whisper.

"Of course," he replied without hesitation. "I'll be right back." He went into his room and put on sweats and a Beyond Limits shirt he got on the first day of the conference. Nothing could prepare him for this moment. It seemed like he was finally getting everything he wanted. Everything seemed to fit perfectly into place now. He returned to Grace on the couch, who was still waiting for him. He thought he was dreaming.

"Just... hold me until I fall asleep. I've been having night-mares lately. I don't want to be alone tonight," she confessed. Erick knew how nightmares could change everything. He felt her drift into a deep sleep, holding her for most of the night until he, too, fell asleep.

He woke up to the sound of Sky and Daniel whispering, giggling, and moving about the adjoining room. He looked over at Grace sleeping, extricated himself from her, and walked over to the kitchen.

"I hope you know what you're doing," Sky whispered as she entered the kitchen. "Isabelle usually gets what she wants, but I'm not sure you're ready to move on from *her*." Her gaze moved from Erick to Grace.

"I know. Isabelle and I are still figuring things out. She's not into labels."

"Well, don't take too long," Sky replied. "That's how messes are created, and someone *will* get hurt. Let's go, Daniel." Sky hugged Erick; Daniel high-fived him; and the couple was on their way. The rain had finally stopped, and soon the sun would explode into the Boston sky.

Erick's phone buzzed on the coffee table, and he went to retrieve it.

Isabelle: Where did you run off to last night? After the power went out, you disappeared. Thought we were supposed to meet up?

Erick: Sorry about that, something came up.

Isabelle: Do you still want to grab breakfast? We can invite Daniel and Sky.

Erick: I'm sorry. They had to leave early, and I have to take care of a few things. I should head back early as well. I'll be in touch.

Isabelle: Okay... something wrong?

Erick: No, I promise. I'll call you later.

Erick changed into joggers, a long-sleeve shirt, and a vest. He needed to get a run in if he was going to sort out the rest of the day. Eventually, he would have to talk to Isabelle about Grace and to Grace about Isabelle. He left a quick note for Grace saying he would return in about an hour.

His feet hit the pre-sunrise cobblestone streets of Boston, and as energy surged through his body, he picked up his speed. Erick didn't think there would be time to talk to Isabelle before he and Grace left, and a decision would have to be made. He was so lost in thought that he didn't see the light-haired girl with the knit cap racing around the corner with AirPods in. They collided with each other, and Erick held her so she wouldn't fall as she let out a small laugh.

"Great minds!" Isabelle's face was inches from his, and he pulled back.

"Isabelle?" Erick's heart rate began to slow down. "I'm so sorry. I didn't see you."

"No harm, no foul."

She stood there, and Erick felt torn.

"Look," Isabelle continued, "you don't have to answer, but I'm guessing the red-head with Sky and Daniel was the former flame you were talking about?"

"Her name is Grace. I've known her since we were kids."

"I'm sensing unresolved stuff with her?" Isabelle's eyes were wide.

"Yes, it's complicated in every sense of the word." Erick closed his eyes. "But my offer hasn't changed. You should visit to see how you could fit into the HigherGround brand."

"I get it. I have no claims on you," Isabelle said. "I just would like a chance to get to know you better." She reached up on her toes, wrapped her arms around Erick, and kissed him lightly on the lips. "Rain check on the breakfast, and safe travels back to Connecticut. You know where to find me if you decide to continue what we started."

Erick was speechless as she took off down the street. The pink sun splashed over the fading clouds as he returned to the hotel. He let himself into his suite quietly and walked to his room, peeling layers of running clothes off and stepping into the shower.

After, he dried off, dressed, and started packing for the trip home. Even as he packed, his mind kept circling back to Isabelle. He had just placed his bags by the door when he heard Grace stirring awake, and the weight of it all pressed harder on his chest. He hadn't asked for this romantic collision, but now he couldn't avoid it.

Chapter 61

Grace woke up with a start. "Erick?" She blinked twice and her eyes adjusted to see Erick's calm, steady eyes.

"Good morning, Grace. How did you sleep?" he asked in a low voice.

"I didn't have the usual nightmares. Where are Sky and Daniel?" she asked.

"They left hours ago."

"Oh, what time do *you* want to leave?" She stood up and stretched her arms.

"How soon can you be ready?"

Grace collected her things and noticed that her shoes were separated. She searched around for her silver-strapped shoe, and her eyes landed on a shiny strap and part of the heel. She grabbed her shoes and put them in her bag before scanning the rooms to make sure she didn't forget anything else. She looked under the couch and in the second bedroom before returning to the living room. Erick was standing by the door, looking at his phone. She wanted to trust him again, but she was still on the fence about everything. *Why did he seem so disinterested in her this morning?* The two-hour drive home could either be productive, or it could give them time to realize that they had too many differences to continue.

Lost in thought, she walked over to the couch and folded up the blanket. Her eyes fell on something shiny in the cushions, and she pulled out a delicate bracelet with a cross on it. *Whose was this?* she wondered. She didn't want to think about Erick having another woman up here and promised herself she wouldn't jump to conclusions without hearing any of the facts. They had agreed to be honest with each other this time.

"Hey, Erick?"

Erick looked up from his phone and asked, "What's up?"

"Is this Sky's bracelet?" Grace held up the delicate jewelry and waited for Erick to respond. When he didn't, she felt the lump in her throat threatening to choke her again.

He moved closer to get a better look at the jewelry and frowned. "Uh, yeah, no, it's actually Isabelle's," Erick said as he took it from her.

"I thought you said she was just a friend," Grace said slowly, shaking her head. *Why was this happening again?* She couldn't help but think about the kiss they shared the night before.

"She was. She *is*." He looked down at his phone again. "Let's get out of here, and I promise we'll talk about everything in the car. I want to beat the afternoon traffic, and they're calling for rain."

They stood side by side in silence as the elevator descended. The air was still thick with their unspoken tension. When the doors opened into the lobby, she was relieved. She noticed he took one last look at the hotel as he opened her door and closed it behind her. They left the hotel and got into Erick's Jeep for the ride home.

He carefully pulled out into traffic and headed toward the highway. "I picked up coffee and some breakfast bars for the trip. "

"Thank you," she said, removing the coffee from the cup

holder and sipping its sweet contents. "It looks like it will be a nice day for a drive if the rain holds off."

Grace winced because she still felt something was off between them. She closed her eyes, hoping the picture in her head of Isabelle and Erick together would go away.

"Yes, maybe spring is coming sooner than we think." Erick sipped from his steel cup, keeping his eyes on the road ahead.

Grace turned to him, unable to continue with the small talk, "I've been thinking about everything. I need to take some… " she began.

"Let me guess." Erick frowned. "You need some more *time.*"

"I was going to say… " Grace looked out of her window in frustration. The way he'd said the word *time* gutted her, and the earlier tension returned. "You're being cruel. God! It's not like you were waiting around for me."

"So you're making this about *me?*" Erick laughed. "You're the one who keeps leaving when you *think* you know everything! Do you know how many times I've tried to pursue a relationship with you and how many times you find some new excuse to leave?" He rolled his eyes. "I don't know how much more I can take."

"That's not fair!" Grace's eyes burned again, the familiar wound of betrayal opening up yet again.

Erick pressed the gas pedal and merged onto the highway. "We could've solved all of this together, but *no!*" He seemed out of sorts this morning, like he might lose his cool at any moment. This was not like him, and she wondered what had changed.

Grace put her hands on her lap, unsure if she even wanted to be with this new version of Erick. He stopped talking, and she thought perhaps it was for the best.

"It's no secret that I've loved you since you walked into Kings Oxford School that first day," Erick conceded, speaking quietly and breaking the thick silence. "I think our problems stem from both of us not communicating what we want and need from each other."

"And *I* think *you're* scared to tell me the truth." Grace pushed down the ache in her heart. "I think you've already moved on with someone else because you don't trust that I'm in it for the long haul. You're not *all in* either. Something happened between you and that woman. You weren't honest with me last year either. Why is the truth so hard? How am I supposed to get past that?"

"I was trying to be a gentleman and give you space to figure out what you wanted after your memory returned." Erick rested his hand between them on the stick shift. "You left me no choice and were very clear about doing it alone. You *never* let me help. Did you expect me to wait for you forever? Remember *I* was the one who put everything on the line with the grand gesture at the book signing. It was pretty clear to me when you ghosted me at the cafe that you were *never* going to be with me."

Grace looked at him for a long time, noticing his beard had grown fuller on his set jawline. She didn't know how to explain what happened and didn't know how they could move beyond this and move forward. They were here now in the present, but everything about them was still caught in the past.

Would they ever be able to bridge the distance between them?

Chapter 62

Erick felt heat rising to his face. With each mile marker he passed, the anger simmered within and threatened to boil over. *How dare she accuse him of moving on? He'd put himself out there for her, made a fool of himself in front a group of people just to show her how much he cared. He waited for her at a cafe that she never showed up to. He didn't run from her... She was always the one running from him, not to mention, she had been in a long-term relationship with his brother!*

His thoughts drifted to the past.

"Grace, while we're getting it all out in the open, let's talk about the biggest elephant in the room. That night at the graduation party... Why *Finn?* Why'd you have to leave with *him?* And before you answer, saying it was Brook, let me remind you that she drugged me with the help of *Finn* just to ruin us. Their plan worked, and you ran away from me." He shook his head, remembering that horrific night.

Grace shifted in the passenger seat, her gaze still fixed on her lap. Their silence was heavy, filled with a decade of distance and unspoken hurt.

"Maybe they were planning our demise, but you were the

one kissing *her*," she started, her voice wavering. "It broke me, Erick. I couldn't face it. I couldn't face you."

"Couldn't or *wouldn't?*" Erick's question came out sharper than he intended. He swallowed hard, trying to steady his voice. "You chose not to talk to me about it. You just vanished with Finn. For ten years, I might add! Somehow, the punishment doesn't fit the crime."

"Because I was scared!" Grace's voice cracked, and she turned to face him. "Scared of the truth, scared of losing what I thought we had. It was easier to run to someone who wanted me without complications. He said everything I needed to hear, which is more than I can say about you! Finn cared about my writing career."

Erick wanted to say, "And how did that work out for you?" but he kept silent. She couldn't have known that Finn would lose his mind and take it out on her. He gripped the steering wheel out of frustration. "You're the one who moved to a new state and started a new life! All of that was based on a lie. Finn and Brook hatched a plan to separate us. My brother didn't love you, not the way I did. Not the way I could. And not once did you try to reach out. Was I really that easy to forget?"

"No, never that," she said quickly and earnestly. "It wasn't about forgetting you. It was about surviving. New York was a chance for me to start over and be someone other than the poor girl in town. I didn't know it then, but I can see now that being with Finn was a mistake. But know this. I *never* stopped thinking about you after I left for New York."

"Finn was my brother, Grace! MY BROTHER! I didn't just lose you that day; I lost him as well. While you carelessly erased me from your life, I had to sit back and watch you live yours with him. I was here, wondering, waiting for a sign that you still cared." The words were bitter in Erick's mouth, but they needed to be said. The questions that had festered for years were finally given voice. It was the beginning of a long-overdue dialogue that would either bridge the divide between them or confirm that some distances were too insurmountable to cross. "Did you ever care about us?"

Grace sank back into her seat, looking small and lost. "I'm sorry, Erick. I was young and selfish, and I was confused. I thought I owed Finn everything since he gave me so much. We were good in the beginning, but when Declan got sick, he started drinking a lot and turned into a monster. He hurt me." She closed her eyes. "He did terrible things, and I didn't know I could get out until my dad called me home."

"He needed me. You *both* needed me!" Erick breathed deeply and calmed down before speaking again. "All that time, all the pain you were in, not once did you consider calling me. I could have helped. I could have helped Finn *and* saved you from his problems." Erick sighed and felt the anger slowly subsiding, leaving a hollow ache in its place.

"I didn't need you to save me. I needed to save myself. As a woman, I needed to find a way to do things on my own. I can't just rely on someone else to save me. This happened when Finn asked to leave with me that day from the graduation party. Eventually, I had to save myself from my own reckless decisions."

Erick's jaw clenched as he replayed the hurts, the misunderstandings, and the distance that had wedged itself solidly between them. Guilt washed over him for not being there for her when Finn was at his lowest point, but she had been the one to shut him out. All those years she allowed Finn to get worse and worse. With all the turmoil inside of him, he still considered the possibility of being in a less complicated relationship with Isabelle. The red glow of brake lights ahead snapped Erick back to the present as he merged into the traffic.

"Does she make you happy?" Grace's question was simple but loaded with years of unspoken emotions.

Erick hesitated, his gaze fixed on the endless stretch of road before them. "She does, in a way that's calm and steady. Not better, just different."

Her gaze drifted away, lost in thought. "What are you saying, Erick? Do we have a future together, or is this it?"

"That's not an easy answer. When you had amnesia, we were

great together, remember?" Erick slowed at the stoplight as it turned yellow and then red.

"I remember everything." Grace forced a smile.

"I have a hard time trying to understand why you couldn't have just stayed and figured it out with me after your memory returned." Erick took a long breath, feeling the weight of their collective history bearing down upon him.

"At some point, Erick, you have to come to terms with the fact that no matter what, I had to save myself and do things on my own. It's how I'm made, honestly. But I'm open to trying a new approach this time around. It would be the only way this relationship could work. Finn beat me down emotionally as well as physically. I didn't feel like I could even trust myself, let alone anyone else. I don't know if you can ever understand that."

Erick mulled over her words, feeling them settle in his chest like puzzle pieces clicking into place. He looked over at her. "We can take it slow, Grace. One day at a time. See where the road leads without trying to control the destination."

"I appreciate that," Grace said, looking out the window as the roads grew closer to the inevitable ending of this long car ride that felt like its own crossroads. "Let's just… be. Be Erick and Grace, whatever that means now."

Erick thought this over. *Was she asking to just be friends? Could he just be friends with Grace?* Would their feelings take them over like they did in the elevator last night? He was unsure how any of this would work, but he would be a fool not to try to see what the next chapter held for both of them. He had waited his whole life to be with her, and he couldn't just walk away now when they were so close.

Chapter 63

race and Erick had argued for a good portion of the two-hour drive, but by the end, some of the heaviness they'd carried from the past had finally been released. She opened a granola bar and offered it to Erick.

"I'm good, thanks." Erick paused before changing their heavy conversation to a lighter one. "So what are you planning to do now that your book tour is over?"

"Honestly? I can't wait to get back to the hiking trails, writing, and helping women through the Healing Hikes Project." She gazed out the window and swallowed small bites of the bar. "I'm still waiting for the Jack Stone case to be closed. The FBI took over the case, and they still have my phone. They accused me of killing him! It was stupid for me to think it would end any other way, but I could never kill someone. It would have been me… "

Grace grew quiet.

"I, for one, am glad you survived that ordeal," Erick said. "Besides, I'm sure they'll realize you're innocent. If you need a lawyer, our family has one. I could make a few phone calls if you want."

"I'll let you know, but I'm sure my mom has contacts as well." Grace took a deep breath before saying, "So what about you? What's next for *Dr. Finn?*"

"I'm going to get back to one-on-one patients." He looked over at her. "It's time for me to slow down a bit on the constant traveling."

"One day at a time," Grace said, feeling relief for the first time in years.

"What are you doing Wednesday night?" Erick's eyes were on the road, but his right hand found hers and held it close.

"Hopefully, something with you," Grace replied as she squeezed his hand.

"Daniel and I are attending a basketball game at a middle school. If you'd like to go, we can invite Sky."

"Sounds like fun, but… " Grace answered, but she frowned as the memory of Isabelle's gold bracelet in Erick's room came crashing back into her mind, bringing with it the jealousy she'd felt earlier that morning. She tried to push the thought away by changing the subject quickly. "Remember when Sky pulled that shotgun on Brook back when she and Finn were tormenting me?"

"How could I forget? Daniel and I talk about it all the time," Erick said, turning off the highway. They both got lost in the memory as a phone call came through on the Bluetooth and flashed UNKNOWN NUMBER. Without hesitation, he hit the answer button. "Erick Finn speaking."

"Hey, Erick," the voice said through the car's speakers. Grace knew instantly who it was, and her stomach churned. *Finn.* The voice sent shivers up her spine.

"What's up, brother?" Erick kept his eyes on the road. "How are you doing at the facility?"

"I'm doing well. The worst of the detoxing is behind me now. Group therapy has been good for me, and I'm learning a lot. A guy here has a therapy dog. His sister runs a school in Texas for training German Shepherds." Finn sounded very upbeat.

"That's great, Finn!" Erick responded. "How much longer do they want you to stay?"

"I'm doing a few more weeks, and then they'll evaluate the situation. I'm not in a hurry to get back to my real life. Brook's lawsuit and all," Finn continued. "Hey, I have to go. My time is short, but I called to see if you wanted to see me on Sunday. They're having a Family Day from 11 a.m. to 3 p.m. You think you can make it?"

"Sure, I can do that."

Erick put his turn signal on and stopped at a red light.

"I appreciate it. I'll let them know you're on the list. See you Sunday," Finn said and hung up.

Grace didn't say anything but felt uncomfortable. She had not seen Finn since that day at HigherGround with Brook when he was impersonating Erick. If Sky hadn't come out, who knows what could have happened?

"You okay over there?" Erick asked, breaking through her thoughts as his fingers tried to reach hers again.

"I'm fine." Grace pulled her hand back and placed both hands on her lap. "Brook and Finn?"

"Uh, they're married, but she's claiming the business is hers. It's a long story. You don't *sound* fine." Erick pulled onto the lane that led to Grace's cottage and parked. He put the Jeep in park and turned to her. "Hey, I thought we had an agreement to be honest with each other."

"You're right." Grace didn't want to have this conversation, but she owed him the truth. "I feel weird hearing you talk to Finn after everything he did to both of us. If I'm being honest, I don't think I can ever forgive him. Finn has never given me a reason to." Grace sighed as the mood had shifted again. After the phone call, the air in the car felt heavy, and she fought to keep the tears at bay.

"Ah, I see." Erick still had his eyes on Grace, and his back leaned against his door. "I get that. It took me some time to forgive him. Forgiveness isn't easy, especially when the hurt is still simmering below the surface. I've been helping him with his sobriety and his legal matters with Brook."

"Oh," Grace said, looking at her lap. She closed her eyes and remembered all the pain Finn had inflicted on her. She felt sick as the memories of his abuse replayed in her mind. Suddenly, she wanted to be *anywhere* but in this Jeep with Erick. Again, she wondered how she and Erick would ever work as a couple. Finn had a way of ruining everything, and Grace didn't trust him not to cause chaos in Erick's life again.

"I hope this doesn't change how you feel about us," Erick said softly.

"I admire you for always knowing and doing the right thing. But this just isn't as easy for me." Grace closed her eyes.

Erick took both of her hands in his and leaned toward her. Grace opened her eyes, saw his sapphire blue eyes sparkling, and wished she could forget about Finn and just hold Erick.

"Thank you for being honest with me." Erick smiled. "It gives me hope."

"I just don't know… "

Grace squeezed her eyes shut and then opened them again.

Erick let go of her hands and ran his hand through his hair. "I have to be honest with you, though." He exhaled a heavy breath. "Finn's my brother, and I'll always be there for him. I hope this isn't a deal breaker for you."

Grace thought for a moment under the weight of his stare. When she didn't say anything, he leaned back in his seat. He reached for her hand once more, but she pulled away again.

"I'm sorry. I can't do this," she said, turning away from him. "It's too much."

"What does *that* mean?" Erick looked gutted.

Grace couldn't overlook this new turn of events. Not after everything she had been through. There was no life she could imagine where Finn would be lurking around every corner. It took her this long to recover from the madness. Grace reached for the door handle.

"Wait!" Erick cried out.

"I'm sorry, Erick. Maybe you've forgiven Finn, and you can

easily accept him back into your life. But he's not my brother. He's my *ex*! And after everything he's done to me, I can't do it. He's your family, your priority. But he's *not* mine. So as long as Finn is in your life, there is no life for *us*."

Erick's mouth flew open, but no words came out.

"Being together was always going to be difficult with our past, but having Finn around is going to make this impossible for me. If you truly loved me, you wouldn't ask this of me. I'm not ready!" Tears began burning Grace's eyes, and she could feel her face getting hot. "You asked for honesty."

"You can't ask me to choose. Not between my family!" Erick found his voice again.

"The same words you said when we graduated!"

Grace wiped her eyes, and they blazed with fury as she shook her head and opened the door to escape this madness.

"Fine," he muttered. He rubbed the back of his neck and stared out the windshield.

"Fine." Grace held her mouth into a tight, straight line. *This would never work.* She wanted to kick herself for even thinking she could make any of this happen with Erick. Even her therapist warned her that it would take time.

"*Fine,*" Erick repeated.

She hesitated with her fingers on the door handle because she knew there was no going back once she left the Jeep. He couldn't possibly understand everything that she'd been through this last year. How could she be with someone who wouldn't give her the time to work through all her trauma? Who would rather throw her back into her trauma by exposing her to Finn whenever he felt like it? There was also the issue of Isabelle and the bracelet she left behind. The incident still burned in Grace's mind.

Right now, she could only think about running far away and never returning. Why were her head and heart always at war? Grace didn't look back as she opened the door, jumped out, and got her bags from the trunk. She headed up the lane to the small cottage and unlocked the door, put her things down, and jumped in the shower. The day started out promising, but the phone call made her remember things she had spent so long trying to forget. How could she love a man who was related to and looked so much like her ex? An ex who wouldn't publish her book. An ex who cheated on her with his assistants. An ex who, when he drank, accused her of cheating on him. The same ex who'd hit her when he was drunk. Despite all of this, she thought she could save Finn. Just like Raven thought she could help Jack Stone.

Grace flinched at the memory of Jack falling from the cliff as it replayed over and over in her mind. Finn had a knack for ruining everything, and once again, he'd ruined her chances with Erick. She knew that being with Erick would be challenging, but she had no idea that the trauma with Finn was still there and raw. Only time would tell if she could move past all that had happened to her. For now, it was her journey and her journey alone.

Chapter 64

Erick looked away from Grace because he didn't want her to see the tears in his eyes, and there was nothing more he could say. As she exited the Jeep and shut the door, it felt final, like she was closing the door to the past and any future they might have had. He turned the key and pressed his foot on the gas pedal. *What was he thinking starting down this road again?*

Instinctively, he drove to HigherGround to pick up Jace. After he parked, Daniel met him at the door. "Hey, Daniel!" Erick always wanted to share good or bad news with his little brother.

"What's up, dude?" Daniel responded. "How was the drive?"

"Not good." Erick rolled his eyes.

"What happened? Did you mess up this relationship already? You've been back for what, five minutes? What is wrong with you?" Daniel teased.

"There's no relationship. Finn called while we were driving back." Erick felt like he had been punched in the gut as he recalled her reaction.

"And you answered it?"

"I did."

"Please tell me you didn't put him on speaker." Daniel cringed.

"Yeah." Erick sighed heavily. "I'm an idiot, but I was driving. I could tell something was wrong. Grace was tense the whole time we spoke. He wanted me to come by for a rehab visit next Sunday. I said I would go to his Family Visitation Day. I just don't think it'll work out this time. Grace is still upset with Finn."

"Well, can you blame her? After all that he did to hurt her physically, emotionally, and God knows what else. You can't expect her to move on anytime soon." Daniel's wisdom was starting to make sense. "I bet she wishes she had amnesia now!"

"Not funny, Daniel. But I get it. I know. I just thought it would work out this time. Somehow. Some way." Erick looked around the apartment. "I'm going home now. Where is Jace?"

"He and Luna are next door with Sky at the studio," Daniel said. "I get to unpack everything."

"Thanks, I'll head over there now," Erick said. He left the apartment and walked over to the HigherGround entrance.

Sky approached him, concern etched on her forehead, her mouth pinched.

"You aren't going to give me a hard time about Isabelle, are you? I know she's your friend, but we are just friends, and maybe we could be more. But this thing with Grace—" Dogs barked outside loudly, suddenly interrupting Erick's thoughts. He turned to the automatic doors and heard tires screeching. The next thing he knew Sky was sprinting past him and out to the parking lot.

"NOOO!!!" Sky screamed as Luna ran outside. Erick felt the danger and turned and ran outside to see what the commotion was.

Daniel rolled up to the scene and was yelling. *"HEY!!!"*

Erick immediately looked around as Sky ran back inside. "What is going on?" Bewildered, Erick's eyes saw the tail lights of a red Lexus and then his eyes focused on the white heap in the parking lot.

It was his dog!

Jace was lying still on the gravel parking lot, blood running down his back leg. Without hesitation, he was at his dog's side holding him. "I got you, buddy!"

Sky returned and ran over to Erick.

"Here," she said, handing him a blanket. "Let's get him to the hospital."

They carefully put Jace in the back of the Jeep, and Erick sped all the way to the Fox Animal Clinic. *Nothing could happen to Jace! Not now. Please, God, help Jace to be okay.*

Erick was speeding the whole way and then slammed on the brakes, abruptly turning into the parking lot, while horns blared in his wake. He threw the gear into park, jumped out of the Jeep, and lifted Jace carefully in his arms as he sprinted through the automatic doors.

His stomach dropped when he entered the veterinary clinic. His beloved dog was in trouble, and he prayed it wasn't too late. "I need some help here!"

Erick's heart raced as a few nurses came running in to help and grabbed Jace. Something was wrong; he could feel it in his bones. He couldn't catch his breath as the room began to spin. The blood drained from his face as they rushed Jace into the back room.

Suddenly, Sky burst into the lobby, gasping for air as she spoke. "We tried to get here as fast as we could!" she said as she caught her breath. Daniel was right beside her. "It was Brook. She came into HigherGround demanding to know where Finn was, and when I wouldn't tell her, she took off. Jace followed her. When she couldn't get the answers she wanted, she sped out of the parking lot and ran over Jace!"

The betrayal and shock were overwhelming as he struggled to process the news. "I did see her red Lexus just as she was leaving. She just backed over him like he was nothing!" Erick was trying to piece together what he had seen when a doctor appeared. She was petite, with chestnut hair, tortoise-shell glasses, and a white coat adorned with the emblem of Fox Animal Clinic. Erick's words got stuck in his throat. He couldn't speak and debated whether to run through the Staff-only clinic doors to reach Jace. Instead, he gasped and cried, *"Please,* I want to see my dog! I *need* to see Jace!"

"I'm Doctor Teresa Fox," she said, offering a polite smile. "Follow me, and I'll bring you to Jace."

She scanned her key card, which opened the large silver doors. Erick could barely speak but managed to nod as he fought back tears.

"Jace is going to be okay," Dr. Fox said briskly, leading him into the exam room where Jace lay on the table.

His brown eyes lit up at the sight of Erick but then dulled into pain as he let out a weak whimper. Erick's heart shattered at the sight of his best friend suffering. He buried his face in Jace's soft fur, trying to hold back sobs. He refused to break away from Jace. The dog's white fur was dotted with dark red blood, and one leg was wrapped up tightly.

"He's suffered a traumatic blunt force trauma. We must get him into surgery," Dr. Fox said sternly. "His hind leg is fractured in multiple places, and you should know that if there isn't enough tissue to put it back together, we may have to amputate. We need consent to do the treatment and start a surgical plan. I'll give you a moment with him while we gather the paperwork. Feel free to review his chart."

The words sent chills down Erick's spine. The thought of Jace losing a limb filled him with unspeakable grief. But at least he was alive.

"Please fix him," Erick begged, determined to do whatever it took to save his faithful companion. Dr. Fox left the room to gather the necessary paperwork.

"Hey, buddy!" Erick said, burying his face into Jace's soft, vanilla fur again. Erick didn't know what else to say and reached for the doctor's notes. He looked over the results and felt confused and angry. He also felt guilty for not being there for Jace all these months while he was traveling. The pit in his stomach would not go away. Erick closed his eyes and allowed the memories to flood in. He remembered bringing him home as a tiny, energetic puppy during those grueling days of Physical Therapy school. Jace had been his constant companion, a furry bundle of joy accompanying him on morning runs. The dog listened intently to his rants about difficult exams and greeted him with boundless enthusiasm each day. They'd take runs sometimes twice a day, and Jace helped him through one of the darkest times when he was having nightmare after another. It felt like he was living in a new nightmare now.

Dr. Fox returned and told Erick his visiting time was up. She led him out of the room, but Erick couldn't resist looking at Jace's pained expression.

Erick returned to the lobby where Sky and Daniel were waiting for him. "They have to do surgery. You guys should go home now. I'll stay here."

"Okay, call us as soon as you know anything!" Daniel hugged his brother as they went to get the car.

Erick nodded and tried to contact Brook, but all calls went straight to voicemail. He could feel the anger building in him, and he didn't think he could keep calm for much longer. He desperately tried to focus on being there for Jace in this critical moment. He did the next best thing he thought he could, pray for his beloved dog and wait.

Erick finally glanced up at the clock on the wall and groaned. It had only been five minutes. Time was moving at a snail's pace. A text came through from Isabelle.

Isabelle: Did you make it home okay?
Erick: Yeah, I did. Thanks for checking.
Isabelle: Good. :) I had a really nice time with you.
Erick: So did I. More than I expected, honestly.
Isabelle: Same. I wasn't ready for it to end.

Oh my God! Could his day get even crazier?

He couldn't deal with any of that right now. The heavy conversation with Grace on the long ride home was wearing on him. His emotions were raw and all over the place. He put away his phone and closed his eyes willing it all to go away. *Jace was all that mattered at this moment.* He couldn't bear the thought of losing him, which was always a possibility.

"Mr. Finn?" Dr. Fox's voice filled his ears.

Erick had dozed off but jumped up immediately to meet the doctor. "How is he?"

"Jace is in recovery. We did everything we could for the leg, but there just wasn't enough viable tissue, and we had to amputate the leg. I'm sorry. You can bring him home in a day or so, but you will have to be super careful and look for any signs of infection, fluid drainage, bleeding, swelling, or redness."

"Okay," Erick said, trying to process everything the veterinarian said. "Of course."

"We must keep him a night or two before you can take him home. Jace might be eager to get up and moving again, even with the sutures still in place. However, I advise keeping an eye on him to prevent additional damage or complications. You must limit his walks to short distances to avoid muscle strain and fatigue. He will quickly get used to walking on three legs. Regular walks help your three-legged pet remain strong, flexible, and trim. I can recommend an animal rehabilitation facility for you. You can go in for a few minutes and come back tomorrow." Dr. Fox shook his hand. "It'll be okay. Jace is still young and strong. We'll reach out to you tomorrow."

Erick went in immediately and saw Jace, who was still groggy from his surgery. "Hey, buddy, it's going to be okay. I promise. I can't stay with you now, but I'll see you tomorrow." He nuzzled his face into the dog's fur and thanked God for saving his life. "I'll come back and get you soon. Rest up, buddy."

With renewed determination, Erick promised himself he would never take a moment for granted again because today was a turning point. He'd already decided to step back from the all-consuming work of research, traveling, and meeting with inventors. He'd been so busy the last few months that it cost him precious time he could never get back. From now on, he would prioritize what mattered and cherish every moment he had with the ones he loved.

Chapter 65

Grace dropped off her bags at home, and then drove straight to the cell phone store. The FBI had kept her phone, the one with the recorded confession, so she had no choice but to start fresh. New phone in hand, and the weight of the past few days pressing down, she decided on a whim to drive to the cemetery where Raven was buried. The sky was blue, with a few wisps of clouds rolling in. Buds were sprouting in the bare trees that lined the family plot, and she realized this was the first time she'd been here since the funeral in the fall when everything had changed for her. She remembered her father, Robin, had called her that day in the office, begging her to come home. She'd been with Finn back then, but the turning point in her life was after Raven's funeral when her dad gave her the journal. Grace had followed the map Raven had hidden in it for her and found the music box with the photos from the top of the summit. At least now, Jack Stone would no longer be a problem.

The door to Grace's car closed with a thud as she made her way to the tombstone where Raven was buried. She laid down a bouquet of purple and yellow irises.

"Well… uh, Mom." It was still hard for her to address Raven as mother, rather than Aunt Raven. "I'm here. I survived all that you warned me about, including Jack Stone." Grace lowered herself to sit on the damp grass next to the tombstone as she shielded her eyes from the sun.

"I just wish you were here. I'm not with Finn anymore." Grace let out a little laugh. "I'm still trying to figure out if I'm any good at this relationship stuff." She picked at the grass absentmindedly. "I have been thinking a lot about family and I'm glad I saw all the places you loved in San Diego. Pala is just as you described, and I hope he's my father. I just want to find my way, Mom. God, it's a scary world out there."

A black raven came and rested on the tombstone, its eyes darting back and forth. Grace sat there holding her breath. "Mom! I need a sign that I'm doing the right thing." The raven looked over at her and then took flight. "I guess you want me to figure it out on my own," she said, as the wind blew her hair across her face. She returned to her car parked on the cemetery's pathway and noticed the raven was still flying around, settling on another gravestone. Out of nowhere, another raven joined it. She stared at the two blackbirds, seeing if she could decipher their movements. From the corner of her eye, Grace saw an older grey-haired couple walking hand in hand. They seemed to appear out of nowhere and crossed in front of her. The sight startled her, as she didn't see which direction they had come from.

Grace believed in signs and was sure this was no coincidence. As she put her car into drive, she left the graveside behind. She pulled up to her cottage, and her mind filled with thoughts of Erick. He never could understand why the phone call bothered her so much. The spark they once had seemed to have extinguished along with any hopes of a future. Instead of going home, she called Faith.

"Hey, Grace, I just got home. Are you okay?" Faith asked.

"Can I come over?" Grace asked, and Faith reminded her

that she was welcome to stop by anytime.

Once Grace arrived at her parents' house, Faith hugged her and let her in the front door. "Come on in. We're in the kitchen. I'm about to make tea. How's your day?"

"It was fine. I went to see Raven today." Grace followed Faith in and hugged her father who was sitting at the kitchen island reading the Hartford Courant newspaper.

"Oh?" Faith pursed her lips. "How are you and Erick? Did you get to see him in Boston?"

"Yes, he won an amazing award, but I think he's moved on with someone else."

"Are you sure?" Robin asked, closing the newspaper.

"I thought we had a connection. We even talked through a lot of things when there was a power outage at the hotel and we were stuck in an elevator."

"What?" Robin frowned. "That must've been crazy!"

"Yeah, it was, but Erick helped me calm down." Grace decided against telling them everything they talked about and the deep kiss they shared in the dark. "He drove me home, and I thought there was a chance we could get back together, but then Finn called while we were in the car. He must be in some sort of rehab facility."

"He finally got the help he needed." Faith sounded nonchalant about it.

"I heard that he married Brook Becker last year." It was no secret that Grace disliked Finn and Brook equally.

"Oh yes, I saw that in the paper a while back. That's an interesting match," Robin added, just as his phone buzzed. "I have to take this. It's one of my suppliers on a job I'm working on. Good to see you, Pumpkin." He kissed her forehead and promised to connect soon. "Hey Lou, let's talk about that white oak piece… " His voice trailed off as he walked toward his wood shop at the back of the house.

"Mom?" Grace looked at her mother. "How did you know Dad was the one?"

Faith didn't answer right away. "Well, honey, we met in school and faced off on a debate team. It wasn't 'love at first sight' but more of a mutual respect. I liked his protective nature, and he hasn't changed a bit. Your father was very different than I was. I loved the easy way he navigated life and how he worked with his hands to make beautiful pieces of wood. He was the first person I would call at the end of a long, grueling day in law school. He was very patient and never got jealous. When I met his father, Bran, I knew that kindness ran in the family. Your grandfather is still helping at the family farm in Wales."

"I wish I had gotten to spend time with him. Did you ever have any reservations about getting married?"

"Of course. I was so independent and driven to finish school and get my law degree. I wanted to help people and make a name for myself. As you know, my parents passed away when I was a senior in high school, and I have been on my own ever since. It was hard."

"Oh," Grace said quietly.

"What's going on, Grace?" Faith asked.

"I just don't know what to do, I guess," Grace stated. "It's just not going to work out between Erick and me. I still have more healing to do, so I made an appointment with Dr. Hopkins to sort it out."

"That's good. It might help. Take all the time you need. I'm here for you whenever you want to talk. Besides, I forgot to tell you. My team did some digging at that San Diego lab. They found no records that matched the one you gave me from Jack Stone."

"Thanks, Mom. I figured as much, and at the end of the day, it doesn't really matter anymore." Grace shrugged. "I have my family, and now that Jack's gone, I can finally feel free." She sipped the last of her tea.

"Everything will all work out the way it should."

"Thanks again, Mom. I love you!" Grace stood up, brought her cup to the sink, and then said her goodbyes.

For the first time that week, Grace felt peace wash over her when she went to bed. She thought about what her mother had said. She would work with the therapist again and get to the root of her problem. Even if Erick didn't want to be a part of her future, this was one chapter she needed to close once and for all. She was back home now; everything hadn't fallen back into place like Grace hoped, but she was done trying to make everything okay for everyone else. She had more healing to do, and that was going to take some time. At least she had her answer now about Erick. He had made his choice to stand with his family again and move on with Isabelle. Grace was going to make peace with being alone once and for all.

Chapter 66

Erick didn't get much sleep, but the following day, he returned to the animal clinic and picked up Jace. He had spent most of the night tossing and turning, worried that he had nearly lost Jace. Replaying the car ride home from Boston, he still couldn't believe everything that had happened and that it had all led to the end of his relationship with Grace.

Once Jace was discharged, Erick carried his dog to the Jeep. Where his leg used to be was now a bundle wrapped in bandages. Despite this, Jace still wagged his tail in excitement when he saw Erick.

"You're going to have to take it easy, buddy. The doctor said no playing around. I'll take good care of you, buddy." On the ride home, Erick hoped he could find the best animal therapist, regardless of the expense.

Erick cleared his work schedule and spent the rest of the week watching over Jace and making sure the stitches stayed in place. It was going to be a long road to recovery, but he believed he was the right person for the job. Sky was going to interview some animal therapists so Jace could start his training in a few weeks. His life had taken a detour, but Jace was going to mend; and Erick spent every waking moment making sure his dog had everything he needed.

When Sunday came, Erick went to see Finn as promised. The wrought-iron gates of the Legacy House swung open, granting him passage to the stately grounds. He noticed the manicured driveway and the towering oak trees that lined the drive, along with the first blooms of daffodils. He stepped out of the car, taking a moment to smooth down his shirt. The air was warmer with the onset of spring, and Erick could hear the laughter and voices of reunited families in the distance. Taking a deep breath, he prepared himself to face whatever version of Finn awaited him. Family Day at the rehabilitation center was about second chances.

Erick stepped through the polished mahogany doors of Legacy House, his footsteps reverberating against the marble flooring in the grand foyer.

"Mr. Finn?" A smooth voice spoke and it echoed in the reception area. He looked up as the director, a woman whose elegant demeanor spoke volumes about the center's clientele, approached.

"Ms. Carter," he responded, extending his hand.

"Your brother has been making exceptional strides," Ms. Carter said as they walked along the marble floors. "Finn's become a beacon for our community here, sharing his experiences and encouraging others. His journey has been quite remarkable."

"Really? That's amazing," Erick reflected, as a sense of pride welled within him. There was hope, then, not just for Finn but also for the fragile ties Erick was trying to mend between them.

"Absolutely," she affirmed, pushing open a set of double French doors that led outside.

Sunlight spilled onto Erick's face as they emerged onto a sprawling patio where tables adorned with white linens and an array of colorful dishes formed a buffet. The scent of roasted meats and fresh bread wafted through the air, mingling with the subtle fragrance of spring blooms that decorated the space.

All around the patio, laughter bubbled up from tables. Erick recognized some of the patients who were celebrities, but now they were simply sons, daughters, siblings, parents, and human beings who needed help. Erick watched the interactions, the cautious hugs, and the hopeful conversations, a collective healing that Legacy House prided itself on nurturing.

"Please, help yourself to some food," Ms. Carter gestured toward the buffet. "Finn will join you shortly."

"Thank you," Erick said, though his appetite seemed to have disappeared since Jace had gotten hurt.

He selected a plate and filled it some salad and a slice of tenderloin. Amidst the clink of silverware and soft strains of background music, Erick was hopeful that today was not just about just supporting and witnessing Finn's rehabilitation but about how scars could eventually fade into stories of survival and strength. He wanted a closer relationship with his brother.

Erick surveyed the meticulously tended gardens, his eyes tracing the paths that wound around vibrant flower beds and a tranquil pond with large orange and white Koi fish circling around. He heard a familiar voice.

"Hey, Erick! You made it!"

Whirling around, Erick turned and saw Finn, who strode over, closing the distance between them. He saw years of strain had receded from Finn's face, replaced with a brightness in his eyes that Erick hadn't seen for decades.

"Look at you," Erick said. "You look great!"

"Feeling better than ever," Finn replied, clapping Erick on the shoulder with a hearty laugh that seemed to come from this newfound sobriety. Erick nodded, understanding that beneath Finn's cheerful surface was a commitment to a new way of life. As they began to walk side by side, Finn started pointing out various features of the facility. Each detail was delivered with enthusiasm, pride in his progress, and gratitude for the place that facilitated it. "Here's where we have group therapy," Finn gestured to a room with large windows that let in a splash of natural light. "And the gym over there—that's been my sanctuary."

"It seems like you've got everything you need here," Erick said, impressed by Finn's dedication to the program at Legacy House.

"Yeah, it's more than just rehab—it's a community," Finn agreed. Then his expression turned contemplative. "But outside these walls, man, I've got mountains to climb. The publishing business... let's just say that chapter is over and with a plot twist. Brook wasn't content with just leaving me; she wanted to take my legacy. I'll have to file for a divorce and sign papers when I return."

"I'm sorry to hear that," Erick murmured, though he wasn't entirely surprised, given Brook's past antics and how she thoughtlessly ran Jace over. "I did see her pompous interview on the news the other day."

A wry grin spread across Finn's face. "Actually, it's a blessing in disguise. I'm thinking about a change, something different, you know?"

"Whatever you decide, you've got my support," Erick affirmed, clapping Finn on the back.

"Thanks, Erick. That means everything." Finn's voice held a note of sincerity that resonated with Erick.

"Speaking of Brook, just the other day she was at HigherGround looking for you. When no one would give her the information, she left in such a hurry that she ran over Jace with her car! They ended up having to amputate it."

"No way!" Finn shook his head in disgust. "Brook should never be allowed to drive! She'll never learn. She is going to kill someone." They continued walking together in shared disgust.

After lunch, Erick said goodbye to Finn. "I'll see you in a few weeks, and we can all help you move into Daniel's."

"Thanks again for everything," Finn said as Erick left.

The valet came out, and he handed Erick the keys to his Jeep. He left Legacy House with a sense of purpose. Finn would handle whatever came next and he couldn't help but feel immense pride for how far Finn had come, despite everything Brook had put him through and the circumstances that led him to this place.

Once he got home, Erick snuggled with Jace and went to sleep. He'd had a great day with Finn, even though the drive home seemed to last forever. Tomorrow, he would go to Higher-Ground and meet the therapist Sky had lined up for Jace. Maybe things were going to turn around for the Finn brothers after all.

Chapter 67

Grace's thoughts seemed to mirror the grey clouds that rolled over the Connecticut landscape. She wrapped her coat tighter around herself as she navigated the cobblestone path leading to a familiar Victorian-style building where her therapist, Dr. Dru Hopkins, had an office. The late March air whirled around and blew her hair across her face. She quickly entered the building and smoothed her hair back into place.

"Good afternoon, Grace," the receptionist greeted her with a smile.

"Hi." Grace returned the greeting and signed the clipboard. "Is Dr. Hopkins ready for me?"

"She sure is. You can go straight in."

Dr. Hopkins opened the door before Grace could even knock. "Grace, come in. Please, sit down," the doctor said, gesturing to the chair across from her mahogany desk.

"Thank you, Dr. Hopkins," Grace managed, sinking into the cushioned seat. She looked around at all the books behind the desk organized neatly in the bookshelves. Grace remembered the first time they'd met at the hospital after the accident.

"I see you've remembered how to walk again! Tell me what brings you back here today?" Dr. Hopkins asked, her pen poised above a notepad.

"Everything's a mess," Grace said, her eyes darting around uncomfortably. "I thought I'd moved past all this—my amnesia and the lies. But it's like I'm trapped in this cycle I can't escape from."

"Let's take it one step at a time," Dr. Hopkins encouraged. "What lies are you referring to?"

"Everyone who claims to have loved me has betrayed me in one way or another," Grace said, feeling the weight of each word. "Finn, he—he was cruel and abusive. For nearly a decade, I lived in a nightmare. He made promises to help my writing career that he couldn't keep. Finn began drinking, crushed by the weight of his father's expectations and past abuse. Eventually, he began to take that out on me."

"Abuse can leave deep wounds, Grace," Dr. Hopkins responded gently. "It's not something you simply move past without scars."

Her hand absently went to her face. "I have plenty of those. But it's more than just Finn. I became obsessed with finding out who my biological father is. It took me to San Diego, where I almost died."

"Can you tell me about that?" Dr. Hopkins asked, her eyes locking onto Grace's with an intensity that made her want to tell her everything.

"I flew to San Diego to see where my mother had taken her last footsteps. I stood on the same edge of the cliff where she had fallen. I looked down at the crashing waves, thinking it would give me answers, and all I had was the name of one of the men she had dated and a journal. His name was Jack Stone, and I suspected that he killed my mother," Grace recalled, her voice breaking with emotion. "I was obsessed with finding Jack, and I couldn't think about anything else. I stopped sleeping and eating. Eventually, I went up to the cliffside to confront him.

Grace recounted the remainder of the story, from Jack's

death to the FBI questioning her. The memories, raw and permanent, suffocated her, and she gasped for air.

"Grace, that must have been awful," Dr. Hopkins said, leaning forward slightly. "But your attempt to save Jack shows your instinct to help others, even when you're in pain yourself."

"They didn't arrest me because they didn't have enough evidence. It makes me sick to think anyone would think I'd hurt someone. I'm still considered a person of interest while the investigation is ongoing."

"Your good intentions were clear, Grace," Dr. Hopkins reassured her. "You reached out to save him. That speaks volumes about your character—more than any speculation ever could." Dr. Hopkins handed her a tissue, and Grace took it gratefully, dabbing at the corners of her eyes.

"Then when I got back, I tried to make things right with this guy I've loved since we were kids. It's a long story, but I fell in love with my physical therapist when I had amnesia. Dr. Erick Finn helped me to learn to walk again, but he lied to me about knowing me when we were in high school. He also just happens to be Finn's twin brother, so that's a lot to process."

"Oh, I see. Let's talk about Erick and Finn," Dr. Hopkins suggested gently. "Your feelings toward them are bound up in all that's happened to you."

Grace nodded, taking a deep breath. "Erick was my first love," she murmured, "my safe haven. But now... I don't know if I can ever go back to that innocence. And Finn—" Her voice hardened with the mention of his name. "He was cruel, and I lost nearly a decade of my life believing in a lie. The worst part was that he took out his anger and frustration on me, not only physically, but also emotionally."

"Trust will take time after healing," Dr. Hopkins acknowledged. "But your heart's capacity for love hasn't diminished, Grace. It's been bruised, yes, but not broken."

"Sometimes, I'm afraid it's shattered into too many pieces to ever fit back together," Grace confessed, looking down at her hands. "Relationships are so difficult for me."

"Even the most fractured things can be mended, given time and patience," Dr. Hopkins said softly. "You're here, aren't you? Seeking understanding and healing."

"Because I don't want to give up," Grace admitted, lifting her gaze. "But how do you trust again when every instinct tells you to build a wall around yourself?"

"It starts by building trust with yourself first. So what about Erick? Do you have an interest in being together?" Dr. Hopkins probed further.

"Whenever I look into Erick's eyes, I see the same kindness that I fell in love with as a young girl. But since they are twins, Finn also has the same eyes. Erick will do anything for his brother, and that's why we broke up. How can I be with Erick when I am still uncomfortable around Finn?"

Dr. Hopkins offered. "Have you spoken to Erick about these concerns?"

"Somewhat," Grace said, rolling her eyes in frustration. "But he's choosing to help his brother over being in a relationship with me. I'm not brave enough yet to face my past."

"Bravery isn't the absence of fear, Grace. It's the decision to move forward despite it," Dr. Hopkins encouraged. "You'll need to find closure with what happened in your past."

"Okay," Grace said, taking in the words that were both comforting and challenging. "I know I can't hide from this forever. It's just so daunting when trust feels like a glass house—one wrong move, and everything shatters again. Who knows if I will ever be able to rebuild bridges or if they will be burnt beyond recognition."

"Trust is indeed delicate," Dr. Hopkins acknowledged, leaning back in her chair. "But remember, trust is built up over time, piece by piece. And sometimes, even when it breaks, you find that the foundation is still there, strong enough to start over. But it's also okay to acknowledge that love isn't always enough to repair what's been broken. Whichever way it goes, your resilience will carry you through. Let's talk about Finn," Dr. Hopkins said, shifting gears. "How are you managing the emotions you feel about him?"

"Mostly, I feel numb," Grace confessed after a few minutes. "Like I'm still waiting to wake up from a bad dream. But then there are moments of anger and intense sadness. It's been a rollercoaster."

"Feelings are often non-linear, especially after trauma." Dr. Hopkins scribbled a note on her pad. "Allow yourself to feel the feelings, Grace. Don't push them away. They're part of healing, part of reframing your story."

That's what this all boiled down to—regaining control, re-writing the narrative that had been forced upon her. She looked up, her eyes clear and more determined. "I think I'm ready to start doing that."

"Remember, Grace, you're not alone," Dr. Hopkins reassured her. "You have support, and though the path may be filled with uncertainty, remember that you're stronger than you think. And whatever decision you make will be the right one for you. We can work on it more if you'd like to meet again?"

"Thank you. Yes, I already scheduled my next appointment," Grace said, her heart lighter than it had been when she first walked in.

"Great! Then we can unravel more of this for you. I also want to recommend a grief counseling group here in town. I think it would be of great benefit to you after all the losses you had this year." Dr. Hopkins handed her a brochure.

As Grace stood to leave, a newfound resolve settled within her as she looked at the brochure. She would go to a meeting and see if it would help. The road ahead might be long and winding, but she would navigate it one step at a time, trusting in her own resilience to guide her way even without Erick this time around.

Chapter 68

Erick met Daniel and Sky the following day at HigherGround to meet Jace's new therapist. Sky, Erick, and Jace walked to one of the larger therapy rooms with a large blue mat. Sky then introduced everyone to Dr. Paul.

When Dr. Paul patted Jace's head and talked calmly to him, Erick instantly knew Sky had chosen the right therapist for his dog.

"Good boy, Jace," Sky said, looking into Jace's eyes. "See, it's all about trust."

"All healthy relationships are built on trust," Erick murmured to himself.

"Are you talking about Jace or Grace?" Daniel inquired as he entered the therapy room.

Joyce, the office manager, followed and approached Erick. She put her hand on his shoulder. "I'm so glad Jace is doing well," she said. "Also, someone is here to see you." She gestured toward the offices.

"Did they give a name?" Erick inquired, his curiosity piqued.

"Isabelle Boyton. She said you invited her, and I asked her to wait for you in your office."

"Thanks, Joyce." Erick gave her a nod of appreciation. "I'll be right back," he said as Sky narrowed her eyes at him. He turned without explanation and then strode down the hall to his office.

Isabelle stood by the large window, her silhouette framed by the gentle morning sunlight. Her highlighted hair cascaded over her shoulders in long waves. When she turned, a warm smile spread across her face.

"Isabelle," Erick said with surprise as he stepped closer to her. "You didn't tell me you were coming."

"Erick, look at what you've built! This place is *incredible*." Isabelle beamed, her eyes reflecting genuine admiration. They embraced briefly, a quick hug that brought back memories of their time in Boston.

"Thanks, I'm glad you think so. It's been quite a journey," Erick replied. "What brings you here? It's been a while since we last caught up. Come on." A hopeful grin tugged at his lips. "Let's catch up while I give you a grand tour. There's a lot more 'magic' to be seen."

"Sounds like fun," Isabelle said. She followed Erick through the expansive studio as she continued. "After the conference, I finished that project I told you about for the Boston University Physical Therapy Center. It's been hectic but so rewarding. And honestly, Erick, I couldn't have done it without the connections you helped me make at the conference."

"That's great to hear, Isabelle. I always knew you'd do amazing things." He pointed out the pool and then waved to Sky, who was in the studio across the hall with Jace. She frowned at him, but then quickly turned back toward Jace's therapist.

Isabelle waved to Sky and then turned to Erick. "With God, all things are possible, right?" She paused before continuing. "How's it all going with the redhead? Or have you finally come to your senses and decided you want *me* by your side when we take on the physical therapy world together?" She teased him with a playful nudge, her eyes twinkling mischievously.

"Actually it didn't work out between us." Erick's lips turned downward in a frown. "About the physical therapy world outreach and conferences, that isn't me anymore. I haven't changed my mind since we talked about this back in Boston. "

"Oh, I thought you would have come to your senses over the last few weeks. Well, it looks like this is the end of the tour." She changed the subject when they found their way back to the front lobby. "I guess I'll be getting back to Boston tomorrow then. It was great seeing you, Dr. Finn." She gave him a quick hug and headed toward the door.

But as her hand pressed the handle, Erick suddenly wanted her to stay. "Isabelle, *wait!*" he called out, prompting her to pause and look back over her shoulder. "How long are you in town for?"

"I just came to visit for the day, but my plans are open. What do you have in mind?" Isabelle stood there looking up at Erick.

He looked back at her and knew he would be a fool if he didn't ask her. Erick was done chasing the past; it was time to think of what might be in front of him. "If you're ever looking for a change of scenery, just let me know. I can help you get a job here or at my newest franchise. I'm also looking for someone to help manage the franchised HigherGrounds if you are interested in something bigger."

Her eyebrows rose in interest, but she held her ground by the door, her hand still resting on the metal handle. "Really?" she asked.

"Absolutely," he said, his voice firm with sincerity. "I like your work ethic and passion. You probably know Sky and Daniel are headed to Georgia at the end of the year, leaving me without a pediatric therapist. There are many opportunities here at HigherGround." Erick hesitated, but he had nothing to lose. "Will you have dinner with me tonight? We can talk more about this."

"I'd love to. I'm staying at the Hilton. You should still have my number. Why don't you text me the details? It was great to see you again. See you soon!" Isabelle smiled widely and exited the main doors.

Erick stood there frozen as he watched her leave. He could feel the sense of possibility, and wondered how all this would work given that he was technically a free man now. He put one foot in front of the other and returned to Jace's session as it was wrapping up. This was his life now, taking care of Jace and looking to the future. No longer was he looking back in the rearview mirror.

Chapter 69

Grace lingered on the church steps that night, open to healing but unsure what this kind of meeting might demand of her. With the brochure in hand that Dr. Hopkins had given her, she walked up the steps and found the meeting room. Metal chairs were aligned in a circle and a refreshment table was placed by the entrance. Several people of varying ages had arrived and were socializing with each other. Before she could change her mind, she went over to the table that had some desserts, coffee, and hot water for tea.

She reached for the last chai tea bag, feeling something she hadn't felt in some time—hope. She wasn't sure how a group of strangers could help, but she was going to give it a chance. She felt someone next to her, and as she looked up, her eye caught a handsome man standing there with his arms crossed and a smirk on his face.

"Hey, that's mine!" His voice was soft, yet deep, the kind of resonance that lingered. Dark, wavy hair fell to his shoulders, a hint of stubble traced his jawline. Strong brows framed a pair of piercing green eyes, and there was a rugged handsomeness to him that felt magnetic. He had to have been in his late thirties or early forties, Grace reasoned. He wore a dark grey long-sleeved cashmere sweater over black jeans, but despite his clean look, he still had that maverick edge.

"Yours? I think you're mistaken." Grace raised an eyebrow, her fingers still grasping the bag of tea. She wasn't going to be intimidated on her first day.

He leaned closer, his eyes playful with fine lines crinkled in the corners. "I've been eyeing that tea since I walked in. It has my name on it."

"Oh really? What's your name? *Chai?*" She rolled her eyes but couldn't hide her amusement as a grin spread across her face.

"The name is Scott. But Chai works, too. It's a universal name." He stepped closer to her and reached over to cover her hand, but Grace still held onto the last chai tea bag and would not let go. *Who does this guy think he is?*

"I'm sure you can find something else. There are so many choices," Grace insisted.

"Okay, let's settle this like adults. Rock, paper, scissors?" Scott's eyes seemed to sparkle brighter as he challenged her to settle this in this playful way.

Grace's gaze lingered on his before she spoke again. "Best out of three," she said, oddly confident and enamored with his persistence. She put the tea bag between them, trusting that he was a man of his word.

They both raised their hands. "On three," Scott said. "One, two, three!"

Grace's hand signified paper. Scott's showed rock. "Yes!" she exclaimed.

"Round one to you. But it's still anyone's game," he said, as they readied their hands for round two. "One, two, three!"

Grace revealed scissors. Scott laughed as his fingers extended into paper.

"Ha! Two to none!" she laughed. This was going to be easier than she expected.

"Last round. I can still win." Scott held her gaze.

"Okay, but I hope your math skills improve because best out of three means I *already* won!" Grace laughed at the absurdity. She'd never been to this meeting before, and this certainly wasn't what she expected. She'd pictured everyone somber, and this was—did she dare say *fun*?

"One, two, three!" He started the game once again.

She squeezed her fingers into a round rock just as two fingers jutted out from him as he threw scissors.

"Three to none! I'm the champion!" She laughed as she retrieved the tea bag, placed it in the paper cup, flipped the lever of the hot water dispenser, and began to fill the cup.

Scott gasped in exaggerated shock, hands on his hips. "You're ruthless. But rules are rules."

"Which means you have to concede that I'm the winner."

He leaned in and gracefully took the cup out of her hand. "Life's too short for rules. That's *my* tea. Thank you."

Grace stood there frozen, eyes wide, and mouth open. "Wait, *what?*"

He brought the cup to his lips, taking a sip. "Delicious. See? Worth letting you win."

"Are you kidding me? You let me win only to take it from me in the end? I won fair and square! You stole it! " She looked around the room to see if anyone else had witnessed this injustice.

"Not quite. I just know how to live." He shrugged and took another sip of the tea.

Grace shook her head, partly annoyed and mostly confused. She wasn't sure if she should be mad or impressed. "That's a bold strategy, Scott."

"Bold is good. I learned that the hard way."

"What do you mean?" She was intrigued now, but kept her hands on her hips in disbelief.

"Please find your seats. We are about to begin," the moderator interrupted the conversations, and the room grew quiet. Grace sat across from Scott, while others filled the rest of the circle.

"Who wants to start?" The moderator, an older woman with cropped salt and pepper hair, looked over the group.

Scott raised his hand and cleared his throat, his eyes scanning across the circle of people. He sipped the tea while looking in victory at Grace. Then he placed the cup on the floor beside his metal chair. "I'm Scott. I lost my wife just over three years ago. It's been… tough, but I've learned that grief becomes part of you. Like a shadow. You can't shake it off, but I've learned how to carry it."

She listened and found herself leaning in, drawn in by the weight of his words.

"It took me all these years to acknowledge my loss, let alone even talk about it. I couldn't leave my house for months. I never thought I'd be here now sharing this, but life is so fragile," he continued, glancing at Grace again. "Sometimes, through the cracks, light comes in and allows joy to return."

She met his gaze, her heart filling with empathy. Sometimes truths came from unexpected strangers.

"After losing my wife, I found a new perspective. Grief isn't all bad. It can bring clarity, and it can teach you to appreciate the little things that you once overlooked. Like sharing a moment of unexpected laughter with a stranger." His eyes met hers, and he smiled at her. "You start to see beauty in the simplest things. Beauty might be hard to see right now. It takes time. But it's there. You just have to look for it. I know it's hard to believe," he said, his tone gentle. "But grief can coexist with joy. You learn fast what matters."

Grace was stunned as she listened to a few others share their stories of grief. The meeting ended, and she looked around as everyone, including her, got up and headed to the refreshment table.

Scott joined her and said, "No tea?"

That same warm, gravelly voice teased her again.

She turned and smirked, "I guess someone took the last one."

"That's a shame. I'd share mine, but I managed to knock it

over when the meeting ended."

"Are you kidding me?" Grace looked incredulous. *This guy is too much.*

"All is fair in tea and war," he mused.

"You have a weird way of looking at things."

He laughed again, "Guess we're both a little strange. Normal is overrated in my book."

"Is that your life philosophy?"

"Maybe. But I'm still winning the tea battle." His smile was bright. She could not look away as their eyes locked for a long moment.

"I'm sorry about your wife," she finally said, looking away.

"Me too," Scott said, his expression softening. "She was my best friend. We shared everything. Tea, adventure, dreams."

Grace nodded, understanding more than she let on. "Sounds like a good life."

"It was. But now I'm here. Figuring it out all over again." He looked past her where the chairs were still in a circle. "Been coming for the last two years. I've never seen you before. Is this your first time?"

"Yes. I'm trying to do the same thing—figure out how all the pieces fit."

"You're in the right place. It's a good group." Scott smiled. "I never got your name, though."

"Grace," she said, holding her hand out to shake his. Before he reached her hand, he showed her two fingers.

"Scissors beats paper!" Scott laughed. "All jokes aside, it was a pleasure meeting you, Grace. I hope I didn't scare you away." He smiled and unexpectedly kissed the top of her hand.

"You didn't." Grace took her hand back and turned toward the door. She found herself wondering more about this mysterious Scott. She hadn't come to this meeting looking for anything new but decided she was going to return next week. Sometimes, a familiar face was enough to keep going. Scott's face and his carefree attitude were quite captivating and she knew she wanted to learn more.

Chapter 70

Erick returned to the cabin with Jace, helping him settle on the soft dog bed he'd bought for him. He grabbed a fresh towel and got into the shower, hoping the water would wash away the dark cloud that had settled over him. *Give yourself a break,* he thought. He'd been through a lot. Jace almost died, and the future he hoped for with Grace was long gone. *Was this how life was always going to be?* he wondered. *A life full of surprises and setbacks?*

As he dressed and gave Jace his dinner, Erick's thoughts drifted to Isabelle. He couldn't help but recall the bustling streets of Boston and all the memories he'd created with Isabelle there. Tonight, he was excited to be meeting her for dinner.

The last rays of daylight reflected off the remaining ice and snow that clung to the bare branches of the New England trees. Erick drove to the Hilton in the capital city of Hartford. Isabelle was waiting for him at the entrance. She'd always had a knack for appearing effortlessly graceful, and her style was impeccable. Tonight was no exception. She was dressed in a short suede skirt over dark tights, a turtleneck, tall knee-high boots, and a flowing scarlet light jacket. Her outfit was completed by a flowing scarlet wool jacket.

"Hey you," she greeted him with a wide grin and then hopped in the Jeep.

"Hey," Erick replied, feeling a flash of nostalgia. "You look great. By the way," he reached into his bomber jacket and pulled out a box. "I've been meaning to give this to you."

"A present for me?" Isabelle smiled and took the box.

"Not exactly, just think you may have lost this when we were in Boston."

Isabelle opened the box and inside was the delicate gold bracelet with the cross on it. "Oh, Erick! Thank you for finding this. My dad gave this to me years ago before he passed, and I thought it was lost forever." She leaned in and kissed him. Then settled back to put her seat belt on.

He drove to the restaurant district and parked the Jeep. They walked side by side, her arm linked with his, through the city side streets to a quaint restaurant tucked away from the main thoroughfare. The establishment had been there for generations, and its decor was cozy with a subtle elegance.

As they settled into their seats, conversation flowed easily. Isabelle spoke animatedly about her recent project at Boston University, her eyes alight with the passion of someone who truly enjoyed the work they loved. Erick listened, captivated. The flickering candlelight illuminated the gold flecks in her eyes.

"So, Boston University," he said, wanting to know more. "That project you mentioned—why don't you tell me more about it?"

Isabelle leaned forward, "It was all about rehabilitation techniques for stroke patients. I focused on integrating the latest technology with traditional methods. It's amazing how much we can help them."

"That sounds incredible. Technology in therapy? I've seen some great results with my prosthetic patients. I use different techniques with each patient. No one size fits all." Erick was enthusiastic. "I still like old-school methods as well."

"The new programs are opening new doors. It's mind-blowing sometimes." Her smile faded slightly. "But truthfully, I'm ready for so much more. I feel stuck in Boston. After I finished school, I got a fellowship and a great job offer. Now, I want to see the world and explore what's out there. Like hiking the Andes Mountains. I'm definitely not meant to stay in just one place." She shrugged, a hint of uncertainty in her tone. "There's so much to explore in the world. It's like, what's next?"

Erick nodded slowly. "I get that. Hiking the Andes does sound cool. But I also love it here in Connecticut. It's quieter, but… it has its charm."

"Charm?" Isabelle chuckled lightly. "Is that what you call it?"

"Maybe. There's something about the small towns. You know everyone, and you can really connect with people." He leaned back and shrugged. "I mean, I grew up here. It's home for me."

"Home can be good, and my mom and step-dad live in Enfield, but…" She trailed off, her gaze drifting to the window. "What if I miss out on something bigger?"

"Bigger?" Erick followed her gaze. "What do you have in mind?"

"Opportunities. Adventure. I don't want to look back and think I played it safe. No regrets."

"But adventure can be anywhere," Erick suggested.

"Like here?" Isabelle gestured around the restaurant. "In a small Italian place?"

Erick smiled. "Exactly. You never know what could happen over a plate of spaghetti."

Just then, the waiter brought over a few steaming plates: classic robust hand-made spaghetti with Grandma's old-style meatballs served with garlic broccoli rabe and another plate of pappardelle with pale pink vodka sauce. A bowl of fresh greens tossed in parmesan Italian dressing was also served family-style.

She laughed, the tension easing slightly. "You have a point. But I need to feel alive, you know?" Isabelle put a little of each pasta and greens on her plate and dusted both with freshly shaved Asiago cheese.

"Alive?" Erick leaned in and made himself a similar plate with half a meatball. "What does that mean for you?"

"Traveling. Taking risks. Meeting new people. Experiences that change me." She hesitated. "Plus reaching new levels in my career."

"Of course. That's key." He paused, choosing his words carefully and taking a bite of food. "But what if Connecticut can give you both? A fresh start and a chance to grow."

"Are you trying to sell me on moving here?" Isabelle's eyes sparkled, and Erick knew he wasn't being subtle.

"Maybe a little." He chuckled and felt the connection building. "I just think it could be a good fit. For both of us."

"For both of us?" She tilted her head. "What do you mean?"

"Wait. Taste this meatball." He put some on his fork and reached over to her. "Isn't it so good? What I'm trying to say is… I'm looking for something real and someone I can settle down with. Find someone to share life with."

"*Settle down?* In your thirties?" Isabelle looked surprised. "Isn't that a bit early?"

"Not for me. I've seen enough of the world to know what I want." He paused, trying to read her expression. "And I think I might have found it."

Isabelle's smile faltered, her voice softening. "You think I'm that person?"

"Maybe." He leaned closer. "But I can't make you stay. Only you can decide where your next adventure takes you."

She bit her lip, contemplating. "It's a lot to consider."

"I know. But I believe in taking chances."

"Like this date?" she asked, her tone teasing but her eyes serious.

"Yeah. Like this date." Erick chuckled nervously.

"Thanks, Erick. I wasn't even sure you were still interested after you left Boston so quickly." Isabelle relaxed slightly, her expression softening. "You're different from what I expected."

"Different, how?"

"More grounded. Real." She paused, glancing down at her glass. "It's refreshing."

"Good to hear." He took a breath, feeling hopeful. "So, what's your next dream adventure?"

Isabelle leaned back, her eyes sparkling again. "Hmm. Maybe a little road trip. Just me, a car, and some good music."

"Oh, where would you be headed?" Erick wiped his mouth with a napkin. He was enjoying this time with Isabelle, flirting with a potential future together, and she seemed to enjoy his company as well.

"I think I know just the place," Isabelle said, smiling at him across the table. "It was actually *your* idea. Tomorrow, I will look for a place to lease while I'm here. Of course, I have to settle things back home, but what you said makes sense."

"Really? Are you sure you don't need more time to think about it?" Erick was stunned. *Could she be that decisive?* "Connecticut would be lucky to have you," he said, and he knew he was the lucky one.

"Maybe we could see each other more often then," she proposed.

"Definitely," Erick agreed quickly, throwing caution to the wind. "Actually, I'm going to a basketball game at the middle school tomorrow night. You should come."

"Sounds fun," Isabelle said, her delight written across her smile.

After he dropped Isabelle off at her hotel, Erick kept thinking about moments from their dinner conversation. Isabelle's laughter soothed his lonely soul, a stark contrast to Grace's recent contact where every discussion seemed like navigating a minefield. With Isabelle, it was just different. He couldn't remember the last time a woman had pursued him.

He recalled how, with Isabelle, there was an ease, an unspoken understanding that life was a series of free-flowing moments rather than a straight path to be followed. He doubted that she would make demands on him that he couldn't meet, nor would she expect him to rearrange his life on a whim. Instead, she shared her thoughts and listened to him with genuine interest. It almost felt too easy and too good to be true.

Erick smiled at the prospect of having her closer in his life. As the stars came out on the clear horizon, Erick felt calmer now and welcomed the promise of spring. He exited the Jeep and went inside the sanctuary of his cabin. He poured a cup of chamomile tea, sat on the couch, and picked up the remote. Jace greeted him by rubbing his body against Erick's legs.

"Hey buddy, I think you're going to like Isabelle," Erick whispered.

Jace looked at Erick and curled up next to his feet on the rug. Erick clicked through the channels, until one caught his attention. "The grand opening of Becker Publishing will take place this fall. We acquired FINNLondon, making us the biggest publishing house on the East Coast and in the U.K.," Brook said, wearing an icy grey pantsuit. Her blonde hair was up in a twist. Erick thought she looked older than he remembered.

"What can we expect from the new management?"

Before she could answer the commentator's question, Erick shut off the television in disgust. Everything Finn had told him was true, and it was clear that Brook never changed. She was always working at some sinister angle. Erick had known her since they were kids, and she had always wanted to be the center of attention at all costs. Sometimes, he believed people could never change unless they really wanted to. He was still angry with her carelessness and all the damage it had caused Daniel. He looked down at Jace who was the latest victim of her recklessness.

He climbed into bed, wondering what was next for him and Isabelle. He wondered if he was even capable of having a normal relationship and how soon all the jumbled feelings about Grace would fade. He had always prioritized his family at all costs, knowing it was the right thing to do. Unlike Grace,

Isabelle was pursuing *him* and now was even considering moving here for him. Maybe this time, things would finally be different.

Chapter 71

race returned to the church the following week. Even though she was skeptical when her therapist had initially recommended this grief group to her, she felt it was a perfect fit after meeting Scott and the other members. She wasn't ready to share her grief yet, but one day she felt she would. She walked over to the refreshment table when the aroma of fresh brewed coffee hit her like a wave. She closed her eyes and recalled being in California again with Pala and his coffee.

Then without warning the traumatic memories returned, always ending with Jack Stone falling over the cliff. That image was like an indelible scar on her brain. She placed her hand on the table to steady herself when she heard a male voice.

"Hey, you okay?"

She turned to see Scott looking pleased with himself.

"Yeah, just… memories."

"Good ones?" he asked, his eyebrows lifted.

"Complicated ones."

Scott paused, then held out a coffee cup with a lid on it, the word Champion was penned in black Sharpie. "I brought you a chai latte. A peace offering."

"A peace offering?"

"Yep. I know it's hard to believe, but I rigged the rock-paper-scissors game last time. I'm admitting defeat."

Grace raised an eyebrow. "You admit then that you cheated?"

"Only a little. But this?" He waved the cup. "This is all above board."

"Mighty generous of you."

"Thought you could use a little sweetness."

Grace's fingers brushed against his as she cautiously took the drink. Then without taking her eyes off Scott, she took a sip of the tea, which was really good, but she wasn't about to admit it to the tea thief himself.

"I promise it's not poisoned."

"Good to know." Grace felt the warmth of the cup on her hands.

"I'm just trying to make things lighter," he said, shrugging. He gestured around the room with one hand.

"It's hard to be light when you're weighed down by loss."

Grace let out a sigh.

"True," he replied. "But you're here, right? That's a start. You're taking the first step. Facing it."

"Maybe I'm just hiding behind a chai latte."

"Hey, whatever works."

His eyes glinted in the dim church lighting.

Grace smiled and took another sip. "This is good."

"Right? It's my secret weapon."

"Your secret weapon?" Grace inquired.

"Tea goes great with bad jokes and awkward moments." He smiled wide with his perfect white teeth.

"Sounds like a winning combination." Grace shot back, amused.

Scott chuckled. "Just don't tell anyone. I have a reputation to maintain."

"Sure, your secret is safe with me. 'The Great Chai Tea Thief,'" She giggled as she whispered the title.

"Exactly. I'm practically a legend." He flipped his hair back.

"Legends need more than just tea."

"True. They do need a good laugh now and then."

She looked down at the cup and confessed, "I haven't laughed this much lately."

"I get that. But it's okay to let it out, even just a little. Laughter shouldn't stop for grief. If you let it, they can coexist."

"Easier said than done." Grace looked at the faces as they filed into the room.

"I never said it was easy. But know that you're not alone."

"Thank you. That means a lot," Grace said, genuinely.

"Good. Now, how about we make a deal?" Scott's eyebrow raised slightly.

"Another deal? Not sure if I can trust you after what you pulled last time." She smoothed her hair self-consciously.

"Next week, if you come back, I'll take you to a real cafe, but only if you promise to bring that great smile of yours."

"Sounds fair."

"Deal then?"

"Does this work on all the women you hit on?" Grace challenged him, because this man had to be too good to be true.

"Nope, you're the first." Scott smiled wide.

"I see." She couldn't help but match his smile. "Deal. But I choose the place."

Scott smiled with a sense of mischief. "Just remember, I'm still the chai latte warrior."

"You mean *thief*. Let the record show that I was the true winner of the tea last time."

"Beautiful and sharp like a lawyer," Scott mused.

"Together, we'll be unstoppable." Grace surprised herself by being so forward. Who knew having a light conversation could be so exhilarating?

"Maybe we could be unstoppable at the cafe down the

street." They exchanged phone numbers and Scott said, "Text me the time that works, and I'll be there."

Grace crossed the room to dispose of her empty cup, and then turned back toward the circle of chairs. Her eyes saw the back of a man who looked familiar and her breath caught in her throat. The man turned, and to her horror, she came face to face with Finn. Immediately, she found a chair next to Scott and tried to regain her composure. She closed her eyes and folded her hands in her lap as she listened to the hum of hushed voices filling the room. The moderator started, but Grace's thoughts were still spinning. But then she heard Finn speak. He answered the group question about how to reconcile with those who have passed.

She reopened her eyes and focused on Finn, who sat across from her, a shadow of the man she once knew. Grace could not look away and was oddly drawn to him as his voice wavered with the weight of unshed tears when he spoke. His vulnerability was captivating.

"I don't know how to forgive my father, now that he's gone," Finn confessed, tracing the outline of an old, circular scar on his forearm. "I have the scars to remember him by, but what I don't get is how I can still be grieving over a man who did this to me."

Grace watched the tremor in Finn's hand as he paused, the scars on his forearm stark against his pale skin. She felt a strange twist in her heart, an unexpected surge of compassion cutting through all layers of resentment and hurt. Their shared past was also marked by Finn's own abusive outbursts toward her, a toxic cycle that had once seemed unbreakable. Yet, here he was, vulnerable, laying bare the quiet parts of his heart.

"Declan was my dad," Finn continued, his gaze lifting now to meet hers. "Sure, he had his demons, but I keep thinking about the good days, you know?"

Grace nodded slowly. Her own grief was just as complex. She understood the conflict and how love could be warped into something almost unrecognizable yet somehow remain love. Once the meeting ended, she immediately slipped out of the room. She didn't want to talk to Finn; and as much as she liked Scott, she wasn't sure if she could ever come back here again.

Chapter 72

Erick left his cabin and drove to Isabelle's hotel. He watched as she gracefully walked through the automatic doors wearing jeans and a light blue sweater. She kept her puffer jacket folded over one arm because the weather was warmer than they expected.

"Hey," Isabelle said as she got into the Jeep.

"Ready?" Erick asked.

"Always!" Isabelle's smile filled the small space.

Erick put the Jeep in gear and contemplated how to start the conversation. "I'm sorry. I never apologized for leaving you in Boston. I never got to explain that I had something to deal with."

"I assume it had something to do with your ex-girlfriend Grace, the redhead," Isabelle said smugly.

"Yeah, I had to find out why she was there and resolve a few things. As I said before, things didn't work out for us in the end."

"Sometimes it's best to leave the past in the past," she said simply, as if it were that easy.

As he braked in front of Daniel and Sky's apartment, he thought about her words. Sky was already outside and down the ramp when she approached the car, and her gaze immediately landed on the passenger seat. Erick hoped they would be okay with his bringing Isabelle instead of Grace.

"Hi Erick," Sky said and then hugged her friend. "Isabelle! I didn't know you were still in town." Sky looked back up at the ramp. "By the way, Daniel's coming. You should sit back here with me." She gestured toward Isabelle to move to the back seat.

Erick gripped the wheel, trying not to notice Daniel and Sky as they exchanged confused glances. He could feel the awkward tension build as Isabelle made her way to the back.

Daniel turned and looked back at Isabelle, raising an eyebrow.

"Got everything, Daniel?" Erick asked pointedly, his eyes conveying a silent message to Daniel that he would not be answering any questions about the date change tonight.

"Yeah. Hello, Isabelle." Putting any judgment aside, Daniel seamlessly changed the subject. "Are you excited about the game and to cheer on Coach Michael?"

"Who's this guy, Michael, and what does he coach?" Isabelle asked.

"Actually, Michael was one of my former patients. He joined the team as an assistant coach mid-season. I thought it would be cool for us all to watch how the team plays with him."

"Erick, is there anyone's life you haven't touched in this small town?" Isabelle was curious.

"Don't let my brother fool you. He isn't that perfect!" Daniel joked.

"Are you done, Daniel?" Erick frowned, but Isabelle chuckled, clearly enjoying the banter. He shook his head, trying to stay focused on the road. "We're here to support the team."

"Of course, Erick, but you need to lighten up and not be so serious about everything. We're here to have fun and see a great game. Rule number one of having fun is not to be so moody! Yes, Erick, that means you. Rule number two: No matter what happens, there will be no frowning tonight. You're an old man now, and all that frowning will eventually make you a curmudgeon one day with even more wrinkles. Tonight is about these kids who have overcome significant adversity. Rule number three: Listen closely, Isabelle. This is important. Doctor 'Too Good' has many followers over here. Don't be discouraged if people throw themselves at him. Just like in the days of Jesus, people will try to touch his garments in hopes of instant healing."

"Seriously, Daniel? Isabelle doesn't need you to give her the play-by-play of my life. And no one thinks I'm Jesus, for God's sake!"

"My brother is so humble. Remember that one time—"

"No, no trips down memory lane!" Erick shook his head rapidly trying to squash this head on.

Daniel tilted his head and smiled. "I mean, he ruminated about everything since we were kids. This isn't major news."

Erick rolled his eyes but couldn't be too angry because he knew Daniel was doing his best to compensate and make light of a situation that might otherwise be more awkward for them all.

"Okay, okay. I'm not uptight all the time," Erick insisted.

Sky choked out a laugh and scoffed, " Just… most of the time."

Isabelle leaned in closer to Sky, whispering loud enough for everyone to hear, "I think he's just learning how to have fun."

Daniel's eyebrows raised in mock surprise. "True, this is a first. Look at you, Erick! Getting all social and stuff. What's next? Karaoke?"

Erick tried to stifle a laugh because he did not want to encourage this awful conversation.

"No karaoke. Nope."

Sky giggled, and Isabelle nudged her.

"Come on, Sky!" Isabelle exclaimed, joining in on the teasing. "We could get him to sing 'Sweet Caroline.'"

"Oh! That would be amazing!" Sky clapped her hands to-ed

egory

Erick glanced back with mock horror in his eyes. "You guys aren't helping my case here."

Isabelle laughed, clearly enjoying the camaraderie. "Honestly, I think it's great. You need to let loose, Erick."

Daniel nodded with a serious look on his face and then chimed in. "Yeah, man. Life's too short to be serious all the time. Especially today! We're going to watch these amazing kids play their hearts out."

"And we get to be part of it!" Sky exclaimed.

Erick finally relaxed and let the excitement seep in. "You're right. Let's just enjoy the game tonight."

Daniel leaned toward the back, a cheeky grin on his face. "You're not going to get all weepy and moody if they lose, are ya?"

Erick shot him a playful glare. "No promises. Good thing you didn't forget the snacks, though!"

"Snacks *do* make everything better," Daniel replied.

Erick navigated the Jeep into the almost full parking lot, the energy around him filled with anticipation. He took a deep breath, a smile building on his face as he glanced in the rearview mirror one last time.

"I'm really happy to be spending time with you guys," Erick said.

"Aw, look at that! Erick's getting sentimental," Daniel teased.

"Not sentimental. Just maybe not so uptight for once."

Erick shot him a glare.

"That's a win, right?" Sky continued the teasing as Daniel pretended to write the score down.

"Erick, not uptight… Call the press. Better yet, should we call a medic?" Daniel jabbed his brother playfully in the arm.

Isabelle laughed, and Erick finally let his guard down.

"You guys are something else. Now can we please focus on finding a parking spot!" Erick begged them.

The Jeep hit a speed bump just then, and Daniel bounced slightly. "Whoa! Keep it steady, Erick."

314

"I think we're all safe. We're practically invincible!" Isabelle declared.

Erick glanced at her, and his expression softened. "Yeah, invincible. I like that."

Daniel looked around with mischief in his eyes as he looked back at Isabelle. "So, Isabelle, if you're invincible, do you think you can handle Erick's extremely uptight nature?"

Sky gasped and pretended to be shocked. "Oh no, the ultimate test!"

Isabelle bit her lip, trying not to laugh. "I guess we'll find out."

Erick shook his head while he tried to find a perfect parking spot. "You guys are too much."

"Here we go! Let's get this game on." Sky punched the air with her fist.

"Yes! Let's do this!" Isabelle cheered.

He allowed himself a small smile, and his heart swelled with this new version of family. He was grateful not just for the camaraderie of this new family but also for the hope this new beginning could bring—the future Erick had desperately prayed for. It wasn't how he planned it at all, but that is how God works sometimes, in unexpected ways.

Chapter 73

Grace finally finished writing her memoir about Raven's life and sent her manuscript to the editor. She glanced at her watch and closed her laptop. Her mind was still tangled in thoughts of Erick and Finn and the chaos that seemed to follow them. A soft sigh escaped her lips when Scott came into her mind. She found his wit a refreshing change of pace in her otherwise stressed life. The room around her felt too quiet and still, and she wondered what was next for her.

She picked up her remote when suddenly a stiff, steady knock on the door jolted Grace from her reverie, sending a flutter of nervousness throughout her body. For a moment, she was afraid it was Finn, but it could also be Erick who might have changed his mind, come to his senses, and realized he had made a terrible mistake. She stared at the door and wondered if she should hide, but her curiosity won in the end. Ripping the bandaid off, she threw the remote on the coffee table and jumped up to answer the door.

"Julie? What in the world are you doing here?" Grace was

stunned when she pulled the door open and saw her old friend.

"Come on, we're going out tonight, and it's my treat!" Julie declared, her voice vibrant with an energy that seemed alien to Grace's current mood. "I haven't seen you in a while, and we need to catch up. I want all the details about California, Erick, and Boston too. I know just the place, and I promised a client I'd go." Grace's heart clenched at the mention of Erick's name.

"Julie, I—" Grace started, but the words caught in her throat.

Understanding crossed Julie's face. "Hey, it's okay," she said softly, squeezing Grace's arm. "We don't have to talk about Erick if you don't want to."

But they both knew they would eventually. Erick was the knot in Grace's life that desperately needed untying, and she was one of the friends Grace could count on to understand. Julie was there for her after the accident in the hospital.

Grace hesitated, but only for a moment and then grabbed her jacket. "Sure, I could use a night out."

Grace was able to relax as Julie's Subaru glided over the road. The soft light from the yellow streetlamps illuminated the road, and Grace stared out the window, lost in thought. Julie was the first to break the silence.

"So what exactly happened in California?" Julie asked as she stopped at the traffic light.

"I thought I could find my father and bring justice for my mother. Instead, I found... Jack Stone."

"Jack Stone? Is he your father?"

Grace shrugged. "I still don't know for sure. But things got really intense. At first, I was hopeful I would find out the truth. But then, everything escalated and spiraled out of control. Then Jack... He just wouldn't back off."

"What happened?"

"He tried to push me off a cliff, but he was the one who fell instead. I didn't push him, but I couldn't save him either." Grace sighed.

"Grace, that's not your fault," Julie said matter-of-factly. "Did you at least find out anything about who your real dad might be?" Julie glanced over in Grace's direction.

Grace looked away. "He gave me a copy of the paternity test, but I still don't know if it was real."

Grace couldn't help thinking about Jack Stone's DNA report. According to that document, he was Grace's biological father, but she didn't want to believe something so terrible. No, she had to focus on what she knew in her heart—it didn't matter who her real father was when she had such love surrounding her from Robin and Pala.

"I met my mother's amazing boyfriend, Pala, at my book signing event. He was the one who bought me a ticket to San Diego. There's a chance he's my dad, and I really liked getting to know him. It's almost like… he knew what I needed before *I* did. And he wanted to protect me, keep me safe. It felt like what a father would do, you know?"

"That's interesting. Did he say anything about him being your dad?"

"Not directly. We submitted a DNA test, but I don't know if any of that matters. I haven't even called him since I've been home."

"I get that," Julie said, nodding her head. "But you have to focus on how far you've come. No matter who your dad is, you're going to be okay. Whenever you feel unsure of the future, just think about the impossible odds you had to overcome just last year."

"That was a dark time," Grace said. "You helped me through it and gave me a glimpse of who I really was." Grace looked at Julie and felt grateful for their relationship. "Hey, how is your mom doing?"

Julie turned down a side street. "She's in a nursing home now. It's been hard."

"I'm sorry," Grace said.

"I was about to accept a new position as a traveling nurse, but I'm postponing that for now so I can be near her. I'd take her home, but she needs round-the-clock care."

"You'll figure it out. I'm so glad we have each other to lean on."

"Agreed. So, what's next for you?" Julie stopped at an intersection. "You and the Doc together now? And how was Boston?"

"I don't want to talk about Boston. Erick and I just didn't work out. All I feel now is this pull to keep moving. The last few years have made me realize I must make it a priority to focus on myself. Not to focus on a man who might not put me first. Everything has changed since I came back."

Grace didn't know where they were going but continued to reminisce. This was exactly what she needed tonight. It wasn't until the structure of a middle school loomed into view, its parking lot filled with vehicles under the glow of streetlights, that Grace returned to the present.

Julie pulled into an empty spot, and as she turned off the engine, an uneasy silence settled between them. Grace's eyes narrowed as a vehicle drove slowly past and parked several rows over—a rugged Jeep just like the one Erick drove. Her heart stopped.

"Hey, look at that!" Julie pointed at the vehicle. "Isn't that Dr. Finn's Jeep?"

Grace felt a chill run down her spine. Her eyes narrowed as she scrutinized the vehicle, recognizing the weathered labrador decal on the side window. It was the same Jeep. The reality of Erick being there, possibly just yards away from her, reignited the anxiety she had been trying so hard to ignore. She fought against the sudden urge to run away and be anywhere else but here. But it was too late; they were already here, and the night had just begun.

Chapter 74

Erick parked the Jeep, removed his seatbelt, and helped everyone out. The trio followed behind Daniel to the side entrance and down the hallway to the gymnasium. Isabelle followed Daniel, but Sky hung back with a confused look.

"What happened with Grace?" she mouthed softly to Erick.

"Not now, Sky. I'll tell you later." Erick quickly caught up to Daniel and Isabelle. He pulled open the heavy gymnasium doors so everyone could navigate the entrance easily. Once inside, a wave of heat enveloped them. The strong scent of polyethylene floor wax and the unmistakable smell of sweating teenagers assaulted their senses.

"Ah, the smell of athletes!" Daniel exclaimed.

"What a goofball!" Sky said, letting out a laugh before kissing Daniel's cheek. "Only you would say that."

"Michael needed a second chance, more than you know," Erick said, as he spotted his former patient from across the court. He watched as the young assistant coach held his clipboard and reviewed plays with the head coach.

"Everyone needs something to drive them forward," Daniel replied, rolling alongside him. "For Michael, it's the game; for you…"

Erick knew he was referring to his complicated relationship status.

"Give it a rest, Daniel. Let's focus on the game," he deflected. It was too soon to be fielding questions about his love life. This was not the time or place.

"Whatever you say," Daniel agreed, though his eyes held a knowing glint. They scanned a perfect spot on the bleachers, the crowd's excitement filling the room. "You're ruminating again."

"Great night, right?" Sky shouted in Isabelle's direction, and Erick was glad for the diversion in the conversation.

"Absolutely," Isabelle said with awe as she watched the young kids warming up.

The rhythmic thumping of basketballs and squeaky sneakers on the polished floor echoed through the school gymnasium. Sky took her seat in the second row of the bleachers, and Daniel rolled his chair to the end of the row next to her. Then Isabelle and Erick sat down. The worn wooden seats creaked, and the anticipation hung in the air like a thick cloud.

"Look at them go," Daniel remarked, his voice lost against all the noise and commotion.

Erick's eyes scanned the activity on the court. He couldn't help but smile when Michael glanced over from the sidelines and waved in his direction. Their eyes held the acknowledgment of a journey traveled together, one that led them both here to this moment. He also knew that God was the reason behind this transformation.

"Looks like Michael's fitting in just fine," Daniel commented, easing his wheelchair slightly forward for a better view.

"Yea—" Erick started to respond when a woman approached the side of the bleachers.

"Excuse me!" a voice came from behind Daniel. Sky stood up, and then Isabelle stood quickly to allow a woman through, but the woman stopped short by Erick. He rose to his feet and then the woman bumped into his side. He looked over to address the situation and found himself face to face with the young woman whose vibrant pink and blonde hair bob swished around her shoulders.

"Hi, I'm Sandra!" she exclaimed, a broad smile revealing her excitement.

"Hello there," Erick replied, momentarily caught off guard. He glanced briefly at Isabelle, who was immediately curious but remained silent, letting Erick navigate this woman himself. He was completely aware of Daniel's eyes on him, knowing he'd have a field day with this later.

Sandra exuded an effervescent energy, and Erick was unsure if he knew this woman. He had seen many people in his practice, but he was sure he would have remembered her. Still, he could not place her face. "Are you here to cheer on the team?" Erick inquired, finding himself intrigued despite the initial disruption.

Her eyes sparkled with enthusiasm. "Absolutely! This game is going to be epic!"

Erick nodded, "They've all worked hard and deserve a good crowd."

"Couldn't agree more," she said, returning her attention to the court, where the players took their positions. The sharp whistle of the referee commanded attention, and then the announcer's voice declared the start of the game. The crowd quieted, the teams took their positions, and the opening buzzer blared. The excitement of the game was underway as the teams dribbled back and forth. The shrill of the referee's whistle sliced through the mounting tension, signaling a timeout.

"He told me what you did for him," Sandra said, her eyes on Erick. "Because of people like you, Michael has a renewed sense of purpose. I wanted to thank you in person for believing in miracles. You're part of his miracle, you know."

The crowd noise grew as the game heated up, yet he felt a sharp pang of internal conflict. He always had a hard time dealing with the praise from past clients. "Michael's come a long way," Erick managed to say, his words barely rising above the cheers as the basketball thudded against the hardwood floor. "Michael, he's the one who put in the effort." Erick gestured toward the court where Michael was intensely observing the players. "All I did was introduce him to Coach Richard."

"I'm going to marry that man. Leg or no leg, he's the most incredible person I've ever met." A whistle cut through their conversation, and the referee called a foul on the floor. Erick's eyes lingered on Michael, who was rallying his team with a passion that resonated deeply within him. Erick leaned forward to see the Highland Huskies execute a flawless play. The ball arced through the air, swishing through the net, and the scoreboard flickered with the addition of two points.

"I'm so happy for you both," Erick shouted, but the thundering applause of the crowd drowned out his words. Seeing Michael on the sidelines, whistle in hand and shouting encouragement to his team was like witnessing a man reborn.

"I'll see you after the game!" Sandra finally moved past Isabelle to another section of bleachers above.

"It's like being with a celebrity," Isabelle shouted into Erick's ear, squeezing his hand.

"He is a celebrity around here!" Sky shouted. And they all sat back and enjoyed the game that was underway.

Chapter 75

Grace felt the weight of Julie's gaze as she unbuckled her seatbelt. They sat there momentarily, and then they both stepped out of the car.

"Of all the places," Grace muttered under her breath and into the chilly wind. "I think this town isn't big enough for us anymore."

Julie rounded the car to join her, eyebrows raised in concern. "Trouble in paradise?" Her voice was a soft, gentle nudge for Grace to share her thoughts.

Grace exhaled into the cool night air. The tightness in her chest had yet to subside. "You could say that," she conceded, her voice carrying the weight of unspoken old wounds.

Julie reached out and touched Grace's arm, causing her to stop in her tracks. "Come on, you can tell me all about it inside." Her smile was bright in the dimly lit lot. "I got tickets from a co-worker, and it's for a good cause. I thought we could have some fun for a change, but we don't have to stay if you don't want to. The Grace I know, though, would never run from a challenge!"

Erick wouldn't expect her to be here, and maybe they could enjoy an uneventful night out. Grace walked forward because Julie was right about her. She would not back down from a challenge. She had every right to be there.

When Grace entered the gymnasium, she was jolted back into the present by the shrill referee's whistle and the sound of a basketball game in full play. Her gaze instinctively swept across the bleachers, and as if by magnetic force, she found Erick among the crowd. The game on the court was a whirlwind of energy. The boys maneuvered their wheelchairs with impressive agility, fiercely battling for the basketball and victory.

Grace saw that Erick's attention was glued to the game, and his ordinarily stoic face was animated with excitement. Her lips twisted wryly when she noticed Isabelle by his side, which shouldn't have surprised her. Still, she wondered how he could move on so fast if he truly loved her the way he said he did.

A tightness constricted Grace's throat. She turned, feeling the walls closing in around her. "I'm sorry, Julie. I can't do this. I need to get some air." She choked out the words with an urgency that couldn't be ignored. Without waiting for a response, Grace pivoted on her heel, leaving behind the echoes of the game. Somehow Erick had suddenly become America's most sought-after bachelor. She stepped outside as the brisk evening air hit Grace's face with the sharpness of a slap. The warm, sunny breeze earlier in the day was gone, which was not unusual for March in New England. She wrapped her arms around herself as she strode back through the parking lot under the pale glow of streetlights.

Julie emerged from the gymnasium and caught up to Grace. "What exactly is going on?"

Grace stopped and turned to Julie. "I just can't do this again. Not with Erick," she said, her voice low. "He made his choice, and has effectively cut me out of his life!" Her words held the weight of unspoken sacrifices and the ache of being relegated to the background of someone else's priorities. "We broke up before we even got started, and now he has women falling all over him, including Isabelle!" The night was silent, filled only by the distant cheering echo inside the gym.

"Who's Isabelle?"

"I went to Boston to surprise him, but he was with her. He denied anything romantic, but I found her bracelet in the suite the night before we drove home together."

Julie's eyes widened. "Whoa, really?"

"I can't make him choose me," she confessed, her voice trembling with raw emotion. "I'm still trying to process all my family issues, including Jack falling off a cliff. Plus, I'm still processing all the stuff Finn did to me in the last decade." She turned away, staring into the darkness, willing her tears to stay put. "I just can't deal with Erick helping with Finn's sobriety now, which is why we can't be together."

Julie reached out, placing a gentle hand on Grace's shoulder. It was a touch that spoke volumes about their friendship. "Grace," Julie said, "that's quite a lot to handle. Have you thought about therapy?"

Exhaling, Grace turned back to face Julie, her gaze steady. "Yes," she admitted, scoffing. "I went to see Dr. Hopkins already, but it'll take more than a couple of sessions to unravel all of this. I went to a grief counseling group a few times as well. I met someone there, but I haven't reached out to him. Also, I saw Finn there."

"Okay, that's a lot to process," Julie said. She frowned. "Finn was at your grief group? That must have been awful. Wait, you met someone there?"

"It was awful seeing Finn again after all this time. Yes, I met a widower named Scott, who has been so supportive and funny." Grace smiled despite her mood.

"Scott? Wow, this is a turn of events. I think going to group therapy for grief is smart."

Grace managed a nod, appreciating the support. It was exactly what Grace needed to hear. "I don't think either of us is looking for anything serious."

"Hmm. I can't wait to meet this Scott!" Julie started walking toward the car. "Come on, let's get out of here."

When they reached Julie's car, Grace slid into the passenger seat. In the quietness of the car, she turned toward Julie. "Thank you," she said. "For tonight. For everything. Sorry we had to leave early."

"I'm starving anyways!" Julie conceded. "Let's go to the cafe and catch up."

As they drove, Grace leaned back against the headrest, closing her eyes for a brief moment, feeling a sense of gratitude for Julie's friendship. Julie had been the one who always stood beside her when others left her behind. With Julie's unwavering support, she realized she was on the path to healing, and eventually, better tomorrows, which may or may not include a handsome stranger named Scott. Only time would tell.

Chapter 76

Erick thought his mind was playing tricks on him when out of the corner of his eye he saw someone who looked like Grace enter the gym. He didn't think it could even be possible because she made it all too clear after their conversation the other night that she wanted nothing to do with him. He'd grown tired of their dance, and when he looked at Isabelle now, he knew it was better for everyone involved if he just moved on.

He had been engrossed in the game and was having a good time cheering as the game went into the second half. Suddenly, the final buzzer sounded, confirming the Huskies' victorious comeback. The final basket sealing the win sent the boys into a wave of action. The team raced onto the court with a Gatorade cooler hoisted high above their heads. Erick watched in awe as they tipped it over their coaches. The icy waterfall drenched Michael and Coach Richard in a sticky orange victory.

"Look at them," Daniel said with admiration. "I'm truly inspired by what some of these kids have overcome."

"Way to go Huskies!" Sky screamed, clearly excited about

the win as the entire crowd stood, the cheering nearly deafening as it echoed throughout the gym.

Erick recalled just how close to death Michael was when he met him at the hospital several weeks ago. Seeing a complete turnaround was nothing short of a miracle. Michael caught Erick's eye across the court, and a silent exchange passed between them—a nod from Michael, a thumbs-up from Erick. It was a moment acknowledging their mutual respect. Erick didn't just see a coach drenched in Gatorade; he saw a man who had fought his way out of depression and into the light of purpose and passion. The team was more than happy. They were inspired, and Michael was a part of that. The sight of it filled Erick with hope. This was about victory as much as it was about second chances.

"What did you think?" Erick asked Isabelle as she wrapped her arms around him while the team began to file off the court.

"It was exciting. You'll have to tell me more because I feel like I walked into a movie halfway through! I'm guessing you inspired that coach to do something he didn't think he could." Isabelle's eyes sparkled, and Erick kissed her in the excitement. It was if he didn't have a care in the world about who was watching.

"You know I can't. Doctor-patient confidentiality. But I am proud of him." He turned toward the court with his arm around Isabelle. He'd enjoyed their time together in Boston, and now it felt like they'd been a couple for a long time. They seemed to be a perfect fit.

As Michael approached their spot at the bleachers, Erick let go of Isabelle to clap Michael on the back. The joy on the young coach's face was more radiant than the championship trophy they'd just won.

"Congratulations on the win, dude!" Daniel said to Michael.

"Great game, Coach!" Erick said sincerely. "You've done something remarkable here."

"Couldn't have done it without you, man," Michael replied genuinely. Erick could only smile in response, knowing full well that the true strength had always been within Michael. "Who is this beautiful woman by your side?"

"This is Isabelle," Erick said proudly.

Micheal's knowing eyes flashed.

"Ah!" He respectfully grasped Isabelle's hand as if he were meeting the First Lady. "Guess we all got a second chance at love. It is my ultimate pleasure to meet you, miss."

"Great game! The pleasure is all mine." Isabelle smiled back at Michael.

"Guess we both got our happy ending. Miracles are all around us!" He winked at Erick. "I see you've met Sandra!"

"We did!" Sandra interjected as she approached the group. "I have to take my man to a celebration party. You are all welcome to come and join the team!" she shouted over the crowd, which was now dispersing out the exits.

"That's okay, we can't stay," Erick said to both of them. "It was lovely to meet you, Sandra."

Michael swung his arm back and fiercely locked hands with Erick in a high-five. Michael left with Sandra as they caught up with the team and Coach Richard who held the large trophy. An unexpected sense of contentment filled Erick's heart as he watched Michael and Sandra disappear into the swell of well-wishers. Building this kind of hope in others was what God had called him to do.

Erick, Isabelle, Sky, and Daniel weaved their way through the crowd and out of the gym as the sounds of celebration echoed behind them. Today was about the Huskies and every soul brave enough to rise above their circumstances. Erick carried that spirit with him as he stepped out into the chilly evening air.

Once everyone was settled into the Jeep, the feeling of excitement returned as they drove back to HigherGround. Nothing was more refreshing and humbling than watching people overcome adversity and celebrate a victory game. He couldn't help but steal glances at Isabelle from the back seat and felt grateful for her support.

The car ride seemed to fly by as they chatted about the

game, with occasional bursts of laughter and playful teasing. After dropping off Sky and Daniel, Erick drove Isabelle back to the hotel, walked her to the door, and pulled her into a passionate kiss.

"I really like it here, Erick. I've decided to give Connecticut a chance. I'm heading back to Boston tomorrow, but I wanted you to know that I put a deposit down on an apartment this morning." Isabelle pulled back briefly. "I move in a few weeks."

"That sounds amazing!"

Erick finally felt that things were falling into place and now there was something he could look forward to. It helped that Isabelle was pursuing him, and it felt amazing as the night whispered promises of an unwritten future ahead.

Chapter 77

"**G**race," Scott called out as she entered the small church room for the grief group meeting. She had decided that Finn was not going to get in her way. Never again.

"Hello, Scott. Nice to see you again." Grace tried to smile. "It's been a minute."

"I'm sorry I didn't get to text you. Work had me all over the state covering stories."

"It's okay. I had a busy week as well. Stories? Are you a journalist?" Grace asked, intrigued.

"Yes, I have a column in the Hartford Courant." Scott looked down at his phone which buzzed over and over. "Sorry, I gotta take this. See you at the meeting."

The meeting started, and Scott found his seat to the right of her. Finn took the seat on her left. Grace sat there frozen, trying to take in another speaker's experience with their loss. She tried not to look over at Finn, but the smell of his cologne, bergamot and cedar, clung to the air, stirring memories she tried to forget. Her face flushed in annoyance that he had shown up to her place of healing. *Why does he have to sit next to me?*

After the meeting, she quickly got up. "I have to go, Scott. Feel free to text me when you have the time," she said with more sarcasm than she had planned.

Scott nodded, and Grace couldn't escape the room fast enough. But then Finn stopped her.

"Grace, please, stop. Just for a second." He reached out for her arm. "Please!"

"You don't get to touch me," she said firmly.

"I apologize." He removed his hand from her elbow and raised his hands in surrender. "But would you consider a moment to talk with me? There's a coffee shop just around the corner."

She eyed him skeptically, wary of reopening old wounds. She sighed, and even though everything in her screamed for her to run, she conceded. "Fine." She gritted her teeth. It's not like he would do anything publicly, and something about him did seem different. Grace was curious what he could possibly want from her. "I'll meet you there."

Once they were seated, he ordered coffee, and she had an iced tea. The waitress came over immediately with filled cups and placed down creamers and sugar. Neither said anything for several minutes as Grace narrowed her eyes at Finn wondering what he could possibly say.

"Remember when you first moved into the loft?" Finn asked, stirring sugar in his coffee absentmindedly.

Grace let out a soft laugh, which surprised her. "How could I forget? Those suites cost seven million dollars." The loft had represented a new life for her and it all had started with him.

"Those early days at NYU," Finn reminisced, a wistful glint in his eyes. "I used to love visiting you on campus."

Grace squeezed the lemon in her iced tea as her thoughts drifted back. "You were relentless," she admitted. "I was happy living in the dorm, free and self-sufficient."

"That's what I loved about you. But of course I was able to change your mind if you recall?" Finn said, leaning forward.

"After you moved in we started our life together."

The assistant job at FINNLondon had been a golden opportunity for Grace to enter the world of publishing. She'd only dreamed of it until this point. He had offered her a future, a partnership both in business and life, and she'd finally be a published author. But of course, that turned out to be one of many promises he wouldn't keep.

"Things were simpler then," Grace murmured, lost in the nostalgia of what had once been.

Finn met her gaze, a silent acknowledgment passing between them. They both knew the destructive path their story had taken.

Grace watched Finn's hands as he folded and unfolded a small, crumpled napkin. They had been laughing moments before, reminiscing about the extravagant dinners and the shopping sprees with purchases from the most exclusive boutiques. She wondered if he had a point in all of this.

"Everything was perfect," Finn sighed, his voice trailing off. He looked out of the window, his eyes focusing on something distant, unseeable. "Until my father got sick."

She remembered those days, too, the creeping dread that filled their loft. Declan's illness had been the turning point of their relationship, but it was what came after that broke them.

"Declan… he despised your influence over me," Finn confessed. "He thought you were pulling me away from him and the family business."

"Is that why—"Grace started to ask but stopped herself. She knew the reason behind Finn's demise. "That was no excuse for what you did."

"I know. It was the pressure," Finn continued. "It became too much. I couldn't please him. I couldn't be who he wanted me to be. So I drank. I drank a lot." His voice was remorseful, and Grace could hear the shame in his voice. "And then I snapped. It wasn't what you deserved. I cheated on you after making you chief editor—a position you earned, by the way, and not because you were with me. I was a coward, honestly.

I couldn't stand up to my father or the bottle. You were, uh, you *are* an amazing writer, Grace. I regret not publishing your first novel. Know that I always believed in you. I did read the one you published last year, *If You Only Knew,* and it was simply brilliant! I've always been envious that you had life figured out. You deserved a better partner and after reading your book, I realized that I failed you in so many ways. I'm truly sorry with all my being. I hope one day you will be able to forgive me, but I understand if you can't."

Grace felt the weight of his confession settle between them, heavy and suffocating. She reached out tentatively, her hand over his clenched fist.

Finn's hand relaxed, and he turned it over to grasp hers briefly, then let go. "I'm newly sober," he said, finally looking at her with clarity in his blue eyes, which she hadn't seen in years. "I want to be clear though. I'm not trying to get back together or anything. My divorce isn't finalized, and I can't afford to think about any new relationships for a while—I need to focus on staying clean and rebuilding myself. Besides," Finn breathed out, as if the words physically pained him, "I know for a fact that Erick is still in love with you. And... I wouldn't want to come between that again, not after everything he has done for me."

"Thank you for telling me, Finn," Grace finally said, doubtful that Erick cared at all at this point. "I'm glad to hear that your sobriety is important. But you should know that Erick has moved on, and it's time for me to do the same. I was thinking about traveling and might even return to California."

Finn nodded. "You have to do what you need to do. I just wanted to let you know how sorry I am for what happened between us. I take full responsibility for all that went wrong. I know I don't deserve your forgiveness."

"I'll keep that in mind. Thank you for the honest conversation. It couldn't have been easy for you."

"Thank you for listening, Grace." Finn stood up. "This is on me." He dropped some bills on the table. "I won't take up any more of your time. I hope you and Erick find your way back together. Isabelle doesn't hold a candle to you, by the way. Take care of yourself."

"Take care of yourself, too, Finn," she replied, watching him walk away, feeling the closure that she didn't know how much she needed until just now.

Chapter 78

Erick spent the weekend moving Finn into Daniel's guest room. The timing worked out. Isabelle was still in Boston packing, and she'd told him she didn't need any help for now.

"How are you and Grace doing?" Finn asked Erick as they stood together looking at the pile of Finn's life's belongings spread out in the tiny space.

"We're not doing anything. It's over." Erick said, setting down the final cardboard box labeled 'Misc.' He never wanted to tell Finn that the real reason for his breakup was because of him. Especially not now when his twin brother was standing amidst the remnants of what was left of his life. "I think this is it."

"I can't believe I'm homeless," Finn murmured. The sound of the busy parking lot next door at HigherGround filtered through the open window.

"Still better than where Brook would have put you," Erick responded as he leaned against the doorframe, arms folded, watching his brother's gaze linger on each unpacked box as if hoping they'd reveal a way out of this mess.

Finn sighed. "Brook was bad news from the beginning, but I couldn't see it while I was still in my addiction. Alcohol cost me everything." There was a gravity to his words because of the upcoming court case that threatened their family's legacy with the future of FINNLondon publishing hanging in the balance.

"Brook's lawsuit is ridiculous," Erick added quietly.

"Ridiculous or not, it's effective." Finn's eyes were glassy, reflecting defeat. "All because I couldn't… " The sentence was left unfinished, and Erick could see Finn getting choked up by the acknowledgment of his failures.

"Hey," Erick interjected, pushing off from the doorway. "You're doing what you need to do now. That's what counts."

Finn glanced at the gold watch his father had given him, and a subtle change flickered across his face. "I have my AA meeting to get to tonight."

"Good," Erick said with a nod. "You need the support, especially now. Moving is a big change."

"Yeah. One day at a time, right?" Finn offered a smile, the first genuine expression Erick had seen all afternoon.

"Exactly. One day at a time."

Silence stretched between them. Erick knew full well Finn's path ahead was long. But he was proud of his brother for making the right choice.

"So, after all these years pining after Grace, you couldn't make it work?" Finn asked, suddenly changing the subject.

"No, we couldn't. Besides, Isabelle and I are together now. She's planning to move here actually."

"Isabelle. Really?" Finn's tone was calm, but his eyes said more. "The girl from Daniel's wedding? She's going to move here from Boston?"

"Yes, Finn, she was living in Boston, but she's looking for a change and she wants to be near me." Erick was getting tired of explaining himself to everyone.

"But you've been in love with Grace since high school! This doesn't make any sense to me."

This was a minefield of a conversation that Erick needed to avoid. "It just didn't work," Erick said. "Why do you keep asking about her?"

"Because I think the real reason you two aren't together is because of me."

Erick winced and chose his words carefully. "Not entirely." He exhaled. It was only partially the truth. "We wanted different things. It's better this way." The dealbreaker was her wanting him to walk away from his family.

Finn nodded slowly, seeming to accept the answer, but Erick could tell that Finn was not entirely convinced.

"We all need to move on," Erick suggested, steering away from the dangerous topic of Grace. "You should get ready for your meeting tonight." He glanced at his phone. "Do you need a ride?"

Finn's eyes were tired, but there was a flicker of resolve. "Yeah," he answered with a slow nod. "My assets are frozen so I no longer have access to the car service."

"Come on. Let's go." Erick nudged Finn out the door. The drive was silent, each lost in their own thoughts. When they finally arrived at the community center, Finn gave Erick a tight-lipped smile before stepping out into the evening air.

Erick joined Finn to offer him support. After the meeting, Finn went to the table for a donut and coffee. He returned with a green tea for Erick, who noticed that Finn appeared slightly more grounded than before.

"Here. You still like that gross green tea?"

"Yup." Erick was surprised Finn remembered anything but himself. It was just more proof that his brother was turning over a new leaf.

"Can we go to the lawyer's office next?" Finn asked when they got into the Jeep again. "I just need to pick up a box of documents for the case and they're open late tonight. It won't take too long."

The ride was short, and when they pulled up outside the brick building, Erick turned off the engine. "I'll wait here. Hey, wasn't there another stop you need to get to?"

"Yes, I've got grief counseling after this. I'll catch a ride back with someone after." Finn seemed distracted.

"Are you sure? It's no trouble—" Erick began, but Finn raised a hand.

"I don't want to be a burden, Erick." Finn's gaze was steady, the set of his jaw determined. "I need to start doing some things on my own."

Erick nodded. "Okay, but you can call me if you need anything. Anything at all."

"Will do," Finn promised, stepping out onto the sidewalk. He didn't look back as he entered the building, leaving Erick alone with his thoughts about how he would navigate things once Isabelle returned and moved into town.

Chapter 79

Grace stepped into Café Bella a few days after Scott had suggested they meet. Her heart pounded. What was she doing going out on a date with this stranger? The jingle of the bell over the door when she walked in signaled that there was no turning back.

She spotted Scott sitting in the same booth she and Erick had sat in many times. He was grinning like a kid in a candy store, waving her down while two cups of hot chocolate sat in front of him with a mountain of whipped cream and a generous dusting of cinnamon on top.

"Surprise!" he said, gesturing to the drink, as she sat down.

She stared at the cinnamon. "I'm allergic to cinnamon," she whispered quietly, trying not to ruin the moment. "It's okay. You didn't know."

Scott chuckled. "How can that be? You love chai tea. Cinnamon is one of the main ingredients. Who told you that you were allergic?"

"My mother was allergic to cinnamon, so she figured I was, too," Grace answered defensively. It felt strange talking about her allergies, especially when she kept thinking that Erick would have known. He even knew the things she had forgotten. *He's not Erick and that's okay,* she thought. She looked up at Scott and realized she desperately wanted to give this man a chance.

Scott laughed again, shaking his head. "Come on, we're not our parents. My dad is lactose intolerant," he said, licking the whipped cream from his spoon. "But I love dairy. No issues here."

"Right," she said, barely restraining herself from sighing. "So you just… ignore all the rules?"

"Exactly! Just because our parents leave us a legacy doesn't mean we can't be different." He leaned back, eyes sparkling. "You should try it. Just one sip."

Just because our parents leave us a legacy doesn't mean we can't be different. Grace wanted to believe that more than anything. She hesitated, her thoughts drifting toward her own father. "Somehow, you remind me of that old story about Adam and Eve. 'Thou shall not surely die.' Are you the devil? What if I have a reaction?"

He shrugged. "Then I'll buy you a different drink. No big deal."

"Easy for you to say." Grace didn't know what to think about this man.

"But think about it. You've been living by those rules for so long. What if you just… changed it up a little?"

Grace picked up the mug, staring at the enticing whipped cream and the fragrant cinnamon on top. "It's not that simple."

"Why not?" he challenged, leaning forward. "You can't let other people or family define you."

She glanced up, catching his intensity. "And you think I should just toss that aside? Like it's nothing?"

"Not 'nothing.' Just… an opportunity to see things differently. Like a fresh start."

She was now unsure if he was talking about the risk of the cinnamon drink or pursuing a new relationship. "Sounds nice in theory."

"But hard in practice," Scott said, softening his tone. "I get it. Really. It's been three years for me since… well, you know."

"Yeah," Grace said, quietly. "And you're here, trying again."

"Exactly. So, why not you?" he urged. "You deserve to enjoy things, Grace. Even if it means breaking a few rules. I'll order another drink if you're not ready. We're here to have fun, but it's really no big deal."

Their eyes locked for a moment. His gaze was intense.

"Okay," she said finally, determination winning her over. "Just a sip."

Scott smiled, triumphant. "That's the spirit."

She took a cautious sip, the sweetness flooding her senses. She waited a minute or so and to her relief, nothing happened.

"See?" he said, grinning. "Not so bad, right?"

Grace picked up the napkin and started coughing. Fear gripped Scott, his eyes wide in terror. She put the napkin down and smirked. "Yeah, not bad," she admitted. "You thought I was dying, didn't you?" she joked.

"I deserved that." He smiled back at her, pleased with this outcome. "You are a quick wit, aren't you? I'm just glad you didn't die. I'd have to rethink my entire life philosophy."

"Drinking hot chocolate when the snow melted weeks ago is just… a little crazy." Grace laughed, enjoying the simplicity of this moment.

"Fair enough." He leaned back, satisfied. "Just remember… life's too short to live in fear or play by the rules."

"Easy to say, harder to do," she replied, her smile wavering.

"True. But starting with small steps can lead to big changes."

"Maybe," she said, the weight of her past still heavy in her chest. "It's harder than it looks to let go of the past."

"I get the sense that you tried to run from your past in order to move forward in your life."

"You have no idea!" Grace looked down at her hot chocolate. "I've been through a lot of challenges over the last decade. After my accident, I had to learn to walk again, I also had amnesia. I lost everything."

"I know how life can rip us apart unexpectedly. But, Grace, you need to embrace it all. Because your past is what makes you—you."

Grace closed her eyes. He had a point. She'd been running this whole time and never seemed to make any progress.

"It takes time," she said, "and not everyone can wait it out."

"The people who care about you will understand that it takes time. I'm glad you're here, aren't you?"

"Yeah, I am." She took another sip of hot chocolate and was impressed by Scott's depth of understanding. She shook her head thinking that Raven had been wrong about the allergy.

"Then that's something. One small step for Grace," Scott smiled and sipped his cocoa.

Grace took another sip, feeling the warmth spread through her body.

Scott was right.

It was time for a change.

And maybe everything she had once believed had never been true.

Chapter 80

Erick spent the next couple of weeks driving Finn around to his various appointments, training one client at HigherGround, and working with Jace's new therapist. He was annoyed with himself for still thinking about Grace. He felt on edge, afraid that he might run into her at any time. He was finishing up with his client when Isabelle texted him that she was back in town, asking him to meet her at the dock behind HigherGround. He slipped outside the studio and saw Isabelle. She wore a buttery yellow floral sundress under a light jean jacket. She had brought a picnic lunch and had a blanket spread over the dock. They hugged and sat down together to eat.

"Wow! This looks great. Does this mean you're all settled in your new apartment?" Erick asked Isabelle, as he sat down opposite her.

"I'm still waiting for a few larger things to arrive this weekend. You wouldn't know anyone who can help me move a few things?" Her eyes flicked up to Erick's, already knowing the answer.

"I could think of someone." Erick winked.

"I bet you can!" Isabelle laughed. Their banter was easy, and the warm sun reflected off the lake. Lost in conversation, Erick looked at his watch, and saw it was getting late. He helped Isabelle pack up the containers in the picnic basket, and they both walked inside HigherGround.

"I just have one report to finish. If you don't mind waiting, we can leave together. It shouldn't take too long." Erick hoped she would stay.

"Sure, I can stay!" Isabelle said quickly.

"What are you two up to?" Sky entered the waiting room, eyeing Isabelle.

"Just getting settled in." Isabelle shrugged.

"I'll be in my office. You and Sky can catch up. I'll come find you later." Erick turned toward the staff door when he heard a voice.

"Dr. Erick?" a young man asked.

"Luke! How is college?" Erick recognized the young man immediately, and he high-fived the former patient.

"It's good. My little brother is here for physical therapy. You remember Raul?"

"Oh, is he okay?" Concern filled Erick's face.

"He'll be okay. Just an old soccer injury. I just wanted to say hello."

"Of course! You look well, and it's always good to see you, Luke. Glad Raul has been coming here. Best of luck at UConn and congratulations on your soccer scholarship."

"Thanks, man." Luke sat down in a chair, looking at his phone.

Erick noticed that Sky and Isabelle were still talking, and then Sky raised her voice. She didn't realize that Erick was behind the large column in the lobby and could hear their conversation.

"What's the real reason you moved here, though? You aren't answering the question!" Sky had her hands on her hips.

"Erick and I are dating. Whether you like it or not, we've

346

become… close."

"You've never been interested in settling down before. What changed?" Sky demanded.

"Erick and I have the same desire to help people, and once he sees that with my help we can take physical therapy to a whole new level, he'll be winning many more awards."

"He has no interest in winning awards or being the face of the company anymore, so that can't be true. What did I tell you about his other girlfriend?" Sky looked around, but Erick was sure she couldn't see him as he leaned against the column out of view. He felt guilty for eavesdropping on the conversation, but where was she going with all of this? "He still loves Grace," Sky declared.

"The red-head? I don't think she's a problem anymore. Seriously, Sky, he deserves more."

"Well, what happened to the other guy you were with?"

"Who, Chris?" Isabelle defended. "He's not my boyfriend anymore. Erick is different, but it's really none of your business."

"I don't think you know Erick at all. He doesn't want that life anymore."

"Just stop. Erick isn't some fragile guy. I know he wants to settle down, but there will be time for all that. He'll want the life he deserves. You'll see. Maybe you should chill out." Isabelle glared at Sky. "And stay in your own lane."

"Isabelle, you need to watch your step. If you interview for a position here at HigherGround, just remember that I have a vote. You are one of my best friends, but Erick is *family*, and I don't know what you're up to."

"We're having fun. Let it go, Sky. Just because you landed a rich man, doesn't mean—"

"I didn't *land* Daniel. We fell in *love*. We were honest and didn't pretend to be something we weren't. I don't care about the family money. I have my own family money." Sky sounded exasperated.

"I'm not after the family *money*, Sky. Erick can decide what he wants. As far as I know, he's already chosen me. We spent a lot of alone time in Boston."

"I don't need to hear about any of that. Let's talk later when I don't have a client waiting," Sky said with a stern look as she opened the staff door with her name tag.

Erick slid into the door behind her before it closed and wondered what that conversation was really all about. He wandered down the side corridor and pulled his phone out just as Sky entered the same corner from the opposite side.

"Oh!" Sky said in shock. "I didn't see you there."

"Did you and Isabelle have a nice chat?" Erick raised his eyebrows as he looked up from his phone and replaced it in the pocket of his khaki pants.

"Sure, I guess." Sky's eyes darted around the hallway.

"Anything I should know?" Erick pried, hoping to find out what was going on with them.

"You know that she was my best friend before I met Daniel, but she can be, uh, determined once she sets her mind on something. She is like a vulture sometimes."

"I see. You don't like that Isabelle set her sights on me. I saw the way you looked at us at the award ceremony. And if I can make one suggestion for the future... A little heads up on your surprise guest would have gone a long way."

Sky shifted on her toes, clearly uncomfortable. "Listen, you're family, and I will always want to protect you. I thought you were still in love with Grace. I wish you had said something before we brought Grace all the way up to Boston. Could you blame Daniel and me for wanting a happy ending for you? Besides, I thought you'd have figured it all out on the ride home together. Have you seriously given up on Grace after all this time?"

"We had a long chat on the way home from Boston. We weren't on the same page about the future we envisioned. She still needed more time to get over Finn and the rest of her past. I told her I can't keep waiting around. That's just something I can't do again. Grace doesn't even know what she wants. Isn't it about time I'm with someone who does?"

"You mean with Isabelle?"

"Why not? Give me one good reason why I shouldn't be with Isabelle?" Erick cocked his head at Sky.

"Okay. She isn't a long-term, 'settle down' kind of girl. That's all I'm going to say, but maybe that's what you need right now. Daniel and I are just worried about you, and we only want the best for you." Sky placed her hand on his arm. "Enjoy your time, but don't get too attached is all I can say. We won't stand in your way."

"Honestly, it doesn't have to be forever. I just need to sort through a few things and enjoy life again, and maybe eventually we can think about the long term."

"I hope you find joy again. I really do. I have a client, but let's chat soon. Just know that Daniel and I love you and only want you to be happy. We'd love for you to have someone here especially when we go to Georgia." Sky left and headed down to the pediatric area.

Erick wondered if he had made the right decision, but he didn't care. He wanted to move on from Grace, and Isabelle wanted help with her career. He didn't see why they both couldn't get what they wanted.

Chapter 81

Grace continued to attend the grief group weekly. She especially enjoyed being with Scott. They'd had a few dates, but he had yet to open up to her about his wife. He had texted her yesterday to tell her that he was going out of town on a story so he might be late for the meeting or he might miss it altogether.

She had agreed to accompany Finn to his next AA meeting. Finn's presence at the grief group no longer bothered her, and their relationship seemed less strained. Today he was dressed in dark cargo shorts and a white T-shirt which were in total contrast to the high-powered suits he wore when they were together.

Together, they walked the two blocks to the nearest meeting, where Finn received a 6-month chip. Grace congratulated him when they stepped out of the community center into the warm and breezy spring air.

"Your family must be so proud of you," Grace said.

"Yeah, I would've asked Erick to come, but he was busy tonight." Finn walked beside her and asked, "So what's up with that guy you've been chatting with at group?"

"No way. You don't get to ask about my personal life."

"Fair point," Finn conceded. "But I'm going to do it anyway. Do you still think about my brother?"

"He's with Isabelle! We've been over this." Grace thought Finn was being naive.

"I briefly met Isabelle at Daniel's wedding," Finn said, lowering his voice. "She's no good for him. She's hiding something, Grace. I can tell." He stopped walking and leaned against the wall of the church. "You know how at FINNLondon, we had to read people—really read them to determine if we should invest in their book. It wasn't just about what they showed us; it was about what they were trying so desperately to conceal. Erick's just lost right now, playing out some misguided fantasy with her," he continued, his tone insistent, almost pleading for her to understand.

"Regardless, I don't know if I'll ever be able to trust Erick again," she confessed quietly. "Trust is not an easy thing to rebuild."

"Erick isn't ready now either," he said, his voice low but clear. "But you two... you're meant to be together. He just reacted to you ghosting him, which by the way was not cool, but I get it. Look, I know that we've had our differences, but I also know that you and Erick should have been together at graduation. I'm also aware that I'm the cause behind all of that, and it's something I regret every single day."

"It's all water under the bridge now," she said, almost to herself, feeling the truth of it settle in. "At some point, we have to choose whether to let the past define us."

Grace noticed a change in Finn's demeanor as if he was shifting gears, preparing to share something significant. Suddenly, he stopped walking. "Listen, Grace," Finn began, his voice filled with concern. "I saw Isabelle with some other guy the other day." His eyes searched hers for a reaction before continuing. "They looked... pretty cozy."

Grace felt he was almost being protective as he reached

into his pocket and retrieved his phone. With a few swipes, he brought up a photo and handed it to her. The image displayed a candid shot of Isabelle, her laughter frozen in time as she leaned intimately into the mystery man beside her.

"I have to look out for my brother," Finn said, as tension creased his brow. "She's not right for him—I can feel it in my gut—but I can't prove anything, and Erick won't listen to me."

Grace looked at the photograph, and although she wanted to help, she knew that ship had sailed. "I can't get involved, Finn," she replied, handing back the phone. Her gaze was steady, even as her heart wavered with uncertainty. "Whatever's going on with Isabelle is not what's keeping us apart." She knew that love wasn't always enough to bridge the distance of two differing souls seeking their own answers.

Finn's gaze was unwavering, his eyes intense with emotion. He shifted his feet. "I know it was because of me," he said softly and looked down at his feet.

The weight of his understanding pressed upon Grace. She looked at him, really looked at him, and saw the man who had once been both her savior and abuser. "Not exactly just you. You can't take all the credit. I have to resolve things for myself before I can be with anyone," she said, grateful that he felt he could be honest with her. "You know that. Like that woman at AA said, 'In order to recover, we can't get there until we know what we're recovering from.'" Grace paused, taking a deep breath.

For the first time, it seemed like Finn had finally seen her for who she really was. It was her resiliency and her ability to sift through all the emotional damage and emerge with the clarity that only came from experience.

"You were always the smartest person I knew," he said with admiration. He opened the door to the church. Their grief group session was about to start.

"Thank you, Finn, and congratulations on making it six months." She touched his arm briefly, acknowledging the distance they had both traveled on their separate journeys. She realized that the path ahead was hers alone, and the smartest choice was to keep moving forward. As they took their seats in the circle and prepared for another meeting, she wondered if she would finally have the courage to speak.

Grace's attention turned to an older gentleman, his silver hair combed neatly to one side, as he cleared his throat and began to unravel his tale. "I'm George. My anniversary is coming up," he looked down. "It would have been our fiftieth… "

As he continued, Grace's attention drifted away, the man's voice fading into the background. She saw Finn across the circle and a memory came to the forefront of her mind. She still would get flashbacks every now and then. In this memory, Grace stood in front of Finn, the sound of silverware and classical music filled her ears. White tablecloths and the decor of fine dining surrounded them as he presented her with a small red box. In the early days, he had a flair for the dramatic when instead of a ring he gave her a promise key. That was ironic because he could never fulfill any of the promises he made. But nonetheless, it was the key to his loft and a new chapter together. His charm was magnetic and when he carried her over the threshold to his loft, as if they were on their honeymoon, she felt so alive. She remembered the whirlwind of living in the biggest apartment she had ever seen. Being Finn's girlfriend was everything she had ever imagined. When he offered her the assistant job at FINNLondon, it was a dream come true. They worked together daily, and he surprised her all the time. Finn had thought of everything.

It was good until it wasn't.

Grace's eyes, misty with the past, returned to the present, where Finn's voice cut through her memories. She watched him, his hands animated as he now spoke to the group. She envied his vulnerability in sharing what was in his heart.

"Being honest is the key," he said, as he talked openly about his sobriety. Here, even with strangers, they were all bound by the common thread of grief. Grace still could not find the courage to express the weight she carried. She knew Finn's story, but hearing it—his truth spoken aloud—was a different experience entirely.

"My dad was no saint. That's for sure. We had our differences," Finn admitted. He was sharing his bitterness and resentment with the group, but Grace felt like he was talking directly to her, and she leaned in, trying to hear every word. "His birthday just passed in April. I didn't even think about it because I still have never forgiven him for all the physical scars he gave me as a child and for the emotional scars I *still* have trying to fill his shoes. He made running a multi-million dollar company look easy. But it wasn't. His shoes were too big to fill. That's when I began to self-medicate with alcohol. It wasn't until I became sober recently that I realized I was avoiding the pain of the past. The worst part about him being gone is that we never had closure. I never knew whether I had finally gained his respect for all the work I had put into the business. Now I'll never know how my father truly felt about me. So on his birthday, I did nothing. I hope I can forgive him one day."

"Thank you, Finn," the moderator said. "Your honesty was a gift to all of us here. Perhaps all of you could consider writing a letter to someone who is no longer with us," she suggested. "You can burn it, keep it, or read it out loud to the group next week."

Grace thought she could write a letter like that and hoped it could give her some closure. At the very least it would give her some direction and an opportunity to put into words all the jumbled-up emotions she harbored.

"Would anyone else like to share?" the facilitator invited, her eyes moving from one face to another, offering the floor to whoever might speak next.

Grace could feel the weight of her own untold story pressing against her lips.

And for the first time, the urgency to speak it aloud.

Chapter 82

rick paused and looked out onto the dusky horizon
after he pulled up to Isabelle's apartment complex
later that evening. Isabelle's presence beside him was
both a comfort and a distraction.

"We need to pick up my brother tonight before we go to
Daniel's for dinner," Erick informed her.

"Tell me again about Finn," she insisted. "I can't remember,
but I think we met at Sky's wedding?"

He turned from the window, his eyes on hers, and he kissed
her. He drove out of the parking lot and focused on the road
ahead. "Yeah he was there. It's been tough," Erick admitted.
"Rehab isn't just about getting clean—it's like tearing down everything you thought you were and trying to piece it all back
together."

Isabelle reached over, her fingers lightly brushing against his
forearm. "But he's doing better now, right?"

"Better is relative." Erick's hand tightened on the steering
wheel. He exhaled slowly under the weight of responsibility. "I
should've seen the signs earlier. His wife, Brook played us all,

but I keep thinking none of this would have happened if I'd been a better brother and just paid more attention."

"Hey," Isabelle interjected, her voice firm. "You can't carry that guilt. Finn's choices are his own. You've done everything you can for him, Erick."

His jaw clenched, and his only response was a silent nod. He wanted to believe her and shed the shame he carried. Guilt was all too familiar for Erick, and he was aware of how hard it was to shake.

"Is there anything else we can do for him?" Isabelle's question cut through his anxious thoughts.

"Give him time and space," he said as if he were talking to himself, "and show him that he's not alone. That's why tonight is important."

"Family dinner, right?" Isabelle turned to him.

"Exactly." Erick managed a half-smile. "Just a casual thing. No pressure. Just us, low key, celebrating Finn's six month sobriety." Isabelle reached over, her hand finding his on the center console, and gave it a reassuring squeeze.

"Then that's what we'll do," she said with conviction. "We'll be there for him. And you don't have to carry all this by yourself, Erick."

He glanced at her with a grateful smile, but his eyes were still dark with concern as her phone buzzed and she quickly typed a message.

"I know," he replied. But did he truly believe it? Could he really unburden himself of the guilt from the weight of his brother's troubles?

"Thank you, Isabelle." He squeezed her hand.

The Jeep eventually slowed to a stop outside the church where the grief group met. Erick turned off the ignition, leaned against the door, took a deep breath, and resolved to do whatever it took to take care of his brother.

The silence around him did nothing to ease the thoughts racing through his mind. He forced himself to look at Isabelle but felt something wasn't right—something he couldn't quite place.

He lowered the window, but the thick humid air hung like a heavy blanket around them. New England weather often fluctuated from freezing cold to hot and humid without notice. The Jeep's top was down, and Erick thought about putting the air conditioning back on. Then, as he drummed his fingers absentmindedly, he wondered if he should go in and get Finn.

"Maybe it's time you let Finn deal with this on his own," Isabelle looked up from her phone. "You can't keep carrying his burdens, Erick. You have to consider your future."

Erick turned to look at her, and in frustration, he pressed his hand against his beard. "I don't know. It's not that simple." He imagined Finn vulnerable and alone with the weight of the world on his shoulders. Erick still felt the urge to lift it off him.

"Sometimes, the best way to help someone is to step back," she gently replied.

He shook his head, but his annoyance lingered. "I've told you before. I'm not interested in advancing my career right now because family must come first." He stared out the windshield at nothing in particular, his gaze unfocused. The oppressive evening heat made the vehicle's interior feel like a sauna, but his mind was elsewhere, tangled up in thoughts about Finn. *Why was she not supporting him on this?*

"I know you feel that way now, but you've already done so much for him, for all of them. This guilt will drive you to madness. You're allowed to think about yourself, too."

Erick sighed. It was a quiet night with only the distant sound of a dog barking. Erick knew Isabelle meant well, but the thought of not helping his brother felt like he was abandoning Finn to face his challenges alone.

"I wasn't paying enough attention all this time because I was too wrapped up in work. None of this would have happened if I was around."

Isabelle reached across the console, her touch light on his arm. "You can't blame yourself for everything, Erick. This situation with Brook… He's a grown man, and he chose her, and now he'll pay the price."

He glanced at her, eyes darkening as he considered her words. Erick was all too familiar with the price of being with a woman like Brook. "I know, but all his assets are frozen. The court case looks like it's going to trial soon. If I'm not there…" He cut himself off, the thought too overwhelming to finish.

"Then what?" Isabelle prompted, her voice soft yet insistent. "What would happen?"

Erick exhaled sharply, a sound of frustration more than resignation. "I don't know. After that, I just… " His sentence trailed off because he couldn't think beyond the impending trial or see beyond all that Finn had been through and the inevitable battles his brother would have to face.

"I'm not suggesting you give up on the people you love, Erick. I just think you should consider having balance," Isabelle said. "Maybe you're looking at this from the wrong angle." Isabelle reached out, her fingers brushing against the back of his hand. "What if there's a way to lighten your load without neglecting Finn?"

He turned slightly to look her in the eyes. "How?" Erick asked.

"HigherGround," she began. "There's no doubt you've built something amazing, Erick. But maybe it's time to let it grow beyond you." Her eyes met his, filled with a mix of encouragement and empathy. "I'm sure there are people out there who would jump at the chance to take your ideas to the next level. People with the resources to expand your vision while giving you the freedom you need. Think about it, Erick. It could be the answer you didn't know you were searching for."

Stunned, Erick could only shake his head. He released the steering wheel, turning fully to face her now. "What are you talking about?" he asked, as the words sounded foreign even to his own ears. Selling HigherGround had never been part of the plan; it was his legacy, his passion. Yet here was Isabelle, presenting it as a solution so casually, totally unaware of all the years he spent creating something special.

The idea caused Erick to swallow hard, trying to switch gears in his mind from Finn's court case to the future of Higher-Ground. Both demanded his full attention. He rubbed the back of his neck as he replayed her words as if it would help connect the dots. Where was this coming from?

"Think about it," Isabelle urged gently, tilting her head to catch his eye. "This sounds like the perfect solution for you, Erick. You can focus on Finn and whatever comes next without losing everything you've built."

Could this be the answer he was looking for? It could allow him to support Finn and, at the same time, free him from the shackles of being the face of HigherGround? Erick exhaled slowly, thinking it felt all too easy and the timing of this was almost too good to be true.

Chapter 83

Grace let out a deep sigh and cleared her throat. She felt the weight of all eyes on her as she looked around the circle and then at Finn, who was watching her intently. "Nearly two years ago, I found out my parents adopted me. This revelation came after learning my birth mother had died suddenly." She paused as her gaze saw Scott slide into the open seat next to her.

"Sorry," he mouthed silently and she was grateful that he had made it just in time.

"She left me a journal and a map that took me to her favorite hiking trail along the edge of a cliff. I had my own near-death experience when I slipped and fell off the same cliff. By some miracle, I survived, but I had forgotten everything." The words caught in her throat as she looked over at Finn, who had never known her story in this detail. Erick and his dog were her saviors. "Before this experience, I'd made some hasty decisions and turned my back on the people who gave everything up to raise me. My biological mother's death brought me home and back to those who truly loved me. But the real miracle came after the

D.S. NASS

fall, and it was the amnesia that gave me a new start," Grace confessed. "It was the forgetting that changed everything. I had to lose myself to find out who I really was. Eventually, most of my memories returned, and I set out on a new path. After I published my first book, my obsession turned into a relentless search to find my biological father, which led me to California earlier this year," she said. "After my book tour, I thought I'd find answers. Instead, I found two very different men, either of whom might be my father. One of them was an evil man named Jack Stone… " She paused as if saying his name would conjure up the devil himself. "He claimed to be my father. He died, but not before he confessed that he murdered my mother. He slipped off of a cliffside, and despite his gut-wrenching confession, I tried to save him, but in the end I couldn't."

Tears welled up in her eyes as she thought of all her unanswered questions. "When someone dies, it's like a chapter that never gets finished. Somehow despite that, life still moves on. What I miss most now is all the time I lost with my mother because that monster cut her life short. No one knows how long we have or how precious life is until it's gone. I felt lost and confused for most of this year," she admitted. "But this group has given me a gift. You've surrounded me with love despite all the loss I've endured, and somehow, it gives me the strength to keep moving forward. I know that's what my mother would've wanted." Grace looked at everyone. "Strength," she repeated, "is not just about holding on, but also knowing when to let go." Her eyes found Finn's and he nodded as if he finally understood. Grace's gaze moved over to Scott who looked at her and handed her one of the tissue boxes that were scattered between the chairs for a time such as this.

"Thank you all," she said simply, her eyes locked on Scott, "for listening, being here, helping me find my way through, and showing me how to be open to whatever comes next."

Grace felt the weight of her past lift after she'd taken a chance and spoke her truth in this circle. It was another step toward healing, and she wasn't alone; she was part of something larger—a community bound by the understanding that growth and renewal could be found even after the most profound loss.

Chapter 84

Erick thought about the practicality of what Isabelle was saying, but the annoyance from earlier returned. He gripped the steering wheel in disbelief and couldn't hold back any longer. "I can't believe you want me to give up my company. It's… it's everything I built."

"But think about it, Erick," she said. "We can grow something new and exciting together. HigherGround can be so much more than just a local brand." She leaned forward, her eyes bright with excitement.

"It's not just a brand to me. It's my life. My family's legacy."

"What about our future? You're so focused on family and the past that you're forgetting we can create an amazing future." Isabelle placed her hand on his thigh.

Erick paused with a sigh. "You're young, and I know you want to travel the world. I want to settle down. Those aren't the same dreams."

"Why can't they be? I mean, why can't we do both?"

Erick looked out the window again. "Because it feels like you're asking me to abandon everything. My brothers, my fam-

"It's not abandonment. It's an opportunity." Isabelle flipped her hair back.

"Opportunity for who? You? You don't get it. Finn is in the middle of a court case. He needs me here." He put his back against the door.

Isabelle crossed her arms. "And what about your dreams? What about your happiness? Daniel and Sky are moving on from here."

"We've been over this. I'm happy, Isabelle. I'm happy here. With my family. The real question is will being with me be enough for *you*?"

Isabelle leaned back in her seat, her eyes downcast. "So, what? You'd rather stay stuck? Do you even *want* a life with me?"

Erick looked at her, "I do! But it feels like you're racing ahead without me. I'm not even sure if I'm the one you want to be with."

"I want to grow. I want to live." Isabelle was insistent.

"I want those things, too. Just… not like this. Not at the cost of everything I hold dear."

"So, what are you saying? You want to stay here forever?"

Erick hesitated. "I don't know. Maybe after the court case I could move to Georgia with Daniel. But… "

"But what?" Isabelle's voice rose a notch.

"Would you come with me?" He barely said the words above a whisper, because he didn't know if he could take the rejection.

"Is that what you really want?" she countered.

"I don't know! It's just… I feel torn, and I don't want to hold you back." He rubbed his beard in frustration.

"So, what's the point of all of this?" Her eyes narrowed at him.

"I want to be with you. But I need to know we're on the same page." Erick gazed at the sky above as if he could find answers there.

"Maybe we need to figure out what that page looks like," she said, looking up, too.

"Yeah." Erick could hardly breathe. "I just wish it didn't feel like an ultimatum." He unbuckled his seatbelt, eager to escape and clear his mind. "Let's talk about it later. The meeting must be over by now, and I need to see what's taking Finn so long to come out."

"Okay, fine." Isabelle conceded.

"Wait here," he said before he closed the door to the Jeep.

Then he walked across the parking lot and through the main entrance. Once inside, he found the meeting room and suddenly stopped cold in his tracks.

His gaze was inexplicably drawn to a burst of red color that stood out against the muted church decor. A woman with fiery red hair braided artfully over one shoulder caught his eye. The sight of her would have been enough to take his breath away, but it was the sound of her laughter, light and free, that stopped his heart. It was Grace, and she was talking with the last person he ever thought she would be talking to, let alone laughing with. *Finn.*

Chapter 85

Grace's heart was lighter after sharing her grief being surrounded by people who were also trying to put themselves back together. The meeting had concluded, and Scott remained in his seat next to her.

"Wow, your story is incredible. You've been through so much."

"You don't know the half of it." Grace stood up and noticed that Finn was talking to another member of the group.

"Would you like to go to dinner tonight?" Scott asked as he stood up. "We can leave from here."

"That sounds intriguing," Grace said. "But can we talk about this later? I need to talk to someone. I won't be long."

"Of course. I'll see what tea they have tonight." Scott winked at Grace and headed to the refreshment table.

Grace walked over to Finn, who was saying good-bye to a woman with a service dog.

"That took courage," Finn said to her. "So I don't know if you heard, but Brook Becker is trying to take over my company." Finn went on to talk about how she hadn't changed a bit. It felt good to laugh about her antics now and compare them to when they were kids. He continued to fill her in on the absurdities of his unraveling life. "Seriously, Grace," Finn said, and he shook his head. "Brook thinks she can handle the same business that I could barely do. It's such a boys' club. They are like sharks out there. I should've been one of those fishermen who worked on those Alaskan boats. It would have been less stressful." Finn scoffed.

Grace felt her head tip back in sheer laughter at the unexpected comment from Finn, even though part of her felt it was wrong to find amusement in someone else's inevitable downfall. They were talking about Brooklyn Becker, after all. This was Finn, a great storyteller himself, his blue eyes wild with the boyish charm she remembered from her youth.

"Remember how she always talked about wanting to get her driver's license?" he continued. "Her dad actually said no because he figured it'd be safer for everyone else on the road. The man had a point. Daniel was her first casualty. Then poor Jace was part of her insanity. He has only three legs now."

"Come on, you're making that up," Grace said, punching him lightly on his shoulder and refusing to take any of this seriously.

"I am not!" He protested, raising a hand as if taking an oath. "Brook Becker: a menace to society, still at large." His hand gestured like he was creating the headline on the front page news. But then his smile turned to a frown.

A sigh escaped Grace as her mouth gaped open. She thought about Daniel in the wheelchair and the beloved dog both of whom Erick loved more than life itself. "Oh my God! Not Jace! You need to get as far away from that woman as possible!" She shook her head in disbelief, trying to reconcile the new feelings she felt for the man in front of her. Was it possible to bond with someone over a common enemy? But this is the same man who, when alcohol took hold, became someone unrecognizable. And yet, here he was, sober and it was still a little disconcerting how he could reach her, despite everything.

"God, I'm glad that chapter is closing." Finn's gaze drifted to the donuts on the table next to them.

"Must feel nice to know you are on the right path," Grace commented as she considered her own journey.

"Nice? It's like being on death row and getting a last-minute pardon." He glanced at her sideways, a smirk playing on his lips. "Once this is all over, I'll do something new and unexpected. Like, become a monk or something."

"Or something," she echoed, her smile returning. For a moment, she allowed herself the luxury of simply enjoying his company. They both laughed at the absurdity of their lives.

He suddenly had a serious and pained look on his face. "The truth is, all joking aside, I really could use your help."

"I'm not sure what I can do," Grace sighed.

"As you already know, Brook is taking me to the cleaners. You don't owe me anything, but you have worked for me for years. I wouldn't ask, but I'm at the end of my rope here. I just want to save my father's legacy and turn it into something meaningful. I thought about walking away, but my brothers reminded me that this is all we have left of the Finn family name. For once, I want to use it for a good cause." Finn looked uncomfortable as if he was asking for too much after everything they had been through. "You don't have to, and I won't blame you for any of it. I never told you that you really were one of the best editors I ever had, and you have an exceptional eye for detail. I have a team of lawyers combing through everything, but it would mean the world to me if you could at least take a look at a few documents. There's a slight chance we missed something. Would you be willing to take a look? I understand if you don't want to. I just don't know what else to do, because if I can't find anything wrong with the documents, then it's over. Will you please help me?"

"Maybe. Can I think about it?" Grace needed time to analyze the consequences of being in Finn's circle again. It was one thing to have a shared moment, but was she ready to let him back into her life and put aside all that had happened?

"Of course. Here's my new number," he said, handing her his card with a number written in ink on the back. "I'm staying with Daniel for a while. Grace, really… I'll understand if it's too much to ask." He tipped his head in gratitude. "I appreciate everything, and if my presence here still makes you uncomfortable, I'll find a new support group for myself."

"I'll let you know if I can help. Keep coming here. I think it's been good for both of us."

"Enjoy your evening," Finn said as he nodded toward Scott. He grabbed a donut and exited the building. Grace stood there, her head spinning with this turn of events. Finn asked her for help, which was so unexpected that she needed time to process how she actually felt about it all.

A woman from the group shook her hand and thanked her for sharing her story. Grace was on the right path, just like Finn was, to something greater. It seemed this healing and growth were painstakingly slow, but she knew in her heart that there was life on the other side of it all. She was filled with gratitude about how far she had come on this journey.

Chapter 86

Erick stood frozen in his spot by the door, observing the unfolding scene. It looked to him like she and Finn were having an intense conversation. He was about to intervene and save Grace, but instead he felt his throat tighten with an unexpected surge of rage. The next thing he saw was Finn reach out to touch Grace's arm, his fingers lingering on her just a moment too long for his liking. He noticed she didn't seem upset at all. In fact, she was actually laughing.

He took a step back as all the emotions sank in and he turned and exited the building into the thick night air. He leaned over, placing his hands on his knees as sharp pains stabbed through his chest. He tried to call out to Isabelle, but the words died on his lips. Survival kicked in as he gasped and then took slow deep breaths until his heart rate returned to normal. When he looked up again, Isabelle was tapping away on her phone, oblivious to the distress and fury that had gripped his heart. He thought about confronting Finn, but that would raise more questions that he wasn't ready to answer. Erick swallowed hard, his gaze shifting back to the doorway, his mind racing with unimaginable thoughts. He closed his eyes and replayed the sight he'd just witnessed. The whole reason he and Grace were not together was because she had explicitly said she hadn't dealt with the trauma Finn had inflicted upon her.

Erick didn't know what to believe anymore. Was any woman he ever cared about then or even now genuine? He felt like a pawn in some cruel game. Isabelle's sudden urge to have him cut his ties with HigherGround and his family didn't sit well with him. But now seeing Finn with Grace changed how he felt about everything. He straightened his back and started down the steps toward the Jeep.

"Hey thanks for the ride." Finn suddenly appeared as he hopped down the steps unaware of Erick's tension.

Erick opened the door to the Jeep and pushed aside Jace's blanket, trying to collect his thoughts. "Of course," he mumbled, still seething. "You remember Isabelle?"

Finn leaned forward, taking in her presence. The corners of his mouth lifted in a cautious smile. "Hello, Isabelle," Finn said, extending his hand toward her. He was acting weird.

Isabelle's gaze lingered on Finn too long. Erick was used to this, but it still irritated him to no end. "Hello, Finn," Isabelle finally responded, her eyes not leaving Finn's face. "Erick, you forgot to mention how much he looks like you." Isabelle laughed as the brothers settled into their seats.

"We get that all the time," Finn replied with his usual charm from the back seat.

Erick's fury about seeing Finn and Grace together returned as he put his foot down on the gas, sending a cloud of dust and gravel in his wake. He maneuvered the car onto the road. Every glance back in Finn's smug face was like staring into a distorted reflection—one that reminded him not just of who he was, but of everything he had tried to leave behind. *Was he cursed?* It felt that way—the same issues and the same faces constantly reappearing no matter how far he ran.

Isabelle's bright and animated voice made him cringe as she spoke of plans and dreams, painting a vivid picture of their future. She talked nonstop about travel, about escaping the small-town life for something grander. Her enthusiasm was infectious yet jarring. It was like he was on the outside looking in at himself.

"Can you believe it, Erick? Next month, we could be hiking through the Andes! It's going to be amazing!" Her eyes sparkled while his darkened.

He nodded, offering a tight smile. "Yeah, that would be amazing," he said, but it lacked conviction. "If we hadn't talked about this already," he added under his breath. But his mind was racing like a movie replaying Grace laughing too much with Finn.

"Just think of the mountains, Erick! The adventure!" Isabelle clearly was not deterred.

He glanced in the rearview mirror as Finn chuckled, "You're not much of a risk-taker, are you, Erick?"

"What's that supposed to mean?" Erick shot back, irritation seeping through every pore of his body.

Finn shrugged, a teasing grin on his face. "You like your safe little bubble. Family, business… predictable, right?"

"There's nothing wrong with taking care of responsibilities," Erick muttered, his eyes focused on the narrow road ahead.

Isabelle looked at Erick, her excitement dimming just a bit. "But, Erick, you're missing out. Life's too short to play it safe all the time."

"Maybe," he said, his voice low. "But some things matter more."

"Come on, man. You need to step out of your comfort zone," Finn urged, but there was a hint of challenge in his tone.

"Maybe I don't want to," Erick shot back, his heart racing. "Maybe I'm fine where I am."

Isabelle leaned forward, sensing the shift in his mood. "It's about finding balance. We can have adventure and still care about those things."

"Sounds easy when you say it," Erick deadpanned.

Silence filled the Jeep. The road stretched on, and Erick felt the tension thickening.

Isabelle smiled. "Just think about it, okay? We'll make memories."

Erick forced a nod, but inside, he felt lost. The thought of Finn with Grace twisted his stomach in knots. Finn was the reason she was even his ex-girlfriend in the first place. He needed clarity, not more chaos.

The dark road ahead distracted him from the pain he was feeling. With every mile they drove, he thought about Finn and Grace being together. *Was Finn up to his old tricks again? Can a leopard ever change its spots?* Erick had no right to feel this way, but seeing Grace with Finn felt like another punch in the gut. Maybe Isabelle was right. This town was too small for all of them. Everyone else was moving on. Why was he the only one who couldn't seem to escape his own thoughts? The more he thought about it the more his desire to start over somewhere else—where he could put distance between himself and the pain—was suddenly becoming the only clear choice he had left.

Chapter 87

"Grace, I'm really proud of you," Scott said as they moved toward the corner of the room. "You shared. That's a big step."

Grace shifted her weight, looking at the ground. "Thanks. I didn't think I could. It just… happened."

"Sometimes it's like that. You just have to let it out," he replied with a hint of understanding in his eyes. "You've been holding onto a lot."

She took a breath. "How about you? You never talk about your wife."

Scott paused, "Yeah. Well, it's complicated. We were high school sweethearts. I thought I had it all figured out."

Grace raised an eyebrow. "What do you mean?"

"I played it safe. Did what my parents wanted. Went to college, got a job, and married the girl I knew most of my life. But we didn't get to live out the life we imagined. Not really," he admitted, his voice quieting. "Then… she got sick. Lost her three years ago. But I lost myself way before then."

"I'm sorry." Her words felt inadequate.

Scott looked around the room and lowered his voice. "I shut everyone out after that. My parents, her parents… everyone. It was easier that way. Just me and the darkness."

"That sounds lonely." Grace looked up at him.

"It was. For a long time, I didn't even get out of bed. Just… stared at the ceiling. But this year, something clicked. I decided I needed to start living again," he said, his voice gaining strength. "I don't want to just exist anymore. I was tired of being numb. I wanted to feel something again." A small smile tugged at his lips. "And I want to take risks. I'm ready to try things. *New* things."

Grace thought about her own hesitance. "But it's scary. Opening up again. Letting someone in." She recalled seeing Finn again after all this time.

"Yeah, it is," Scott replied, his tone serious. "But isn't it scarier to stay stuck? To miss out on what could be?"

She hesitated, chewing on her lip. "I don't know. I mean, what if it hurts again?" Her thoughts turned to seeing Isabelle on stage with Erick.

"Pain is part of living, Grace. But so is joy. You can't have one without the other," he said, his eyes locking onto hers. "Trust me. I've learned the hard way. Let's go to dinner."

Her heart raced. "With you? Is that… a risk?"

"It could be. But you won't know unless you try," he said. "I'm not asking for forever. Just one meal. One conversation."

Grace considered that. A simple meal. It felt both inviting and terrifying. "Okay. Dinner. But only if you promise to share more with me."

"Deal," Scott said with a bit of excitement in his tone. "Sounds like a plan. Meet me outside in five minutes. I'll drive."

Grace agreed and left the church, stopping short of the parking lot as she watched Finn get into a Jeep that she wished she didn't recognize. The Jeep screeched as it lurched forward, leaving a dust cloud behind them. Her gaze followed the vehicle as Isabelle's golden hair fluttered through the open window.

"Ready? I'm the Bronco over here," Scott said, leading to his vehicle. "Hop in."

As they drove, the familiarity of the town's storefronts and street corners reminded Grace of her past. She needed more than just a change of scenery; she needed a life without complications.

"I made reservations," Scott said as he pulled out of the parking lot.

"You were *that* certain I'd say yes?" Grace asked amused.

"Maybe!" Scott winked at her. "You're in for an experience of a lifetime."

"You really are one confident man!" Grace laughed.

Once they arrived at the non-descript storefront, Scott walked her inside to a dimly lit room. "Wow, it's really dark in here," she said, glancing around but seeing very little. There were soft candles in glass ball centerpieces on the table, and patrons were talking loudly at times, but then, oddly, not at all. What had she got herself into?

Scott placed his hand on the small of her back guiding her. "Yeah, it's part of the experience. Just wait." Before she could respond, a man dressed in a tux appeared. He smiled warmly and gestured for them to follow.

She held onto Scott's arm and whispered, "Are you sure about this place? I feel underdressed."

He smiled back with reassurance. "You look perfect, trust me. You'll love it."

They reached a small table, and the maître d' pulled out her chair. Grace sat down, still unsure. "I have trust issues, you know."

"Don't worry, I got you," Scott said, "just focus on the experience."

Suddenly out of nowhere, the servers wrapped silk scarves around their eyes. Grace gasped. "What is happening? Now I can't see anything."

"Just relax and let go," Scott said, squeezing her hand. "Trust me," he said once again.

Chapter 88

E rick slammed on his brakes as he pulled into his re-
served parking spot adjacent to Daniel's apartment.
"You might want to get those brakes checked,"
Finn joked as rain started beating down.

After Erick put the roof of the Jeep back on, his gaze remained locked on the rearview mirror. He had given his very
soul to drag Finn out of the abyss, and he couldn't believe that
this was how he repaid him. His mind replayed Grace laughing
with his brother. Then he remembered Isabelle's offer, hanging
over him like a noose around his neck. He looked through the
windshield at the sign, *Dr. Erick Finn*. Isabelle was already exiting the vehicle and quickly ran up the ramp to Daniel's apartment where Sky let her inside.

Finn strode toward the ramp, unaware of Erick's smoldering
gaze behind him. Erick caught up and put his hand out to pull
Finn back.

"What is it?" Finn looked puzzled.

The air between the brothers felt charged, heavy with unspoken accusations.

"What kind of game are you playing?" Erick hurled the accusation at Finn without holding back.

Finn met Erick's glare with a dismissive shake of his head, the movement slow and deliberate.

"What game are *you* playing?" he countered with a challenge in his tone. "Why are you with Isabelle when you are *clearly* not over Grace?"

The mention of Grace's name opened an old wound. Erick tightened his jaw and clenched his hands into fists. "You don't know anything! Isabelle and I are together," Erick shot back. "She and I have so much in common that we just fit." Erick's eyes burned into his brother's, challenging Finn even though Erick himself wasn't convinced. Did they truly fit together?

Finn's eyes narrowed as the tension heightened to dangerous levels between them. "You sound like you're trying to convince yourself. I'm good at reading people, and I know she's hiding something. I didn't want to say anything, but because of everything you've done for me, I owe you the truth. I saw something that you should know about." Finn leaned in closer, dropping his voice. "I saw Isabelle a few days ago with some older guy at the cafe in town. When she went to the restroom, the guy made a phone call and said the words 'I have someone on the inside of HigherGround.' I walked by, and he clearly thought I was you. He looked nervous and hung up the phone immediately. He ran out of Cafè Bella so fast I thought he'd robbed the place. Suspicious, no?"

The revelation struck Erick like a slap in the face, sending a shock wave of betrayal through his system. "She's not cheating on me, Finn. Isabelle is just trying to get me to expand and help me with HigherGround." Erick's voice grew louder. The possibility of Isabelle using him made his blood boil, yet a part of him resisted the accusation, the part that still clung to the hope that she was different and that Finn was just up to his old tricks again. Erick stood up taller, jaw clenched, and he could feel a vein throbbing in his temple as Finn continued.

"HigherGround is what you built. Since when have you ever

needed help with your business?"

The statement hit Erick like a brick. It was his vision that had breathed life into HigherGround. But what did Finn know about any of this? How did this get turned around? Finn was the problem, not him. Without a second thought and in a swift motion propelled by rage, Erick shoved his brother back until Finn's spine met the unforgiving concrete wall next to the doorway with a loud thud. Erick's breath came in ragged gasps. "This is about you, not me! What the *hell* are you up to with Grace?" The words came out like bullets and were just as deadly. For a fleeting second, Erick searched his brother's face for a flicker of guilt, for any sign that would betray Finn's true intentions.

Finn's eyes narrowed, and with a sudden burst of force, he defiantly fought back and shoved Erick's chest, breaking the iron grip that pinned him against the wall. "You need to back the hell up!" he spat out.

The push sent Erick stumbling back, throwing him off balance. "After everything I have done for you—hell, what I gave up for you!" The veins in his neck stood out as he screamed at Finn with disgust. "You haven't changed at all, have you?"

The door to the apartment burst open. Erick's wild gaze, along with Finn's defiant stance, was like a powder keg, and this was not going to end well.

"Do we have a problem here?" Daniel's authoritative voice cut through the tension. He glared at his older brothers, his disapproval written all over his face with his piercing stare. "Get inside, *both* of you!" he ordered, rolling his wheelchair back to allow them to pass. "And I don't want to hear another word from either of you unless y'all want to apologize."

The truce Daniel was imposing on them caused Erick to swallow hard and come to his senses. With one last glare at Finn, who remained silent, Erick followed Daniel into the apartment where the scent of herbs and spices filled his nose, bringing him back to reality.

The door closed behind all of them with a soft click, and Daniel maneuvered his wheelchair to the kitchen, where Sky and Isabelle were also having a heated conversation. Erick was concerned about what was going to happen next.

"Is anyone going to tell me what's going on?" Daniel demanded.

"I'm not feeling well," Finn said, heading into the guest room.

"Dinner is just about ready." Sky stepped back from Isabelle and gestured to Daniel to meet her on the patio, leaving Erick alone in the kitchen with Isabelle.

He closed his eyes and wondered what he was doing there and how everything had escalated so quickly.

Chapter 89

Grace's heart was pounding, and she started to panic. "Scott, I can't see anything!" What was she thinking, running off with this man without telling anyone? Realization took hold when she knew that she could take the scarf off and run if she had to. All this letting go was terrifying.

"I got you. Just enjoy." Scott's voice was smooth and calming as he reached for her hand. "I'll give you the first taste."

She took a deep breath, feeling his warmth. "Okay, I'll try."

As the first course arrived, Scott gently fed her a bite. "Here, just focus on the texture and the flavors."

She hesitated but then opened her mouth. The flavors exploded, first sweet then tangy. "Wow, that's amazing."

Scott grinned. "Told you. What do you think it is?"

"I have no idea what it is! But it's delicious. Maybe mango." Grace leaned back, starting to relax. She could hear other guests murmuring every now and then, and she was able to sense whenever someone walked by.

"It's nice to let someone else take care of you, isn't it?" Scott sounded serious.

"Yeah, it is," she admitted, as she felt her shoulders relax.

As the next course came, he continued to feed her, each bite bringing more joy than the last. "So, you promised you'd tell me about your wife," she said, curiosity sparking. She felt around for her own utensils and touched the plate. Her finger touched something squishy. Grace licked her finger and when he didn't respond right away, she could feel the mood shifting slightly.

"Megan was... incredible. We had this storybook romance. Met in high school. It felt like a movie. We rarely fought and we were like two sides of the same coin, always in sync."

Grace listened, intrigued. "What was your wedding like?"

"It was perfect. She wore this breathtaking white dress. I remember thinking... how'd I get so lucky?" There was a hint of sadness in his voice.

"What happened?" she asked gently.

"Then we discovered she was pregnant. We were thrilled. Then... well, things changed. Meg had some kind of fast-growing cancer, and the doctors gave us an unthinkable choice. In the end, I lost them both. There was a gene we could have tested for, but we didn't know."

Grace felt a pang of sympathy. "I'm sorry," she whispered thinking about her own fertility.

"It's okay. Life happens. You just find a way to adapt. You keep moving forward. It's taken me a long time to figure out there is life after grief."

"And now? Do you find it sometimes hard to move on?" she asked.

He took a moment. "Sometimes. But I want to find happiness again, even if it's scary."

She nodded. "It is scary. But maybe it's worth it."

"Exactly." She felt him lean in closer, and his voice lowered. "I'm glad you're here."

Grace was glad as well, and she couldn't agree more. "Me too."

She savored each bite as the final course arrived, feeling

more alive than she had in a long time. "This is the best meal I've ever had, and I can't tell you what any of it was," she said giggling in surprise.

"Glad to hear it."

"Maybe we should do this more often," Grace said, hopeful that he felt the same way.

"Definitely," Scott replied and felt for her hand and squeezed it again. "I'd like that a lot. I've made a list of things I need to do before the end of the year. A bucket list, if you will. But it would be more fun sharing those experiences with someone. Maybe you could be that someone, if you're up to it." In that dark room, with the world outside fading away, they formed a connection.

After dinner, he gently removed the silk scarf from her eyes and drove her back to her car. He got out and leaned in for a deep passionate kiss. Grace wanted more, but Scott pulled away and said, "I'd like to see you again. Maybe sometime soon, you'll want to go on an adventure with me." He ran his fingers through her hair.

"What do you have in mind?" Grace said breathlessly. His lips met hers again, and a surge of excitement rose inside her.

Chapter 90

Erick stood in the small kitchen alone with Isabelle. He didn't know what to say, and it felt like his whole world was upside down. He needed to get some air. Sky and Daniel had already headed outside to the patio.

"Come on Erick, let's go out to the patio," Isabelle suggested.

"I need to ask you a question," Erick said, hanging back.

"What's up?" Isabelle turned around.

"Finn said you were with some guy at the Café Bella the other day."

"What?" Isabelle asked, her eyes widening in disbelief.

"He said you were looking pretty cozy… "

"Finn is trying to break us up, Erick. Can't you see? Besides, doesn't he have a history of causing drama?"

"So you're not cheating on me?" Erick asked.

"No! Why would you say that?" Isabelle took Erick's hand into hers. "Do you really trust your brother's word over mine?"

"I'm just trying to get the facts," Erick said. "So you didn't meet with anyone at at the Café Bella last week?"

"Why would I lie about that?" Isabelle shook her head. "I'm with *you*, Erick. If anyone should be concerned, it should be me. You're the one who is still hung up on your ex-girlfriend!"

"Her lies pour out smoother than wine." Finn entered the kitchen behind Erick, his hands gesturing wildly. "You're seriously going to stand there and deny that you were with that guy?" When she just stood there, he turned to face Erick. "Look. I know our relationship has been rocky most of our lives, but I promise you, I know what I saw. He had dark hair with grey at his temples and was wearing a blue Beyond Limits polo." He shoved the photo on his phone into Erick's view.

Isabelle crossed her arms in front of her and huffed, "Oh, *that* meeting? That was just business."

Erick scoffed when he saw who was in the photo. So, Isabelle *had* met with someone. "Are you talking about Chris Callahan? You've been cheating on me with Callahan?"

"What? *No!*" Isabelle stammered. "That's absurd. It was only business, I *swear!* We met at the conference, and then he reached out last week because he had a proposal for you, Erick."

"It all makes sense now." Erick sighed at the realization as he recalled the phone call he had with Callahan prior to going to Boston. He looked at Isabelle, "So if the proposal was for me, why didn't you tell me Chris Callahan was in town?" His fury subsided for the moment, but he was going to get to the bottom of all of this.

Isabelle took a step back and sipped the rest of her white wine. Her eyes were wide, but her expression shifted; the corners of her mouth curled into a smile. "I wanted it to be a surprise," she began, choosing her words carefully. "Because he's willing to give you a very substantial offer to buy—"

"What?" Sky choked out incredulously. She had suddenly appeared in the kitchen.

Erick's jaw tightened as he tried to process this unexpected piece of the puzzle that was his life. Erick struggled to maintain his composure. "I'm not selling HigherGround, nor have I had any time to think about any of this," he managed to say. "I sure as hell didn't need to hear all of this from *Finn*. *You* should have told me."

Isabelle scanned the room, the casual tilt of her head dismissing the seriousness of Erick's accusation. "I thought we were celebrating tonight."

Erick fought to keep the anger from his voice as he looked at Finn. "That was the original idea."

"Hey, I thought you should know." Finn shrugged and announced, "Anyway, I'm not much in the mood to celebrate anymore. I'm going to call it a night."

Isabelle stepped closer to Erick, her movements fluid and graceful, and she wrapped her arms around his waist as Finn disappeared into the guest room.

"I'm sorry," she murmured against the fabric of his shirt, her breath warm on his skin. "I was trying to surprise you. I meant no harm," she said with regret. Erick felt the faint touch of her fingers as they traced the contour of his back, seeking to soothe him with her touch.

Erick glanced over Isabelle's head at Sky, his eyes seeking understanding and forgiveness.

"I'm sorry about dinner," he said, "and for everything else."

His gaze shifted from Sky to Isabelle "I'm not feeling well. I think I'll go." He looked down at Isabelle. "Do you need a ride back to your apartment, or do you want to stay, Isabelle?"

When she didn't respond right away, he stepped away from Isabelle's embrace. Erick called out to his dog. "Come on Jacey boy!"

Isabelle's voice cut through the awkwardness as she placed the wine glass on the table

"Wait, I'll go with you!" Turning toward Sky and Daniel, "I'm truly sorry, for all this," she gushed, her eyes downcast.

Daniel nodded, an understanding between him and Erick that only years of shared history could have built. He rolled closer. "Dude," he pleaded. "Call me later, alright?"

Once outside, Erick, Jace, and Isabelle ran through the rain to his Jeep. He put his seatbelt on and exhaled slowly as Jace quietly settled down on his blanket in the back. Isabelle sat silently beside Erick.

"I need you to slow down a bit," Erick said, finally breaking the silence. His voice was raspy with fatigue. "I need to think about what I want to do. Tonight was about Finn's sobriety, not about the business or even about us. We somehow lost sight of this."

Isabelle shifted in her seat, turning to face him with an expression of concern. "Selling your business doesn't happen over night," she said softly.

"*Please,* Isabelle," Erick pleaded as he shook his head. "I just need time to process everything. I thought we were getting closer, but now I fear we are on two completely different pages of thought on what we want our life to look like."

Erick was at a crossroads, and he knew it. There was only one thing he could do in this situation, and he wondered why God felt so far away from him right now. He navigated the streets on autopilot, his thoughts a jumbled mess as the rain came down in sheets.

Isabelle turned toward him. "We can go as slow as you want. It doesn't matter what we do as long as we're together."

"I'm trying to believe that," he began, his voice rough with emotion. "And if we are truly together, why are you doing business deals with Callahan behind my back?" His eyes found Isabelle's briefly begging for understanding. "I really do care for you, Isabelle, but I'm just under a lot of stress right now. I need time to see where God is taking me."

The journey across town passed slowly in silence except for the squeak of the wipers gliding across the windshield. When they finally arrived at Isabelle's apartment, she turned to him as he parked the Jeep, her eyes searching his face. "Come in. I'll make you feel better," she suggested gently.

Erick's response came slowly, his fatigue evident in the sagging of his shoulders and the resignation in his voice. "Not tonight." His voice cracked slightly, revealing the depth of his weariness. "I need space. I'll call you when I'm ready to talk."

"Of course," she said softly. She opened the door, and Erick watched as Isabelle stepped out of the Jeep. She glanced over her shoulder, her hair and face soaked with the rain. "Take as much time as you need."

The door closed, leaving him alone with his thoughts and the quiet company of Jace sleeping in the back seat as she disappeared into the building.

Chapter 91

Grace stood by the fireplace in Scott's living room. His home was a quintessential New England Colonial with dark wooden floors. The farmhouse charm and decor looked like a spread in Architectural Digest magazine. Her breath caught as her gaze locked on a magnificent large framed wedding photo of Scott and Megan looking so much in love. The room started spinning, and Grace suddenly felt dizzy, just as Scott entered, holding two glasses of wine.

He handed her a glass, smiling, but his eyes lingered on the photo, too. "Cheers," he said clinking his glass with Grace's.

"Thanks," Grace said, her eyes drawn to to the enormous photo as if Megan was there in the room with them.

"Yeah, that was a great day," he reminisced, staring at his wedding picture.

"I can see you both were really happy," Grace whispered as she sipped her wine.

"We were. Megan had a way of lighting up a room." He wrapped his arms around Grace as if they were looking at beautiful scenery instead of his dead wife.

She took another sip and looked around the room. "All these things are hers?"

"I guess I haven't wanted to change it too much. It feels like… part of her is still here."

Grace looked down at her glass and swirled the wine. She hesitated, then spoke. "Well… it's just… I mean, you two look like you had quite a life together."

"We did. But that life ended." Scott exhaled and ran his hand through his hair.

Grace bit her lip, unsure how to proceed. "And you're ready to start a new one? With me? But I see her everywhere. It's hard not to feel that you're not quite ready."

"I'm sorry. This was a mistake." Scott sighed.

"No, I'm glad you brought me here. I can see how much she meant to you, and I think we both just need some time." She took a deep breath, and the tension eased slightly.

"I agree. Time is good." Scott put his wine glass down on the mantle. "I should take you back to your car."

They hastily got into the Bronco, and Scott drove her to the church parking lot where her old sedan was the only car left. He leaned over and kissed her again.

Scott sat back in his seat as he let a breath out. "So, about that guy at the grief group… Finn, was it?"

Grace rolled her eyes. "Can we not talk about him?"

"Just curious. You two seemed… close."

"We were once." Grace looked out the window. "Does it matter?"

"Yes, it does. I'm trying to get to know you."

"We met at Kings Oxford School. But I ended up dating his brother, Erick.

"Then after we graduated, I dated Finn."

"Ah, so he *is* your ex!" Scott looked amused now. "There must be something still there?"

"It didn't end well," Grace confessed as she fidgeted with her hands. This was not how she thought this evening was going to turn out.

"Wait, you dated *both* of the brothers?"

"It was a long time ago. Love has been complicated for me. Erick got tired of waiting for me to change and get over my past."

"But if you only love someone hoping they'll change, that's not really love, is it? Love should be about accepting the other person completely, flaws and all."

Scott had a point, and as much as she wanted to get to know him better, she wasn't sure she could compete with the ghost of his wife. She had her *own* ghosts to deal with.

He looked her in the eye. "True. Change is risky. But what about your family?"

Grace shook her head. "They're complicated. I'm definitely not ready to dive into that."

"No diving? You're missing out."

"I've done enough diving into memories for one day."

"How about a new adventure then? Tomorrow, skydiving."

"Skydiving? That's on your bucket list?" Her eyes were wide now.

"Come on," Scott said. "It'll be fun. Just you and me taking a step forward."

"What if I fall?"

"Then I'll catch you, but falling is kinda the whole point." Scott looked amused.

Grace got out of the Bronco after Scott said he would pick her up at seven the next morning.

"Okay, sure. Let's do it. What could possibly go wrong?"

Chapter 92

Erick watched as Isabelle walked through the main entrance to her apartment. She disappeared from view, and Jace shifted in the back seat, a low whine breaking the silence. Erick put the Jeep in gear and navigated the familiar roads back to his cabin. Erick's mind raced as Grace's words came back to him, hauntingly similar to his most recent plea to Isabelle for time and space. He realized he was seeking the same understanding that Grace had sought from him. He needed time to find all the answers—about Finn's newfound connection with Grace and Isabelle's unexpected dealings with Callahan. He reached back and patted Jace once more, a silent promise that they would face whatever came next together.

Once home in the cabin, Erick fed Jace dinner and filled his water bowl. Then he called Daniel.

"Hey." Erick said, sounding defeated.

"What's happening with you? Sky and I are concerned."

"Too many things to count." Erick took a deep breath. "Isabelle found a buyer for HigherGround."

"I didn't know you were selling," Daniel said slowly.

"I'm not."

"I guess that explains why Sky and Isabelle seem to be at odds lately. Does this affect our plans for Georgia in the winter?"

Erick just shook his head. "Nothing has changed about that."

"But there must be something else that has you so rattled?" Daniel insisted.

"Yeah, I was supposed to pick up Finn at his grief counseling group. After everything Finn had put us all through, I thought he had changed for good this time."

"He seemed better, don't you agree?" When Erick didn't respond right away, Daniel asked, "What has he done?"

"Finn was with Grace. They were acting like they were together."

"What?" Daniel gasped. "No way, man! That can't be true."

"I know, but I saw it with my own eyes." Erick ran his hand through his hair.

"There has to be some explanation. Did he say they were *together* together?"

"No, he denied it all. But that's what he does. I'm so tired of giving everything to people who just want to take more and more from me." Erick was resigned. "I think Isabelle and Callahan have been planning this takeover since the conference. I can feel something is definitely wrong here. Maybe I *will* sell and follow you guys to Georgia. Start a new life, a quiet one."

"Ah, I'm so sorry, dude. But before you make any rash decisions, let's figure out what's really going on here. I'm certain that things are not what they seem with Finn. He talked to me about moving out as soon as possible. He feels like he's a burden on us. That doesn't sound like someone out to get you." Daniel took a breath as if he was going to say something difficult. "You aren't going to like hearing this, but maybe you're the one that has it wrong here. We don't know the whole story. There's no way Finn would reconnect with Grace romantically. For God's sake, he knows... heck we *all* know you still are in love with her!"

"I am not in love with Grace! But Daniel… it was crazy. I have a hard time seeing it any other way. The only reason Grace and I broke up was because she couldn't forgive what Finn had done to her. I told her I was supporting Finn through his sobriety, and she chose not to stay because of that. Yet she seemed perfectly fine tonight." Erick squeezed his eyes shut and collapsed in defeat on his bed with the phone pressed to his ear.

"Either way, you really need to talk to both of them," Daniel said. "Betrayal cuts deep, but there's no way he's dating Grace behind your back. Sorry all this seems to be happening all at once. It sounds overwhelming. You know I'll always be there for you, but if I'm being honest, it sounds to me like you need to go for a run and maybe spend some time in prayer. That has always worked for you before."

"You're right." Erick sighed and looked over at Jace at the foot of the bed. "You're *always* right. I need to do that now. Thanks for listening."

"Anytime," Daniel said, and before hanging up he left him with these words. "Everything will work out as it should. You'll know what to do next."

It was late and Erick was exhausted, so he took a shower and went to bed. He woke before the sun was up and decided to go to the place where he could pour his heart out and receive the clarity he so desperately needed.

"Let's go, Jace!" Erick called to his dog. He pulled his rain jacket on and together they ran into the woods on the familiar trail to untangle the pains that life had thrown at him time and time again.

Chapter 93

Grace sat in the cramped cabin of the small airplane, her heart racing as she stared at the safety video playing on a screen. The small plane rattled as it climbed into the clear, bright, blue sky. She wasn't sure it even felt safe on the plane, let alone jumping out of it. It was supposed to be thrilling, this skydiving adventure with Scott, yet all she could focus on was the tightness in her chest and the overwhelming fear which pressed down on her. *What am I thinking? This has to be the worst decision I've made yet.*

"Would you look at that!" Scott leaned closer, his eyes wide with adventure as he pointed at the video. "Did you see how they just floated down after the freefall? It's like flying!"

"More like plummeting," Grace muttered under her breath, her palms sweaty. She hadn't expected the fear to come crashing in like this.

"Hey," he said softly, his voice warm like the morning sunlight that streamed into the small windows. "You okay?"

Grace grimaced, and her stomach twisted. "Yeah, just a little nervous. I mean, we're jumping out of a perfectly good airplane. Heights are no longer my thing, obviously."

"You're not wrong," he chuckled. "But think about it! You're leaving comfort behind, and that's a big step. I know you're ready for this."

She bit her lip, glancing back at the screen. The instructor was smiling, an overly enthusiastic grin that felt like a lie.

"I'm not ready," Grace said. "What if I can't do it?"

Scott leaned in closer, his shoulder brushing against hers. "Just breathe. Focus on the moment. Do you remember how you felt when you first rode a roller coaster? This is going to be even better."

The plane lurched, and Grace's breath caught in her throat. "This isn't even close to riding a roller coaster!"

"Just wait until you're free falling. You'll feel alive!" he promised, but her heartbeat was banging in her ears along with the loud engine of the plane.

As the plane ascended higher, the knot in her stomach grew. The guide began strapping her into the harness, and panic surged through her veins like wildfire. "I can tell you've never done this before."

She shot back at him, "I can't do this!" then gasped, her voice trembling.

"Grace, look at me." Scott's eyes locked onto hers, intense and steady. "You can. You're stronger than you think. Just take a deep breath."

The wind whistled through the now open door of the plane, and she was afraid to look down at the ground. The roar of the engine only heightened her sense of dread. "Scott, I—"

"Trust me," he urged, his hand gripping her forearm. "I'll be right there with you. You're going to love it."

Her heart felt like it was going to explode as her guide motioned to her, signaling it was time. Grace swallowed hard, her throat dry. The nausea rolled over her in waves, threatening to overwhelm her.

"This is a terrible idea," she muttered as she looked down at the ground.

"Now or never!" Scott shouted, his grin wide and infectious. He was so confident, so sure of himself. It made her feel small and uncertain, yet somehow, she wanted to be brave for him.

Before she could fully process what was happening, the guide shoved her forward, and with a sudden rush, they were tumbling into the open air. The wind whooshed past her ears, the world below disappearing in a blur as she tumbled round and round. It felt like being yanked from reality, thrown into a world where nothing made sense.

Flashbacks of falling from the cliff filled her mind but then suddenly disappeared. Her fears turned into exhilaration and blue sky. The sensation was surreal. It didn't feel like falling. It really was more like... flying! A sense of freedom wrapped around her and her heart rate began to slow down. "I can't believe this!" she yelled back. Her voice swallowed whole against the rush of the wind.

The parachute deployed with a gentle tug, and suddenly, everything slowed. They floated, suspended in the sky, the world sprawled beneath them. The chaos of the freefall faded, replaced by soft air around her, and she looked over at Scott as his parachute opened.

Grace gasped in awe, the thrill of the moment washing over her like a wave. "I can't believe I'm really doing this!"

"You're doing great!" the guide shouted in her ear from behind her as they prepared to meet the ground.

And there, in the vastness of the sky, Grace felt something shift inside her. Maybe it wasn't just about facing her fears; it was about discovering herself, piece by exhilarating piece.

Chapter 94

Erick returned from his run, the humid, fog-thickened air clinging to his skin. He bounded up the stairs of his deck toward the cabin, Jace trotting beside him, panting softly. A familiar heaviness settled in his chest as he approached the door. Just then, he noticed it was slightly ajar and frowned. Erick was sure he locked the door, which meant someone was inside. He carefully pushed the door open, ready to face his intruder, with Jace right by his side.

But then, Jace began barking excitedly and wagging his tail as if he knew the trespasser.

"Hey, Jacey-boy!" Finn said, leaning down to pet the dog. He smiled in a way that had always irked Erick, especially in moments like this.

"You're lucky I didn't have a weapon," Erick said. He was annoyed Finn was here but was glad he didn't have an actual intruder.

"I found the key under the mat," Finn said. "I thought I'd wait for you."

"Sure, just come in *uninvited*," Erick snapped, trying to keep his irritation in check. He dropped his keys on the table. "What do you want, Finn?" He turned his back on his brother, filling up Jace's water bowl, and then he filled a glass of water for himself, not offering any to his unexpected guest.

Finn took a step forward, his expression shifting to something more serious. "I wanted to talk. About everything. Clear the air."

Erick rolled his eyes. "What's there to talk about? You've already done enough damage with the whole Grace situation."

"I know," Finn admitted, his voice softening. "Look, I didn't know she was in the same grief group. But... I have to say I'm glad she was." Finn continued as Erick narrowed his eyes. "I think sometimes you forget how long Grace and I were together."

Erick folded his arms and shifted from foot to foot. What was Finn getting at here?

"Even so," Finn shook his head, "it's as if we hardly knew each other. This group has helped us both to see each other's perspective and clear up some issues from our past. I was only trying to make amends for the way I treated her for all those years. But I don't have any romantic interest in her now, and I know she doesn't have any in me, either. I was honest in the group, and when she shared her side of the story, I finally understood how deeply I had hurt her. And the worst part was, that person wasn't even the real me. That person I was—the abused, insecure, lonely version of myself—is someone I *never* want to be again. Look, I know I messed up, and I'm not here to fight. I'm here to mend our relationship because you're my brother, my *twin*, and I honestly care about you."

Erick didn't respond. He couldn't. He was truly speechless. Finn continued, closing the silence between them. "Anyway, and more importantly, you and Grace belong together."

"Finn... " Erick began.

"Please don't deny it. You know it, and I know it. And I'm sure she has feelings for you, too. The only two people who don't seem to know it are you and Grace."

Jace whined softly, sensing the tension in the room. Erick knelt down to scratch his dog behind the ears, avoiding Finn's gaze. "It doesn't matter anymore. She's moved on, and I'm moving to Georgia, Finn. Maybe even going there with Isabelle. We're starting a new chapter." He wasn't sure if anything was going to actually work out, but this was the best plan he could think of. This town was suffocating him, and he needed a fresh start away from Grace.

"Guess we all are moving on. I'm planning a trip to Texas after the trial," Finn confessed and ran his hand through his hair in frustration. "I want to look into getting a therapy dog and visiting a friend from rehab. I need to re-focus on myself."

"Good for you," Erick said, looking defeated. He still felt the weight of their past. "But for God's sake, Finn, why are you here *now*?"

Finn sighed. "I just… I don't want us to be at odds anymore. Can we just drop the whole Grace thing? Focus on what's next for us?"

Erick hesitated, but he realized Finn had come to him vulnerable and willing to mend their relationship. If Erick didn't do that, he was going against everything he stood for. Forgiveness was his salvation. He felt the walls he had built around his heart starting to come down. "I guess we can try."

"Try?" Finn echoed, a flicker of hope in his eyes.

"Yeah, try," Erick said, his voice grumpy but softer. "We've got enough to deal with Brook and the trial."

"Agreed," Finn said, smiling with relief.

Erick moved over and hugged his brother. "It'll take some time for me to rebuild our trust, but you are my brother, and I want us to put the past behind us."

"That is exactly what I came here for. Thank you." Finn slapped his brother on the back. "Now… you got any food in this tiny house?"

Erick laughed as he shook his head and took out a carton of eggs from the fridge. This was what he had always wanted, everyone getting along. There was still uncertainty with Isabelle, Finn's upcoming trial, and Daniel moving to Georgia. But as he moved around the kitchen, he felt something for the first time in a long time. Maybe things were finally going to work out for the Finn brothers. It filled his heart with joy for the first time in a long while.

Chapter 95

Grace wrapped her hand around her cup of tea allowing the warmth to calm her racing heart. Scott sat across from her in a booth at a cozy diner called Maverick's, the smell of bacon and coffee filling the air.

"Can you believe we actually did that? I thought I'd lose my stomach halfway down." Scott put a forkful of eggs in his mouth. The waitress dropped off a large stack of steaming pancakes between them. "Thank you!"

"Right? I was sure I'd freeze up. But jumping out of a plane? It felt… *freeing!*"

"I'm so proud of you for facing your fears and doing it anyway," Scott said.

"I guess that's true. Still, I can't believe they let me jump. It's barely been two years since my surgery." Grace took a sip of her tea. "What's next for you? Exploring the pyramids in Egypt?" Grace blushed and stabbed at a pancake, her appetite returning.

"Yes, let's add that to the list." Scott pulled out a leather-bound journal and a pen and crossed off Skydiving on the list when his phone rang. "I'll be right back, okay?" He pressed the phone to his ear and stepped out of the diner.

Grace watched him leave and then turned her attention to the planes that took off with passengers awaiting their jump. Every day with Scott was more exhilarating than the next. She looked down at the open journal and then looked outside at Scott who was still engaged in his phone conversation. Carefully, she slid the journal over to her side of the table and turned it around. Her heart raced, but her shoulders slumped when she saw the flowery writing.

When I'm gone, promise me you will live your life in a way that we never got to. I'll always be with you and looking down from above knowing you are living life to its fullest. This is my wish for you. Here is a list to get you started.

Adventure of your choice

~~Skydiving~~

Cliff Jumping

Cage Shark Diving

Backpack

Long Road Trip Coast to Coast

~~Experience dining in the dark~~

Grace couldn't believe her eyes. This was a message from Megan beyond the grave. Her eyes fell down the list and looked at the next page. The final adventure she had planned for him.

Find someone to share it with

Quickly she pushed the journal back to his side of the table and shortly after, Scott returned with a big grin on his face.

"I have news!" Scott said, sliding back into the booth. When the waitress returned to drop off the bill, he handed her his credit card. "Thank you."

"What is it?" Grace asked, and pulled out some bills of her

own, but Scott waved her away.

"I have an appointment with an agent later. I'm putting my house up for sale or rent, and I quit my job at the Hartford Courant."

"That explains a lot!" Grace smiled.

"Yeah," he shrugged. "I want to write for myself now. I'm already working on a memoir."

"Is that so? That makes two of us."

"You're a writer, too?" Scott slid several pancakes onto his plate and dug in.

"I just finished with my second book about my mother's legacy. Wait, you're really leaving your house? Just like that?" Grace recalled the perfect house that Megan had decorated impeccably.

"Yeah. I figured, why not? Life's too short to just sit around."

"That's… bold. What if it doesn't work out?"

"What's the worst that could happen? I could rent it out or find another job. But I can't keep waiting around for life to happen. I've spent months after the funeral not being able to get out of bed." Scott looked down at his plate. "I was hoping to ask you a question." Scott paused and looked intensely at her. "What if you came with me on an epic road trip? We could hit some spots on my list together." He picked up his notebook.

"A road trip? Just like that? Don't you have obligations?" She sat back in the booth, stunned. But Scott's offer seemed way too good to be true. The fact that he hadn't warned her about the shrine at his house or that he was hiding the fact that he was following his late wife's quest, not his own, still confused her.

"Yeah, I have some loose ends that need to be tied up. That's why I'm leaving at the end of the month. Could be fun. You can't live in fear, Grace. You just jumped out of a plane!" Scott stabbed another pancake and flopped it down on his plate eager to dive in. "No pressure, of course."

"Maybe." Grace didn't know what to think of this man. Her experience with men caused her a lot of pain in the last decade. *Could she trust herself? Could she trust this man?*

"Then we'll figure it out together. Look, I'm planning to go to the fundraiser at the church this weekend. It supports the youth group and mission trips. You should come."

"I'll think about the road trip, but the fundraiser is something I'd like to go to, for sure," Grace said. "I'm grateful for the meetings, and I'd like to give back."

They finished their breakfast, and after Scott drove her back to the cottage, she looked up to the clear sky, recalling her exhilaration from earlier that morning. The sun shone brighter now above the clouds as Grace stepped out of Scott's Bronco, her feet planted firmly on the ground. The path ahead was uncertain, but one thing was clear: it was time for Grace to find her way home, wherever that may be. She knew who she was now: a survivor, an author, a woman reborn from the ashes of her past. And with that knowledge came power—the power to decide her destiny, to perhaps break free from the gravitational pull of the Finn brothers and this small-town life.

It was time to go, to seek the space where her spirit could soar, and she was grateful that Scott would be a part of it all. Grace turned and went inside, the door closing behind her. It was time to write a new story.

Chapter 96

E rick arrived at the bake sale for the fundraiser at the church that Saturday afternoon. Isabelle had invited him over a week ago, and he needed to clear the air since they hadn't spoken since Daniel's dinner party. Finn texted him that morning that he was going to the church fundraiser and had something important to show him.

The church hall was buzzing with activity. Tables with white tablecloths were lined up, and the smell of fresh baked goods filled the air. Erick walked up to Isabelle who was arranging some items on her table.

"Hey," he said.

"Didn't think you'd come." Isabelle glared in his direction.

"A promise is a promise." Erick threw his hands up in defeat. "Look, Isabelle, I acted out of line the other day. I'm sorry. I know you were just trying to help." He wasn't all in with her future plans and was still uncertain about her relationship with Callahan. He hoped Isabelle could be trusted, but he also knew that time would have a way of revealing everything. When he reached for a cinnamon roll, Isabelle slapped his hand and then pointed to the donation box.

"That's for the kids! Pay first," Isabelle teased. "It is a bake *sale*!"

"This should cover it." Erick placed a large bill in the box and then put his hand out and waited. She handed him one of the pastries wrapped in a napkin as more people approached the table. "I'd like to talk to you more, but this really isn't the time or place. I see you're busy and my brother is over there. Can we meet up after?"

"I'm not going to wait *forever*," Isabelle said sarcastically.

Erick stuffed the roll in his mouth ignoring her jab and made his way over to Finn, who was talking to a dark-haired woman holding a leash attached to a calm German Shepherd.

Finn looked up as Erick approached. "Hey, man. I'm glad you're here. We need to talk. But first, this is Rachel, and *this* is Buddy." At the mention of his name, the dog perked up.

Erick knelt down to the German Shepherd to pet him, but stopped short when he saw the vest where not only his name was embroidered, but it also said WORKING DOG. "My apologies, Rachel. I didn't realize he was working. What a beautiful dog you have here."

"No worries, he helps me to stay calm when he senses I'm in a crisis."

"I see. Very nice to meet you both."

"Same. Buddy and I are going over to the pet treats table. He's earned a break. I'll catch up with you later," Rachel said and she and the dog left the brothers alone.

"I realized I never truly apologized when I jumped to conclusions the other day about Grace. I'm sorry," Erick said, smiling over at Finn. "So is the girl with the dog what you wanted to show me?"

"Apology accepted, but I wish you would admit that I was right about you still having feelings for Grace," Finn countered.

"We've been over this. I'm still with Isabelle."

"Even after she lied to you about Callahan? And since when

do you need help with HigherGround? Do you understand that Isabelle's just using you?" Finn looked behind Erick and back at his brother. "You need to see this, Erick. Look at what Callahan's been up to."

Finn unfolded a printed piece of paper from his pocket and handed it to his brother. Erick skimmed the document, which was an article from a newspaper.

"They paint him as the savior of small medical facilities," Erick said, keeping his eyes fixed on the article."But… it's all smoke and mirrors."

"Rising costs, forced closures," Finn added. "He standardizes care, but it's a cover-up. Makes him look good, but—"

"But the people who suffer? Like they don't count?" Erick was getting annoyed with all this. "I know all about this. People were discussing it at the conference in Boston."

"Exactly. With Callahan, it's all about the image. And look at this." Finn handed Erick another print out.

Erick stared at the paper and asked, "What's this?"

"Isabelle's private Instagram account. Don't ask how I got it, just… just look."

Erick looked down at the small photos of Isabelle and Chris Callahan together way before Daniel's wedding and a photo of the two of them under the Beyond Limits banner during the conference. They did look like a couple.

"Unbelievable," Erick said, shaking his head.

"Look, maybe there's nothing to it, or maybe… it's a worst-case scenario. Either way, tread lightly with Isabelle until you find out all the facts. And promise me you'll talk to Grace one last time before you move on." Finn put his arms on his brother's shoulders as his eyes fell on something across the room. "Actually, the timing couldn't be more perfect." He spun Erick around, and Erick finally realized who Finn was looking at. Her red hair drew him in immediately and took his breath away. Grace was there in the flesh. He had two questions pop into his mind: *Why was she here, and why on earth was she talking to Isabelle?*

Chapter 97

G race stepped into the church's main room that was filled with several vendors, bakery items, pet treats, books, and assorted candles. As she scanned the crowd over for Scott, she noticed an unusual sight toward the back of the room. First, Finn and Erick were in the middle of what looked like a heated discussion. *Great.* She should've known that they both would be at the event. But then she saw Erick's girlfriend, Isabelle, and she felt a sinking sensation in her gut. *Here goes nothing,* she thought as she shrugged and went over to the bakery tables where arrays of pastries, croissants, and cinnamon rolls were displayed artfully. *Drop the money in and leave,* she thought. *Don't make eye contact.* But as Grace dropped cash into the fundraiser box, she couldn't help but lift her gaze toward Isabelle. *Ms. Perfect is standing here looking down at everyone, and she doesn't look like she would ever eat any of the food she is selling.*

Isabelle looked up, surprise flickering across her face. "Oh! Grace, isn't it?"

"That's me," Grace replied. *Keep it short.*

"Thanks for the donation."

"Of course."

Isabelle offered her a cinnamon roll, and Grace took it, glancing around. "Wow, it sure is busy. How's the event going?"

Isabelle's smile faded. "You know, just your typical fundraiser. Are you here alone?"

"I came for the fundraiser, Isabelle. Not sure what you are implying."

Grace watched as Isabelle's eyes darted toward Erick and then back to her.

"Is that the only reason?" Isabelle asked, throwing Grace off balance for a second with the accusation.

"I'm not here to stalk you and Erick, Isabelle. I'm here with someone else." Grace glanced in the direction of the Finn brothers and decided enough was enough. She didn't need anyone questioning her integrity. It couldn't hurt to say exactly what she was thinking. "Besides, what do you care? From what I heard, you're with some other guy, so how serious could your relationship with Erick be?"

Isabelle's eyebrows caved, her eyes narrowing. "You have no idea what you're talking about."

"Oh, but I think I do. I know how deeply Erick cares for people. He's so trusting. Maybe too trusting. But you?" Grace surprised even herself with her rant. "If there's one thing I know, it's that you're not the right fit for him. Not even close."

Isabelle smirked, "You think you know him better than I do?"

"I've known him for years. In that time, I've watched him give everything to everyone. It's one of the things I used to love about him. You act like you're some kind of prize, but you're just a distraction."

"*Distraction?*" Isabelle said haughtily. "Get over yourself. I'm not just some *fling*."

Grace shrugged. "Erick deserves someone real. Someone who won't play games. I know you're just using him. And that's cruel. The Finns deserve better than the likes of you."

"And who made *you* the moral authority?" Isabelle crossed

her arms as the crowd moved past her table.

"I'm not. But when I see bullshit… like you pretending to be Christian and give a damn about people I care about, it gets to me." Grace was not backing down.

"Maybe you're just scared he realized he deserves more than what *you* could give him. Someone who knows what she wants and isn't afraid to go after it." Isabelle looked around. "So where's your date? Or are you just *pretending* to have one?"

"Not that it's any of your business, but his name is Scott." Grace looked around.

"Scott Townsend?" Isabelle challenged.

"You know him?" Grace frowned. *Of course Ms. Perfect knew all the men.*

"I've seen him around at church." Isabelle stood up straighter. "He's a widower."

"It doesn't matter to me. We all have a past." Grace stood her ground. "But don't try to change the subject. Erick will never put up with betrayal," she shrugged. "You'll see."

"You should be careful yourself," Isabelle said. "You know, Scott and his wife were very close. No one thinks he'll ever get over her. She was so beautiful, and well, a love like that… you can't replace it." Isabelle smiled, satisfied that she dropped that little nugget of information.

"Unlike you, I don't feel the need to change anyone I care about." Grace put her hands on her hips. "I've moved on. You should too. You *don't* belong here." Grace shook her head at this ridiculous conversation.

"Moved on? Or just still pretending?" Isabelle's tone was sharp, and then she smiled. "Speak of the devil."

Grace looked in the direction Isabelle was facing and saw Scott enter the building. She regained her composure, knowing that Isabelle was just trying to get under her skin.

"The only person pretending is you." Grace realized this exchange was going nowhere, and wanted to grab Scott and leave now. She lifted the cinnamon roll to take a bite, but stopped short. "You know what? Maybe we both just need to settle this once and for all—"

Suddenly, a hand shot out. It was in her periphery, and Grace was stunned when it slapped her hand with so much force that the roll went flying in the air. It felt like time had suspended as all eyes followed the pastry which hung in the air briefly until hit the floor with a splat.

Chapter 98

Erick was trying to process all of what Finn was saying. Everyone had tried to warn Erick about Callahan. Finn was right about everything he had suspected about Isabelle. He decided to confront her, but when he turned in Isabelle's direction, he saw Grace. She and Isabelle were arguing, and he didn't know what to do, so he stood there paralyzed, watching the scene unfold.

Isabelle handed Grace a large cinnamon roll. *She isn't actually going to eat that. Grace is just being nice.* Suddenly, the conversation started to get louder and he could not look away. How could he go over there? He was still upset about finding out Isabelle had played him this whole time. Just then, the unthinkable happened, and Grace leaned in to take a bite of the cinnamon roll.

"Noooo!" he yelled and without a second thought, he sprinted across the room. He smacked Grace's hand hard, which sent the roll flying in one swift movement, landing in a heap by her feet. It all felt like a movie scene in slow motion.

"What the—?" Grace said, her eyes wild with anger as she

stared directly at Erick.

"Are you out of your mind?" he shrieked and stuttered. "You can't... she can't... she could die!" His outburst caused everyone in the room to look over.

A man with shoulder length brown hair walked over, "Is there a problem here? Finn is it?"

Erick glared at the man. "The name is Erick and *you* are?"

"I'm—" The man got cut off because Erick didn't care who he thought he was.

"What were you thinking?" Erick turned back to Isabelle, his panic still in his voice. "Cinnamon could kill her!"

"Let's take a breath here." Finn arrived by his brother's side. He intervened by gently putting his hand on Erick's chest.

Isabelle's confusion turned to irritation. "How am I supposed to know that? The sign here says to tell us if you have any allergic concerns. It's not like I'm trying to kill her or anyone else."

"Grace isn't allergic to cinnamon," the unknown man chimed in.

"Why are you still talking?" Erick snapped at the man. He broke free from Finn's grip. "Who the hell are you??"

"We need to calm down, Erick," Finn warned. "It's a bake sale. And we're in a church."

"The name's Scott Townsend." Scott moved closer to Grace in an oddly protective way that Erick didn't see coming. His stomach knotted more as he watched Scott put his hand on her arm right in front of him. "Are you okay?" The man lowered his voice as he spoke to Grace.

"I'm fine. It was just an honest mistake." Grace looked over at Isabelle and then at Erick. "Isabelle didn't know, and besides, it turns out my mother didn't leave me with that allergy after all."

Erick was stunned at this revelation. "Are you sure it's safe?"

"You need to chill, man. This is not the time or place for this." Scott turned to Grace. "Want to get out of here?"

"Sure, I'll meet you outside. I just need a minute," Grace said, and Scott reluctantly left the church room.

"Are we good here?" Finn asked Erick whose jaw was set.

"It's fine." Erick had made a mess of everything once again, and he had had enough. He was tired of trying to make everything right when everything felt so wrong. Finn walked away slowly with Grace and there was nothing he could do or say about it.

"Why would I try to *kill* your ex-girlfriend?" Isabelle demanded an answer from Erick.

"I never said you were trying to kill her. I was just… " Erick squeezed his eyes shut.

"Playing the hero again?" Isabelle now had her hands on her hips.

Erick gestured to the room. "Thank God she wasn't allergic! Or I'd be calling 911." He sighed and shook his head. "I can't be here right now."

"Because you still have feelings for your ex?" Isabelle challenged.

"Give it a rest, Isabelle. You want to know why I'm really upset right now? I know everything. You and Callahan were together this whole time. You both played me at the conference. You tipped your hand when you asked me to give up the things that mean the most to me."

"Erick, please… " Isabelle said, looking around to make sure no one was listening.

"No, Isabelle. No. You need to tell me right now. Was any of this real?"

"Yes, Erick. Yes. But now is hardly the time or place to talk about this." Isabelle looked over at Finn and then over at Grace across the room.

"Why? Are you afraid the good people of this church will realize what a scam artist you are?" he wanted to say, but he didn't. Instead, he said, "I'm not sure anything you could say would change my mind at this point. I've been wrong about everything it seems. You lied about Callahan and broke my trust. And because of that, I think we should take a break."

"Erick, let's just talk about this later. Please, I love you."

"No. I need time to figure out what I'm doing with my life."
Erick was done. Done with all the insanity. All he wanted was to
see Daniel and figure out how soon they all could start packing.
The trial was coming up quickly, but after that there would be
nothing tying him here anymore.

Isabelle just stared at him with her mouth open in disbelief
as he turned and walked out of the church. He didn't look back,
and he wouldn't.

Chapter 99

Grace left the scene feeling sick to her gut about everything. She walked over to a less crowded area of the church with Finn as her heart rate started to settle down.

"Hey, are you sure you're okay?" Finn asked, concerned.

"I'm fine," she said again.

"Sorry you had to deal with all that. Things escalated quickly."

"Yeah, things got crazy so fast. I just want to get out of there."

"I'm glad you're okay. Look," he said, running his fingers through his hair. "I hate to bring it up again, but have you considered helping me out with the case against Brook? No pressure, just curious."

"I have a lot going on this month with my new book and other things." *There were other things, like being with Scott.* "I'd like to hear more about the project before I can decide."

"Sure. I just only need a few hours of your time to look over some legal documents."

"When do you need my answer?"

"As soon as you can. The court date is coming up fast. It would mean a lot if you could help."

"I understand. Okay, I'll let you know." Grace turned to leave when she heard Finn call out to her.

"Grace?"

"Yeah?" She turned around to see his concerned face.

"It's none of my business, but forget about Isabelle. Erick will figure it all out in his own time. I just wish you both could see what I see. I hope it's not too late."

"I'm sorry, but I can't have this conversation with you right now." Grace felt a pain in her heart as she knew Scott was waiting for her. The time was approaching where she would have to make a decision that would change all their destinies going forward. She would be lying if she didn't admit her heart skipped a beat at Finn's revelation about Erick still having feelings for her. It didn't matter now, and she didn't want to wait around there any longer. "I have to go, but I'll let you know if I can find the time to help you with your case."

"I'll be waiting." Finn nodded to her, and she left the church building.

Grace stood in the parking lot and looked around for Scott's Bronco, but it wasn't in the lot. She finally found him waving to her as he stood by a sleek black motorcycle while holding out an extra helmet.

"Let's go for a drive," Scott suggested extending the extra helmet for her.

"You're full of surprises!" Grace hesitantly took the helmet. "Just so you know, this is my first time on a motorcycle."

"Well, then you're in for an experience of a lifetime. There will be many more firsts if you stick with me."

"This is what you say everytime I see you," Grace said. She put her helmet on, her red hair cascading down her back. He put his on and tapped the seat behind him. She got on the back of the bike and wrapped her hands around his waist, and the bike took off. It wasn't just exhilarating feeling so close to the road, but being this close to Scott was just as exciting.

They pulled up to Red Hill Lookout Point where the view in front of them was spectacular. The trees were lush and dark green while scented lavender fields swayed in the wind. They could see the patchwork of green and brown fields and jagged, grey-toned rock formations that ran up the sides of surrounding cliffs. Grace took her helmet off and stared out over the landscape, lost in thought as she sat behind Scott on the bike. This was her home, but why did it feel like she was gazing out at some unknown landscape? Just being with Scott made her see things in a different light.

"Can you believe this view? I mean, it's stunning, isn't it? Just look at it!" Scott's excitement was contagious. "Can you imagine experiencing more views like this every day. This is what we have to look forward to when we leave here and start our adventure."

"It all sounds amazing, Scott." Grace let go of his waist and could feel his passion for living a life without limits. Once the bike was parked, they walked over to the ledge. "But at some point you have to come up for air." She knew there had to be a catch to this magical existence.

"Not anytime soon. I'm having too much fun. So, I have news." He turned to her with a serious look on his face as he reached for her hands. "The real estate agent called. She has a solid cash offer on the house, and I'm ready to accept. The money from the house would be enough to cover all our expenses until my freelance writing pays off."

"That was really fast," Grace said, unable to hide the surprise in her voice. Her eyes darted toward Scott who let go of her hands and moved behind her. He wrapped his strong arms around her, his warm breath on her neck.

"Yes, it is. But I think it's meant to be." Scott paused for a moment before continuing, speaking into her ear softly. "Grace, you're the most exciting woman I've met. I've only known you a short time, but you strike me as a woman who doesn't play by the rules, and you look like you love the wind in your hair as much as I do."

"It's still a huge decision," Grace insisted as she stared ahead at the landscape.

"Grace," he said, moving in front of her now, his brown eyes sparkling as they locked on hers. "Imagine waking up to the sunrise over a pristine lake, the world still and quiet. Just you and me, sipping coffee and planning our next adventure."

She watched him, the way his eyes danced with each word. It was easy to be swept up in his passion, but beneath that excitement was the weight of her decision ahead. Finn was counting on her to stand by him in court. Brook Becker was ruthless; Finn needed all the support he could get. Yet here was Scott, offering a chance at freedom, a chance to escape her past once and for all.

"Scott, I… " Grace started, her voice faltering. "I don't know if I can just leave everything behind."

"Why not?" he challenged, wrapping his arms around her in a protective hug. "You've been playing it safe for too long. Think of the stories we could write while we complete that bucket list. You know, your mom would want you to *live*, not just exist." Scott stepped back to face her, pausing before he continued. "I read your book. It was exhilarating to read the parts of the diary written by a woman who wanted freedom more than life itself!"

At first, Grace looked surprised but then smiled at the mention of her mother, Raven, who had always been an adventurer herself. Raven had often told her to embrace life, to chase after dreams; but it was easier said than done. "It's not that simple," she replied, her voice barely above a whisper. "I have commitments, people who depend on me."

Scott's expression softened slightly, but his determination remained. "And what about you? What do you want, Grace? You could be free—swimming in oceans, hiking snowy or desert mountains, relaxing in hot tubs after a long day of exploring. We could make memories and write together, just like your mom always wanted for you."

The imagery he painted was enticing. She could almost see it: the glistening water, the laughter shared between them, the thrill of new experiences. But then her mind flickered back to the courtroom, the tension that would fill the air as the Finn brothers fought for their lives against Brook Becker's agenda to take everything good away from them. She felt obligated to help them, to be there when it mattered most.

"I just don't know if I can walk away from everything," she said, shaking her head. "The Finns need me. They've fought so hard, and I can't just abandon them."

"Grace, you won't be *abandoning* anyone. Those who really love you wouldn't hold you back from the freedom you deserve," Scott argued, his voice rising slightly in frustration. "You're choosing to *live!* You deserve to have a life full of spontaneity and joy. Think of it as a fresh start. We can write about our adventures, share them with the world. It would be cathartic."

Grace was silent, weighing the options over in her head. She looked up at Scott. Who was this man offering her everything she had ever wanted? What was the catch? The catch was clear. If she left, she could never look back.

Scott crouched down, his gaze steady. "What if you stay here and never know what could have been? Life is unpredictable; it's messy. But it's also beautiful." He turned her face toward him gently and kissed her deeply.

Grace's heart raced, caught between the thrill of Scott's vision and the responsibilities that weighed heavily on her shoulders. She felt a storm of emotions swirling inside her. "I just... I need time to think," she said finally, her voice shaking after the kiss.

"Of course," Scott replied, standing up and giving her space. "But please, just... whatever you choose, make sure it's your choice and not one of the *Finn* brothers' choices. I hope you'll listen to your heart. And I hope your heart chooses to chase sunsets with me. Life is like an ocean. You ride the waves or let them crash over you. If you stay still, you'll drown. It's because of you, Grace, I feel ready to move on from Megan. I thought maybe you were ready to do the same thing."

As she looked into his earnest eyes, Grace realized that the choice before her was one of the most significant she would ever face. Would she choose the safety of the known, or the exhilarating uncertainty of the unknown?

"Meet me at Café Bella a week from Thursday at noon. If you're not there, then I'll know what you decided." He leaned in and kissed her again. "I want you with me when I leave, Grace. And I'm not trying to pressure you, but I'm going to leave *with* or *without* you. The choice is all yours, love."

They mounted the motorcycle once again, donned their helmets, and drove back to the church where her car was. Grace kissed Scott goodbye and said that she would be in touch. A choice would have to be made, and for the first time, she was going to make the right decision for herself even if it meant hurting someone she cared about deeply.

Chapter 100

Erick sat in his Jeep, trying to process everything that had happened. A loud noise resembling a motorcycle engine startled him out of his thoughts and he looked up just in time to see Grace on the back of a bike with that guy. What was his name? Scott Townsend. She'd moved on and everything he thought they'd had together was gone just like the dust cloud that the cycle left in its wake.

The week flew by, and Erick was even more certain that he wanted to follow Daniel and Sky to Georgia. Things hadn't turned out the way he had expected with Isabelle and he'd kept his distance.

After meeting with his client, Erick went to look for Daniel at the indoor pool. Steam from the heated pool clouded the windows, and the sharp scent of chlorine filled his nostrils. He found Daniel organizing the pool equipment, with Jace lying beside him.

"Hey, Daniel!" Erick called out as Jace bounded over to Erick.

"Hey, bro."

"So, I was thinking of heading down to Georgia after the trial, maybe find a place of my own there and get things ready for you guys."

Daniel looked up, eyebrows raised. "You serious? You'd leave everything here?"

"Yeah. Just... I don't know. It feels like the right time." Erick shrugged. "Maybe a fresh start, you know? After all that went wrong with Isabelle."

Daniel chuckled softly. "Fresh start? Or running away?"

"Maybe a bit of both," Erick admitted. "But I like the idea of being closer to you and Sky. I'm going to miss you guys."

Daniel paused, his expression shifting. "You know, it's not just us. You've got to think about what *you* want."

"I want to be with my family. That should count for something." Erick knew this much was never going to change.

"Sure, but what about Grace?" Daniel's eyes narrowed slightly.

Erick sighed, shaking his head and folding his arms. "That ship has sailed. She's moved on with some dude named Scott."

"Sometimes, it's not about the past. It's about closure." Daniel shrugged. "You could find out where she stands and if she feels the same?"

"And what if she doesn't and my heart gets ripped out *again?*" He shook his head, frustration building. "I'm done with that. It's like losing a limb!" Erick crossed his arms. "She's happy with Scott. I can't be the guy who crashes their party. She took the time to make amends with Finn. So if she still wanted to be with me, she'd have found me by now and told me."

Daniel pushed forward, leaning in. "You're not crashing anything, and she thinks you're with Isabelle. *Are* you still with Isabelle?" Daniel asked.

"I don't know if I can be after everything. I need to tell her that and sooner than later."

"What are you waiting for?" Daniel was asking all the hard questions.

"Do you really think there's a chance with Grace?" Erick

asked.

"Well, Grace did try to surprise you in Boston. I'd say you don't know until you have that conversation with her. There's nothing wrong with being honest. Isn't that what love is about?"

"Love? What do *you* know about love?" Erick regretted the words, the heat rising in his cheeks. "You're married to the only girl you've ever loved, you have no idea what it's like for me."

Daniel took a deep breath. "I've been listening to you talk about Grace for half my life. Sure, I've been lucky in finding Sky, but I've seen love break apart, and I've seen it heal. Sky and I have our differences. We fight about stuff all the time, but at the end of the day, we're honest with each other. You have to take risks. You can't just run from it. You play it too safe, man."

"I don't want to risk it. Not again." Erick looked away, the steam swirling around him like a fog. "I'm tired of being a fool."

"Being a fool means you care," Daniel said, his voice steady. "It's better than being someone who lives in a box and takes no risks in life."

"Maybe. But I like it safe." Erick's eyes met Daniel's. "You don't know what it's like to be left behind and losing everything."

"Losing isn't the point! It's about learning." Daniel gestured with his hands, emphasizing his words. "I know a lot about losing." He gestured at his wheelchair. "I know that you don't mean anything you're saying right now to me. God, Erick just be willing to try. Even if it hurts."

"Easy for you to say. You have Sky. You've already got someone who loves you."

"I didn't always." Daniel got quiet. "You remember before I met Sky I barely could do anything. I was so depressed and devastated by my injury. It wasn't like I could even talk to you about it. The guilt was already killing you, and I didn't want to be a burden and pile on. Dude, I felt abandoned by everyone and I barely wanted to live. I held it in, all that time we were living together. Then Sky came into my life. Even then I didn't think someone like her could ever love me because I was half a man. It took time, and you get clear on what matters fast when it is a matter of survival. And yeah, it was painful, because she could have laughed at me. I asked her to play video games with me and everything changed that night. All of it… was worth it." Daniel's voice was emotional. "You can't let fear keep you from finding happiness."

"For the record, I've never abandoned you. I had no idea what you were going through. I'm so sorry you ever felt that you couldn't talk to me about what you felt then." Erick let out a slow breath and couldn't imagine what would have happened to his little brother because he wasn't paying attention when it mattered most. "I've made so many mistakes, I don't deserve happiness right now. I just want… peace." He shoved his hands into his pockets.

"Peace isn't found in running away," Daniel replied gently. "It's found in facing what's really there. You need to tell both Isabelle and Grace the truth."

Jace stirred at Erick's feet, as if sensing the tension. Erick reached down, scratching behind his ears, seeking comfort in the familiar gesture. "Look, I'll think about it," Erick finally said, his voice softer.

"Good," Daniel replied, a smile widening across his face. "That's all I'm asking."

"Alright. But I can't promise anything."

"Never said you had to." Daniel grinned. "Just remember, love can be messy. But it's also worth the chaos. I just don't want to see you have any regrets."

Erick nodded slowly, the weight of the conversation lingering like the steam on the windows. "Yeah, I'll keep that in mind."

"I've gotta head out. It's our anniversary tonight, and I'm taking Sky out to dinner."

"Happy Anniversary! I have some things to take care of here. Catch ya later, Daniel."

Daniel waved and headed out of the room just as Jace jumped in the pool. "No!" Erick cried out his voice echoing in the empty space. The golden lab swam across the pool, and he noticed that even missing one leg he swam like a champ. Jace then flawlessly exited the pool and shook his body expelling water everywhere.

"Now, you're all wet and I have to clean the pool!" Erick had to laugh. "But I'm impressed with your adaptability. Maybe you're teaching me something." He realized that losing Grace felt like he'd been living without an appendage. If Jace could live a full life with a missing leg, then just maybe he could, too.

Chapter 101

Grace and Scott went on a whirlwind of exciting dates. Once, he attempted to teach her how to surf, but she ended up wiping out multiple times and then stayed on the beach. They had a romantic picnic and a bonfire that night right on the beach, ending a perfect day. Other than trying out another new restaurant in town, he had been preoccupied with the selling of Megan's things and preparing for the closing. He didn't pressure her to tell him her decision and gave her space to do what she felt she needed to do. Today she had a small group scheduled to take on her Healing Hikes project. Summer was coming to a close in New England and there was a cool hint of fall in the breeze, signaling a subtle shift in the season.

In a few days, she would meet up with Scott at Cafè Bella to plan their next chapter together. She'd have to walk away from everything here and not look back, but Grace had begun thinking that there was no reason she couldn't do both. She could give Finn a few hours of her time, help him with his case, and then she could leave guilt free with Scott.

Grace made a quick decision and texted Finn.

Grace: I can be there this afternoon.
Finn: Great, and thank you!

The irony of what would happen this morning with her group was not lost on her. The purpose of these hikes was to help others let go of what weighed them down. When she arrived at the trailhead, she unloaded three medium-sized backpacks from the trunk, then pulled out a small folding wagon. Next, she placed several medium round rocks into the wagon, which were the basis of this journey. Grace arranged the first aid kit and water bottles in a fourth backpack, and she slung it over her back. Car doors closed with a thud, announcing the arrival of the three women who had signed up for the hike. As they approached Grace, their eyes were wide, darting between Grace and the wagon of stones.

"Hey, everyone! How are we doing today?" Her voice held a warmth that came from knowing that the outcome of this adventure was going to be profound.

Chelsea, Sharmon, and Ryleigh sounded both apprehensive and excited. With each name ticked off her list, Grace felt the weight of responsibility settle further on her shoulders.

"Okay, I got all the signed waivers online, and we're all set to go," Grace instructed. "The hike is roughly four miles there and back, but we'll be making four stops on the way to the top. We're on this journey together. We continue as a group and we end as a group. Understand? Any questions?"

Nods of agreement met her words with an unspoken pact forming between them. None of the women asked any questions, and then Grace passed each woman an empty backpack.

"Now, each of you will choose your four stones," Grace continued, gesturing toward the wagon. "They are not super heavy, but all together it will be about ten pounds."

The women circled the wagon, each selecting stones for the journey. Grace watched their faces intently until they took their chosen stones. Each stone would represent struggles that they would let go by day's end.

Grace surveyed the women, their backs adjusting under the new weight. Next, she handed them each a washable marker. "Now, on each rock, I want you to write down something that's really been on your mind, something you're having a hard time letting go of."

The women nodded, each lost in thought. "Remember, you don't have to share what's on the rock," Grace reassured them, sensing the vulnerability of the moment. "The more honest you are, the better the experience."

A collective chatter started as they helped each other load the stones into the packs. Grace watched with empathy, knowing all too well the courage it took to carry such loads. She, too, picked up two rocks, feeling their weight in her hands before placing them in her own pack alongside the water and first aid kit.

The trail welcomed them, and the early morning light played across their path, lighting the way forward. Upon reaching the first stop, Grace directed, "Take one rock out," and she did the same.

Chelsea stepped forward, her eyes glistening, and gently placed her stone beside a large pink and beige mushroom. She bowed her head for a moment, a silent farewell to her burden, a rock with the word *DAD* on it. The others stood by waiting their turn.

Sharmon followed, her voice ringing clear as she declared, "I want to let go of my stressful job!" Her proclamation was met with an affirming murmur of amen.

Next, Ryleigh set her stone down. It said simply *Baby girl.* "I gave up my child when I was sixteen." The others circled around her. "Because my parents made me feel ashamed."

Grace put her stone down with the word *Family* written down on it. "This stone represents my pursuit to find my biological family, but it also means I have let go of what I expected family to be. Family doesn't have to be blood related. What's important is that they just love you for who you are."

The group continued on and made some more stops. At the last stop, they placed their final stones. Grace stood before her final stone. It bore a name that struck a chord in her heart —Finn. Memories of pain and betrayal flooded her mind. Her soul cried out for release as she whispered the words, "I forgive you." It was a declaration that went against all of her instincts. For years, Grace had carried the weight of Finn's addiction to women and alcohol that left her broken and scarred. But despite it all, her heart was mended with the support of her new family. She thought of Robin, Faith, Pala, Julie, and maybe even Scott. She was grateful for all their support. She wiped the tears as she let go of it all.

Grace's thoughts were interrupted when Ryleigh called out as she pointed out the view from the summit peak, her tone conveying the depth of her awe.

"Hey look at this!"

A profound hush settled over the group as they gazed at the panoramic view before them. The peak of New England fall was not coming for a few weeks, but what Grace saw now was still breathtaking. The sun's rays filtered through the canopy of trees, casting a golden glow over the town below. The hills were shades of green and vibrant floral colors stretched as far as the eye could see. The last of the lavender carried its scent in the wind, and large sunflowers facing the sun resembled a vibrant brushstroke of brown and yellow against the blue sky.

"God's own masterpiece," Sharmon murmured, echoing the reverence that seemed to hold them all captive.

"It's gorgeous," Chelsea agreed, the word a simple yet powerful affirmation of the moment.

Grace nodded, her spirit lighter than ever with newfound clarity. As she looked up, she saw a large black raven take flight and smiled, knowing Raven was with her always. Years ago, this spot revealed her unexpected heritage, which seemed to pale in comparison to all the new family she had surrounding her now.

They began their descent away from the summit, each step

bringing them back to the rest of their lives. The trail looped back toward the world below, and Grace could not help but smile.

In that clearing, among the stones cast aside, there was a remarkable shift—the weight of their collective sorrow began to lighten, making room for hope, forgiveness, and a future that awaited them beyond the summit. Grace's breaths grew deeper as she recalled how this had been the same rugged path that had once betrayed her, where gravity had pulled her down in an unforgiving plunge. Around her, the women's conversation flowed easier as if they'd known each other for years. The camaraderie deepened between them with their shared and carried burdens, not just in their packs, but deep within each of their hearts. Grace felt free and excited about life like never before. Her next stop was to help Finn, and then there would be nothing holding her back from the life that she deserved.

Chapter 102

Erick and Jace jumped into the Jeep and headed over to Isabelle's apartment. He agreed with Daniel about talking to Isabelle. He wanted to get closure and to break it off with her for good.

He parked and with all the windows down, told Jace to wait for him. He went inside and knocked on her door, but no one answered. A young man came into the hallway and stared at Erick.

"Excuse me," he said, moving around Erick. Then the man put his key in the lock. "Can I help you with something?"

"I'm trying to locate Isabelle. Is this her apartment?" Erick was confused, but he was sure he had the right number.

"Come in," the young man said. "I'm Steve. I just moved in here a few days ago." Erick noticed the half-open boxes. There was no trace of Isabelle. "I'm guessing she was the previous tennant."

"Do you know where she went?" Erick asked, stunned by the news.

The young man shrugged, a look of pity crossing his face.

"I'm sorry, man. I really don't. My neighbor said she just packed up and left. Didn't say much to anyone. Are you Erick Finn by any chance?"

Erick's mouth opened and shut quickly. "Yes, how did you know?"

Steve walked around the kitchen aisle and opened a drawer. He pulled out a white envelope with Erick Finn written in script on the front and handed it to Erick.

He took the envelope from Steve, his heart pounding in his chest as he glanced at the young man. "Thank you, Steve. I'll be on my way. Sorry to have bothered you."

"No worries, man. Good luck," he said, but Erick was already out the door and in the hallway.

The hallway felt suffocating, the air thick with unspoken words and unresolved feelings. His mind raced. Weeks had passed since the bake sale disaster, and it was clear that he had waited too long to sort things out with Isabelle.

Erick's grip tightened around the envelope, a wave of desperation crashing over him. He tore it open, wondering what other explanation she could give him when the truth was finally out there. He unfolded the letter, his breath catching in his throat as he began to read the words.

Dear Erick,

I'm sorry everything ended the way it did. I wish you could believe me when I say I had fallen for you. I do feel guilty because it was never supposed to go this far. It's true that I've been seeing Chris Callahan for awhile now. He asked me to help him with some business deals. When I agreed, I barely knew you. Once you asked me to stay, I felt I needed to end it with Chris. He threatened me that he would tell you about my part in all this if I didn't get you to agree to sell HigherGound. I started to believe that we could work together and build a future together. You were different than anyone I had ever dated. Maybe in another life we could have worked out, but you did warn me in Boston that you weren't ready for anything serious.

I want you to know that I realized that deceiving you

was wrong. In the end I got in too deep knowing full well you were still in love with Grace. Chris insisted we close the deal and that if I stuck with it, we all could get what we wanted in the end. But I wanted YOU Erick, not just part of you, but all of you. I wanted to believe that our time together meant something. I've never met anyone like you, but I need to walk away. You deserve someone who is honest and I'm sorry it turned out the way it did. I think it is the best for all of us. Goodbye, Erick. I'll never forget you.

God bless,
Isabelle

Relieved, he folded the letter and shoved it in his cargo shorts and left the building.

Jace whimpered softly in the back of the Jeep while Erick sat there thinking about everything that had happened. He dialed Finn's number, but it went straight to voicemail. He knew Daniel was at work, but he needed to talk to someone about Isabelle's letter. Erick went home and started packing for Georgia. When he was finished, he would go and see Finn because with the trial around the corner, this may be the last time they'd be together for a while.

Chapter 103

Grace drove to Finn's apartment next to Higher-Ground. He was waiting for her with the door open. She noticed his dark hair was unusually long and pulled back with a hair tie. She looked around on high alert, wondering if she would run into Erick, but she only saw strangers leaving or arriving at the physical therapy studio.

Once inside, she quickly noted all the scattered files on the hardwood floor. The sound of the air conditioner kicked on.

"It looks like a paper bomb exploded," she joked, stepping over a manila folder.

He cracked a smile, his eyes crinkling in the corners. "Welcome to the capital of chaos," he said, handing her a stack of documents. "I'm glad you're here. You were one of the best editors I have ever met, and if anyone could find a detail out of place, it would be you."

"I'll do my best." Grace quickly got to work.

As they settled into their task of focusing on all the fine print, the time passed rapidly.

"Can I ask," Grace began, breaking the silence, "how you

and Brook ended up together?"

Finn paused. "Life is so unexpected sometimes. We were having fun, nothing serious," he started, his voice tinged with sadness. "Then, there was talk of a baby, and even though kids were never in my game plan, I thought maybe here's my shot—to do things right, be different than my old man."

"With Brook, though?" Grace's eyebrows lifted as she watched him closely and shook her head.

"I made a mistake. Drinking causes you to make the worst decisions. Now I have to start over with nothing." Finn sighed, leaning back against the couch. "I just want something better for myself, and for FINNLondon. Maybe even make a difference for others."

"Then that's what you should do," Grace commented.

"Right now, it's just a thought." He gestured helplessly at the paper-strewn floor. "Brook's bleeding the company dry, and all assets are frozen until the trial's over. 'Brooklyn Becker versus Dominic Finn'. Here's the petition." Finn handed her some of the legal notices. "I'm hanging by a thread," he admitted, "while I try to salvage what's left of my life. Starting with sobriety—it's still new."

"We're not done yet," she said, reaching for another document. "Let's find that loophole."

They dove back into the papers, their focus sharpening as they sifted through financial statements and legal jargon.

"When I was a kid, all I ever wanted was to impress my father," Finn said as he perused one of the documents. "Even though that was never going to happen. Once my mother passed, my dad's focus was all about making a profit at any cost. He drank heavily and used women. Now, I want to change my behavior so I'm no longer like him."

"You're nothing like Declan," Grace said firmly. "You turned your life around."

"Maybe." Finn ran a hand through his hair pushing the strands out of his face. "I need a hair cut before court."

Grace organized the documents in piles across the glass coffee table as the sunlight poured through the apartment's window. She knew she and Finn were in for a difficult task, but she was prepared for battle. She leaned forward to examine a particularly lengthy document.

"It sure is hot today," she said, making small talk as she collected her hair into a hair tie, forming a messy bun.

Finn nodded as he sat adjacent to her, going through his stack of papers. Then he paused, his gaze lifting from the documents to Grace with intensity. "I saw you there," he said, his voice low.

Grace felt both curiosity and apprehension, but unable to resist, she looked up, her eyes wide, searching Finn's face for clarity. "What? Where?" she asked.

"Years ago, in our yard," he began, his voice steady. "Brook and Erick were drinking champagne, laughing in that carefree way we only could when we were kids. I tried to tell them about Declan burning me and his emotional abuse, but they never believed me." Finn's gaze dropped for a moment, a shadow crossing his face. "You were hiding behind that tree."

The scene unfolded in Grace's mind like an old movie. She vividly remembered that day when she had ventured on their property, hiding behind a tree, the prickly bark against her skin as she observed the Finn boys and Brook having a heated conversation.

"I had no idea you saw me," she said. "That was the day I realized there were two of you. That you were twins."

"Yes we are. But we are different in so many ways," Finn murmured. "We did fall for the same girl. Erick always was head over heels for you." He glanced up at her, the regret in his eyes unmistakable. "I also knew Brook wanted him, so I thought I could manipulate the situation and change the outcome in our favor." He sighed, the sound heavy with remorse. "I was wrong. I am truly sorry for all that."

Grace winced at his confession, the sincerity in his tone evident of all the work he had put into his sobriety and new life. She noticed the lines of his face had deepened over the last decade. She shuffled the legal documents into neatly aligned edges and sorted them into different piles.

"Erick was devastated when you guys broke up early this year." His voice was softer now, and from what Grace could tell, Finn was also being protective of Erick. "Of course he never told me why. I thought for sure you two were going to stay together this time around."

Grace stopped what she was doing. The memories of going to Boston, the elevator, Isabelle, and the phone call from Finn on the way home sealed the final blow to their future. Erick's words haunted her.

"Whatever is going on with Isabelle isn't what's keeping us apart."

The words were a line drawn in the sand. Grace knew that sometimes love wasn't enough. "Like I told you, I have to resolve things before I can be with anyone," she said, remembering Finn was on the same journey. "You know that better than anyone."

"It's not my place," Finn continued, shifting awkwardly in his seat, "but you should go easier on him. He's very sensitive."

Grace felt Finn's gaze, the unspoken plea for empathy for a brother he cared about despite everything. "Well," she finally said after gathering her thoughts. "We've both moved on, so there's nothing I can do now."

Finn leaned back and exhaled slowly. "I know the real reason you two aren't together and it's me," he said softly. "I just want you to know I meant it. I won't get in the way this time."

She raised an eyebrow, silent, prompting him to continue.

"He's helped me when I was at my lowest, and I didn't deserve a second chance." Finn's voice cracked slightly. "Hell, I'm surprised you even want to be seen with me."

The confession had a ring of honesty to it. Grace looked at Finn, really looked at him, and saw not just her former abuser or the man who had once conspired against her happiness but a person—a flawed, complicated human being wanting nothing from her but redemption.

"Your past actions," Grace started, choosing her words with care, "they may not be easily forgotten. But I know people can change if they want to. We all deserve a chance to prove that."

She also wanted a chance to change and become the person she was meant to be even if it meant starting over in an unknown place with someone new and leaving all the past behind. Tonight, after she did this one last thing for Finn, she could see herself moving on with Scott and being a part of his great adventures.

Chapter 104

Erick felt the heat of the late afternoon sun as it shone down on his face. Isabelle's letter burned in his pocket as he knocked on Daniel's apartment door, and Finn answered with a look of surprise on his face. Jace barked happily and ran past Finn into the apartment.

"I didn't know you were coming over today," Finn said sheepishly and stepped aside as Erick followed Jace inside. The blood drained from his face as his gaze followed Jace, who bounded over to a woman on the floor surrounded by papers in the living room. *What was Grace doing here?*

"What the–?" Erick felt his face turn red hot. He was there to talk to Finn and discuss the letter. Yet here Finn was alone with Grace *again*. "I thought you said…What is she doing here?" His fist clenched, and Erick felt his whole resolve shatter as his world tilted on its axis for the second time that day.

Finn looked from Grace to Erick. "Come on, let's talk outside." Finn led Erick back outside.

"Are you kidding me? You said… Why??!!" Erick wanted to choke his brother again but just paced back and forth on the ramp instead.

"Dude, calm down, it's not what it looks like! I asked her to help me with the case against Brook because she might be able to see something we missed. When she worked for me she was damn good at finding things. Plus, Grace despises Brook just as much as we do." Finn pleaded with Erick. "I swear that I'm not stealing her from you!" Finn put his hand on Erick's shoulder. "I really don't want to upset you. I had no idea you were stopping by or I would have warned you."

"I'm trying to do the right thing here. I know that our time is short and this is our last chance to hang out for a while." Erick felt the anger dissipating as he prayed for his next words. "I was hoping you'd like to chill on the beach today with me and Jace. I didn't realize you had plans. Maybe I should just go." He looked toward the ramp and down to the Jeep as if assessing how long it would take him to escape.

"I think that is a great idea, and I would love to go with you. I just need a little bit of time and then we can take a break. I'm this close to figuring out that Brook doesn't have a right to dad's company. Dad gave it to me before we were married." Finn smoothed his hair. "I just keep coming up empty-handed. Maybe I should just prepare to lose the company and build a new legacy."

"No!" Erick was tired of all of this losing. Finn might be playing him, but he had to trust him at some point. He shook the thought from his mind. Finn had changed, and now his twin brother needed him more than ever. Erick had the sudden realization that he had been the one who was acting crazy, and maybe the problem wasn't Finn, but *him*. Daniel had told him as much. He had to try to put his feelings aside because this was his family, and he was done losing what mattered to him. "Our family has suffered long enough," Erick asserted. "We take back what was stolen from us, and we do it together as a *family*. We'll find a way, even if it is the last thing I do."

"Thank you," Finn said, placing his hand on his brother's shoulder. "You don't know how much this means to me, and I appreciate how much you've helped me."

Erick replied with a nod, and then braced himself to face Grace as he and Finn entered the apartment once more. Erick found Jace lying beside Grace's feet getting belly rubs.

"Oh, look at you! You are one brave and smart doggie!" she cooed in his ear and looked up at the brothers. "Sorry, I couldn't resist."

Erick squeezed his eyes shut. *God please give me the strength.* He needed to lower his blood pressure if this arrangement was going to yield any results to defeat the dragon known as Brook. He rubbed his forehead and sat down on the opposite side of the coffee table joining the battle.

Erick averted his eyes from Grace, aware that the pain of losing her was still raw in his chest. "How can I help?"

"Okay, so we've divided up all the papers I signed after the wedding date last summer and the documents that I signed before the wedding. These other papers are random business transactions, and those over there are all the monetary financial transactions over the first six months of our marriage, including the wedding expenses." Finn sat down next to Jace, pointing to each pile. "We go to trial in a few days so we need to find the needle in the haystack. We're missing something. I can feel it."

Grace looked over at Erick and said, "You're a smart business owner. You might be able to spot something wrong in the financials. I noticed that a large sum of money was moved over the day after the wedding. But it might not mean anything."

"That was to cover all the expenses of the wedding, the marriage license, the officiant, the caterer, and miscellaneous stuff," Finn explained.

"I see the receipts for all these items but none for the officiant or the license fee to the town clerk," Grace said.

"That's weird. I have to look up who officiated the ceremony in my contact list. I'll be right back. You guys are cool, right? I can leave you two alone for five minutes." Finn looked sternly at Erick.

"Of course, we can be in the same room." Erick frowned.

"We're just fine," Grace agreed.

They continued looking over the transactions and compared them to the receipts. "That was a good catch," Erick conceded. *Why did he feel drawn to her whenever they were in the same room?* He hated himself for being such an idiot, knowing full well she'd already moved on.

"Thank you. I'm glad to help." She looked down at her hands and paused as if she was looking for just the right words. An uncomfortable silence filled the room before Grace continued. "Finn told me that he's interested in going to Texas to see a friend from rehab, and I hoped he might meet someone new, you know, someone who is *not* Brook. But he has no interest in any serious relationships during his first year of sobriety. "

"AA recommends waiting about a year," Erick said. He looked into her emerald eyes and felt a calmness he hadn't felt in weeks. "I'm sure Finn is grateful for your help."

"It's the least I could do. For what it's worth, he and I have moved on from our past issues. He is really making a change in his life this time by working on his issues as well. You should be proud of him," Grace admitted.

"I know. I see it, too. Listen, can we talk—"

"So, get this," Finn interrupted, "the officiant doesn't have any copies of the records and said he never got a check from us and never filed the marriage license. We must have forgotten. I told him I would take care of the bill as soon as I could since Brook has my assets all tied up." Finn looked radiant and was beaming. "I called the county clerk's office. You're never going to believe what they said. This changes everything!"

Erick couldn't help but smile as he looked at Grace and then back at Finn while he waited for what came next. It had been ages since he heard good news, and they really all could use some right about now.

Chapter 105

Grace was excited to hear what Finn said, but her thoughts kept nagging her about Erick's behavior earlier. She'd never seen him so full of rage like that before. His usual, calm demeanor was gone, and he looked like a madman. Seeing Erick so unhinged gave her an unsettling feeling.

In contrast, Finn was so chill about everything and so un-expectedly thoughtful of her feelings. It was as if these two swapped bodies. She would figure out one of these days what was going on, but for now, she looked up at Finn, waiting for him to tell them what the town clerk said that would change everything.

"So I was waiting on hold for the supervisor to get on the phone. They said no marriage license was ever filed with our names. This matches the officiant's story who never filed the paperwork due to our lack of payment." Finn gestured to the piles on the table. "There is no copy of any marriage certificate in any of these papers. So, I called our lawyer, Amy Nass, and left a message for her to call us back. But if I'm right," Finn said, as he picked up an unopened envelope and ripped it open, "this has to be a past due notice from the officiant."

"You two were never legally married!" Grace jumped up and hugged Finn and then Erick.

Erick hugged her back awkwardly and then high-fived Finn.

"I hope this works out," Erick said, "but court is never a slam dunk. There's always something unexpected, and Brook could still win. I also talked to law enforcement about her hit and run with Jace, and they won't do anything."

"I think we found what we were looking for, no matter what the court determines. Let's go celebrate at the beach!" Finn shouted. "Who's in?"

Jace jumped up and barked his low bark and hit Erick with his excited wagging tail. "I'll drive!" Erick led everyone to the Jeep.

Grace felt the warmth of the sun on her with the Jeep's top down, as she sat up front and smoothed her blue sundress. She didn't care that Isabelle had claimed Erick and this seat earlier. This was a moment in time she never thought would happen. She was going out with *both* Finn brothers to celebrate their potential shared victory against Brook in the coming days.

As Erick drove them to the closest dog-friendly beach about a half an hour away, she wondered how they got to this place where all three of them could be in the same car, let alone the same room together. The day was beautiful, and Jace was excited when they parked and they headed down to the water.

"The salt water will be good for Jace's healing," he said to Grace. She and Erick took turns throwing a ball to Jace. The golden labrador jumped into the ocean chasing the ball.

Grace ran up the dunes and threw down a towel to sit down on as she took a swig of water from her bottle. Erick tossed the ball to Finn, who continued to play with Jace while Erick sat down next to Grace, removed his shoes, and watched the horizon and the ebb and flow of the ocean. Each wave seemed to wash away another layer of time, bringing him closer to those youthful days before graduation when they'd been two carefree souls racing along this same shore. Here they were again, as if the universe insisted on folding time back upon itself.

Grace observed Finn laughing as he ran into the ocean after the golden lab, cheering Jace on. This was the most exhilarating day and the first time she'd felt peace with not just Finn, but with her feelings for Erick.

"Remember how you convinced me to go out in the ocean? I thought you'd left me," Grace mused, as she stood up and ran to the water's edge.

"I remember *everything*, Grace." Erick caught up to her. The swell of the foamy water circled their feet and covered them with a wet sand. "You went under the waves right about there, right?" Erick pointed to a spot just beyond the breakers. "Do you remember what I said to you when you started to go under?"

Grace rolled her eyes, and smiled. "You said my favorite words. 'I got you.' I know. I've lost count of how many times you've saved me."

"Who's counting? But if I'm being honest, I think you are a smart and capable woman who no longer needs saving." When he said these words, Grace knew that he finally understood.

As the sun began to set lower on the horizon, it cast an orange glow that seemed to set the ocean ablaze. In its light, Erick and Grace felt like children again, recalling old times. They would savor these fleeting and rare moments. Jacey boy and Finn ran over to them.

"Is it okay if I take Jace over to the ice cream truck?" Finn asked, laughing at Jace shaking his fur and spraying everyone in the process.

"Of course," Erick responded. "What a perfect day. Now we just need to get good news about the trial and then Brook can go find someone else to bother." Turning toward Grace, he asked, "Whatever happened with your case with the FBI?"

Grace knew that she also had issues with the legal system when she was in San Diego and when she thought the FBI was going to pin Jack Stone's death on her. "Funny you should ask because up until a week ago, I thought I could still go to jail for a crime I didn't commit. The FBI agent called me last week and let me know the results of Jake Stone's autopsy. They found the body, but there was nothing significant that would indicate a sign of foul play. Rebekah's other brother, Dovid, came forward. He apparently worked with Jack Stone and told the FBI everything he knows. He admitted to knowing about all Jack's schemes against his family, Raven, and myself. Lawyers are working on getting his sister Rebekah pardoned. She was serving a lifetime sentence for what Jack did to his parents. Bottom line, they don't have any evidence to convict me of anything. I am free, finally free!"

"That is great news!" Erick hugged Grace tight without hesitation this time, catching her off guard.

Holding him this close was almost more than she could bear. When she let go, she could see the sorrow in his eyes, but she also felt the electricity she'd always felt being so near to him.

"I think things are looking up," Grace agreed. "For all of us."

Jace bounded back with Finn who held the ice cream cup to the dog's mouth, letting him lap it up. Darker clouds began to roll in, and they headed back to Daniel's apartment.

Grace said good-bye to the Finn brothers and got into her sedan. As she backed out of HigherGround, thoughts of what she was leaving behind became jumbled inside her head about where the next step in her journey would take her.

Chapter 106

Erick leaned against the Jeep, arms crossed, watching Grace drive away as the sun set over the hills of Connecticut. It could only be a miracle from God that the three of them could celebrate today.

Finn lingered a moment by Erick's side, then cleared his throat. "So, did you finally tell her how you feel?" Finn asked, studying Erick's face.

"No," Erick replied, shaking his head, which was filled with the memory of her on the back of a motorcycle, her arms secure around another man. "She was crystal clear at the bake sale that she'd moved on with Scott whatever his name was."

Finn shifted on his feet. "But... ?"

"There's nothing more to say. I'm heading home to pack. I purchased the last flight to Georgia the evening after the trial."

"Georgia? You're not going to wait?" Finn looked confused.

"Wait for what? Even if I stayed here, I'd still need to go to Georgia and set up everything for Daniel and Sky at some point. The plan is that we're all moving in a few months. But don't worry, Daniel said you could stay here in the apartment as long as you need."

Finn nodded slowly. "Let's go inside for a second." Once inside, Finn closed the door. "I'm grateful for the place. After the trial I'm planning on flying to visit Texas to clear my head and all. My rehab buddy that I told you about recommended I come out and see the therapy dog center."

"Good idea," Erick said, though his voice was distant. "After the trial is over, we can decide how we want to spend the rest of our lives."

Finn hesitated. "The London partners are offering to buy me out if we win."

"Is that what you want? What about our father's legacy?" Erick sighed.

"I don't ever want to be the person I was when I was running the company. I'm not sure if we will win at the trial, but things need to change regardless of the outcome. I want to do something positive for a change or use the money for something greater than just publishing. Speaking of change, I think not telling Grace how you feel is a mistake," Finn said quietly.

"Maybe. But I've chased her long enough." Erick pulled out the envelope, his hands clenched. "Besides, I'm still processing my last breakup. Isabelle left town and all I got was this letter."

"Isabelle's gone?" Finn raised an eyebrow. "What does the letter say?"

Erick unfolded the letter, and read it aloud to Finn. The words were just as painful as the first time he had read it. Not because Isabelle had left, but that she'd played him. Despite her claims that she cared about him, learning that the entire relationship had been orchestrated by Chris Callahan, and that she had been seeing him behind Erick's back, made Erick realize he could no longer give his trust so freely. Brook, Isabelle… they were cut from the same mold. Grace was different; she was the only one who saw Erick for who he truly was, and now she was gone, too.

Erick's emotions stirred within him. Isabelle's confession about Chris Callahan and HigherGround cut the deepest. All the time they'd spent together, Erick had believed that it had meant something to her as well, but the letter painted a different reality. Isabelle needed someone who would take risks with her, who wouldn't hesitate to chase something bigger than the life he so stubbornly protected. In the end, of course, she'd gone back to Chris, who shared her drive and her vision for an exciting career and life. The truth clawed at him, and it was undeniable that Erick hadn't just lost Isabelle because of her dreams or Chris's ambition. He'd lost her because she was right about him. And he didn't know how to live with that. This was why he needed to move away.

"Whoa that *is* pretty heavy," Finn said, breaking through his thoughts.

Erick scoffed, "What does she want me to do; stand by and not help those in need?"

"She does have a point. You tend to go too far. Don't get me wrong, it's because of your help that I was able to get on my feet. But now it's important that we all need to figure out things on our own. When you really love someone, you give them the space to grow and learn. Just like you did with Grace. You gave her the space because deep down you love her."

Both Finn and Isabelle were right, that he had never truly moved on, but there was no more time for wallowing. "Well, that may be the case, but I'm done chasing the ghost of Grace. If she really wanted to be together, she would have told me. I can't compete with that adrenaline junkie, Scott. I have responsibilities. I'd rather be alone for the rest of my life than be with someone who only wants to use or change me. These women just don't get me."

Finn frowned. "That's harsh."

"Yeah, but it's true. If Grace really wanted me, she'd find a way to get over the past. It just has never worked out with us for one reason or another."

Finn crossed his arms, "And you're okay with that?"

"I'm not okay with any of it. I'm just over it all. I just... I can't keep waiting."

"Moving on is harder than it sounds," Finn said, voice low.

"Tell me about it," Erick replied, his gaze drifting. "But I have to try. For myself."

"After the trial, we'll figure it all out," Finn said. "I do believe it's time for all of us to move on."

"Yeah. It feels like I'm on a hamster wheel going nowhere. But it's time to get off."

Finn nodded, realizing the weight of Erick's words. "Sometimes moving on also means letting go."

"Exactly," Erick said, folding the letter back into the envelope. "I'm ready for the next chapter, whatever that looks like, but I just can't do it here with all these reminders."

"Now that you're not with Isabelle, I believe more than ever that you need to tell Grace how you feel. I know you don't want to open up those old wounds, but maybe if you just write her a letter. You don't have to actually give it to her." Finn shrugged. "We did this exercise in rehab and in grief counseling. It really works. It'll feel like a weight has been lifted off your shoulders. Trust me." He handed Erick a pen and a blank piece of paper. "I'll give you some space."

Erick took a deep breath and hugged his brother. "Look at us! We've put our differences aside and we are stronger than ever. I'll write this one last letter and then there is no stopping us. We'll put Brook Becker in her place. No one messes with the Finn brothers."

Finn left the room and Erick sat down at the kitchen table and, for one final time, he let his thoughts pour out. Then he folded it up and placed it into an envelope and laid it down on the counter. Just then his phone rang, "Hello?"

It was Joyce on the line.

"Hey, Erick, can you and Finn come over to HigherGround right now? The lawyer is looking for you guys." She spoke in a hushed voice as she said, "She's talking on the phone to someone about new evidence, and I think there's a witness who came forward. You and Finn should get here right away."

"On my way!"

Erick hung up the phone just as Finn entered the room.

"We gotta go!" Erick said, explaining the situation as he headed for the door.

They quickly left the apartment and sprinted through the parking lot. It was time to let go of the past, make a plan to defeat Brook, and finally get the justice they deserved.

Chapter 107

Grace was ready to finally move on from the Finn brothers. The early rays of the morning sun filtered softly through the curtains of her cozy cottage, casting warm light across her small living room. After weeks of tension and uncertainty, she finally felt a sense of clarity. The previous week had been the tipping point. She had discovered the evidence in the paperwork at Finn's, the literal missing piece that might change everything for the case against Brook Becker. Celebrating with the brothers on the beach was so surreal, and she knew deep down that she would miss them.

Today, she was packing for a life of adventure with Scott, and her heart raced at the thought of starting over. All the chapters of a new life were waiting for her just beyond these familiar walls. She took a moment to appreciate the sacred space she had created for herself over the last two years. This place had held her secrets, her dreams, and her heartaches. Now, as she glanced around, she felt a thrill of excitement at the thought of all the new experiences Scott had to offer. She was also apprehensive about what lay ahead, but with her mother's memoir finished, she knew publishing it would open more doors for her.

Her gaze fell on the first book that she published. She was proud that *If You Only Knew* had been a great success. Grace picked it up and held it close. This book was her story and Erick's, but the names had been changed, and so had she. He would always hold a special place in her heart. It was now time to let go of all that was and embrace all that could be. She jumped at the unexpected hard knock on the door. "Hello?" she answered, returning to the present.

"Hey, Grace! It's Finn," came his familiar voice. "Sorry it's so early."

"Come in. Is everything okay?" Grace narrowed her eyes. Then she stepped aside to let him in. He wore a very expensive-looking dark charcoal suit, dark tie, and a white pocket square. His hair was cut short and his face was cleanly shaven.

"Everything is fine. I just wanted to thank you in person for all your help with the paperwork. I really couldn't have done it without you." He removed his sunglasses and looked around the small cottage.

Grace smiled, feeling a swell of pride. "You look ready for the court battle! I'm glad I could help, Finn. It was the least I could do." She adjusted his tie for him, a habit she had done many times before.

"I was wondering," he continued, "did you and Erick ever talk?"

She sighed softly and stepped back, remembering the peace they had found at the beach together, just last week. "Finn, there's really nothing left to talk about."

Finn's voice turned serious. "I respectfully disagree. Don't you want closure?"

Grace felt the familiar ache in her chest, but she shook it off. "I appreciate that, Finn. Really. But I'm ready for my next adventure… with Scott. We leave this afternoon for our road trip."

"I understand. Speaking of adventures," Finn said, "I'll be traveling to Texas in a few days. Just wanted to wish you well on your journey. And remember, if you need anything, I'm just a call away. I'll help you in a heartbeat."

"Thank you, Finn. That means a lot," Grace said knowing they had come a long way.

"So, since you're leaving today, does that mean you aren't coming to court today?" The corner of Finn's lips turned downward, showing his disappointment.

"I'm going to meet up with Scott in a few hours actually." Her gaze shifted to her suitcase in the middle of the floor.

"I see." He hugged her and then whispered in her ear, "Take care, Grace." She could hear the sincerity in his voice. He kissed her head and moved away from her. "You deserve all the happiness in the world."

"Goodbye, Finn!" Her heart filled with mixed emotions.

"There's just one more thing," Finn said, reaching into his light jacket. "You should have this."

"What is it?" Grace asked and took the envelope from him.

"Just me making things right for once. It's just like your book title, and I think you should know all the facts before you go. Be safe and call if you need anything." Finn winked and left the cottage.

She looked at the envelope. It was a plain envelope, and she squinted at it for a moment. Her phone rang, and she put the envelope down.

"Hi, Mom." Grace looked around the room to see if she had everything. "I know you're concerned. I'll be fine, I promise."

"Pumpkin," Robin got on the line. "Please be safe and check in with us often. I hope you'll be back for Thanksgiving."

"I will try, but no promises on where I will be then."

"Okay, we love you. We really appreciate you sharing your location with us. We will miss you. Please call anytime!"

Grace hung up the phone and looked around her little cottage. A wave of sadness rushed through her. She shook it off. *Everything is as it should be. My hope is that you will find all that you are looking for in this world.* She could hear Raven's voice flowing through her as she wheeled her suitcase to her old sedan that had always been there for her. She thought about getting a new one when she got back. *If* she ever came back. Would she ever come back? Living life on the road seemed so magical. But now she wasn't sure what lay ahead. Maybe that was the whole point.

She closed the door, loaded her suitcase, and then felt in her pocket. No phone. Grace went back inside the small cottage. When the door opened, the strong breeze blew in, sending the envelope Finn had given her to the floor. She picked it up. Then she headed back to her car and stared at the envelope. *Nothing good can come from this,* she thought to herself. In the end, curiosity won, and she ripped it open and began to read.

My Dearest Grace,

Trying to find the words to express how much you mean to me feels like trying to capture the ocean in a small bottle. My stupid brother Finn asked me to write this letter, and I agreed, only because I know you'll never read this. So here goes. You and I have been through it, haven't we? From the first time I saw you at the lockers in high school, my life changed its trajectory.

From the moment I looked into your bright emerald eyes, I knew with a certainty that shook me to my core, that you were the one. I've actually never stopped loving you. If I could build a time machine and rewind time, knowing everything I know now, I would do it all again, but I would never have taken that drink at the graduation party and I would have stood up to my father and protected you from Finn.

Every hurdle, every hardship, every minute of this last year, I'd endure it all just to be near you one more time. What I'd do differently this time, though, would be to tell you how I felt when I was with you. Your very existence fills me with insurmountable joy. I'm truly sorry for all the lies I told you when you were recovering. It still weighs on me. But even with the shame of it all, I would do it a thousand times over just to be near you, to hold your hand, to see the flicker of life return to your eyes when you learned to walk again. And if losing you meant keeping you safe, I'd set my feelings aside. Know that I would do anything for you. I know none of this makes sense, but honestly, my life no longer makes any sense since you've been gone.

Your hair is like an autumn sunset captured in wild silken strands. Even after all this time you still take my breath away when I see you. You make me a better man, Grace. You inspire me, challenge me, and have loved me with an intense fierceness I never thought possible. But what we had is more real than anything in this world. I think of the story you wrote, OUR story that is now permanently in print and forever burned in my heart. You believed in me when we were mere kids and believed in us, enough to share our love story with the world. And with that, it feels like we have a chance, a real chance, for a better ending. I'd do anything for just another minute with you. I've loved you a thousand lifetimes over, and I have no right to ask you for anything. But this ending of our dance doesn't seem right. In fact it seems so incredibly wrong! I want adventure, too. I'll never be the guy who could whisk you off to endless magical places with no roots, no familiar place to come back to, but I do love adventure and romance. As long as it's with you.

I want to scale mountains and taste everything life has to offer, but if you aren't by my side, all the colors would seem muted. With all the hurt I have caused you, I deserve to be alone.

Remember when we looked at the stars on the rooftop all those years ago? I believe with all of my heart that our love story was written there in the stars. Grace, you are the only woman I've ever truly loved. My heart has held a permanent space for you, even though time moved on and our distances grew. It has always been you. I'm in awe of your resilience and so proud of who you have become. You know who you are now and where you're going. I wish you all the happiness the world has to offer.

Grace, my love, my life, would you consider letting us finally write the new story with an ending we deserve? I pray to God that one day we will find each other again.

With all my love, always and eternally yours,
Erick

Grace folded up the letter and wiped her eyes. She knew

two things were true, Erick was being more honest than she had ever known, and Finn had no right to share his private thoughts with her. Yet, she was glad he did, as it caused her to pause and think about what she was doing. She turned the key and her old car sputtered to life. She was ready to start her new chapter and pressed the gas pedal and drove down the lane and out to the main road. It was high time that she focused on herself. She took her next steps very carefully as she stepped out of the car and closed the door with a thud. Everything was about to change. She smiled, reached out to the door in front of her. There was no looking back now.

Chapter 108

Erick sat behind the defendant's table at the court-house near where Finn and the family attorney were sitting. The courtroom was dark, but the sun shone through the large windows. To his left were Daniel and Sky. Today was the day they had been preparing and waiting for, and now they were inside the courtroom where the atmosphere was tense and the air thick with anticipation. The plaintiff's attorney had already called his witnesses, showed the evidence, and authenticated Finn's signature on the paperwork. Brook looked pleased with herself.

Now it was their turn to submit their case. It had already been a long and stressful morning, but Amy Nass was ready to end this once and for all.

Amy stood up. "Your honor, defense would like to call Brooklyn Becker to the stand."

Brook looked at Erick briefly and then she turned to her father sitting behind them. James Becker nodded to her that he approved. Erick watched her take her place on the stand and swear her oath to the bailiff to tell the truth.

Amy approached the witness with confidence and her notes in hand. "Good afternoon, Ms. Becker," Amy began, her voice steady and clear. "Do you have a vendetta against the Finn family?"

"Objection your honor! Leading the witness!" Brook's lawyer was on his feet.

"Sustained."

"I'll rephrase. We have security footage showing you driving away and running over the Finn family dog, leaving him with only three legs. Do you deny this?"

"Your honor!"

"I'll withdraw the question." Amy looked over at Finn and flashed a victory smile. "Ms. Becker... is there a reason you didn't take the Finn name after your marriage to Dominic Finn?"

"I told Finn I was not interested in changing my name." Brook rolled her eyes.

"Finn?" Amy looks up confused.

"Dominic goes by his last name, Finn. Everyone knows that." Brook picked a loose thread from her pant suit..

"I see. Let's talk about your marriage. We can start with the wedding. Did you hire a wedding planner or did you organize the wedding yourself at Finn Manor?"

"I planned the entire thing. There wasn't enough time to hire a planner. Events are my specialty, and I handled every detail down to the napkins," Brook said in a very cocky tone. "It was beautiful and intimate. What can I say? I know how to throw a party!" she answered proudly. "We had flowers, a great setup—"

"Ms. Becker," Amy interrupted, her tone authoritative, "The wedding was an outdoor ceremony, correct?"

"Yes," Brooklyn replied confidently. "It was perfect, if I do say so myself."

Amy nodded. "I'd like to submit Exhibit A for the court's review." She handed a bundle of documents to the judge, who glanced through them before nodding in approval. Next, she handed Brook and her attorney a copy as well.

"Objection!" The plaintiff's attorney leapt to his feet. "This is the first we have seen any of this!"

"Please approach the bench," the judge demanded.

Erick looked over at Daniel and Finn. This was the smoking gun Grace had found for the case, and he knew where this was headed. No one could hear what the judge was saying, but they remained hopeful the evidence wouldn't get thrown out.

"Objection overruled," the judge declared and gave permission for Amy to proceed with questioning.

"Now, Ms. Becker," Amy continued, her gaze piercing. "These documents include the financials and receipts from your wedding." She gave Brook one of the papers. "Have you seen these documents before?"

"Yes, it's a spreadsheet of all the expenses for the wedding and the paid receipts."

"So you can confirm this is a complete list of the expenses for yours and Dominic Finn's wedding?"

"Yes, this was a small simple wedding." Brook shrugged.

"Can you read aloud for the court the highlighted portion of this document."

"Pastor Urick Lewis, officiant, $875.00," Brook read out loud.

Amy handed her the copied documents each showing paid receipts. "Can you tell the court what you are looking at here?"

"Objection! Relevance! Your honor, Ms. Nass is wasting the court's time. The wedding has nothing to do with FINNLondon."

"Sustained. Ms. Nass, where are you going with this?"

"Your honor, the plaintiff is suing my client based on the fact that because they are legally married, she is entitled to all the assets. I'm pursuing a foundation for cause with this evidence."

"You have a short leash, get to the point quickly." The judge peered at everyone over his spectacles.

"Ms. Becker, have you had a chance to look through the expenses and receipts?"

"Yes, so what? Is it a crime to have a small wedding?" Brook narrowed her eyes at Amy. "I'm not as self-indulgent as everyone thinks."

"No crime in any of that. But I have more questions. So, after the ceremony, did you file the marriage license with the county clerk's office?"

"Yes, that was all a part of the process. We applied and then the officiant, Mr. Hewitt, filed it the next day."

"Were you aware that the officiant never received payment? Please take another look at those papers and maybe you can explain to the court why there is no receipt or why payment was never sent?" Amy raised her voice a notch.

"What?" Brook fumbled through all the papers. "Of course they were paid. So what if we lost one receipt, who cares! That proves nothing."

"I can call Mr. Hewitt to the stand if you like. He's here in the courtroom, and he will testify that he was never paid."

"So what, that changes nothing." Brook looked nervously at the back of the courtroom.

"Let's focus on the facts, shall we? There's no receipt for this officiant and therefore proves that Mr. Hewitt was never paid. Is it possible you forgot to pay the officiant who performed at your wedding?"

"I guess it could have been the case or we just lost the receipt."

Amy, unwavering, moved to her next point. "I'd like to submit Exhibits B and C, your honor." She handed another set of documents to the judge, who examined them closely.

"Ms. Becker," Amy continued, "the first of these documents is a 'PAST DUE' notice from the officiant dated exactly six months after the ceremony, showing this bill was not paid. The other document shows the list of marriage licenses received on the day of the wedding, as well as two months later. Notably, there is no record of a marriage license being filed for you and Mr. Finn. In the state of Connecticut Statute Section 46b-34: the statute that states a marriage license must be filed within 65 days of the wedding date to be valid and the person who performs the marriage must certify the marriage on the license and return it to the registrar at the county clerk's office where you got married within the first week of the month after the marriage."

Brook's face flushed. "Well, I… I don't know! Maybe there was some sort of clerical error?" she exclaimed, her voice rising defensively. "It doesn't mean anything!"

"Doesn't mean anything?" Amy echoed incredulously. "You're claiming ownership of the FINNLondon Publishing company and its assets based on your marriage to Dominic Finn, yet you have no official or legal record of that marriage. Without a valid marriage license, you have no legal rights to his assets or the publishing company."

The courtroom fell silent, and Brooklyn's confidence wavered. She opened her mouth, ready to protest, but the words caught in her throat. "I—"

"Ms. Becker," Amy interrupted with a sharp tone. She leaned forward slightly. "Please answer the question directly. If you were in charge of all the details, then why was there no payment made, and if the payment was made, why was there no receipt? If your marriage license was filed on time, your names would be listed in the town clerk's public records, and they were not."

Brook shifted uncomfortably in her seat. "I have no idea. But, that's… that's not fair! We were married! We applied for the license before the wedding and just because there's no paper filed doesn't mean it didn't happen!"

"Your Honor, I object to the relevance of this line of questioning," the plaintiff's attorney shouted again.

"Mr. Spector, we talked about this already." The judge looked over the papers again. "This is my courtroom, and I've allowed it. Please continue Ms. Nass."

Turning back to Brook, Amy pressed, "Ms. Becker, you are not legally married and yet you are pursuing false legal claims against Mr. Finn because you have something personal against the Finn family. Your honor," Amy said, turning to the judge, "given the absence of any legal documentation of a valid marriage license being filed and the lack of evidence supporting

Ms. Becker's claims, Ms. Becker has no legal claim to any assets related to that marriage, including ownership of FINNLondon Publishing. I move that this case be dismissed. "

The courtroom fell silent as the gravity of Amy's words settled in. Brook's confidence had evaporated, replaced by an unmistakable sense of dread. All eyes turned to the judge, waiting for the final verdict.

Chapter 109

Grace opened the door and quietly slipped into the back of the courtroom just as Brook was called to the stand. Finn had turned around at that moment and their eyes met. He nodded his head and closed his eyes out of respect for her showing up today. She saw Erick, Daniel, and Sky sitting in the first row. Their attorney was presenting the evidence that Grace had found last week helping Finn and Erick sort through all the documents. Earlier that day, she met with Scott to tell him she was not going with him after all. It would have been a huge mistake to follow a grieving man—who was still chasing the ghost of his dead wife—across the county. It was the honesty of Erick's private words written in the letter that Finn gave her that made her realize what she wanted most.

"I need both attorneys to meet me in chambers immediately. Brook, you need to remain in your seat. Everyone else remain where you are." The judge stood up in his black robe and entered through a side door, followed by the lawyers.

Grace saw Erick stand up, while Daniel and Sky were whispering to each other. Finn gestured with a tilt of his head, and

Erick looked directly to the back of the courtroom and their eyes met. He shrugged and put his hands up. She wanted to talk to him, but what was the point when he and Isabelle were still together? Although she did wonder why Isabelle wasn't there. What kind of girlfriend wouldn't show up in court to support her boyfriend's family? Before she could say or do anything, the judge returned to the courtroom. The lawyers remained standing, and Brook looked up from her seat.

"Given the witness's inability to provide evidence of a legal marriage, coupled with the lack of county records contradicting her claim, I'm forced to uphold the law. The plaintiff's entire claim to ownership of the shares of FINNLondon rests on her alleged marital status, which we've now proven to be false. This case is dismissed!" The judge hit the gavel twice.

"Daddy, wait!" Brook, embarrassed, got down from the stand humiliated and chased after her father who had left the courtroom clearly displeased with the outcome.

The verdict had just come in, and Brook's smug confidence crumbled for the whole world to see. The Finn family hugged each other as Grace got up, left the courtroom, and found her way to the restroom. Once inside, she washed her hands, reapplied lipstick, but then she heard the door bang.

"Well, well, well!" a voice from behind her called out. Brook leaned against the wall, her sneer sharp enough to cut glass. "You all think you've won." Brook spat, her voice dripping with venom. "But *I'm* the one who dodged a bullet. Those Finn brothers? They've got nothing I want."

Grace's jaw tightened. She didn't owe Brook a response, but the words slipped out anyway. "Why'd you have to run over the dog, Brook?"

Brook's laugh was harsh, grating. "That mutt is a menace. Should've been put down years ago."

Grace shook her head, her voice steady but cold. "People like *you* should be put down. You lost today. And people like *you* will *always* lose."

Brook's eyes narrowed, her lips curling into a bitter smile.

"Oh, please. You think you're so high and mighty? Erick's moved on. Isabelle's been in the picture since Daniel's wedding. You're on the outside, Grace. Always have been. Poor little carpenter's girl."

Grace's chest tightened, but she didn't flinch. "At least my dad loves me unconditionally. Good luck with *yours*."

She turned to leave, but Brook's voice stopped her. "You think you're better than me? Finn and I have been pulling the strings on everything all these years. You think this is over? Not by a longshot."

Grace froze, her hand on the door. She didn't look back. "Do your worst, Brook. You'll never win. Guess you didn't end up with a Finn after all."

"Neither did you!" Brook's evil laughter was sharp and hollow, but Grace didn't look back as she allowed the door to swing shut behind her, leaving Brook alone once and for all. There was only one thing left to do. She knew what she wanted, and Grace walked down the hallway, her steps firm, her head held high, and her mind clear. She had come to terms with the past, and it was time to move forward with a future she was ready for now. She looked around and then quietly reentered the courtroom but stopped short when she saw it was empty. Grace turned sharply at the voice behind her. Her heart skipped a beat. Finn stood there, a faint smile tugging at his lips.

"Looking for someone?" he asked, his tone light but with an edge she couldn't quite place.

She exhaled, her shoulders relaxing as she turned to the familiar face. "Congratulations, Finn." She stepped forward and hugged him, her voice muffled against his shoulder. "Ding dong, the witch is dead."

He laughed, a short, sharp sound. "Ha! You can say that again." He tilted his head and spoke lower. "Hey, it means a lot that you came today. I'm glad you changed your mind. And honestly, your deduction skills? They were the tipping point in the case. I can't thank you enough."

Grace shrugged, her smile softening. "It was the least I could do." She looked down at her sandals, suddenly self-conscious. "Is Erick still here, by any chance?"

Finn shook his head. "Nah. He took Daniel and Sky home. He's getting ready for his flight to Georgia tonight. I just finished up with my lawyer. Come on. Let's get out of here," Finn suggested and they went outside and stood on the stone court steps. People were walking around, and traffic was starting to build on the streets below.

"Georgia?" Grace looked confused. "What's in Georgia?"

"He's getting everything set up at his franchise of Higher-Ground. For when Daniel and Sky move there. Plus, Sky's family are all in Georgia."

"Oh." Grace nodded slowly, her gaze drifting toward the courthouse steps. "I'll catch him when he comes back, then." She glanced over his shoulder, where James Becker was steering Brook out of the courthouse, his voice sharp and cruel.

"What a disappointment you are to this family," James said, pulling on his daughter's elbow.

Finn's voice dropped, low and careful. "I don't know if he's coming back."

Grace's head snapped toward him. "He and Isabelle are starting over there?"

Finn winced. "It's not my place to say, but… after everything, I sort of owe you one. Isabelle's gone. She admitted to dating someone else the whole time they were together. Just like Brook, Isabelle tried to steal HigherGround by giving it to her partner."

Grace blinked, stunned. "What?"

Finn leaned in, his voice barely above a whisper. "He's pretty upset. Listen, if you care for him at all, you might be able to still catch him before he leaves. Convince him to stay or at least say goodbye. He needs closure, Grace. *Desperately.* You both do."

She stared at him, her mind racing. "I… I don't know—"

Finn cut her off. "I know you still love him, but I'll stay out of it. Just stop talking to me and get over to his cabin while there is still time. This might be your only chance. I couldn't live with myself if I'm the reason *again* you missed your chance to be together."

Grace glanced back at the courthouse, then at Finn. His expression was unreadable, but his eyes held a quiet pleading and urgency. She hugged him tight. Her eyes stung, but she wouldn't cry.

"That's why you gave me the letter. Thank you, Finn. You really are amazing. I won't ever forget what you did for me. For us."

With time running out, she turned and walked away. Her heart pounded in her chest as she reached her car and realized everything had brought her to this moment. It felt like everything truly was about to change, but this time it was different, and her gut told her that this time it just felt right.

Chapter 110

Erick dropped off Daniel and Sky and returned to his cabin after the court case had concluded. His gaze fell on the half-filled open moving boxes. He put his suitcase on the bed and turned to his dresser, carefully moving folded shirts, shorts, and pants into the suitcase. His hand felt the familiar frame that contained the picture of Grace that she'd given him in high school. Jace whined as if the suitcase were an omen.

"I know, Jacey boy. I have to go, but I'll be back for you. We'll all be together soon. I'm pretty sure God's still at work and has a plan for my future." He rubbed Jace's fur and then went outside to load the car. He checked his watch as he walked up to the porch. He had a few hours before he had to leave for the airport where the red-eye flight would take him to Atlanta. "You and me boy on our next adventure." Jace laid down on the porch as Erick watched the sun lower in the horizon.

Next he looked around and had an idea. He found the ladder on the west side of the cabin and climbed up the house and carefully balanced himself and sat on the roof. He laid back and watched the last few minutes of the sunset and reflected on the last couple of years. When he heard Jace bark, Erick stood up on the roof, the cool evening air brushing against his weathered face. Jace's barking broke the silence again, sharp and insistent. He turned, squinting toward the edge of the property. And there she was—Grace—walking up the path, her hair illuminated by the faded light. His chest tightened.

"Erick?" Her voice carried up to him

"I'll be right there," he called back, already moving toward the ladder. But before he could climb down, she was already halfway up to him, her hands gripping the rungs.

"I need your help." Grace looked up smiling in his direction, her hand outstretched.

"I thought you'd never ask!" He laughed and then reached out, helping her find her footing on the uneven shingles. She settled beside him, her legs straight out next to his. For a moment, neither of them spoke. The horizon was like a painting in the late summer sky, with hues of orange and purple above the treeline.

"I heard you're leaving," she said, finally, her tone casual but her eyes fixed on him. "Maybe for good."

He nodded, his gaze dropping to his hands. "Yeah. Atlanta. Got a fresh start waiting for me there, I guess."

Grace tilted her head, studying him. "You don't sound too sure about it."

He shrugged, a half-smile tugging at his lips. "Guess I'm not. But... nothing's worked out here. Not with you. Not with Isabelle. Finn is moving on, and I just figured it's time to try something new."

She looked away, her fingers tracing the edge of the roof. "I get that. Running away feels easier sometimes."

"I'm not running," he said quickly, then paused. "Okay, maybe I am. But it's not just about that. I think... I think maybe God's got something better planned for me. Something I can't see yet."

Grace turned to him, her expression softening. "You always

did have this way of seeing the bigger picture. Even when we were kids. Remember Finn Manor? That night on the roof?"

He chuckled, the memory flooding back. "Yeah. You gave me that photo. Still have it, by the way."

Her eyes widened, a flicker of surprise crossing her face. "You kept it?"

"Of course I did. It meant something to me. Still does," his voice dropped, quieter now. "Aren't you supposed to be on a road trip with Scott?"

Grace looked down, her fingers fidgeting with her light jacket. "I'm not with Scott anymore," she said abruptly, as if the words had been waiting to spill out.

Erick blinked, caught off guard. "What? What happened?"

"I walked away. I wanted to write my own story not live in someone else's. Skydiving… it gave me clarity. Letting go of everything that didn't matter. And Finn, he told me to talk to you. Said I'd regret it if I didn't. He was very persuasive."

He stared at her, his mind racing. "I know he is that and more. Funny, he said the same thing to me, to talk to you."

"Why didn't you?" she shot back.

"You asked me for time and space. Then you were with Scott," he said, not able to take his eyes off hers. "I had to respect that."

Grace shook her head, a small, rueful smile playing on her lips. "You always were too good for your own good, Erick. But here's the thing—life keeps bringing me back to you. No matter where I go, no matter how far I run. You're like my north star. My lighthouse in all the storms where I always find my way home to you."

The words hung in the air, heavy with meaning. Erick felt his resolve waver, the walls he'd built around his heart cracking under the weight of her honesty.

"Grace…" he started, but she cut him off, leaning in closer.

"I read your letter," she interrupted.

"*Finn*…" Erick scoffed. "He's like a dog with a bone."

"I'm not running anymore," she said, her voice barely above

a whisper. "Not from you or your family. Not from this. I will follow you to the ends of the earth, if I have to. Even Georgia to be with you."

He hesitated, his breath catching in his throat. Then, slowly, he reached out, his hand brushing against hers. Their fingers intertwined, and for the first time in decades, everything felt right. He pulled her to him as if his life depended on it, his hands soft on her face and then in her hair. As they deepened their kiss, the world around them faded into the background. The sun was below the horizon now, and the stars flickered to life. And for a moment, Erick forgot about Georgia, about the boxes, about everything except the woman beside him.

When they finally pulled apart, Grace rested her head on his shoulder, her voice soft but steady. "So… what now?"

For the first time in a long time, Erick felt like he was exactly where he was meant to be. Grace was right, nothing could ever stand in their way now, and he realized that no matter what he had ever done, all the paths had always led back to her.

He smiled, a sense of calm settling over him. "Now… we figure it out. Together. Come with me."

He stood up and held out his hand for hers to take *now* and *forever*.

Epilogue

race and Erick were married shortly after they returned from Georgia. They had a quiet intimate ceremony on the docks of HigherGround where Pala walked Grace halfway down the aisle. Then Robin walked her the rest of the way. Two years after the wedding, they built a larger house next to Erick's cabin and prayed for a child of their own, but nothing seemed to work. One day a woman contacted Erick about supporting an adoption agency for children with disabilities after Grace suffered her first miscarriage. Together they brought home Willow, a twelve-year-old girl who grew up in foster care her whole life because she had a prosthetic leg.

Against all odds, Grace and Erick also welcomed Sunshine into their family the following fall. She was a beautiful baby girl who had fiery red hair, just like her mother. They named her Sunshine, a symbol of hope and love that had been present throughout their journey together. On that day in that moment, all their struggles seemed worth it as they held their precious baby girl in their arms.

Erick's cabin was converted into an office for Grace to work at the new Legacy Foundation. She helped with the adoption process of children with different disabilities to find homes and the medical care they needed. Her second book entitled *The Raven's Journey* was on the New York Times bestseller list.

On the morning of Sunshine's fifth birthday, the little red-head tore through the house; her shriek piercing the quiet afternoon on that early fall day. Sunshine stomped up the stairs, and Willow ambled after her, her new prosthetic leg never slowing her down as she climbed the wooden staircase with ease.

Grace looked up from arranging wildflowers for that night's dinner party. Her dining table would be filled once again with laughter and family from all over. Her grandfather, Bran, flew in from Wales. Pala, Robin, Faith, along with Daniel, Sky and their adopted son, Derrick, were coming as well. Finn and his girlfriend, Rachel, were also joining them along with Grace's friend, Julie.

Grace laid out the table cloth and made sure there were enough place settings. She wanted everything to look especially nice. This was a day to celebrate miracles. Suddenly she heard a crash from above.

"Girls! What in the world is going on up there?" Grace called, and she swiftly ran up the stairs toward the source of the commotion.

"Willow won't give it back!" Sunshine's wail floated from Grace and Erick's bedroom.

"Give *what* back?" Grace entered her room. Willow, her face flushed with frustration, clutched a delicate wooden music box to her chest while Sunshine, cheeks streaked with tears, desperately reaching for it.

"Willow, that belongs to me," Grace said sternly, extending her hand.

She begrudgingly handed the box to her mother. Willow exclaimed, "She almost dropped it!"

Suddenly Sunshine lunged toward her sister, sending the

music box tumbling out of Willow's hands, spilling onto the tile floor with a hollow sound. The lid popped open, and the warped tune of "You are my Sunshine" hung ghostly in the air. A folded up envelope fluttered out.

"Oops," Sunshine muttered, eyes wide, but then she began crying.

"Careful!" Grace moved quickly, but the small, folded envelope slipped from the music box's inner compartment and was now on the ground, catching her attention. Her heart skipped a beat as she recognized the faded lettering on the front: "DNA Results - Pala."

"Mom, what is it?" Willow asked, her anger momentarily forgotten.

Grace picked up the envelope, a heavy sigh escaping her. "This is from a long time ago." She looked at her daughters, seeing curiosity spark in their eyes.

"Tell us," Sunshine urged, pulling on Grace's sleeve.

"Alright," Grace relented, ushering them to the living room. She settled onto the couch, the girls snuggling close on either side. "Your Grandma Raven left me this treasure before she passed away—left it at the summit." Grace smiled at the memory. "Daddy and I took you hiking there before, remember?"

"Was Grandma a pirate?" Sunshine asked, her imagination running wild.

Grace chuckled softly. "No, my love, she was an adventurer though. And she believed in leaving something meaningful behind—a legacy."

"Then what's in the envelope?" Willow pressed, her maturity beyond her years.

"Test results," Grace replied wondering why this would show up now. "But some things—we learn to live without knowing. It's the journey that matters more than the destination."

Sunshine yawned, her interest waning as the story lacked the pirates and treasures she'd hoped for. "Can we go get our dresses now? I want to wear the pink one that Mom-Mom got me."

"Me too," Willow said, standing and stretching. "Let's get

ready for the party."

"Go on, you two," Grace said smiling as she watched them scamper off. On a whim, she opened the envelope, and it said what she already knew in her heart.

Pala was a perfect match.

Grace tucked it inside the box and placed it high up in her closet.

Hours later, the family gathered around the dinner table, and laughter filled the room. Grace's grandfather sat next to Robin and Faith, who were very proud grandparents. They sat next to Sunshine and Willow. Next to them was Pala who also flew in from San Diego for the event. Grace's friend Julie sat between her and Joyce. Joyce's husband, Don, took the seat beside his wife, completing the circle around the table. Daniel and Sky walked over and found their places next to Erick. They sang 'Happy Birthday' to Sunshine, and Grace passed around pieces of cake.

"Remember when I told you that Daniel got accepted into that stem cell treatment?" Sky asked Erick and Grace.

"Of course," Grace said. "We were hopeful."

"I think it's working. He has made so much progress already with a cane," Sky added.

Daniel had Derrick in his lap who was giggling and stealing food off his father's plate. "This little guy is going to be running before we know it. I just want to keep up with him."

"Finn, tell them our announcement," Rachel urged as she left to get their birthday present for Sunshine.

"The Finn Manor has been recently renovated and just received an award for one of the best addiction treatment centers in Connecticut. We also built a kennel to train therapy dogs on the property."

"That is quite an accomplishment," Grace said knowing how far he had come with his sobriety.

Rachel came in with a young German Shepherd who was calm and sure of himself and she handed the leash to Finn.

"Jacey Boy isn't getting any younger, and dogs do better in

packs. As you know we train dogs, this one we picked out for you guys because he can look after the girls and Jace. His name is Diesel."

Sunshine shrieked and cuddled the puppy. "You're my Diesel!"

"What a beautiful family you have here!" Julie exclaimed.

Erick raised his glass of apple cider, catching Grace's eye. "To the family!" he toasted. She noticed his salt and pepper beard glinting in the candlelight.

"To the family," Grace echoed, her gaze drifting over each beloved face. A sense of profound gratitude washed over her for the life they had built. She wished Raven could be with them now.

"Mommy, when can I have more cake?" Sunshine's question brought Grace back to the moment, and she cut a generous piece for the birthday girl.

"Anything for you, my little ray of light," Grace murmured.

As conversations bubbled around them, the room became alive with the warmth of shared stories and dreams. Grace and Erick took a moment to absorb it all—the sights, the sounds, the feeling of completeness. This was their legacy. Every choice and every step had led them here to this moment.

The laughter at the dinner table tapered into a comfortable hum of contentment. Grace looked over at Erick, whose gaze was on everyone they loved. Everyone's expressions were illuminated by the soft glow of the flicker of candlelight.

"Mommy, when can we open presents?" Sunshine pleaded, her pale blue eyes gleaming with the boundless energy of youth.

"Soon, Sunshine," Grace said, putting her hand on her daughter's arm.

"You should hear what Dad and I are doing at the Higher-Ground studio." Willow beamed because working with her dad was a dream, and she, too, enjoyed helping people.

"Willow is doing so well with the patients," Erick said, pride evident in his voice.

Just then, the doorbell echoed through the house. Willow,

ever the spirited soul, leaped from her chair with teenage eager-
ness. "I'll get it!"

Jace followed and barked excitedly, careful not to knock her
over. Grace exchanged a knowing glance with Erick as their
daughter's footsteps pattered across the floor.

"Who could that be?" Erick wondered aloud, his dark blue
eyes flickering with curiosity as he stood up and followed Willow. He was so proud of how far she had come.

Grace stood up, the sound of the front door opening and
closing, followed by muffled voices that drifted back toward the
dining room as Willow reentered with a boy with shaggy black
hair.

"Andrew, isn't it?" She smiled warmly at the neighbor boy,
noting his sheepish grin and how his eyes darted around the
room, taking in the festive scene.

"Yep, that's me," Andrew replied, hands shoved into the
pockets of his jeans. "Sorry to intrude. I was just, uh, looking
for my dog. He has a habit of…"

"Yeah, I'm sure he's somewhere in our yard." Erick finished
for him, the corners of his mouth twitching upward in amusement and annoyance. He held Grace with one arm at the dining room entrance, cautiously observing his daughter with this
young man.

"Please, join us," Grace offered getting another chair next
to Willow.

"Thank you, Mrs. Finn," Andrew said, his voice sincere.
"That's really kind of you."

"Here we go again," Erick chuckled under her breath. His
words meant only for Grace, and she smirked at the irony of
their daughter's crush as she set the table for their unexpected
guest.

Life, with all its mysteries and romances, continued to unfold in the most beautifully miraculous, and unpredictable ways.
Here, under the roof of the home that Erick and Grace had
built together, their house was now filled with warmth and the
people they loved. They honored those who had passed but

were still living in their hearts. They both knew that whatever lay ahead for them, they would embrace it together. This wasn't just their destiny. It was their *mended legacy* for generations to come.

The end.

DISCUSSION QUESTIONS

Character and Relationship Dynamics

Grace and Erick's relationship is repeatedly challenged. What are the core issues preventing them from achieving lasting happiness? Are these issues primarily internal (personal flaws) or external (circumstances and other people)?

Grace and Erick have a history of starting and stopping. After seeing Erick with Isabelle, Grace experiences the feeling of betrayal from the past. How has their history shaped their reactions and decisions in this latest installment of their story?

Are her responses justified, or is she projecting past experiences onto new situations?

How does Finn's presence impact both Grace and Erick individually and their relationship? Is his role one of conflict or a catalyst for growth, and how does this differ from his character in Mended?

Consider Isabelle's role in the story. Is she simply a "rebound" or does she represent something deeper for Erick? How does the relationship between Erick and his twin brother, Finn, influence Erick's choices and relationships, particularly with Grace?

Isabelle plays a significant role. What were your initial impressions of her character? Did you believe her motives were genuine?

Scott enters Grace's life and offers her a different perspective. What does he represent to Grace in contrast to Erick?

What are your initial thoughts on Scott and his role in Grace's journey of healing? What does he represent to Grace in contrast to Erick? What does Grace gain from her interactions with him?

Themes

The book explores themes of forgiveness, betrayal, and second chances. How are these themes interwoven throughout the narrative, particularly in the context of Grace and Erick's relationship?

The concept of "legacy" is present in both Finn's court case and the characters' personal histories. What does legacy mean in this story, and how does it impact the characters' choices? The story mentions Grace's fear that her father's blood in her veins could make her unlovable. Is this a rational fear? Where do you think this fear stems from? Is it purely about her father, or is there something deeper at play? Do you think Grace finds what she's looking for in San Diego? Does she get definitive answers to her questions? What is the biggest lesson Grace learns on her trip to San Diego, and how does she evolve as a character?

Plot and Story Structure

Were you surprised by Grace's decision to go to San Diego and leave ErickIf you were in Grace's shoes, would you have made the same decisions? Why or why not? again when Finn re-entered the picture? Did you find her reaction believable?

Discuss the significance of the power outage in the elevator scene. How does this event contribute to Grace and Erick's reconciliation?

Do you think the introduction of Scott as a love interest is an effective way to challenge Grace and move her forward?

What are your predictions for the ending of the story? Will Grace and Erick ultimately find their way back to each other, or is it time for them to move on?

Does this book effectively leave you hanging off the cliff wanting to read more?

Personal Reflections:

Which character do you most identify with, and why? Have you ever experienced a situation similar to the challenges faced by Grace and Erick?

What is your definition of true love, and does this book reflect your view?

Did this book change your perspective on forgiveness, reconciliation, or the importance of facing one's fears?

What message do you think the author is trying to convey through Grace's and Erick's story? What is the biggest question you were left with when you finished the book?

Thoughts about the ending.

ABOUT THE AUTHOR

D.S. Nass is the author of *Mended*, a heartfelt debut novel inspired by her love of reading, writing, and the healing power of nature. A native of central Connecticut, she now lives in southern New Jersey with her husband, Jason. Together they have a beautiful family of five children, two beloved dogs—Jacey Boy, a golden Labrador retriever, and Diesel, a loyal German Shepherd—and are proud grandparents to two sweet granddaughters, Daisy and Scarlett.

Deborah earned her degree from Central Connecticut State University and considers her faith and family the most important parts of her life. When she's not writing or hiking her favorite local trails, you can find her laughing with friends, enjoying time with her granddaughters, or working hard to inspire young readers in the community.

Mended and *Mended Legacy* were born out of Deborah's passion for stories that explore transformation, resilience, and redemption. She writes with the hope that her words will offer comfort, courage, and a faith connection to readers walking their own winding paths.